Bookworm III

The Best Laid Plans

ALSO BY CHRISTOPHER G. NUTTALL

The Mind's Eye

Bookworm series
Bookworm
Bookworm II: The Very Ugly Duckling

Dizzy Spells series
A Life Less Ordinary

Royal Sorceress series
The Royal Sorceress
The Great Game
Necropolis

Inverse Shadows Universe
Sufficiently Advanced Technology

Bookworm III
The Best Laid Plans

Christopher G. Nuttall

Elsewhen Press

Bookworm III: The Best Laid Plans
First published in Great Britain by Elsewhen Press, 2015
An imprint of Alnpete Limited

Elsewhen Press, PO Box 757, Dartford, Kent DA2 7TQ
www.elsewhen.press
British Library Cataloguing in Publication Data.
A catalogue record for this book is available from the British Library.
ISBN 978-1-908168-66-5 Print edition
ISBN 978-1-908168-76-4 eBook edition

Designed and formatted by Elsewhen Press

To Eric Jalil Nuttall, my son

Prologue

The Golden City was on edge.

Inquisitor Cass could feel it as she strode through the streets, her long black robes spinning out around her, marking her as an Inquisitor to all who cared to stare. The handful of people on the streets were careful not to stare, even though she was morbidly certain they would have ogled her if she'd been wearing something – anything – else. She'd left the Peerless School a full year ahead of her contemporaries and looked ridiculously young for her position. But then, being underestimated was always an advantage.

She smiled to the guards as she reached the walls surrounding the Golden Palace, then stepped through the wards, feeling the waves of magic protecting the Grand Sorceress shimmering against her personal protections before they parted, allowing her to enter the complex. The guards nodded respectfully to her – they had no magic and were really only there for show – and stood back, trusting in the Grand Sorceress's wards to keep out the really dangerous threats. Cass kept walking forward, allowing the magic surrounding the Golden Palace to guide her steps. Slowly, inch by inch, it led her through a long corridor and into the antechamber, outside the Throne Room. There were more guards standing there, watching the long line of petitioners who had somehow managed to slip into the building in hopes of seeking an audience with the Grand Sorceress. Judging from the looks some of them aimed at Cass when they thought she wasn't looking, their persistence wasn't getting them anywhere.

The stone door swung open, allowing her into the Throne Room. As always, the sheer magnificence of the room took her breath away. The walls were covered in gold, while the floors were solid marble, engraved with golden images of the great heroes of the Necromantic Wars. In the exact centre of the room, surrounded by silver runes of power, was the Golden Throne itself. Cass felt the tug of the magic shimmering around the Throne and had to force herself to pull away. When there had been an Emperor in the Golden City, she was sure, his presence had been enough to dominate the chamber. Now ...

The Grand Sorceress, Lady Light Spinner, sat at a small table, positioned neatly in the shadow of the Golden Throne. Her face was hidden behind a veil, as always, but her posture was tense, while her hand signed documents in a swift, almost frantic manner, suggesting she too was on edge. It was hard to blame her, Cass knew. During her elevation, a Dark Wizard had done significant damage to the Golden City, while only scant days ago several Great Houses had collapsed into chaos. The Empire was weaker than it had been for centuries.

"Wait," Light Spinner ordered.

Cass went down on one knee, then forced herself to remain calm, despite her puzzlement at having been summoned to the palace. Junior Inquisitors were rarely called before the Grand Sorceress unless they had done something truly spectacular ... or fallen flat on their faces, embarrassing both themselves and their trainers. But Cass knew that she had done neither, not recently. She'd done her duty ...

The Grand Sorceress looked up at her, suddenly. "You may rise," she said. "And speak freely."

"Thank you," Cass said.

She wondered, absently, what the Grand Sorceress made of her. At twenty-five, she was the youngest Inquisitor on active duty – and certainly the prettiest, with long blonde hair that framed a heart-shaped face. The Grand Sorceress wouldn't have hidden her face, Cass was sure, if there hadn't been a good reason to hide. But why? Even the Inquisition didn't know why the Grand Sorceress chose to wear the veil.

"You swore your oaths to the Grand Sorcerer," Light Spinner said. "Did you not?"

"Yes," Cass said. "I did."

She frowned at the question. Light Spinner, the Grand Sorceress, *knew* she'd sworn the Inquisitor Oaths. Cass couldn't have entered the Watchtower without having sworn the oaths and bound herself to their service. And, as Grand Sorceress, Light Spinner was entitled to her obedience. Cass could no more have disobeyed a direct order from the Grand Sorceress than she could have chosen to ignore a magic-abusing fool in the streets.

"I have a specific task for you," the Grand Sorceress said. "It will require you to be released from your oaths, should you accept."

Cass blinked, genuinely shocked. The Inquisitors were all powerful magicians – and very well trained. Their oaths kept them from being anything more than the Grand Sorcerer's enforcers, rather than joining other magicians in the endless battle for supremacy. For the Grand Sorceress to *release* her from her oaths ... it made no sense. Cass could have carried out almost any order the Grand Sorceress chose to give *without* being freed from her sworn words.

"My Lady," she said, carefully. "I ..."

The Grand Sorceress held up one gloved hand. "There are issues you need to understand," she said. "Johan Conidian is alive."

Cass felt an odd flicker of fear. There were ways to strip a magician of his or her magic, if necessary, but they required careful rituals and complex spellwork. Johan Conidian, on the other hand, had developed a form of magic that allowed him to take a person's magic *without* the rituals, something that had terrified every magician who had heard about it. They lived in a world where magic was power, she knew. How could they be faulted for being terrified when they sensed that they could lose their power?

And that everyone they were mean to would be mean to them, once they were powerless, Cass thought, silently.

"I am sending him and Elaine, the Head Librarian, out of the city," Light Spinner continued. "They will not be able to attend the Conference" – she gave an odd little chuckle – "but instead they will be carrying out a mission for me. You will accompany them and provide what assistance you can."

"But not as an Inquisitor," Cass said, slowly.

"No," Light Spinner agreed. "You will go as an independent magician."

Cass considered it, reluctantly. The Inquisitors were among the most capable magicians in the world – and she'd worked hard to join their ranks. It had been far from easy, not when the Senior Inquisitors had taken great pride in pushing the younger volunteers to breaking point, hoping to force out anyone who could break before it was too late. And it was always harder for a woman ... she'd survived, somehow, and gained her robe and staff. The thought of simply abandoning her achievement was horrific.

But she could see the Grand Sorceress's point. The oaths she'd sworn would push her in a certain direction, once she was face-to-face with Johan Conidian. His magic was new and utterly unprecedented, as far as anyone could tell. She had a duty to take him to the Watchtower or simply kill him, before he fell into unfriendly hands. If the last few months had taught her anything, it was that the peace and stability of the last fifty years was proving to be an illusion.

And she knew her duty.

"I will, if you will release me," she said. She hesitated, then took the skull ring off her finger and dropped it into her pocket. "Can I retake the oaths afterwards?"

"If you wish to return to the Inquisitors, you may retake the oaths," Light Spinner said.

Cass bowed her head, then stepped forward when Light Spinner rose to her feet. The oaths were suddenly *very* prominent within her mind, sworn words that were woven into her magic by old rituals. Obey the Emperor – and the Grand Sorcerer. It was the only way to ensure stability, she knew, given how many magicians were prepared to fight for power. The Grand Sorcerer wasn't just the most powerful magician in the world, as far as anyone knew; he or she was supported by a corps of other powerful magicians. It was hard for anyone to challenge the Inquisitors.

"In the name of the Emperor, wherever he may be, I release you from your oaths," Light Spinner said. "I ..."

Cass barely heard her as magic suddenly shimmered around her. The oaths had been part of her for years, long enough that she'd forgotten what it was like to be free of them, to be free of a compulsion she had accepted willingly as part of her job. Now ... magic danced and twisted, reminding her that she was a powerful magician ... and that she was free. It would be easy, now, to do whatever she liked, to be the ultimate spoilt brat. Magic made it so easy ...

She reached into her pocket and took the ring. It burned against her flesh the moment she touched it, growing hotter and hotter every second. Only Inquisitors could wear the rings.

"I will take that," Light Spinner said. "It will be held in trust for you. And I suggest you change or glamour your clothes."

"Thank you," Cass said, placing the ring on the table. It felt as if she had given up a piece of herself. Moments later, her black robes became a simple pair of trousers and a shirt. She'd worn plain clothes often enough, but this was different. She might never be an Inquisitor again. "Please give it to my superiors if I don't return."

She took a deep breath, then calmed herself. The job still needed to be done, even if she was no longer bound by her oaths.

"I thank you," she said, formally. She had never heard of an Inquisitor being released from the oaths before, if only because they rarely lived long enough to retire. Now ... it was growing harder to remember why she had sworn the oaths in the first place. "And I will carry out your *requests*."

"Good," the Grand Sorceress said. She motioned for Cass to follow her out of the giant chamber, into a smaller office lined with giant bookshelves. "This is what I want you to do."

Chapter One

The chamber under the Great Library was *crammed* with books.

Elaine let out a sigh as she surveyed the groaning tables, utterly heaving with books, maps and records recovered from a dozen smaller libraries within the city. Some of them dated back to the Necromantic Wars, when the Witch-King had been first hero, then villain; others were much younger, either copies of copies or outright fakes. The dusty tomes all *looked* old – some of them clearly hadn't been touched for years – but a quick inspection was often enough to reveal that they weren't what they seemed. It was astonishing, really, just how many Great Houses had seen fit to embellish their roles in building the empire over the years.

Or maybe it isn't astonishing at all, Elaine thought, as she ran her fingers through her long brown hair. *Grand Sorcerers come and go, but the Great Houses last forever.*

She looked down at one of the tomes and cursed its author under her breath. The knowledge in her head was enough to tell her that the writer had been making it up as he went along, although anyone could have worked it out for himself if he'd read the book with a critical eye. There were at least nine outright contradictions within the book, while one whole segment was devoted to discussing a ritual that Elaine knew wouldn't actually work, no matter how enthusiastically the participants danced naked under the moonlight. Apparently, it was an old family ritual, but Elaine had her doubts. *She* rather suspected it had been written by a dirty old man.

Walking to the next table, she looked down at the maps they'd recovered from one of the Great Houses. Some of them showed recognisable continents; others, more detailed, showed the world as it had been before the Necromantic Wars. Elaine scribbled down notes to herself in her notebook, hoping a quick comparison with a modern map would show her lands familiar to the Witch-King. If they found a place he considered secure, she was sure, they would find his lich. And then they could destroy him before it was too late.

She shook her head, then stepped past the table and looked down at a mirror, lying in one of the half-empty boxes. It sparkled with magic when she tested it, but none of the spells seemed to do more than alter the reflected image. On impulse, she picked it up and studied her reflection, watching as the mirror showed her how she could improve her looks, if she was prepared to put in the time and effort. Shaking her head, she put it down on the table again. The mirror had probably been crafted for some minor daughter, someone who wouldn't be expected to achieve anything beyond looking pretty and marrying well. No one else would have the time to primp and preen every day.

Not when they could use glamours instead, she thought, coldly. The mirror hadn't been designed by a skilled magician, she was sure. It hadn't noticed the glamour covering her eyes, let alone made suggestions for improvement. But there was no real improvement, she was sure, for eyes that glowed a brilliant red. All she could do was keep them hidden and pray no one looked past the glamour. Red eyes were *not* a good sign.

The next set of texts were copies of ones in the Great Library. She made a note of their titles, then marked them down to be returned to their owners. None of the owners had been *pleased* to give up their private libraries, after all, but the Grand Sorceress had been insistent. Elaine hoped – prayed – that none of them realised that *she* had requested access to their libraries, if only because she didn't need more enemies. Being a Privy Councillor made Elaine a target for anyone who wanted power, even though she was hardly the Grand Sorceress. And if they'd known just how much knowledge was locked in her head ...

She sighed, rubbing her forehead. Some of the knowledge had faded, but everything to do with magic was as sharp and clear as it had been on the day she'd woken up and discovered just what had happened to her. The Great Library, repository for every last piece of magical knowledge in the Empire, had been copied and dumped into her head, including thousands upon thousands of forbidden spells that successive Grand Sorcerers had kept under lock and key. She knew she'd been lucky not to be executed, after the truth of her parentage had come out, but there were days when she wondered if she had *really* been lucky. No matter what precautions she took, she knew – all too well – that she was vulnerable to a more powerful magician.

They don't know, she told herself.

But she knew one person – entity – who *did* know. The Witch-King had spent centuries manipulating events within the Empire, preparing for his rebirth. They'd been lucky to stave off his first assault on the Golden City and no one had heard anything from him since, but she knew it was just a matter of time. And yet, the Witch-King was functionally immortal. He could pull in his horns and wait for another couple of hundred years before he made another play for power, by which time everyone who knew he was still alive would be dead. How did one fight an entity who thought in decades and spent centuries crafting his plans?

She sighed again, feeling a headache building up under her skin. The headaches had been growing more frequent as she'd delved into the tomes, looking for something – anything – that would cut the search short, but there was nothing. She'd even spent hours reviewing history, looking for traces of the Witch-King's influence, only to discover that it was largely impossible to tell what might have been his work and what was nothing more than a coincidence. All she'd ended up with, for her trouble, was a series of headaches and a hundred conspiracy theories. *Anything* could be the Witch-King, anything at all. The only thing that kept her from giving up was the certain knowledge that if the Witch-King was as omniscient as he seemed, he would have won by now.

The wards surrounding the Great Library shimmered, once, then sent her an alert. Johan had left his apartment, right next to hers, and was making his way down towards the underground chamber. The labyrinth spell prepared itself to grip him, leaving him walking in circles endlessly until Elaine or one of the other librarians could come to see who had tried to enter the private sections of the library. She hastily told the spell to let him through, then reached out with her mind, trying to sense Johan's presence. The knowledge in her head told her she should be able to sense his presence anywhere, whenever she wanted to know where he was or what he was doing. But she barely sensed the merest flicker of his presence until he stepped into the chamber.

Elaine greeted him with a tired smile. Johan Conidian was tall and handsome – and, until very recently, Powerless. His family had practically kept him a prisoner until he'd developed magic, a very strange form of magic. Elaine had studied his power extensively, since the first day he'd used his magic, and yet she had no idea how it worked. Or, for that matter, why the apprenticeship bond hadn't been sealed. They had sworn willingly, after all; he had accepted her as his mistress, even though it was rare for a female to take a male apprentice or vice versa. But the bond hadn't formed properly.

"Johan," she said. "Have you started to pack?"

"Yes, *mother*," Johan said. He stopped, a moment later, his face filling with horror. "I ..."

Elaine stepped forward and rested her hand on his shoulder, trying to provide what comfort she could. Johan was emotionally unstable, unsurprisingly; his family had either viewed him as a cripple or a burden ... and *always* as an embarrassment. There were times when he was as mature as Elaine herself and times when he acted rather like a five-year-old, his mood swinging rapidly between happiness and tantrums. Elaine wondered, sometimes, if the reason the apprenticeship bond had remained incomplete had something to do with Johan's mental state. It was impossible to take an apprentice who hadn't passed puberty ...

... And while Johan was physically seventeen, his mental age was harder to determine.

It's not impossible, her thoughts mocked her. *It's just forbidden.*

She gritted her teeth. More and more, the knowledge in her head was popping up to the forefront of her mind, pulled by the merest thought. Every time she thought about the limits of magic, something would emerge from the back of her mind, pointing out that the limits weren't what she thought they were. If there was a power imbalance between an adult master and apprentice, it would be far, far worse if the apprentice happened to be a child. And then the master would have to cope with the child passing through puberty ...

"Elaine?" Johan asked. "Are you all right?"

"I think so," Elaine lied. The knowledge wasn't painful, but the understandings it brought bubbling up into her mind often were. Her teachers had never taught her how much had been buried by the Grand Sorcerers over the years, just to prevent it being abused. And she knew it all. "And yourself?"

Johan sobered. His family had been devastated – and, even though they'd been horrible to him, she knew part of him regretted it. It was quite possible the Conidian Family would never truly recover, not now that so many of its members were Powerless or dead. The senior surviving member – Charity Conidian – was only eighteen years old. How could she hold the family together in the wake of such a disaster?

And to think his father wanted Johan to take over as Prime Heir, Elaine thought. She couldn't blame the Conidian for wanting someone – anyone – to replace his bullying braggart of an older son. But Johan had been Powerless ... until he wasn't. *But he couldn't have handled it either.*

She shook her head, dismissing the thought.

"I think we have a rough plan for our travels," she said. "The Travellers will take us up to the borderlands, at least, and then we will have to proceed on our own."

"That's what I came to tell you," Johan said. "Your friend has arrived."

"Daria?" Elaine asked. "She finally made it back?"

"Yep," Johan said. "I asked your assistant to let her into your office while I came to fetch you."

"You could just have sent a note," Elaine reminded him, dryly. A normal apprentice would have been able to call his master, just by using the apprenticeship bond. Johan didn't seem to have that option. "Or sent one of the staff down here."

"I just wanted to look around," Johan admitted. "This place ... I could have been happy here."

Elaine felt a sudden, bitter stab of sympathy. Johan was bright, smart enough to rise high in the world, even without magic. But his family had kept him a virtual prisoner, not daring to let him run free for fear of what their enemies would do to him – and them, through him. He might have been Powerless, for no reason anyone could determine, but he still had the Conidian bloodline. A career in the Great Library would have suited both of them, if Johan had had even a spark of magic ...

... And now he had power and far too much unwanted attention.

They think he's dead, Elaine reminded herself. Light Spinner was the only other person who knew Johan was still alive. *Let them think he was a freakish accident ...*

She cursed mentally. Inquisitor Dread had told her that several known Powerless had wound up dead over the last few days, either through being murdered by their families or being accidentally killed when the families were trying to trigger their powers. If, of course, Johan *wasn't* just a freak accident. The hell of it was that there was no way any of the murderers could ever be punished. Their fathers held absolute authority over their children until they came into their magic. In hindsight, the marvel was that Johan had survived so long.

"I *was* happy here," Elaine said. "And now I will have to leave."

Books had been her constant companions, first at the orphanage and then at the Peerless School. Fiction had allowed her to dream of other worlds; facts had allowed her to master magic and pass her tests, even if she lacked the raw power of her classmates. Daria had often accused her of lacking ambition, but – in truth – she had never really wanted to do anything other than work with books. Working at the Great Library had satisfied her, even if she had been a recluse with few friends.

And then she'd become the Bookworm. And then she'd been rewarded – and punished – by being made Head Librarian.

She wasn't blind to Light Spinner's political manoeuvrings. Elaine represented a danger to the Empire, after all; indeed, she was mildly surprised that the Grand Sorceress hadn't killed her out of hand. Placing Elaine in the Great Library, even making her a Privy Councillor, had been a way to make use of her, as well as rewarding her for her efforts. But it also kept her firmly under control. The Head Librarian could never leave the city.

But I already have left the city, Elaine thought, ruefully. *And now I may be leaving for good.*

She'd never *wanted* to leave the Golden City. She wasn't one of the hardy explorers who had mapped the world, or one of the warrior-magicians who had built the Empire, or even one of the farmers who had tamed the land and purged it of magical influences. Being Head Librarian had been all she'd ever wanted, even if it did mean spending far too long in pointless meetings. The idea of leaving, of severing the connection between herself and the ancient building, was terrifying. And yet she had no choice. No one else could search for the Witch-King.

It would be easier, she thought, *if we knew how he influenced people.*

Johan cleared his throat, breaking into her thoughts. "Are you listening to me?"

Elaine felt her cheeks redden. "I was distracted," she said. "I'm sorry."

"My father used to do that too," Johan said, softly. "He never actually listened to a word I said."

"I'm sorry," Elaine repeated, embarrassed. "What did you say?"

"Just that I think your friend was antsy," Johan said. "You really should go see her now."

"She always is," Elaine said. Living with Daria in an apartment had been an education, even if she'd missed a single essential truth about her redheaded friend. Daria moved like lightning, hopping from one boyfriend to the next, darting around so quickly that Elaine couldn't hope to keep track of her affairs. "But she's also a very decent person."

And a werewolf, she added, in the privacy of her own thoughts. *How in the name of all the gods did I manage to miss that?*

She took one last look around the chamber, then linked into the wards and issued a series of orders. The chamber would be locked down until she returned, ensuring that the ancient books and scrolls would remain safe and untouched. She hid a smirk as she looked at one chest of books, remembering what the owner had told Inquisitor Dread. Only people who shared his bloodline could read the books, he'd warned; anyone else risked everything from blindness to death. But it was astonishing just how easily such protective charms could be put aside if one knew how ...

And that is why they would want to kill me, if they knew what I could do, Elaine thought, grimly. *I know far too much about how magic actually works.*

Johan followed her out the door and closed it firmly behind him. Elaine took a moment to check that the wards were firmly in place, then led the way up through the book-lined corridors to the private apartments. As always, the corridors thronged with students and visiting magicians, including dozens of Court Wizards. They might have been summoned to attend the Grand Conference of Court Wizards, where they would pay homage to Lady Light Spinner, but they were taking advantage of the visit to catch up on their reading. Elaine didn't blame them, not really. If there was one advantage to having to leave the Golden City, it was not having to attend the conference.

She frowned as she heard the sound of two students fighting, followed by shimmering alerts from the wards as they started to hurl hexes at one another. Two librarians moved in to separate the two before they could do real damage, then drag them both out of the library and dump them onto the streets. Elaine rolled her eyes in disgust – had she been as desperate to get the books first when she'd been a student? – then reminded herself that exams were coming soon. The students had to be panicking.

Shouldn't have spent all that time having fun instead of studying, she reprimanded them silently. *Now you have to fight to catch up ...*

They passed through another set of wards, then stepped through the door into Elaine's private office. Daria was sitting cross-legged in one of the chairs, her face twisted into a bored expression. The bookshelves lining the walls didn't impress her, Elaine knew, but then they never had. Daria wouldn't be happy unless she was doing something, anything. There was nothing in the room for her.

"Elaine," Daria said, standing in one smooth motion. "It's good to see you again."

"And you," Elaine said, as Daria enfolded her in a hug. Her friend smelt strongly of perfume, which she used to dampen her scent. "I've missed you."

"Yeah," Daria said. "Elaine, I'm afraid I've got bad news."

Chapter Two

Johan had seen many beautiful girls in his time, despite effectively being kept prisoner by his family. His mother and sisters had been beautiful, the girls his father wanted to marry to his brothers had been beautiful ... but there had been something about them that had been *fake*, unreal. They'd used glamours, he suspected, to make themselves look attractive, matching their appearance to their target's tastes. It had always struck him as a kind of fraud.

But Daria was stunning. Short-cropped red hair dominated a face with large, dark eyes and pale, blemish-free skin. She wore a long grey robe that was tight around her chest, then spilled out to hide her legs completely. He couldn't help staring at her, even though there was something oddly canine about her eyes. And the way she moved, as she stood and hugged her friend, was smooth and almost inhuman.

A werewolf, he thought, suddenly. A new-made werewolf wouldn't show any traces of the curse on his or her body, but a born werewolf would show hints of her true nature. He fought down the urge to panic, reminding himself sharply that born werewolves enjoyed much better control over their nature than made werewolves. Besides, he knew what it was like to be an outcast. The gods knew his family had treated him as their secret shame for years.

"And you must be Johan," Daria said, as she let go of Elaine. Her voice was sultry, sending shivers down Johan's spine. "I've heard a great deal about you."

"All lies," Johan managed. He'd heard enough of the rumours concerning him to know that most of them were complete nonsense. "I'm just her apprentice."

"I'm glad to hear it," Daria said, briskly. She held out a hand, which Johan shook firmly, in the manner he'd been taught. There were tiny hairs covering the back of her hand, so fine as to be almost invisible. It was another sign of her true nature. "Elaine needs a male presence in her life."

Johan felt his face turn bright red. He didn't look at Elaine, but he sensed her embarrassment through the bond they shared. And she *would* be embarrassed ... he cursed mentally, wondering why *that* aspect of the link had to be the one that actually worked. There were some definite advantages to not sharing a full apprenticeship bond – he didn't like the thought of a person being able to control him at will – but he'd always had a stronger sense of her than she'd had of him. It just didn't make sense.

Elaine cleared her throat, loudly. "He's my apprentice, not my boyfriend," she said, as Daria let go of Johan's hand. The irritation echoing through the link was overpowering the embarrassment, barely. "And you should know better."

"Of course, Your Nobleness," Daria said, archly. "I beg your pardon, Your Nobleness. I ask for your forgiveness, Your Nobleness ..."

"Oh, shut up," Elaine said.

Johan concealed his amusement with an effort. It was hard to see what the two girls actually had in common; Elaine was shy, almost a recluse, while Daria was outgoing and friendly. And yet, they did seem to have a solid friendship, one that had survived Elaine's elevation to the Privy Council. Perhaps they grounded each other, he told himself, or perhaps it was their differences that made the friendship work. Daria reminded Elaine that there was more to life than books, while Elaine allowed Daria to relax and actually do something serious with her life. Or maybe he was completely wrong.

Daria clamped her hands over her mouth, then bulged out her cheeks. Elaine snorted rudely, then motioned for her friend to sit down. Johan sat on the sofa and tried to keep his eyes off Daria, fearing that the apprenticeship bond would choose that moment to start working properly. The last thing he wanted was for his mistress to know he was lusting after her best friend.

She must be used to it, his thoughts mocked him. It was clear, now, why Daria wore her robes. She could shift into wolf form without them getting in the way and, with a little care, could shift back into a human without running around naked. *Daria is gorgeous.*

Oh, shut up, he told himself, angrily.

He looked around the office as Elaine moved a pile of books from one chair and sat down, heavily. The room was crammed with books, ranging from magical textbooks that had been added to reading lists for next year, to various tomes that hopeful authors had sent to the Head Librarian, requesting their inclusion on the library shelves. Johan had devoured as many of the textbooks as he could, in-between studying with Elaine and trying to determine the exact nature of his powers, but he hadn't found them as helpful as he'd expected. His magic just didn't seem to behave according to the normal rules.

But you weren't allowed to read them at home, his thoughts reminded him. His father had reluctantly enforced the law forbidding non-magicians from touching books of magic, but at least he'd been kind about it. Jamal had taken great delight in rubbing Johan's nose in the fact there were books he would never be able to read. *And now you're making up for lost time*.

He scowled as he remembered his elder brother, the now-powerless brother. The gods alone knew what had happened to him; Elaine had said, rather dryly, that Jamal had left the city, shortly after the Inquisitors had released him from custody. Johan honestly wasn't too surprised. Jamal had been horrible to just about everyone who wasn't a social superior – there hadn't been many of those – and his victims would want a little revenge. The thought of Jamal turned into their plaything was darkly amusing. Jamal had, after all, treated Johan as *his* plaything.

"The seers have been having dreams of impending disaster," Daria said. There was an edge in her voice that cut through Johan's thoughts, bringing them back to reality. "They don't want to stay in the city any longer than strictly necessary."

"I'm not sure I blame them," Elaine said. "What are they dreaming?"

"Nothing specific," Daria said. "But they still want to leave."

Johan looked at Daria, trying hard to keep his eyes on her face. "Don't they see actual events in their dreams?"

"The Sight doesn't work like that," Daria said. There was a hint of annoyance in her tone, although it didn't seem to be directed at Johan. "They never see specific events, merely hints and insights into the future – and feelings, of course. In this case, they've been telling everyone who will listen to them that they have a sense of impending disaster."

Johan looked at Elaine. "Is this reliable?"

Elaine frowned. "Sometimes," she said.

She didn't seem inclined to say anything else, but Johan could sense her worry through the bond. True Seers were rare, very rare. His father had once told him – more accurately, he'd told Jamal while Johan was in earshot – that a True Seer would be snatched up by the Grand Sorcerer, if his powers were proven to be real. But most Seers tended to only see hints of the future, little details that could be anything ... and then use hindsight to *prove* they'd been right all along. Jamal had sneered at the concept and, for once, Johan had to agree. A prediction about meeting a tall handsome stranger could be spun in any direction, with a little ingenuity, while the absence of specifics made it impossible to disprove the prediction.

But people still believed their personal futures could be mapped out for them, if they asked the right fortune teller. Johan's father had sneered at the concept, pointing out that it rarely worked as advertised – and when it did, the results were sometimes unpleasant. Once told, a future would come true, even if it was nightmarish. Johan didn't pretend to understand how ignorance could be bliss, but he wasn't going to dismiss his father's warning. There were some fields of magic that, no matter what anyone said, were poorly understood.

"They were warning the Travellers to abandon Loch Leven," Daria said. "They kept having shadowy dreams of impending disaster. A few weeks later, the city was struck by an earthquake that left most of the buildings in ruins. None of the City-Fathers had listened, of course."

"Of course," Elaine agreed.

"Stupid bastards," Daria said. "They might not trust us, but they should know we don't lie."

She got up and started to pace. Johan found himself staring

again as he realised just how well the robe clung to her body as she moved. It showed no bare flesh, but it revealed the shape of her limbs and buttocks ... embarrassed, he tore his eyes away and found himself looking at Elaine. Her face was impassive, but he could sense a flicker of amusement through the bond, mixed with embarrassment. He looked down at the wooden floor instead, telling himself it was safer. At least there was nothing on the floor to distract him.

"The gaffer wants to leave the city immediately," Daria said. "I managed to convince him to wait a couple of hours, so I could come fetch you. Do you still want to come with us?"

"... Yes," Elaine said. The hesitation that echoed through the bond was surprisingly strong, suggesting she was truly reluctant to leave. "We just need to finish packing, then I need to hand the wards over to Vane. She can hold them until the Grand Sorceress selects my successor."

Johan frowned. "Why not just give the job to her permanently?"

"She might," Elaine said. She shrugged. "But I don't get to choose who will succeed me."

Johan nodded. If some of Elaine's tales about her predecessor as Head Librarian were true, not every Head Librarian had taken up the job willingly. *He* wouldn't have been happy to remain confined to the city, not after his family had treated him as a prisoner, but Elaine was different. She was unadventurous and shy, so much so that Vane – her Deputy – handled almost all of her personal contacts. The library staff sometimes had to wonder if their Head Librarian truly existed.

Don't be silly, he told himself. *They know she exists.*

Daria cleared her throat. "They will be leaving in two hours," she warned. "Can you be ready by then?"

"I think so," Elaine said. "I would prefer not to travel on the Iron Dragons."

"Then start packing," Daria said. "Hurry."

Elaine reached for a sheet of paper, sketched out a note for Vane, then tapped it with her wand. Johan watched, feeling a glimmer of awe, as the paper rose into the air and disappeared through an air vent. Wherever Vane was, the note would find her. It was less spectacular than other magic he'd seen – his brother had been fond of using him as a target for all kinds of spells – but he had to admire her precise control. Most magicians were more than a little sloppy when it came to using magic, spending it freely. But then, Elaine had very little power of her own.

And a little less would have seen her excluded from the Peerless School, Johan thought. He understood the frustration Elaine sometimes felt, even though she was the most knowledgeable magician alive. She had to be focused and utterly precise, while her peers could achieve everything she could and more by waving wands around at random. And yet, given time to think and plan, she made a formidable opponent.

"Go pack," Elaine ordered. "Daria and I will wait for you here."

Johan nodded, then rose and headed through the door. Outside, a handful of library assistants were carting boxes of books past him, using spells to manoeuvre the crates through the air. Johan shivered – that spell had been used to play with him, once upon a time – then allowed them to pass him before he walked down to his apartment. The ward Elaine had placed on it, keyed specifically to keep the rest of his family out, glowed as he approached, recognising his presence. If his father, or Charity, or anyone else who was related to him had tried to enter, the wards would have taken offence. The results would not have been pleasant.

And serve them right, Johan thought, as he opened the door. *I don't want anything to do with them.*

He pushed the thought aside, then stepped into the room. It was larger than his bedroom in House Conidian, dominated by a bed large enough for two people. Elaine had told him that the apartments were normally assigned to visiting scholars, who apparently liked their comforts. Johan had – barely – managed to avoid asking if those comforts included women from the city. He knew, thanks to Jamal's boasting, just how easy it was to find a whore to share one's bed for the night, even though he'd never done it himself.

And Daria would look nice on the bed, he told himself, before he angrily thrust the thought away from him. Daria was older than him by at least four years, assuming she and Elaine were the same age, and a born werewolf. She would have the enhanced sense of smell common to all werewolves ... he cringed in sudden horror as he realised she would know what he was thinking or feeling. His scent would change every time he looked at her ...

Shaking his head, he reached for his bag and checked his clothes. Elaine had told him to bring as little as possible, so he'd packed two sets of clothing, a couple of books and a small bag of money. Thankfully, his vault in the City Bank hadn't been sealed or handed back to Charity, in her new position as Family Head. Johan couldn't help wondering if Charity had ever *known* that their father had attempted to bribe Johan into returning to the family fold ... or if she expected the vault to remain closed until she was ready to demand access. The bankers wouldn't be in a hurry to tell her it existed, after all. They gained more from leaving the money in the bank, under their loving care.

And I should write out a will, Johan thought, although he'd been discouraged from doing anything of the sort. *Something that will leave my money to someone – anyone – else.*

He sighed as he picked up the bag, then took one last look around the chamber. It was plain and simple, but it was *his*, the first place he'd felt truly secure. Jamal and his other siblings, even Charity, hadn't hesitated to make his room at home into a nightmare, hiding magical booby traps everywhere. He still remembered the two days he'd spent as a stone with shuddering horror, even though his father had eventually tracked him down. And none of the others had ever been punished for their crimes against him ...

The memory made him shiver, helplessly. He hastily put the bag down, then closed his eyes and concentrated on a mental discipline Elaine had taught him. It seemed to come easier, now that he was her apprentice; perhaps a little of her precision had rubbed off on him. But he was always aware of her presence at the back of his mind, like being able to sense the sun through clouds and rain. It was strange to realise that she wasn't aware of *him*, even though she *should* have been. The books he'd read, when he'd been trying to decide if he should become her apprentice, had warned that his mistress would be able to compel him to obey, if necessary. But the bond he shared with Elaine didn't seem to be able to do anything of the sort.

He pushed the thought to one side, opened his eyes and picked up the bag again. Tossing it over his shoulder, he strode out of the room, closing the door behind him with a thud. He didn't bother to reset the ward. There was nothing left in the room he cared about, not really. He'd never had many possessions at home and he'd brought none of them with him when he'd left for good. His life had never really given him the chance to become attached to anything, certainly nothing material. He'd never been able to tell when one of his few possessions would be booby-trapped and turned into a weapon against him.

He walked back into Elaine's office and placed the bag on the floor. "I'm ready," he said, simply. "When do we go?"

"Now," Daria said. She rose in one smooth motion, then picked up Johan's bag effortlessly and peered at it suspiciously. "I hope you listened to your mistress about what you could and couldn't bring?"

"I'm not religious," Johan said. Elaine had warned him not to bring any religious artefacts with him, pointing out that the Travellers would not approve. "I don't have any icons to bring."

"Good," Daria said. "Elaine?"

"I'll join you in an hour or so," Elaine said. "Johan will tell you when I'm on my way."

"How nice," Daria said. She gave Johan a smile that made his heart beat faster. "You have a young man who can't get you out of his mind."

Johan felt a surge of embarrassment from Elaine ... and, when he looked up, he saw that her pale cheeks were bright red.

"Thank you," Elaine said, tartly.

Daria giggled, then motioned for Johan to follow her out of the door, carrying the bag in one hand. Johan hesitated, torn between taking it from her and being reluctant to get any closer while his scent was still detectable. She would know he was lusting after her ...

"I'll see you soon," Elaine promised. "Don't do anything I

wouldn't do."

"That doesn't leave much for him *to* do," Daria called back. "Bye!"

Johan sighed, then allowed her to lead him out of the office and down towards the nearest exit.

Chapter Three

Charity Conidian felt uncomfortably like a fake as the carriage came to a halt outside the gates, allowing her to climb out of the vehicle right in front of the Imperial Palace. The lines of petitioners, many of whom had been waiting there for hours if not days, turned to stare at her as the gates opened, allowing her to enter the building. She kept her face as impassive as she could, sensing hundreds of faces glowering at her. *They* had been waiting for hours and she was being allowed to enter the moment she arrived? It was hard for her to blame them for being annoyed.

Your father would merely have sneered at them, her thoughts reminded her. No one said anything out loud, of course. Her golden robes marked her as someone of substance. *He wouldn't have doubted his right to move ahead for a second.*

She cursed her father mentally as she walked through the gates and up to the massive pair of stone doors. Magic crackled around her, reminding her – as if she'd needed the reminder – that she was walking into the lair of the Grand Sorceress herself, a woman with the power to do *anything* she liked to Charity and what remained of her family. No one would come to their defence, not after the ... *incident* at House Conidian. Her father was effectively dead – being Powerless was worse than dead – and his network of clients had been shattered, while the sharks were already gathering. If she couldn't salvage something from the wreckage, the Conidian Family would die.

But she didn't know *how*! Jamal – wherever he was now – had been the Prime Heir, while Charity had been primed for an arranged marriage to someone who suited her father's interests. It hadn't been something she *wanted*, but she'd accepted it ever since she'd learnt to understand how the world worked. The family came first, always. And if it meant she had to share her bed with an elderly warlock who had interests her father wished to share, she had no choice, but to obey. The only consolation had been the certain knowledge that there would always be a place for her at House Conidian. But now even that was gone.

She looked up as she heard someone walking towards her with calm, measured footsteps and saw a tall blonde-haired girl, in her early twenties if Charity was any judge. The girl nodded to her, then walked past. Charity stopped and turned to stare at her as she left the palace, wondering just who she was. Her father had made sure she knew all the movers and shakers in the Golden City, as well as their children, and she didn't recognise the blonde. It was possible she'd been brought up outside the city, yet everyone who wielded political power *had* to spend some time inside the Golden City. And she should have known ...

"My Lady," a voice said. She turned to see a middle-aged man, wearing a slave collar around his neck. "You are requested to wait in the antechamber."

Charity nodded, not trusting herself to speak. Her father had been a powerful magician, the master of a spider's web of influence ranging from the Imperial Palace to the Southern Lands, and a Privy Councillor. *He* could have demanded an immediate interview with the Grand Sorceress and been seen at once; *she* had to wait, just so she knew her place. But she was almost grateful for the chance to collect herself, she decided, as she was shown into the antechamber. The girl looking back at her from the mirror was almost a stranger ...

She rubbed her eyes, bitterly. Once, looking good as well as strongly magical had seemed a good thing. She had to attract suitors, after all, suitors who might be prepared to trade power and influence for her hand in marriage. Now, she looked weak and mournful, her large blue eyes making her look childlike. There was no point in trying to hide behind a glamour, not now. She simply didn't feel like putting the effort forward to construct one. And she couldn't help wondering, as she sat and forced herself to calm down, just what the Grand Sorceress wanted. The chance to cripple one of the Great Houses might well seem ideal, from her point of view.

Not that we're much of a threat any longer, she thought, bitterly. Her father and Jamal were Powerless and Johan was dead, while her younger siblings were too young to influence events. If she failed to keep the family together, the gods alone knew what would happen to the children. Jay wouldn't come of age for another two years and the others were younger still. *We'll be lucky to keep even a fragment of our power.*

She looked down at her hand. It was shaking. Johan's fault, of course, although he hadn't meant to do anything of the sort. She'd been turned into animals and objects before – Jamal had picked on her too – but Johan's power had left her deeply shaken. He might not have known it – she hoped he hadn't known it – yet his power had blanked her out, almost completely. She hadn't just been forced into the shape of a rat; she'd *been* a rat. The experience had almost destroyed her confidence completely.

The slave cleared his throat. "Can I get you something to drink, My Lady?"

"No, thank you," Charity said. She wanted a glass of brandy desperately, but she needed a clear head when she faced the Grand Sorceress. "I will be fine."

She had to wait for nearly half an hour before a different slave appeared and beckoned her forward, leading her into the Throne Room. Charity hadn't been in the giant chamber since the family had moved to the Golden City, when she'd been presented to the Grand Sorceress, but it hadn't changed. The Golden Throne was still glowing with magic, linked into the powerful wards surrounding the palace. Charity couldn't help admiring the sheer level of workmanship that had gone into crafting the Throne. There was no one alive who could build the like.

Her father had once told her that entire fields of magic had been forbidden, then forgotten, never to be rediscovered. Charity hadn't really believed him, but now, looking at the Throne, she wondered if he'd been right all along. The Throne was not only soaked in magic, she saw; it was linked so firmly into the Golden City itself that it would be impossible to remove, or even to reprogram. No one who was not a member of the Imperial Family could sit in the

Throne and live.

"Charity Conidian," the Grand Sorceress said, in her raspy voice. "Come forward, into the light."

Charity obeyed. The Grand Sorceress was sitting below the Throne, half-hidden in the waves of magic billowing around it. As always, her body was hidden and shapeless behind the veil, suggesting that she had something to hide. If she was truly as staggeringly beautiful as the rumours said, Charity was sure, she would have flaunted it to the entire world. Instead, she chose to hide. It suggested there was something about her that would shock everyone, if they learnt the truth. But she kept that thought to herself. Irritating the Grand Sorceress didn't tend to lead to a long and happy life.

She went down on one knee, then bowed her head. "I came as you commanded, Your Supremacy," she said. There were many ways to address a Grand Sorcerer, but she knew she didn't dare show any form of defiance. "And I look forward to serving you."

"I'm sure you do," the Grand Sorceress rasped. "How is House Conidian?"

Charity gritted her teeth. "Weak, but recovering," she lied. In reality, she wasn't sure if she could keep the house in the Golden City. Perhaps it was time to retreat back to the countryside and spend the next few decades rebuilding the family. "We will survive."

"I am glad to hear it," the Grand Sorceress said. There was a hint of ... *something*, perhaps amusement, in her tone. Lady Light Spinner *was* from a rival Great House, after all. If the Conidian Family took a fall, her family would be strengthened. "And your younger children?"

"Well enough," Charity said. She'd called the younger siblings back to the house, just to keep them out of the firing line. "Jay is in his fourth year at the Peerless School, while his younger siblings are enduring their first."

She shuddered, bitterly. The full powers of a Family Head had descended on her, no matter how ill-prepared she was for them. She could command her younger siblings as she saw fit, with no regard for their feelings. The only blessing was that Jamal was no longer in a position to claim leadership of the family. *He* would have had her married off to one of his cronies before she could muster a single word of protest. And she dreaded to think what he would have done if she *had* managed to object. She would have been better off abandoning the family completely.

"How nice," the Grand Sorceress said. "I ...

She broke off, then rose to her feet. "What are *you* doing here?"

Charity turned her head, then jumped. Vlad Deferens was standing at the edge of the room, smirking at them. Charity had never liked him, even when he'd been working with her father; he'd always given her the impression that he was leering at her behind her back. And when she'd looked up his homeland, she'd realised why. She'd never understood why her father had seen him as a potential ally, even though he *was* a Privy Councillor and a powerful magician. He was just too uncivilised to be trusted.

He was a tall, powerfully-built man, wearing a red tunic and kilt that exposed his bare arms and legs, revealing his muscles to anyone watching. His dark hair was long and unkempt, his beard just long enough to be difficult to comb. His eyes, as dark as his hair, sparkled with mischievous light. She couldn't help the impression, as he looked at her, that he was undressing her with his mind. No doubt he was one of the magicians who had learnt stripping spells and used them in the Peerless School. The Administrator might hand out harsh punishments for anyone caught in the act, but he'd never been able to stamp out the practice completely. In the end, all it had done was encourage the girls to learn more protective spells.

"You shouldn't be here," the Grand Sorceress snapped. Magic crackled around her, more magic than Charity could summon at a moment's notice. "How did you get through my wards?"

"It's easy to walk though the wards if you happen to be superior," Deferens said. He had a rich plummy voice, which couldn't quite disguise the scorn. "Or if you happen to know one of the great secrets of the universe."

Charity took a step backwards ... and another, and another, until she was pressed against the far wall. Magic was boiling around the Grand Sorceress now, barely held in check by her indomitable will. And to think that her father had thought he could manipulate her ... Charity shivered, fighting down the urge to turn and run for her life. She'd known the Grand Sorceress was powerful – Lady Light Spinner was the strongest magician known to exist – but she'd never really understood *how* powerful. A flick of her wrist could obliterate Charity as easily as she might step on a bug.

And yet Vlad Deferens had walked through the Grand Sorceress's wards as if they hadn't even existed.

"There are no secrets that would let you past my wards," the Grand Sorceress said. "How did you enter my palace?"

Charity knew she was right. Warding had been a particular speciality of hers – Jamal had encouraged her to learn how to protect herself and her property as quickly as possible – and even though any ward could be broken with enough magic, it would definitely have sounded the alert before it snapped. By all the gods, there were plenty of ways to set up wards to monitor the other wards and alert spells to monitor *those*. And the Imperial Palace was *crawling* with wards, some so ancient that they predated the first Grand Sorcerer. There was no way a team of highly-experienced ward-crackers – or even Inquisitors – could have broken the wards without sounding an alarm. Light Spinner should have had hours to prepare her counterstroke as the wards were weakened, then finally broken ...

"You *wanted* to surrender to me," Deferens said. He leered at the Grand Sorceress, a filthy expression that made Charity feel unclean – and she wasn't even the target! "And so your wards let me through."

Magic billowed around the Grand Sorceress as she took a step forward. "You will leave this place, now," she hissed. "Or fight me in the heart of my power."

Charity shivered in fear. Magic was flaring around both of them now, enough magic to do real damage to the Imperial Palace if they started fighting in earnest. It was hard to tell which of them was the strongest, but it hardly mattered. She knew there would be little left of the palace if they fought ... and there would be nothing left of her. Carefully, she looked towards the door ...

... And Deferens looked at her. And she found her feet frozen to the floor.

"I merely wish to claim my right," Deferens said, as he turned his gaze back to the Grand Sorceress. "You cannot deny me that, can you?"

The Grand Sorceress took another step forward. "What right do you wish to claim?"

Deferens indicated the Golden Throne. "I wish to take my rightful place."

Charity stopped casting counter-spells – none of which seemed to do anything more than waste energy – and stared at Deferens in disbelief. Only a member of the Imperial Bloodline could sit in the Golden Throne and the Imperial Bloodline had been extinct for centuries, as far as anyone knew. The Privy Council might be obliged, by their oaths, to allow anyone who wanted to sit in the Golden Throne a chance, but there had been few takers. It wasn't really surprising. A fake would die the second he sat on the Throne.

Let him do it, she thought, vindictively. *The Throne will kill him.*

But Deferens wasn't stupid, a nagging thought at the back of her mind reminded her. Surely, he would know the dangers of taking the Throne ...

"If you wish," the Grand Sorceress said. Her voice was tight, utterly emotionless, but Charity was sure she was worried. She had to know the dangers too, but her oaths wouldn't let her stop him. "Please. Take a seat, if you dare."

Deferens smiled a victorious smile, then stepped up onto the podium, turned, and sat down on the Golden Throne. Magic blazed around it for a long second – Charity thought that he was about to die – and then the entire palace shook, violently. She screamed in pain as the wards suddenly pressed down on her with terrifying force, then pulled back so quickly that she couldn't help wondering if she'd imagined the whole thing. And yet, her feet were still stuck to the floor ...

"I claim my right as Emperor," Deferens said. He sat on the Throne, illuminated by shimmering golden light. The radiance was magic, Charity realised, because she couldn't take her eyes off him. And it played with her emotions, causing her to feel respect, awe ... and fear. "Kneel."

There was so much power in his words that Charity found herself on her knees before quite realising that her body had started to move. Light Spinner started to kneel, then stopped herself, magic flaring around her. Deferens snorted rudely, then drew on the wards. Charity covered her eyes hastily as light flared through the room, the wards pushing down on their former mistress. There was a scream, then darkness fell like a hammer. And then a thin chuckle echoed through the room.

"You can open your eyes now," Deferens said.

Charity obeyed, helplessly. Deferens was standing in front of Light Spinner, who was still ... too still. He looked down at the veil for a moment, then pulled it free in one savage gesture, revealing a stony face. Charity found it hard to grasp what she was seeing. The Grand Sorceress had been turned to stone! And her face was warped and twisted ...

"So that was what she was trying to hide," Deferens said. He ran his hand over Light Spinner's chin, smiling unpleasantly. "She must have been a very bad girl in her youth."

Charity swallowed as he turned his attention to her. "And you? Are you such a bad girl?"

"No," Charity said.

Deferens turned and walked back towards the Throne. It seemed to have changed, somehow, now that a true heir to the bloodline had taken his seat. Charity tried to move, but her legs refused to obey. It was hard to tell if he'd trapped her in place or she was simply too scared to move a muscle. Sheer terror kept her rooted to the spot.

"You have a choice," Deferens said. "You can serve me, loyally and faithfully, or you can join her. Which do you choose?"

Charity thought about it, somehow calming her thoughts. There was no way she could fight him, not even without the wards backing him up. Light Spinner hadn't been able to fend off the wards and she had been the most powerful magician in the city. She glanced at the warped statue and shuddered, helplessly. That fate – or worse – would be hers if she refused to submit.

But if she *did* join him, what would he make her do? The thought was terrifying, her imagination providing all kinds of possibilities. And yet, she would have a chance to escape, if she waited for the right moment. And maybe she could steer him in more positive directions.

"I will serve you," she said, and bowed her head.

Vlad Deferens – Emperor Vlad I – started to laugh.

Chapter Four

Elaine shook her head in embarrassed amusement as Daria and Johan departed, then rose and started to make her way through the Great Library for the last time. Daria, perhaps because she'd been born and raised among the Travellers, had no sense of the appropriate. Johan was her apprentice, not her boyfriend, and even if they hadn't shared that bond, he was still four years younger than her. It would be inappropriate for her to even consider such a liaison.

But you have to admit he's handsome, her thoughts mocked her. *And he wasn't scared by your eyes.*

She scowled at the thought, angrily. She'd never had a boyfriend at the Peerless School – her low magic levels and constant bullying had seen to that – and she'd only ever had one relationship since, which had faltered as soon as her lover had seen her eyes. Red eyes, *glowing* red eyes, meant tainted magic; they were rarely a good sign. Even a mundane like Bee had known to be scared of them ... and she might have understood, if he'd left someone else. But he'd left her ...

Magic danced around her as she walked through a pair of wards and into the lower chambers, where the magic shimmering through the building was focused. She closed her eyes as soon as she stepped into the chamber, reaching out to touch the wards and perform one last scan of the building for trouble. As always, a number of students had rediscovered a dozen ways to try to cheat in their exams, no doubt convinced that no one else had ever discovered how to use magic to cheat. A handful of others were bending rather than breaking the rules outright; she silently applauded them for exploiting the loopholes, then prayed they wouldn't bend the rules any further. Cheating wasn't just forbidden at the Peerless School; it was *pointless*. No amount of cheating could help a cheater prosper when he or she had to actually use what they'd learnt in the real world.

Idiots, she thought. Mastering the theoretical parts of magic had never been difficult for her, she remembered; it was the practical exams that had almost killed her. *They can't hope to fool the anti-cheating wards on the testing chambers.*

She frowned as the wards reported a handful of dark – or at least grey – artefacts, then sent orders for her staff to investigate. The wards had been tightened up considerably since she'd become Head Librarian, but most wizards tended to consider such wards a challenge to break rather than a warning sign. It wasn't as if she could bar people from the library for anything short of serious misconduct, she reminded herself, even though there were quite a few students who should probably be denied access to the library. Their conduct outside the school had been appalling.

But it won't be my problem for much longer, she told herself. *And someone else will have to worry about it.*

She opened her eyes, then walked into the next chamber. It was piled high with books, mostly older textbooks that had been donated by former students to the librarians. Most of them were out of date, Elaine knew, and therefore largely useless to the current generation of students. She had a feeling that most of them would be shipped to the smaller magical training establishments, if they weren't sold to private tutors. By then, the *next* set of donated books would probably have arrived. There was no shortage of books in the lower levels that hadn't been inspected, let alone tagged or marked for disposal.

Beyond the old textbooks, there was a collection of romance novels someone had sent in, probably as a joke. Elaine sighed – the Great Library stored magical books, not *all* books – and then picked up the first one and glanced at it. The lurid cover made no bones about the content; it showed a smiling woman, naked from the waist up, standing on the beach, while a nude man approached her. Elaine had read a couple of similar books when she'd been very – very – bored at the Peerless School, where the female students had passed them around as if they were forbidden fruit. And yet, they tended to follow the same basic formula. A tiny amount of setting, a pair of characters ... and then chapter after chapter of steamy sex, followed by misunderstandings and fights, and then more sex. She snorted, then put the book back down on the table. The set would probably end up being passed to a cheap bookshop for disposal.

She walked through the next door and stepped into the warding chamber itself. Magic crackled around her, then fell back once it had verified her identity. No one, apart from the Head Librarian and the Grand Sorcerer could enter the chamber without permission, at the risk of their lives. The wards that protected the Great Library were ancient, dating from the days before the First Necromantic War. And that had been thousands of years ago.

"I won't be here again," Elaine said, out loud. She hadn't been the Head Librarian for long, yet it was hard to remember a time when she *hadn't* carried the library's wards in her mind, when she had only been a mere worker in the building. "If I return, I will be ... what?"

It wasn't a pleasant thought. The post of Head Librarian had been ideal, as far as she'd been concerned; she would have happily given up her seat on the Privy Council, if it had meant she could spend more time in the library. Vane could handle the face-to-face issues, Elaine knew, while she could hide in the stacks or inspect new material brought into the library. It wasn't as if she *had* to show herself ... she could happily have lost herself in the labyrinth under the public floors, using the magic to sustain herself. No one would ever have to see her again.

Daria would have dragged you out, eventually, her thoughts mocked her. *And you already have too many problems facing people.*

"I know," she said, answering herself. "But I would have been happy."

She pushed the thought aside, then walked up to the crystal orb resting in the exact centre of the chamber. The designers had known how to build wards in ways their successors had forgotten, ensuring that nothing short of a truly staggering level of force could destroy the Great Library. There were so many protections worked into the defences that even Elaine had trouble seeing how they all interacted, from the ones that shielded the books from harm to the ones that prevented decay. No matter how dusty a tome was when it entered the library, it was unable to decay further until the librarians had inspected the damage and decided how best to handle it.

Bracing herself, she stepped up to the orb and touched it lightly. Instantly, the magic solidified around her and peered into her mind, leaving her feeling naked as it inspected her on a very intimate level. Long seconds passed before the feeling retreated, allowing her to inspect the innermost workings of the Great Library's wards. From here, she could make all the changes she wanted and none but the Grand Sorceress could gainsay her. And, with her knowledge of how the wards actually worked, she might well be able to seal the building off from everyone. But it would leave her trapped inside ...

She pushed the temptation aside and started to work. Vane was already added to the wards, of course, as her deputy. All she really had to do was prime the system, then add Vane once she arrived in the chamber. And then Vane could carry the wards until the Grand Sorceress appointed Elaine's successor. Vane had thought that Elaine would be back, sooner or later, but Elaine had told her otherwise. Even if they succeeded in finding the Witch-King and destroying him for good, they would still have to worry about Johan's true nature being revealed. It would be better if they found a place to stay out of the way and hid there, indefinitely.

And, her thoughts mocked her, *would Johan want to stay with you for the rest of his life?*

The wards shimmered, suddenly, as a message was sent through them to her. "My Lady," the desk attendant said, "there are two Inquisitors here to see you."

Elaine sucked in her breath, then glanced at her watch. The Travellers were punctual to the extreme; if they said they would leave in two hours, they meant it. They weren't parked very far from the Great Library – the Golden City was tiny, hemmed in by the mountains – but the task of handing the wards to Vane would take nearly an hour. She would have to help Vane through the early stages of the transition, after all ...

... But she couldn't refuse to see the Inquisitors.

"I'm on my way," she said. "Show them to my office" – she

paused, trying to think if she'd left anything incriminating in plain view – "and offer them drinks, if they want it."

"Yes, My Lady," the desk attendant said.

Elaine sighed, then pulled back from the orb. As always, there was a sense of disorientation whenever she let go of the supervisory wards, as if she'd been staring into a bright light that had suddenly blinked out of existence. There were stories of people who built themselves elaborate wards and had then been unable to disengage their minds, as if the wards were so much a part of them that they just couldn't let go. The Great Library wasn't that personal – the building was over a thousand years old, far older than Elaine herself – but if it had been, Elaine suspected she would have found it impossible to go. Even now, the thought of permanently separating herself from the library was horrific.

Muttering curses under her breath, she turned and walked out of the chamber, stepping through the labyrinth as though it wasn't there. Vane was waiting outside, her pretty face torn between anticipation and fear. If she served well enough as Head Librarian, she might inherit the job permanently, but it would destroy any hopes she had of a career outside the Great Library. But then, as a younger daughter of a lesser house, she couldn't reasonably expect anything greater.

And I became Head Librarian, Elaine thought. There was no requirement for aristocratic birth to serve in the Great Library. Compared to Elaine, or her predecessor, Vane looked ideal for the job. *I was a no-kin orphan and Miss Prim was a thief.*

"My Lady," Vane said. "What do you think they *want*?"

"The Inquisitors?" Elaine asked. "I have no idea."

She shrugged, expressively. Inquisitors were hardly uncommon visitors to the Great Library, either investigating reports of magic being misused or researching precedents for court cases in the Watchtower. And Inquisitor Dread, at least, was a friend, insofar as Inquisitors could have friends. She'd come to rely on him more than she cared to admit.

"I'll speak to them, then meet you back here," she said. Hopefully, she could dismiss the Inquisitors quickly. Otherwise, she would have to send a message asking Johan to come back to the library, leaving them to find some other way to leave the city. "Just wait for me here."

"Of course, My Lady," Vane said.

Elaine sighed inwardly – Vane was the kind of girl she'd always envied and hated at the Peerless School, even if she *was* a decent person – and then turned and walked up the corridor, back towards her office. The passageways were empty now, not entirely to her surprise; no one, not even an innocent student, wanted to be anywhere near an Inquisitor. Their black robes brought back memories of crimes long forgotten, crimes that were objectively minor, but subjectively terrible. And if an Inquisitor felt like interrogating someone, he could ...

... And only the Grand Sorceress, his ultimate superior, could say no.

She sighed, again. Memories that weren't hers – memories that were really composites from a thousand books – rose up within her mind, mocking her. There were good reasons for the Inquisitors to exist, she knew, reasons that could not be taken lightly. And yet she'd resented her first meeting with Dread, knowing that he could have made it a great deal worse. In truth, she'd managed to escape very lightly.

And you practically lied to him, her thoughts reminded her. *He could have arrested or killed you for that, couldn't he?*

Someone had stuck a ward on her office door, warning all and sundry to keep out unless they had permission to enter. Elaine braced herself, then pushed against the ward. Unsurprisingly, it yielded at once. Someone had keyed it specifically to allow her to enter the room, without resistance. A quick check revealed that the ward was also keyed to prevent her from leaving the room, at least without an Inquisitor. She was growing to be an expert at dismantling wards, but it would take her several minutes and her wand to remove the ward to the point she could make her escape. By then, the Inquisitors would catch her.

Bracing herself, feeling a cold trickle of uncertainty prickling down the back of her spine, Elaine walked forward, into her office.

"Gentlemen," she said.

She'd hoped to see Dread or one of the other Inquisitors she knew personally. Instead, both of them were unfamiliar, their faces half-hidden behind glamours. She would have known who they were, if she'd known them personally; instead, their faces were blurred slightly, just enough to make identification impossible. They were both strongly muscular men, wearing black hooded robes and carrying staffs; one of them was standing in front of her desk, while the other was standing against the far wall. It looked faintly absurd to her, but she kept that thought off her face with an effort. This was clearly more serious than she had realised.

The Grand Sorceress must have sent them, Elaine thought. It was the only explanation that made sense. *But why?*

"Gentlemen," she said. "I'm afraid this will have to be a short conversation."

"It will," one of the Inquisitors said. "Lady Elaine No-Kin?"

Elaine nodded, although she was only a Lady by courtesy. And, while she knew who her father was now, it wasn't something she wanted to acknowledge. Technically, there should have been a reference to Johan in her name too, but she hadn't added it officially. Too many people would have wondered why she bothered when Johan was supposed to be dead.

"Yes," she said, clearly. "Might I ask ..."

The Inquisitor took a step forward, tapping his staff against the floor. "By direct order of His Majesty the Emperor," he said, "you are under arrest."

Elaine stared at him, dimly aware that the other Inquisitor was moving up and around behind her. The Emperor? There was no Emperor – and there hadn't been an Emperor for over a thousand years. But the Inquisitors seemed perfectly serious – she glanced at their hands, just to check they were wearing the skull-rings of *real* Inquisitors – and then back up at the leader's face. There was no hint of humour or amusement in his cold stare. He genuinely believed what he was saying.

She finally managed to speak. "There is *no* Emperor."

"The Emperor has returned and assumed his Throne," the second Inquisitor said. His voice was completely flat, revealing nothing of his thoughts or feelings. But if he was telling the truth, Elaine knew, what he felt was immaterial. Inquisitors were sworn to obey the Emperor before all else, even the Grand Sorceress. "And he has ordered your arrest."

The Witch-King, Elaine thought, mutely. Rumour had given the last Emperor thousands upon thousands of royal bastards, although – as that *had* been over a thousand years ago – the tales had probably grown in the telling. Anyone who actually shared the Imperial Bloodline probably wouldn't know it, unless they sat in the Golden Throne ... and, as the Throne killed anyone who *didn't* share the bloodline, there were few people willing to risk their lives on the slight chance of becoming supreme ruler of the world. But the Witch-King, with his genius for plans that stretched over millennia, could have preserved some of the bloodline in a remote part of the world ...

... And then brought a distant descendant forward to claim his birthright.

"I see," she said, hopelessly stunned. She tried desperately to play for time, utterly unsure of what to do. What had happened to Light Spinner? Surely *she* would not tamely surrender power to a *faux* Emperor. "And the Grand Sorceress?"

"The Grand Sorceress has been removed from power," the Inquisitor said, firmly. "She is no longer any of your concern."

He made a simple gesture with his hand. Elaine's wand leapt from her belt and into his hand; he glanced down at it for a long moment, then dropped it into a pocket on his robes. She took a step backwards, only to walk right into the Inquisitor behind her. He caught her arms and tugged them behind her back, holding her firmly in place. His protections shimmered against her magic, making it impossible for her to cast any spells. She wanted to struggle, but he was holding her too tightly to escape.

The first Inquisitor removed a wand from his belt and pointed it at Elaine's face. It glinted silver, which set off alarm bells in Elaine's head. There were spells – nasty spells – that could only be cast with a silver wand. Panic shot through her mind as she realised what he intended to do, but she was held too tightly to allow her to break free. There was a sudden flare of magic ...

... And a spell crashed right into her mind.

Chapter Five

Elaine almost lost the fight within the first five seconds.

The spell would have beaten her if she'd been a normal magician, the reflective part of her mind noted, even as she fought desperately to ward it away from her soul. Any normal magician, faced with a compulsion and obedience spell, would attempt to push it back, focusing their mind on the intruder until it was forced out of their thoughts. But *this* spell, known only to Inquisitors – and Elaine – actually took advantage of standard countermeasures. Concentrating on the spell would only make it more powerful and dangerous.

She staggered as the spell infested her mind, burning through her protections with a chilling casual ease. The spell, only written down in the Black Vault, was powerful, *too* powerful. It didn't just burn through her thoughts, it sought to twist them permanently. And it had been forbidden, then largely forgotten, because its effects were far too close to permanent. Even if she managed to thrust it out of her mind, it would leave its calling card on her thoughts.

"She's resisting," she heard one of the Inquisitors said, in tones of awe. "I thought that was impossible."

"You were told to take her seriously," the other Inquisitor said. His grip on her wrists hadn't slacked, even for a second. "She was a Privy Councillor. The Grand Sorceress wouldn't have appointed her to the council if she hadn't been quite remarkable."

Elaine barely heard them over the roaring in her mind. The spell was howling through her thoughts, forcing her to acknowledge its presence – and every time she admitted to herself it was there, it weakened her defences. No wonder it was so hard to remove, she noted; it didn't just take over her body and soul, it left them permanently warped, if the spell wasn't removed in time. Even the Inquisitors only used it as a last-ditch method for compelling obedience, not least because there were hundreds of other spells that didn't have such ghastly side-effects. But the Emperor – whoever he was – had to be taking her seriously.

It was hard, so hard, to protect the innermost recesses of her mind without looking at the threat, but she had no choice. The tidal waves washing against her defences only had power if she thought about them, yet it was almost impossible to build her barricades without knowing what she was facing. It was like picking her way through a room with her eyes pressed firmly shut, knowing that opening them meant death. If she hadn't spent months building up new and interesting ways to make the magic she had go further, it would have beaten her.

It's a draw, she told herself, as she opened her eyes. *The spell is held at bay, but I can't force it out of my mind.*

"The spell holds her," the first Inquisitor said. He waved his wand at Elaine's head, scanning the magic running through her body. "Barely."

"But enough," the second Inquisitor said. He let go of Elaine's wrists, allowing her to stand limp. "Search the room for anything interesting."

Elaine barely felt anything as her captor checked her pockets, removing the pair of notebooks and pens she kept with her at all times, then ran his hands over her body calmly and professionally. It felt almost as if she was watching it happen to someone else, as if she were detached from her own body, as if it was almost a dream. The Inquisitor removed the ankle chain she wore, then placed it and the notebooks in his robes. Once, she would have been outraged at losing her chain. Now, it was hard to feel anything.

The spell is working its way into my thoughts, she realised. Stalemated in its first attempt to overwhelm her, the spell was oozing its way around her defences, hunting for weaknesses and gaps it could exploit. She dreaded to think what would happen when the time came to fall asleep. Her defences wouldn't hold under ceaseless pressure and when she woke up, she would be a slave. Unless they removed the spell first ...

Or I find a way to do it, she thought. But it was so hard to concentrate without weakening her defences. She cursed the spell's inventor in her thoughts – she couldn't imagine what sort of monster would devise and use such a spell – then started to probe though her stockpiles of knowledge. *There's no other way to escape.*

She tried to reach out, to touch the library's wards. But the link refused to form.

"You will come with us," the first Inquisitor said. "You will walk normally, but you will speak to no one as we leave the library and travel to the palace."

Elaine felt her body twitch, then start to obey. The haze infesting her thoughts made it impossible to resist, even if she had been able to consider it. If she'd put up any sort of fight, she knew all too well, they would have hammered her into the ground and then dragged her to the palace. Besides, the spell was in control of her body, at least to some degree. She was obeying their commands, after all. It was a horrific sensation, all the worse for knowing that the spell was doing permanent damage. She might never truly recover.

She forced herself to concentrate on building additional defences as her body walked through the door and out into the corridor. The Inquisitors followed her, walking as if they were merely accompanying her on her travels, rather than escorting a prisoner. Part of her mind found that absurdly hopeful – she would have been too embarrassed to show her face if she'd been marched through the streets in handcuffs – but the rest of her knew better. It wasn't as if anyone would come to her rescue, even if they *had* known something was wrong. The Inquisitors weren't just capable magicians, they were *powerful*. It was what allowed them to uphold the system that underpinned the Empire.

A handful of students gaped at the Inquisitors as they walked through the lobby, then hastily scattered. They probably had guilty consciences, Elaine thought sourly; couldn't they tell that something was very wrong? But the spell controlling her limbs made it impossible for anyone to tell that she wasn't moving under her own power ... she cursed herself again for recognising the spell's existence. Every time she noted it was there, it gained an advantage in the struggle to take over her soul.

Cold air slapped her face as they walked outside, reminding

her that the spells that kept the Golden City temperate all year had failed. Light Spinner had been working to fix them, she recalled as she shivered helplessly, but the spells were so old and ingrained into the city that even a team of dedicated workers couldn't fix them. Fashions had changed, Elaine noted, seeing just how many people were wrapped up warmly on the streets. Once, students of both sexes had worn revealing clothes, showing off their bodies. Now, almost everyone was wearing heavy woollen jumpers, charmed to keep the cold away. She had a feeling that there were plenty of students who mourned the change in the weather.

One of the Inquisitors cast a warming spell as the wind started to blow against her face, pushing back her hair. Elaine was almost grateful, even though she knew it was just a courtesy rather than a gesture of apology for arresting her. She gritted her teeth as the spell made her walk onwards, wondering absently why so few people were paying attention to her and her unwanted companions. But then, anyone who paid attention to Inquisitors risked attracting their attention in return.

Everyone is guilty of something, Dread had once said, cynically. *And so they hide from us whenever they can.*

She wondered, suddenly, what had happened to Dread, before reminding herself she should be grateful for his absence. Dread had sworn the same oaths as her companions, oaths that would bind him to obey the Emperor ... whoever he was. If he'd been with them, *he* would have had to cast the spell ... she would have seen it as a betrayal, even though he would have had no choice. Inquisitors were rarely released from their oaths – it had only happened a handful of times in their thousand-year history – and they were *never* disobedient. The oaths wouldn't let them disobey.

It's worse than that, she reminded herself. *The oaths become part of them to the point they can no longer comprehend why they want to disobey. Or why they should disobey.*

She gritted her teeth as she felt the spell surging against her protections. There were horror stories – and true stories that were worse – about what happened when someone was careless in swearing oaths. It was easy, chillingly so, to swear to do something lethal ... or to obey without question, no matter what one was told to do. Or to allow an oath to warp one's mind beyond repair. One of the stories that had never made it out of the Black Vault had talked about a man who had sworn to marry a particular woman – and when he'd found her again, he'd practically kidnapped and raped her. It hadn't had a happy ending.

Snow started to drift down from the heavens as they turned the corner and started to walk towards the Imperial Palace. Elaine sucked in her breath, despite the chill, as she felt the magic radiating around the building, even at this distance. The wards had once been solid but largely impersonal, even when the Grand Sorceress had been in residence. Now, they were bound to a single will. Elaine had known there *was* an Emperor from the moment the Inquisitors had mentioned it, but she hadn't really believed them. But now there was no escaping the truth.

The line of petitioners desperate to see the Grand Sorceress was gone, she noted, and there was blood on the ground. It didn't take a deductive genius to realise that they'd been chased away, probably by the Inquisitors. She wanted to believe that no one had been really hurt, but the blood suggested otherwise. If Light Spinner had been growing more and more impatient with the petitioners, what would her successor make of them?

It was hard to speak. Her mouth didn't seem to want to work properly. But she needed to know.

"The people who were here," she said. "What happened to them?"

"You will be silent," the first Inquisitor ordered. "Shut your mouth."

Elaine's mouth shut with a snap as the spell did its work. She wanted to glare at the Inquisitor, but it wouldn't allow her even that piece of freedom. Instead, all she could do was follow them through the gates – the wards washing over them as they entered – and walk up to the doors. Inside, the walls were lined with soldiers, wearing dark-grey tunics she didn't recognise. They looked tough, incredibly disciplined. And they were clearly prepared for trouble, as they were carrying swords, clubs and shields. Not enough to stand against magic, she knew, but enough to keep the mundane population in check.

But who *were* they? And where had they come from?

The thought nagged at her mind as she was escorted down a long flight of stairs. The Grand Sorcerers had never built up large armies, nor had they permitted any of their subject rulers to muster more troops than was strictly necessary. They'd never *needed* armies, after all, not since the Necromantic Wars. And military power in the hands of subject rulers could cause trouble, even lead some of them to consider revolt. But whoever had become Emperor had clearly prepared for trouble. He'd brought a small army with him when he'd conquered the city.

She tried to recall what little she'd been taught about the Imperial Family, before it had been declared extinct, but there was nothing useful, apart from a list of names. So far back, it was hard to separate truth from legends – or disinformation, spread by later enemies. The Emperor was supposed to have thousands of bastard children, but none of them had come forward to claim the Throne. Now, it was quite possible that none of his descendants – assuming they knew what they were – *could* claim the Throne. How close did someone have to be to the Imperial Bloodline for the Throne to accept them? The spells on the Throne might not accept someone who was a tenth-generation descendant of one of the Emperors.

That would be a recipe for Civil War, she thought, recalling one of the disputes between kingdoms that the Privy Council had had to settle. There had been two heirs, each from cadet branches of the royal family, each with a decent claim to power. In the end, they'd effectively picked one at random. *If just anyone could claim the Throne, provided they had a trace of the bloodline, there would be no way to separate out who had the best claim.*

A door opened, drawing her thoughts back to reality.

"You will wait in this room," the first Inquisitor ordered. "You will not attempt to leave until we come back for you."

He pushed Elaine inside, gently. It was a luxurious chamber, but she wasn't fooled; it was, to all intents and purposes, a holding cell. The Grand Sorcerers – and Emperors, she assumed – had used them to house prisoners with enough status to merit careful treatment, even if they were guilty as sin. She stepped inside, her body obedient to their commands, and looked around, admiring just how carefully the room had been crafted for its purpose. There were comfortable seats, a drinks cabinet, a small set of books and two additional doors, which she assumed led to the bathroom and the bedroom. But there was nothing she could use to break out of the chamber, even if she had had full control of her body. The door was firmly closed and guarded by a powerful set of wards.

She managed to walk over to the sofa and sit down, her entire body trembling as though it were drunk – or drugged. The spell seemed to have receded into the back of her mind, but it was still there, still trying to infest her thoughts. Cursing it under her breath, she closed her eyes and concentrated on her defences. She had expected the spell to have made some headway, but she was shocked when she realised just how many of her defences it had broken down. Hastily, she started to repair the wards as best she could, while solidifying the protections around her mind.

Good thing I don't have a proper link to Johan, she thought, bitterly. *The spell would probably have infested him too ...*

The thought was horrific. Johan had almost no mental defences, compared to her. She didn't want to think about what would happen if someone cast the same spell on him, unless his odd magic somehow repelled it. But where was he? Daria had taken him to the camp and then ... she cursed under her breath. What would happen when Elaine failed to show up as planned? Would they take Johan and leave, or abandon him in the Golden City? And what would Daria do? She could ask at the Great Library ... and then ... what would she be told? It wasn't as if anyone knew Elaine was under arrest.

They saw me leave with two Inquisitors, she reminded herself. *And I must have looked awful.*

She pushed the thought away. It would be better, much better, if Johan and Daria stayed well away from the Imperial

Palace.   Everyone thought Johan was dead, after all; the Emperor would be less than pleased to discover that he was still alive. Or did he already know? He had command of the Palace's wards, after all, and they would have recorded everything that took place within the building.   Had he thought to review everything Light Spinner had done during her time in office? *Could* he review everything or ... or would the wards force him to scan everything in real time? If the latter, reviewing everything would be an impossible task ...

And who in the name of all the gods *was* he?

The Witch-King had to be involved, Elaine was sure. No one else could hide a branch of the Imperial Bloodline from view for generations, perhaps supervising their breeding without letting them know just who and what they were. She tried to calculate the odds in favour of it being a coincidence, and gave up after ten minutes of pointless contemplation. No, the Witch-King had to be involved, which meant that the entire Golden City – and the Inquisitors – were effectively in the hands of the enemy. And they'd never seen it coming.

We knew the bastard could make plans over generations, Elaine told herself. *He was alive, a living breathing human, when the last Emperor sat on the Throne. Why didn't we consider the possibility of him preserving and protecting a surviving member of the Imperial Bloodline?*

Because it was unthinkable, her own thoughts answered her. *We were all taught that the Imperial Bloodline was dead and gone. It never occurred to us to think otherwise.*

Bitterly, she sat back and concentrated on erecting more defences. Despair would simply help the spell force its way into her mind, she knew, and when her defences fell she would be lost forever.   She had to hold on and pray, somehow, that she could find a way to escape before it was too late. But with her magic tied up in fending off the spell, she knew it would be difficult ...

And if she fell asleep, it would be the end.

Chapter Six

"This is really something," Johan said.

Daria turned to look at him. "It is?"

"Yes," Johan said, as he looked at the carriages. "It is."

Johan had grown up in a family where duty was everything, where his older brother was expected to carry on the family name and his younger siblings were expected to marry people who could bring new assets to the family. Their father had trained them to do their part for the family – apart from Johan, who had been considered the family embarrassment at best and a potential disaster at worst. There had been little true love in the family, he knew; truly loving parents would not have allowed them to grow into warped little humans. They had cared more for the family name than for the children who would bear it.

But the Travellers *were* a loving family. The kids ran around happily, while the older children and adults actually worked together. It was almost as if there were dozens of parents for each child, as if whoever had actually birthed the child didn't matter. He saw a child fall and scrape his knee, then get comforted by the nearest pair of adults ... and then go right back to having fun. It was something he had never known in his former home.

"I'm glad you feel that way," Daria said, after a moment. "You and Elaine will be sharing a carriage, I'm afraid, so please check it out" – she jabbed a finger at one of the carriages – "and let me know if it's suitable."

Johan nodded, then walked over to the carriage. A handful of boys and girls, all roughly his age, were sitting in front of it, chatting as they read sheets of paper. He couldn't help thinking that the girls were prettier than his sisters, even though they weren't using glamours to hide any tiny imperfections on their faces. But they were also definitely werewolves ... indeed, almost all of the Travellers were werewolves. He wasn't just looking at a family, he told himself; he was looking at a *pack*. There was no such thing as a lone wolf.

He forced himself to look away from the girls as they started to giggle – like Daria, they could smell the change in his scent – and climbed up into the carriage. On the outside, it was surprisingly small; inside, it was remarkably roomy. Someone had clearly been using magic to enhance the space inside, he realised; it wasn't as impressive as parts of the Great Library, but it was easily large enough for two people. The small collection of pots and pans hanging from the ceiling caught his eye and he looked up at them, then smiled. Hopefully, neither Elaine nor himself would be expected to cook. Their adventures in the mountains had convinced him that he would never make a good chef.

We're going to be undressing together, he thought, and flushed. Maybe Daria had a point, putting them together, but it was going to be embarrassing as hell. *I'll leave her alone to change, then change myself, if we do.*

He sat down on the bed, then closed his eyes and tried to feel for Elaine's presence. It was the furthest they'd been apart since forming the apprenticeship bond, but he could still feel her in the back of his mind. He smiled to himself, feeling an odd sense of reassurance just from knowing the bond was there. Elaine could no more abandon him than she could cut off one of her own hands. The bond, for all that it was weighted in favour of the master – or mistress, in this case – carried obligations of its own.

"Assuming they apply to us too," he muttered to himself. "The rules seem to be different for me."

He sighed. There were times when he wished his magic was *normal*, just like the magic of his brothers and sisters. The bond not forming properly didn't strike him as a good sign. He'd spoken to a couple of apprentices who had visited the library and both of them had shared a much more intimate link with their masters than he enjoyed with Elaine. But it was better – by far – than being Powerless. His family would have kept him prisoner indefinitely, he suspected, or they would have killed him eventually. There had been quite a few children listed in the books who had vanished from the records, somewhere around the time they would have attended the Peerless School. Had they been sent for private tutoring ... or had they been killed for being Powerless? There was no way to know.

And then he felt a sudden shockwave of alarm from Elaine.

He jumped to his feet ... and banged his skull against the low ceiling. Cursing, he rubbed his head with one hand as he tried to reach out to Elaine. But there was nothing, beyond a sense that something was very, very wrong. Elaine's presence was always light and ghostly in his mind, as if she was nothing more than a dream or a figment of his imagination, but now it had faded almost to nothingness. He was aware of her when she slept, he knew; he'd never sensed any change in the bond. But now ... was she dead?

There was a tap on the door. "Are you alright?"

Johan gritted his teeth against the pain, then opened the door. A young girl, barely older than himself, was standing outside, her white hair spilling down over her chest. She'd been one of the children outside, he recalled, probably one of the ones who had giggled at him. But right now it hardly mattered.

"I don't think so," he said. "Can you fetch Daria? Now."

He jumped out of the carriage as the girl sped away, feeling his head spinning in pain. It was difficult to separate his own thoughts and feelings from Elaine's, despite the simple fact that they were two different people. Some of the weirder cautionary tales about apprenticeship bonds had warned that two people could blur together, if they didn't keep a barrier between themselves at all times. It hadn't seemed possible, to Johan, because Elaine was very definitely a woman, but now he had his doubts. He sat down on the ground and forced himself to focus his mind. The pain didn't make it easy.

"Johan," Daria said. He looked up to see her standing, looming over him. "What happened?"

"Something's wrong with Elaine," Johan said. The pain was fading now, but the sense of her presence was also faint. He had no idea what could produce such an effect. According to the books, apprenticeship bonds could *not* be accidentally broken, short of one partner dying while the other survived. And it was next to impossible to sever a bond before time even if both parties consented. "She's in trouble."

Daria's eyes narrowed. "And you know that how?"

"We have a bond," Johan reminded her. "And now she's very faint in my mind."

"The Mothers and Fathers want to leave," Daria muttered. She held out a hand to Johan. "I think we may have to go with them or let them go without us."

Johan took her hand and allowed her to help him to his feet. She was strong, stronger than he'd realised. He'd known that werewolves had enhanced senses of smell, even in human form, but he hadn't known they were physically strong too. Up close, her scent was almost overpowering, a wild scent that played hell with his mind. Part of him wanted to stay close to her; the remainder wanted to run, to leave her far behind. It was easy to remember, now, that werewolves were predators. And to understand why they were feared.

"We can't leave Elaine here," he said, trying to sound firm. A lifetime in his family's house had taught him never to try to assert himself. Even the spellbound maids had enjoyed more magic than himself. "I *won't* leave her here."

"Nor will I," Daria assured him. She let go of his hand, then turned and started to stride towards the largest carriage. "Come with me."

Johan followed her as she walked up to the carriage and then around it, to where a group of men and women were chatting. It was an odd sight; there were times when the group seemed to defer to one or two members and times when they just argued and argued, as if there was no one really in charge. Johan recalled, from what little he'd read, that werewolf packs tended to have an alpha male and an alpha female, but – being partly human – there was a great deal of competition for the posts. He couldn't help wondering how they settled arguments amongst themselves without one of the combatants dying. Maybe they fought to first blood instead.

He hung back as Daria spoke to the group, her face somehow seeming more canine than ever. It was spooky, almost; werewolves were bound by their curse, if he recalled correctly. They had free will and human-level intelligence, yet they also had wolfish patterns in their behaviour that were very hard to break. Judging from the way the pack elders shifted in their circle, it was quite likely that some of them thought – or felt – that Daria shouldn't have interrupted.

Daria looked back at him. "They want to go now."

"Then they can go," Johan said. Elaine was more important than leaving the city with the Travellers. They could make their way to another city and then make contact with the Travellers there, or even hire horses from the closest Iron Dragon station to the badlands. "I need to go after Elaine ..."

A loud trumpet blew, silencing debate. Some of the wolves covered their ears – to them, the trumpet had been intolerably loud – while others howled in shock. The children, running between carriages in a wild game of catch, snapped into wolf forms and howled too, sending up a terrifying racket. Johan almost panicked – he'd read too many stories of howling wolves – as the werewolves huddled together, then relaxed as the parents urged them back into human forms. Daria caught his arm and tugged him away from them, towards a tall man carrying a trumpet in one hand and a scroll in the other.

"A herald?" Johan asked. He hadn't seen one since the day they'd arrived in the city, when one of them had announced the arrival of the Conidian Family to anyone who cared to listen. "What's he doing here?"

Daria shrugged.

The herald slowly unfolded his scroll, his every action suggesting that he was well aware of his own importance. Johan eyed the man's uniform – a red, yellow and green creation that looked alarmingly like a trifle – and carefully kept his amusement to himself. Whoever had designed the uniforms had either been a sadist or had wanted to make damn sure that the wearer would be instantly recognised. Johan rather hoped the herald was paid good money for his efforts. Few people would want to wear such a uniform unless they were insulted with a fairly considerable bribe.

"Hear Ye, Hear Ye," the herald said. His voice was loud enough to carry over the howling from the baby werewolves, probably augmented by some kind of charm. "Hear Ye. By the Grace of the gods – all hail the gods – our Emperor has returned to the city and claimed his Throne. All hail Emperor Vlad of the Golden City!"

Johan gaped at him. An Emperor? The genealogy tables his father had made him memorise, before he'd been confirmed as completely lacking in magic, had said there were no living members of the Imperial Bloodline in existence. And if they *had* been in existence, they wouldn't have lived long enough to claim the Golden Throne. The Grand Sorcerers had been in power long enough to take precautions against any upstarts coming forward to take everything they'd built up over the years. Johan had no doubt, given how he'd been treated by his family, that any *genuine* descendant of the last Emperor would have spent the rest of his days croaking on a lily pad, if he was lucky. Or he might simply have been killed out of hand.

"By order of the Emperor, none may leave the city," the herald continued. "Remain in your homes" – he cast a disdainful look at the carriages – "until his rule is established, then you may do as you see fit. All hail the Emperor!"

The herald blew his trumpet again, then rolled up the scroll and turned to leave. Johan hesitated, then ran after him. The man turned to face Johan, his face unpleasantly sweaty with fear. Clearly, he'd drawn the short straw when he'd been sent to inform the Travellers – and everyone else in the less pleasant parts of the city. And yet, there had been a time when Johan would have happily traded places with him, even if it *had* meant facing angry werewolves.

"You said there is an Emperor," he said. "How?"

The herald eyed him, as Johan's father had done when he had asked a particularly stupid question. "The Emperor took the Golden Throne," he said, in tones Johan wouldn't have used to address his youngest sister. But then, his sister had turned him into a doll more than once and played with him. "He has assumed control of the city."

Johan swallowed. He didn't know how anyone could have taken the Throne, but he suspected the worst. Had someone tricked the Golden Throne? Was that even possible? The Golden Throne was ancient, old enough to be impossible to alter without risking one's complete destruction. Or was there a *real* Emperor seated on the Throne? What did that mean for the city?

"Thank you," he said. He took a breath, then asked the next question. "Who is the Emperor? I mean ... who was he before he assumed power?"

The herald cleared his throat meaningfully. Johan scowled in sudden understanding, then produced a gold coin from his pocket and dropped it into the herald's waiting hand. The man smiled, made the coin vanish in a way that had nothing to do with magic, then leant forward.

"He was Privy Councillor Vlad Deferens," he said. "And now he is the Emperor."

He bowed, then turned and strode off, leaving Johan staring after him in shock. Elaine had told him about Vlad Deferens, but nothing she'd said had been very good. The man had been raised in a fashion that made *Johan's* father seem nice and normal ... and he'd made one bid for supreme power before, back when the previous Grand Sorcerer had died. And if Elaine was right, his hatred of women was legendary. The gods knew his homeland saw an exodus of female magicians every year. How had he been able to cope knowing that the supreme ruler of the world was female?

He must have killed her, he thought. *Or imprisoned her. Somehow.*

"Johan?" Daria said. "What did he say?"

"Vlad Deferens is the new Emperor," Johan said. He was still too stunned to think straight, but certain things were clear. As a Privy Councillor, Deferens might have known Elaine's true nature. She would be a valuable prize ... as well as a woman in a position of power. The bastard could kill two birds with one spell by taking her prisoner. "And Elaine has to be his prisoner."

He cleared his throat. "We have to go after her."

"We can't stay here," Daria said, more practically. "But we need a plan before we try to break into the Watchtower."

She held up a hand. "I'm going to speak with the elders," she said. "You stay here and think."

Johan watched her go, admiring the way her robe tightened around her buttocks, then closed his eyes and tried to reach out to Elaine. But he felt nothing, apart from a faint sense of her presence. Had she been drugged? Or had she been turned into something inanimate? Or ... there were too many possibilities, all of them bad. Elaine was tougher than she looked, but she could be broken; *anyone* could be broken. And once Vlad Deferens got her to talk, he'd know that Johan was still alive.

And he will see me as a threat, Johan thought. He'd never quite come to terms with realising that powerful magicians, the ones who had scorned him as a Powerless, had feared and hated him when they'd discovered he could steal their powers. Vlad Deferens would have Johan killed, once he got his hands on him. *I have to remain out of sight.*

Daria returned, looking grim. "They want us to leave," she said. "I think they're planning to head for the tunnels now, before the city is closed completely."

"They'll have closed the tunnels by now," Johan predicted, grimly. There were only a handful of ways in and out of the Golden City, unless someone wanted to try climbing the mountains. "They'd have done that before they told everyone about the change in power."

"And everyone will want to leave," Daria agreed. She sighed, then shook her head. "I think we'd better find somewhere safe to hide, then think about our next step."

Johan scowled at her. He wanted to find Elaine, now. But he knew she was right. Elaine had to be well-guarded, wherever she was, and they would need a plan – and allies – to get her before Vlad Deferens could turn her into a slave. Or simply kill her out of hand. As Emperor, he would have access to the Black Vault, after all. He might decide he didn't *need* the knowledge crammed in her head.

"Very well," he said, with ill grace. "Where are we going?"

"Somewhere few dare go, even now," Daria said. She turned and started to walk away from the carriages. "Coming?"

After a moment, Johan followed her.

Chapter Seven

It felt like an eternity before the Inquisitors returned to the holding chamber, long enough for Elaine to erect a whole new series of mental defences. They wouldn't hold forever, she knew all too well, but at least they would preserve her mental integrity long enough to allow her to think and plan without opening herself to the spell. The spell itself seemed content to keep control of her body, while biding its time. She was chillingly aware that it was just waiting for her to run out of magic and collapse before it took her over completely.

"On your feet," the Inquisitor ordered. "Are you presentable?"

Elaine glowered at him as her body obeyed orders and rose. She had never been particularly vain, not like Daria or Millicent, but she was sure she wasn't at her best. Her face was probably showing signs of her inner struggle, her robes were torn and dirtied and her hair was completely out of line. The idea of being *presentable* was absurd, given the circumstances.

"Probably not," she snarled, feeling the compulsion to answer the question welling up within her. The spell's inventor had a *lot* to answer for. "But unless you're willing to give me a proper bathroom and a pair of stylists, this is the best I can do."

The thought made her temper worsen. Elaine had never really believed in the gods, but there was a certain amount of satisfaction to be had in listing the hundreds of different hells and imagining which one might be playing host to the demented spell-inventor and everyone who had ever listened to him. The Inquisitor didn't seem concerned by her comment – he'd probably heard worse every day of his career – and merely took her by the arm, then frog-marched her out of the holding chamber. Elaine wondered why he didn't just issue orders and let the spell do its dirty work, then pushed the thought aside as she was half-pulled up the stairs and down towards the Throne Room. The vast army of soldiers she'd seen when she'd entered was gone.

She looked up at the Inquisitor and dared a question. "Where have the soldiers gone?"

"Out on the streets," the Inquisitor answered. "The population must be kept under control."

Elaine blinked in surprise. She'd expected nothing more than a command to shut up – again – or a slap across the face. Instead, she'd received an answer. She puzzled over it as the Inquisitor led her through a pair of doors, wondering if the Inquisitor was resisting his oaths on some level. No matter the oaths he'd sworn, he couldn't be entirely happy about finding himself the servant of a new Emperor. At least the Grand Sorceress had been intelligent as well as powerful and capable.

They entered the antechamber and waited, patiently. It didn't seem to have changed much from when Elaine had last visited, apart from a handful of portraits that had been placed on the walls. They were showing legendary emperors, characters who were as much myth as reality, people who were the very distant ancestors of the man sitting on the Golden Throne, waiting for her. The newcomer had to have put them up, Elaine decided, as she studied the nearest portrait. Light Spinner wouldn't have wanted to remind anyone that there had been a time before the Grand Sorcerers.

Not that anyone would have doubted it, Elaine thought, coldly. *There is always a beginning and an end.*

She pushed the thought aside as the doorway leading to the Throne Room swung open, seemingly of its own accord. Magic washed out at her, scanning her down to her component atoms, then pulled back, allowing her to enter the chamber. The Inquisitor gave her a push, then marched beside her as she stepped through the door. This time, the Golden Throne was glowing, emitting a radiance that was only visible to someone with magic ... and a man was seated on the Throne, lounging there as if he had every right to belong. And his face ...

Elaine stopped, dead. Vlad Deferens.

"Ah, *Elaine*," Deferens said, with faux courtesy. "Come in, come in."

Elaine cursed under her breath as her legs did as they were commanded. She walked forward until she was standing right in front of the Throne, staring at it – and its occupant – as if they were the only people in the room. There was something about the magic that caught her attention and pulled her to it, almost effortlessly. Everyone had *known* the Grand Sorceress and her predecessors were powerful magicians, and knew not to push them too far, but the Emperors inherited their positions through birth. The Throne helped keep their followers humble.

"It must be a surprise to see me here," Deferens said. "Or did you expect me all along?"

"No," Elaine said, truthfully. "I didn't expect to see you."

"You never took me seriously," Deferens commented. His voice hardened. "Did you?"

Elaine winced. She'd disliked Deferens from the moment she'd first heard of him, when she'd learnt about his views on women. If given unlimited power, Deferens would reduce women to servitude, if they were lucky. She didn't understand how *anyone* could harbour such misogynist thoughts, but he came from an entire *country* of misogynists. Humiliating him in public, when she'd thought she would die as soon as the whole affair was over and there was a new Grand Sorcerer, had seemed a good idea at the time.

"I always took you seriously," she said. "I just never liked you."

"And now I am the Emperor," Deferens said.

Elaine half-closed her eyes in the hopes it would make it easier to see, but it didn't work. The radiance from the Throne was magical, after all. It wasn't something she could just block out, as long as magic ran in her blood. The Golden Throne was far more than just a seat, she knew; it was something more, something protective. And it couldn't be fooled. If Deferens had been accepted by the Throne, he was the rightful heir.

"Tell me something," she said. "When did you know you were the heir?"

Deferens frowned. "I have always known," he said. "My

family have cherished the bloodline for a thousand years."

"But when did you *know*?" Elaine repeated. "How did you learn?"

And who, she asked herself, *am I talking to right now?*

She leant forward, studying Deferens closely. He had always been unkempt, prancing around in skimpy clothes so he could show off his muscled arms and legs, but now there was something a little different about him. Deferens had an ... edge to him that hadn't been there before, she was sure. And that edge meant that he might have been touched by the Witch-King.

Or touched by the Golden Throne, she thought. *Who knows what the Throne does to successful candidates.*

"I just knew," Deferens said.

Elaine shook her head, slowly. She would bet her small fortune that Deferens *hadn't* known, until he'd been nudged into taking the Golden Throne. His family would be protected by their ignorance – and their distance from the Golden City. And their warped social structure might have been designed to allow the Witch-King to breed them, as a dog-breeder might breed his dogs. By controlling the women so precisely, the Witch-King might have been able to ensure that Deferens had precisely the right link to the Imperial Bloodline that he needed to take the Throne.

And we told ourselves that we were so clever when we blocked his first attempt to grab the Throne, she thought, bitterly. How did one beat an opponent who had literally centuries to lay his plans? *Did Kane lay waste to part of the city just to cover the Witch-King's plans?*

She yelped as a sharp smack exploded against her bottom. "As I was saying," Deferens said, as the Inquisitor stepped backwards, "I now rule the world."

"So it would seem," Elaine said, resisting the urge to rub her behind. "You don't rule everyone, not yet."

Deferens smirked. "It's only a matter of time," he said. His expression became ugly. "And now it is time for *you* to pledge your loyalty."

"Go to one of the hells and stay there," Elaine snapped.

He surprised her by laughing. "The spell my puppets used on you will wear you down, eventually," he said. "You will be worse than an oath-sworn servant then, my dear Elaine; you will be a slave, a helpless slave, unable to resist even the slightest order. You, of all the people in this city, know it. Swear to me and you will maintain at least *some* freedom."

Elaine bit her lip. He was right, she knew. Sooner or later, she would have to sleep – and when she opened her eyes, she would be as obedient and helpless as Deferens could possibly want. But she would still have a chance to beat the spell, if she could sit down and focus for a few hours, before it was too late. Swearing an oath of loyalty to him would destroy any chance of resistance for good.

"Never," she said.

"In a day or two, perhaps less," Deferens said. "Perhaps *much* less."

He rose to his feet and leered down at her. The radiance faded slightly, allowing Elaine to tear her attention away from him and look around. A young girl – Charity Conidian, she thought – was kneeling in the shadow of the Golden Throne, her eyes wide with fear. Despite her own condition, Elaine felt a stab of sympathy. Charity had probably been bullied into offering Deferens her oath, even though she was technically a Family Head. She would now be nothing more than his slave, as long as her magic held out.

"You should look over there," Deferens said. He pointed one long finger into a dark corner, where something lurked in the shadows. "What do you make of it?"

Elaine frowned, puzzled by the abrupt change in subject. The object looked humanoid, but too still to be a living human. An animate statue? There were legends about statues that only moved when one wasn't looking, legends that various sorcerers had tried to make real after realising what wonderful guards they would make. But only the very greatest of them could animate a single statue, let alone protect it from counterspells cast by roving thieves.

"Let me show you," Deferens said. He cast a spell, crafting a beam of light which he shone into the corner. "Now what do you see?"

Elaine stared in horror as she realised that it was no statue. She was, as far as she knew, the only living person who knew what Light Spinner looked like, under her veil. The Grand

Sorceress had experimented with wild magic, in her younger days, and she'd been lucky. She'd *only* escaped with heavy scarring, scarring that – like Elaine's eyes – no amount of magic could hope to fix. And she'd hidden her face for fear of what would happen if people knew she'd been scarred so badly. It was hard, Elaine knew, to blame her. People who were touched by wild magic tended to go insane very quickly.

And the statue wasn't *of* Light Spinner, it *was* Light Spinner.

She stepped forward, drawn by a compulsion she didn't recognise, until she was touching the stone. Normally, there would have been a shimmer of magic around any transfigured object, human or animal. But the statue had only the faintest glimmerings of magic, suggesting that the spell hadn't just petrified Light Spinner, it had locked her so firmly in place that even her thoughts had shut down completely. Perhaps it was a mercy, Elaine knew. Being an object, even for a few brief moments, could be terrifying.

Deferens caught her shoulder, his touch making her want to cringe away. "Impressed?"

Elaine pulled herself free of him. "What have you done to her?"

"Merely taken what was mine," Deferens said. "And now ... will you swear to me?"

"No," Elaine said.

"I could *order* you to swear to me," Deferens leered.

"I don't think it would work," Elaine said. Oaths didn't take unless they were sworn willingly, although there were plenty of ways the line between willing and unwilling could be fudged by an unscrupulous sorcerer. "And besides, as you say, your spell would leave me helpless anyway."

Deferens gave her a puzzled look. For the first time, she thought she saw a glimmer of respect in his eyes.

"And you would sooner be broken completely than swear to me?" he asked. "You have very strange priorities."

"Go to the hells," Elaine said.

She braced herself, expecting torture or drugs, anything that could break her will and allow the spell to do its work. Instead, Deferens merely laughed.

"I could kill you," he said.

"I doubt it," Elaine said. Taunting him might get her killed, but that wouldn't be such a bad thing, not really. She knew she couldn't hold out for long if they brought out the thumbscrews. "You wouldn't get the knowledge in my mind if you blew me into little pieces, would you? You need to keep me alive."

"And I can promise you humiliation after humiliation when the spell completes its work," Deferens hissed, angrily. "Can you imagine how you could be used when I wasn't tapping your brains?"

Elaine wondered how hard he'd had to bite back a killing spell. If half the rumours Daria had dug up, while she was laying bets on the outcome of the competition to choose the next Grand Sorcerer, were true, Deferens had never taken any cheek from anyone ... unless, of course, he'd needed them. He had a certain charm, Light Spinner had once admitted, that was surprisingly disarming. But not when he held all the cards.

"Better make sure you don't accidentally kill me," Elaine taunted. "Where would you be then?"

Deferens glowered down at her, then pointed a finger at the wall. "Stand there ... no, *kneel* there," he ordered. "And watch as I consolidate my power."

Elaine obeyed, helplessly. He was trying to rub in just how helpless she was and, she had to admit, it was working. Her body did as it was told, while her mind was under siege. The longer she stayed awake, the weaker she'd be and, eventually, she would fall. She was mildly surprised he hadn't knocked her out, but he probably had no idea what would happen if she was forced to sleep. Very little was actually known about the long-term effects of the spell because it normally worked at lightning speed.

She turned as she reached the wall and knelt, then watched grimly as Charity rose to her feet and headed towards the door. Deferens himself sat on the Throne, drawing strength from the power shimmering through the Palace's wards, and waited. Moments later, the first of the city councillors stepped through the door and stared at Deferens. His comrades followed him into the Throne Room, their faces slack with shock.

They never expected to deal with a real Emperor, Elaine thought. *None of us saw this coming.*

She gritted her teeth as the councillors chattered amongst themselves, then walked slowly towards the Throne and prostrated themselves before it, following protocol that had gone out of fashion when the last Emperor had died. They – or rather their predecessors – had made a deal with the Grand Sorcerers; they would continue to run the city, while respecting the Grand Sorcerer's authority. As the Grand Sorcerers hadn't wanted the hassle of running the Golden City, they'd agreed to the deal. But now ... who knew what an Emperor would want to do? And one so magically powerful?

"You may rise," Deferens said. "Do you respect my right as Emperor?"

"Yes, Your Majesty," the Council Leader said, quickly. It would have been suicide to say anything else. "You have taken for yourself the Golden Throne. As such, we are honour-bound to recognise your lineage."

"Then I thank you," Deferens said. There was no hint of irony in his tone. "Your positions are confirmed, my councillors, and will remain in your families, as long as you obey. Should you not obey, your families will be banished from the Golden City and exiled to far-flung islands."

A fate worse than death, Elaine thought, sardonically.

She sighed, inwardly. It was, for them. The Golden City was their home – and the centre of power for the entire Empire. To leave the cramped city, confined by the mountains, would mean abandoning the power their families had built up over the generations. Even if they proved to be big fish outside the city, almost anywhere else within the Empire, they would still be small fry compared to those who remained in the Golden City. No wonder Johan's father had spent so much money on moving into the city, after Kane had killed so many of the city's previous residents. It was his one shot at propelling his family right into the very highest levels of power.

And it would have succeeded too, Elaine thought, *if he'd treated Johan a little better.*

Her knees were aching by the time the last of the supplicants had entered the Throne Room, pledged his loyalty – there didn't seem to be any women among them – and retreated back into the antechamber. She distracted herself by setting up new defences, even though she knew it was just a matter of time before she lost control – and herself.

"You can take her back to her quarters," Deferens ordered Charity, gesturing with one hand towards Elaine. "And make sure she doesn't do anything stupid, like trying to kill herself."

"Yes, Your Majesty," Charity said.

Elaine swore, mentally, as Charity beckoned her forward. Suicide was wrong, but the thought had crossed her mind as a last resort. How far had she fallen, she wondered, if she was praying for someone *not* to order her to preserve her own life?

"Come with me," Charity said.

Helplessly, Elaine obeyed.

Chapter Eight

Charity had met the Head Librarian twice; once, when she'd asked her father to give her a little help with her studies and once, again, when Johan's strange powers had emerged from wherever they'd been hiding. She had never really understood why the Grand Sorceress had given Elaine No-Kin the job, although she supposed as a Privy Councillor there must be more to her than there seemed. But the position would have ideally suited someone from one of the Great Houses ...

Now, the Head Librarian was following her like a dog following her master, shaking with the force of the internal struggle in her mind. Charity shuddered in sympathy; the oaths she'd sworn to the Emperor nagged at her mind, but at least they weren't infesting her thoughts and warping them into helpless servitude. She still had freedom of thought, even a considerable amount of true freedom, as long as she didn't disobey or defy the Emperor. The Head Librarian would be nothing more than a puppet in a scant few hours.

"I'm sorry," she muttered, "but resistance was futile."

"He's mad – worse than mad," the Head Librarian said. Her voice sounded harsh, broken. "What were you thinking when you pledged yourself to him?"

"I was thinking that I wanted to survive," Charity snapped back at her. Intentionally or not, Johan had robbed her of her confidence. "He would have killed me as easily as he killed the Grand Sorceress."

"It might have been better if you had been killed," the Head Librarian said. "He's a monster."

Charity nodded in bitter agreement. She'd watched Emperor Vlad – her thoughts wouldn't allow her to call him anything else – ever since she'd sworn her oaths and she'd seen hints of the monster he was, lurking below the surface. He'd brought soldiers to the Golden City, given orders for them to clear the streets using whatever methods were necessary ... and humiliated a pair of female Inquisitors. It was madness, but he'd done it anyway. She'd been left with the uneasy thought that she'd sworn endless loyalty and obedience to a madman.

"I had no choice," she said.

"There's always a choice," the Head Librarian said.

"Shut up," Charity hissed. The Head Librarian's mouth closed with an audible *snap*. "I don't have to listen to your ... to your condescension!"

She cursed her father and both of her oldest brothers under her breath. Why couldn't her father have given her proper training? By all the gods, why hadn't he disowned Jamal after the third or fourth complaint about his behaviour and declared *her* the Prime Heir instead? She could have had months, perhaps years, to learn how to handle the family magic and the skills of being a Family Head, rather than having to improvise when the world blew up in her face. Now ... now, to all intents and purposes, House Conidian no longer existed as anything other than an adjunct to the Emperor. Her younger siblings would have no choice but to follow her lead.

It was better than having her mind slowly worn down, she told herself. But only by degree.

They reached the holding chamber and opened the door, revealing a surprisingly luxurious room. Charity sighed, recalling how some of the bad boys of High Society were placed under house arrest rather than being held in the Watchtower, then motioned for the Head Librarian to walk into the chamber. She obeyed, her muscles moving oddly as the spell gripped her mind tighter and tighter. Charity watched as she reached the centre of the room and stopped, dead. The spell would hold her there until it had completed its task ...

"You may move freely, as long as you do not leave this apartment," Charity said, feeling another flicker of sympathy. Who would have thought that such a mousy little girl could hold out against such a spell? Or show the nerve to defy the Emperor on his throne? "What does the Emperor want with you?"

"He wants power," the Head Librarian said. "And I can give him power."

"But you can't resist forever," Charity said. The Emperor had gloated that the spell his Inquisitors had orders to use would eventually burn through the strongest mental defences, no matter how much magic the victim had to burn. "The spell will leave you a vegetable. Why not give him what he wants?"

"That's your oaths talking," the Head Librarian pointed out, snidely. "It isn't enough for him to claim your obedience, Charity. He wants you to be his mindless supporter too."

Charity felt a hot flush of anger. What did the Head Librarian, a girl of no family, know about the obligations that bound her to the Emperor? Or what she'd had to do to hold the family together, now her father and oldest brother were effectively dead? The vultures had been gathering, pecking at the corpse, when she'd gone to the Imperial Palace. There had been no choice, but to ally herself with the Emperor. The family needed a powerful protector.

"Shut up," she snapped, again.

Charity fought hard to keep a grip on her anger. She could issue any orders she liked, she knew, and the Head Librarian would obey. The spell would see to her obedience. But she knew, too, that Johan had turned so violently against his family because they'd mistreated him, when they thought they could. There was no point in humiliating the girl facing her, not now. She would belong to the Emperor soon enough.

"Stay here," she said. "Do not leave this room."

She turned and marched out of the door, then banged it closed behind her. There were a handful of bolts on the door – the only thing that marked it as a prison – and she slammed them shut with every sense of satisfaction. The Head Librarian would remain bound until her defences were completely gone, whereupon she would be helpless. She would never have the ability to think for herself again.

Good, Charity thought, vindictively.

A pair of guards appeared at the end of the corridor and she waved them forward. "Guard this door," she ordered, when they eyed her suspiciously. They weren't guardsmen from the Golden City, but part of the force the Emperor had brought with him from his homeland. "No one is to enter or leave without the Emperor's permission."

They looked surprised that she was issuing orders – in their homeland, women were never permitted to issue orders to men – but they did as they were told. Charity nodded to herself, then hurried back down the corridor, heading towards the Throne Room. A small army of enslaved workmen were already at work, taking down the portraits of various sorcerers of renown and replacing them with ancient paintings of past Emperors, all over a thousand years old and worth more than a house in the Golden City. She paused as she caught sight of one of them and smiled as she realised just how closely Emperor Vlad resembled his long-gone ancestor. Perhaps, if the paintings had been placed in a gallery and made open to the public, someone would have remarked on it a long time ago.

She hurried past the workmen and into the Throne Room, where a small line of suppliants were bowing before the Emperor. Most of them were tradesmen, responsible for binding the Empire together into a coherent entity; the remainder were magicians who ran their own businesses, rather than working directly for the Grand Sorceress or one of the Great Houses. Jamal had always sneered at them, but their father had pointed out that the businessmen often had specialities and freedoms that the Great Houses couldn't afford to overlook. Her brother had not been impressed.

"Lady Charity," the Emperor said. He looked down at the suppliants. "You may all wait in the antechamber."

None of the suppliants looked very happy, but they knew better than to argue. Anyone who wanted to disagree with the Emperor only had to look at the statue of Light Spinner to change their mind, or have it changed for them by one of their companions. The Emperor was likely to be even less patient with dissent than the Grand Sorcerers, who had often considered it a wasted week if they couldn't kill or humiliate one person personally. Even Light Spinner had had to make a few examples of idiots willing to question her in the early days of her reign.

Charity went down on both knees and lowered her gaze as the Emperor looked back at her. It was strange, part of her mind noted, how it was becoming increasingly hard to remember that there had been a time before the Emperor. Had it really been less than a *day* since he'd taken the Golden Throne? Everything before the moment he'd sat down seemed almost like a dream, even though she knew it was all too real. The oaths might be twisting her mind ...

... And the truly frightening thing about the whole concept was that she *wasn't* scared of the thought.

"Your Majesty," she murmured.

"I have sent messengers to the remaining Great Houses," the Emperor said. His voice was rich with amusement, amusement he didn't bother to try to hide. Powerful he might have been, but he lacked the bloodline of any of the Great Houses. They'd always looked down on true outsiders. Now, they had to do homage to the man they'd scorned. "They will assemble in the Blue Tower, where you will speak my words to them."

Charity blinked in surprise. "You won't speak to them yourself?"

"Let them get used to the idea of bowing before me," the Emperor said, firmly. "You will carry my words to them."

Her father would probably have understood instantly, Charity reflected. It took her several minutes to work her way through the multitude of possible meanings. The Emperor might be sending her as his messenger to underline her new status as his ... assistant, or he might be showing his contempt by sending her, rather than going himself. Perhaps he wanted to do both, she told herself. Or maybe he just didn't want to be bothered with the Great Houses any more than strictly necessary. He had to know they would resent his rise to power.

They're not going to like it at all, Charity thought. *At least they knew where they stood with the Grand Sorcerers.*

The Emperor smirked at her, then started to outline what he wanted her to say. None of his words were very compromising, although he did manage to hint that he would recognise the Great Houses as being part of his court if they behaved themselves. Charity shuddered to think of what her father would have said, if faced with such demands, but there was no way she could refuse her orders. Instead, she bowed her head, then rose to her feet and backed out of the Throne Room. Turning her back on the Emperor would have been an unforgivable insult.

She turned the moment she entered the antechamber, then walked through the maze of corridors towards the giant doors that opened into the gardens. Even the Emperor had only a tiny garden – it wasn't worthy of the name, compared to the lands her family had owned before they'd moved to the Golden City – but it was larger than any other private garden within the city. The Golden City was just too cramped to allow even the aristocracy to clear large spaces of land for themselves.

Snow was drifting from high overhead as she stepped through the doors and out into the open air. She cast a warming charm around herself, then hurried towards the Blue Tower, safe and secluded at the other end of the gardens. The sight took her breath away as she stumbled through the snow; the tower was made of stone, but sheathed in blue marble. Rumour had it, if she recalled correctly, that one of the previous Grand Sorcerers had used it for secret liaisons with his conquests, which had included every aristocratic or magical woman in the Golden City. Charity rather doubted it; Jamal might have been a complete idiot when it came to women – and their parents had often required a great deal of very expensive soothing – but the Grand Sorcerer wouldn't have time to chase every woman he saw. He wouldn't have any time for ruling!

Inside, it was warm and surprisingly – or perhaps not surprisingly – comfortable. Charity shrugged off the snow that had settled on her robes, then looked around at the handful of powerful magicians facing her. Most of them came from families that were old when the Empire itself was young, tracing their ancestry back over thousands of years. A couple were dirt poor, but still strong in magic and land. And bloodlines ... she knew her father, with his eye for a good deal, might well have tried to marry her to one of their sons. Or even to the Family Head himself.

"I thank you for coming," she said. "The Emperor is most

pleased."

She kept her face expressionless with an effort. She'd never faced powerful aristocrats like these before, not on her own. All she'd been expected to do, when her father had hosted guests in their house, was look pretty, do as she was told and try to catch their eyes without being too forward about it. And she hadn't been particularly good at it.

"The Emperor," Lord Falcate said. She vaguely remembered him being a Privy Councillor under Light Spinner, which had made him one of the most powerful men in the Empire. "Do we really have an Emperor?"

"The Golden Throne has accepted him," Charity said, bluntly. "None but the Imperial Bloodline may sit there and live."

"Yes, we *know*," Lord Falcate said. It was one of the first things children were taught, even the magic-less kids who barely had a year or two of schooling before they went to work. "I do not believe it, though."

"I swear that it is true," Charity said.

"We all felt the shift in the magic," Lord Ahlstrom said, tartly. "We must concede that an Emperor has finally resurfaced."

Charity took a breath. "I have already pledged myself to his service," she said. "As such, I bring a message from him to you."

She frowned at their expressions. No doubt they'd hoped to loot House Conidian before she managed to secure all of the family's property, which would have included the children. Her younger siblings were too young to marry, but not too young to enter into marriage contracts that would have given their prospective parents-in-law too much influence and power over their lives. And over what they could claim as their share of their family's former assets ...

... But if she was working for the Emperor, they would be safer leaving what remained of her family alone.

"The Emperor is grateful for your service in keeping the magic-users of the city under control," she said. A pleasant statement and a threat, rolled into one. No one could hope to forget that it was the *Inquisitors* who kept magic-users under control. "As such, he is prepared to renew your Charters of

Power, which were drawn from the early days of the first Grand Sorcerer. However, he requests proof of your goodwill and loyalty."

"I hope he is not expecting us to swear any unlimited oaths," Lord Ahlstrom snapped.

"No, My Lord," Charity said. "He is requesting that you – that each of the magical families – hand over a child, someone who can be trained to serve the Emperor."

And serve as a hostage, she thought.

She shivered. It wasn't an uncommon practice for hostages to be exchanged, particularly when two rival families tried to come to terms despite years of mistrust and outright hatred on both sides. Charity had half-expected to spend a year or two in the house of a rival family herself, when her father had been negotiating a complex long-term agreement with them. But, in the end, the talks had broken down. She'd been relieved, if she recalled correctly. A later breakdown of the agreement would have meant her certain death.

"The Emperor wants one of our children?" Lord Ahlstrom demanded. He sounded shocked at the mere thought. None of the Grand Sorcerers had insisted on taking hostages. "Is he mad?"

"The Emperor wishes to have nothing but good relations with you," Charity said. As far as she knew, that was actually true. "However, you will have to accept the supremacy of the Imperial Bloodline."

She paused. "Those of your children who go to work in the Imperial Palace will also have access to the Emperor," she added. "They will have the chance to seek positions of power."

They looked doubtful, but accepting. It *was* unusual to hand over a hostage without receiving another in return, yet the Emperor was on a fundamentally different level from any of the Great Houses. And besides, law and custom allowed the hostages plenty of leeway to write to their families. There would be a chance for them to try to manipulate the Emperor, as the years wore on. It wasn't a bad bargain ... as long as they were prepared to toe the line. If they weren't, the hostages would be the first to die.

"I will present my young daughter," Lord Ahlstrom said,

finally. "She will take up a place in the Imperial Palace."

Because she's your fifth child, Charity thought cynically, as the others made similar promises. None of them offered a senior family member. The firstborn children, the Prime Heirs, would never be used as hostages, even if there were no other candidates, but even second or third children had their uses. *You might mourn her death, but it wouldn't damage your family.*

"Thank you," she said, out loud. "The Emperor will be pleased."

Chapter Nine

Johan hadn't spent anything like enough time on the streets, not when his father had rarely allowed him to leave the house, but even he could tell that an air of fear and uncertainty was settling over the Golden City. The streets were normally crammed with people, even when the snow was falling; now, they were almost deserted, with only a handful of men and women walking to and from their homes. They looked around almost furtively as they moved, as if they expected to be attacked at any moment. Johan had a feeling they might have had a point.

"Over here," Daria hissed. Her nose wrinkled as she sniffed, loudly. "Someone is coming."

Johan frowned – the blizzard was growing stronger – but he trusted her nose. She pulled him into a darkened alleyway and tapped her lips, warning him to keep quiet. Moments later, a line of soldiers marched out of the snowstorm, heading down towards the mountains that marked the edge of the city. They wore fighting armour, rather than the ceremonial gear he'd seen on the City Guard, and carried swords and shields. It looked, very much, as if they were going to war.

He felt his frown deepen as he caught sight of the emblem on their shields. It wasn't the standard wand and staff that represented the Empire, but a sun shining brightly in the sky, representing ... what? He had the oddest feeling that he'd seen something like it before, perhaps in one of the books he'd devoured when he'd still held out hopes of being able to make his own way in the world. But the memory refused to surface as the soldiers marched onwards and vanished into the snow.

"No one should be able to bring an army here," Daria muttered. "But someone did."

Johan turned to look at her. She seemed unbothered by the

cold – a werewolf wouldn't be bothered by changes in temperature – but deeply worried.

"They weren't the City Guard," he said. "They were *real* soldiers."

"Yeah," Daria said. "So where did they come from?"

She slipped onwards, leading the way up the street and through one of the markets. Johan had always enjoyed markets as a young man, but this one was eerie. The stalls were empty, their owners either hiding for the night in their homes or huddled in the pub, discussing the situation with their mates. A handful of vagrants were trying to sleep under the stalls, relying on the wood for shelter; Johan had the uneasy feeling that many of them would freeze to death in the coming days, if the snowstorms grew worse. Daria ignored the sight and kept walking, heading onwards into the poorer parts of the city. Every so often, she pulled Johan aside as soldiers walked past, clearly on patrol. Sometimes, they had prisoners with them as they walked.

"They're keeping the streets clear," Daria muttered. "They must be desperate to keep the citizens from talking to one another."

Johan nodded, sourly. He'd thrilled to tales of war from the days before the Empire, although his father had often pointed out that most of the stories were glorified. The good guys never lost a man, while the bad guys died in their thousands ... and it was remarkably sterile. Johan had seen more blood when he'd cut his finger than any of the characters in the stories had ever seen. And yet, he could have made it as a soldier. Or a guardsman. Or even an accountant working for the bureaucrats. If only he'd been allowed a chance ...

But there was nothing fun about being under military occupation.

"Hey!" A voice snapped. "Stop right there."

"Shit," Daria muttered, yanking Johan down yet another alleyway. The sound of pounding footsteps told them that they hadn't managed to hide in time. "Keep moving ..."

They ran out of the alleyway and straight into another group of soldiers. Johan cursed under his breath as the men turned to face them, their grim expressions becoming tighter when they laid eyes on Daria. He reached for his magic. The soldiers froze solid, literally. Daria gaped at him, then tugged him forward, leaving the soldiers behind. Johan honestly wasn't sure if they would be fine, or if whatever he had done to them was permanent. No one, not even Elaine, had managed to get a handle on how his powers really worked.

"They would have carried protective charms," Daria said, as they ran through the slippery streets. "And you managed to overpower them."

"I think so," Johan said, doubtfully. Normal protections didn't seem to stop *his* magic. "But the next person we run into might be an Inquisitor."

"Probably, knowing my luck," Daria said. She paused. "Can you make us invisible?"

"I don't know," Johan said. There were hundreds of invisibility spells, but his magic didn't follow the usual rules. "I can try."

Daria shook her head. "Just keep walking," she said. "And hope we get there before those soldiers get better, or their friends find them there."

Johan shuddered as they walked. Being transfigured had always been terrifying, even though the spells Jamal and his other siblings used wore off, eventually. His powers, on the other hand ... nothing about them quite made sense. Even Elaine hadn't been able to undo some of his work, despite her vast knowledge of the way magic worked. It was quite possible that he'd frozen the soldiers for good.

And there was another mystery. Elaine – and Jamal, and Charity, and every other regular magician – exhausted themselves when they cast spells. Jamal, whatever else could be said about him, had been a powerful magician ... and even *he* had tired, when he cast complex spells. But as far as Johan could tell, his powers didn't seem to cost him anything, not even a bout of weariness. The power just seemed to come from nowhere.

"It makes no sense," Elaine had said, weeks ago. "You should be getting the power from *somewhere*, but where?"

Daria glanced back at him. "Do you know where we are?"

"No," Johan said, shortly. The Golden City might be small

– it took barely half an hour to walk from one side to the other – but he'd never had the opportunity to memorise a map, let alone explore as extensively as he would have liked. "Where are we?"

He looked around, doubtfully. The Golden City was so cramped that even a small house was staggeringly expensive. His father had moaned about the cost often enough, looking for ways to avoid paying a small fortune each year just to maintain the house. But here ... the houses looked weird, as if they'd been submerged in water and then left to dry in the open air. There was a scent of decay in the air, and ... and strange sensations that left a chill running down his spine. He couldn't help noticing that the snow was refusing to lie on certain houses.

"This used to be called the Blight," Daria explained. "Some idiot was casting forbidden spells and he managed to unleash a tidal wave of wild magic, which rendered the entire area uninhabitable. Only a desperate person would risk hiding in the houses here, because he might go to sleep and wake up in a completely different form. Elaine did something here and cleansed it of most of the wild magic."

"I ... see," Johan said. His father had said something about it once, he recalled, but he hadn't been paying attention. And Elaine was hardly the sort to blow her own trumpet and brag about her achievements. "If it's safe, why aren't people moving in?"

"Some bits are still unsafe," Daria said. "But the areas that *are* safe, Johan, belong to the Grand Sorceress. She was allowing the richest families in the Empire to bid on completely new lots, within the Golden City. The bids were still going up, the last I heard."

She stopped in front of a house and pulled a small wooden wand from her pocket, then waved it twice in the air. "This should be safe enough," she said. "And very few people will come here, fortunately."

The door opened with a creak, revealing a very strange room. Johan blinked in shock as he realised that nothing quite made sense, as if he'd stepped into a room decorated with funhouse mirrors. The walls looked oddly out of place, while the furniture seemed warped and twisted. And yet it all still seemed remarkably intact.

"They'll want to knock the whole building down and start again," Daria said, as she closed the door behind them. "No one would want to live here permanently."

She paused, then glanced into the fireplace. "Do you know how to build a fire?"

"Barely," Johan said. He'd built fires with Elaine when they'd been living away from the city, but Elaine had told him not to try to light one using his magic. "Can you light it?"

"Probably," Daria said. She picked up a warped chair, two of its legs clearly longer than the other two, and started to break it into pieces of wood. "Put these in the fireplace, along with anything else that might burn, then give me a shout."

Johan obeyed, glancing around for something lighter than pieces of wood. A pile of broadsheets lay in one corner; the paper looked all right, he discovered when he picked it up, but the writing was in a language that was completely unfamiliar. He frowned at the sight – the Empire had used the same written language for so long that there were few native speakers or writers of anything else – and then started to tear the paper up for the fire. The next set of pages showed images of strange creatures with giant eyes, long tentacles and nasty expressions. None of them seemed to resemble anything he knew to exist. Shaking his head, he carried the paper over to the fire, dropped it into the fireplace and built up a small pile of paper and wood.

"Add this to the top," Daria said, as she came back into the room. She was carrying a small grey object in one hand, cradling it gently. "It should have been burned years ago."

Johan took the object and looked down. It was so badly warped that it took him several seconds to realise it was a doll, one hand-carved by someone who had loved the doll's owner. He felt a sudden pang of grief for the missing child, wondering if she had escaped the wave of wild magic or if she had died beside the doll. She'd been a lucky girl, he decided, as he placed the doll on top of the fire. Even Jamal hadn't had anything made with his father's hands.

"We burn our dolls when we reach adulthood," Daria said,

as she pointed the wand at the fire and cast a spell. There was a flicker of fire, then the paper caught, sending flames crackling through the grate. "It's supposed to mark the day we cast off our inner child and embrace the adult world."

Johan held his hands in front of the flames, enjoying the heat. "Is that a Traveller ritual?"

"Yeah," Daria said. "I was very surprised when Elaine showed me the doll she had kept from the orphanage."

"I can't imagine my sisters burning their dolls," Johan said, with a shiver. He'd *been* their doll often enough. "They were really expensive."

He shrugged. "Do men have dolls too?"

Daria gave him a sharp look. "Boys tend to have stuffed animals," she said, tightly. "They bury them when they are ready to become men."

"I don't know much about the Travellers," Johan admitted. "What happens when you want to get married?"

"There's normally a big gathering every year or so," Daria explained. She rubbed her hands together, then reached for her bag. "You will generally be introduced to prospective husbands there – or brides, if you're a man. Everyone looks for the one who *smells* right to them – if they find that person, they take them off somewhere under the moonlight and wait to see if romance takes hold."

Johan considered it. "What happens if you don't smell right to the person who smells right to you?"

"It rarely happens," Daria said.

She shrugged. "If the romance lasts, the woman generally joins the man's pack, although not always," she added. "There's always jostling between the newcomer and the established pack leaders until the new order is established. Or sometimes the happy couple sets off on their own and forms an entirely new pack. It does happen."

Johan smiled. "And what happens if the romance *doesn't* last?"

"They peacefully separate," Daria said. "What sort of idiot would stay with a man who doesn't love her?"

"Too many in High Society," Johan said. His mother had always had a cold relationship with his father, even though they *had* managed to produce seven children. "They prefer the status of being married to the right person rather than picking someone they actually *love*."

"Idiots," Daria said.

She opened her bag, then produced a large piece of bread and two slices of cheese. "I couldn't grab much before we left," she said, by way of apology. "You should really eat."

"I can't eat alone," Johan said. "I ..."

"There's no shortage of rats around," Daria said. "You eat the bread and cheese. I'm going hunting."

She stood, walked to the centre of the room and shrank, rapidly. Johan stared as her robe fell down over her body, concealing the final stages of the transformation into a small wolf. She emerged moments later from beneath the folds and winked at him, then headed towards the door. If he hadn't known she was a werewolf, he would have mistaken her for a large and very well trained dog. Despite not having any hands, she managed to open the door ... and stop, dead.

"I come in peace," a female voice said. "Really."

Daria growled, a sound that sent shivers down Johan's spine. She was a werewolf, with all the strength of the breed, and he had been staring at her as if she were a normal girl? All of a sudden, he understood why werewolves were shunned, when they weren't feared or hated by the general population. They might have looked human, when the full moon wasn't dominating the sky, but they were very different.

The newcomer stepped into the house and smiled at Johan. She was tall, with long blonde hair, and wore a dark cloak that concealed her body. A simple wooden wand hung from her belt, beside a potions gourd and a device that Johan didn't recognise. He'd never been able to sense magic, not the way his family could, but he had no difficulty in recognising her as a powerful magician. She had the same air of supreme self-confidence that he'd seen in too many graduates of the Peerless School. Elaine was the only one he knew who didn't show that attitude.

"I ... I am Cass," she said, simply. Her voice was tightly controlled; friendly, without being *too* friendly. Oddly, Johan was reminded of a distant relative who had been forced to host a funeral for her husband, even though she'd genuinely loved him. "I've been sent to help you."

Daria snapped back into human form and crossed her arms under her bare breasts, seemingly unbothered by her nudity. Johan looked away, hastily. Naked, Daria was very different to any of the pictures he'd seen in the books he'd stolen from Jamal. Jamal had liked thin girls, but Daria was strongly muscled, with very little fat on her body.

"I remember you," Daria said. "You're an Inquisitor."

"I was," Cass said. She held up her hands for inspection. There was no skull-ring present. "I was released from my oaths."

Daria barked a harsh laugh. "What did you do? Get caught in bed with the Grand Sorceress's son?"

"The Grand Sorceress felt that the Head Librarian would need some assistance," Cass said, tartly. "And she saw fit to release me from my oaths."

She stepped forward and closed the door behind her. "This wasn't a bad place to hide," she said, "but we can't stay here indefinitely."

"And what," Daria growled, "makes you think *you* are staying with us?"

Cass shrugged, then looked at Johan. "Can you make contact with your mistress?"

"The bond doesn't work very well," Johan confessed. It wasn't something Elaine had been keen to advertise. The gods alone knew what Charity would make of it, if she ever found out that Johan was still alive. "I can sense her; she's still alive, but not much else."

"I can probably help you link to her properly," Cass said. She opened her cloak, revealing a dark shirt, long trousers and a pouch. "And I brought food."

Daria glared at her, then stamped back to where her robe had fallen and pulled it over her head. Johan couldn't help feeling relieved. It was hard not to stare at her, but he knew she would be aware of his interest and ... and he probably didn't smell right to her.

She turned to stare at Cass as soon as she was decently covered. "How did you find us?"

"I was watching you when you were with your family," Cass said, flatly. She pulled the pouch off her belt, then started to reach into it. The pouch was clearly far bigger on the inside than the outside, as it rapidly proved to contain several large pieces of meat and bread, as well as bottles of water. "I was planning to meet you once the Head Librarian arrived and introduce myself, but once you went running off on your own I had to follow you."

"I never sensed you," Daria growled.

"I'm very good at what I do," Cass said. She gave Daria a smile, then turned her attention to Johan. "Eat as much as you can, young man. We have some meditation to try."

Chapter Ten

Elaine wasn't fooled by the spell's seeming dormancy. It was waiting for her to fall asleep, or to lower her defences, or something else that would give it the opportunity to claim her mind and soul. Worse, it still held her body in an iron grip; she had freedom of movement within the holding chamber, she'd discovered, but any attempt to leave via the door simply led to her body locking up and refusing to move. Charity Conidian's orders had been too specific to allow Elaine any leeway at all.

She probably has plenty of experience ordering slaves around, Elaine thought, darkly. *How many slaves did her family have under their roof?*

Scowling, she inspected the drinks cabinet in the hope of finding water or juice. The only thing she found that was remotely drinkable was a very light wine, but she knew better than to drink anything that might lower her ability to resist. There were no shortage of spells for removing alcohol from liquid, yet even trying to cast a basic spell would drain her magic to dangerous levels. She didn't dare take the risk. Instead, she found a pair of oranges held in a preservation spell and ate them both. They would keep her going, for the moment.

She walked back to the sofa and sat down, skimming through the vast reserves of information in her mind. What made the spell so dangerous? And how could it best be broken? There was little encouraging within her mind, nothing she hadn't already reviewed while waiting to see the Emperor. To dismantle the spell from the inside, she would have to embrace it ... and, if she failed even slightly, she would fall under its influence completely, body and soul. But she was starting to feel as though there was no choice.

Closing her eyes, she started to meditate, marshalling her reserves for the battle ahead. In some ways, her limited magic was actually an asset; the spell had had much less to absorb into its own matrix and throw back at her. But in other ways, she simply didn't have the reserves to hold it off long enough to pick it apart. The more she looked at it, the more she hated the idea of trying to force it out of her mind. And yet, she knew there was no choice ...

Johan, she thought. The link between them was almost impossible to feel, even when she was meditating, her mind closed off to all distractions. It tore at her more than she cared to admit; Johan could sense her, to some degree, but she couldn't sense him at all. Who knew what would happen if they spent time apart? Would the weak link break or would it merely go dormant? And what would happen when her defences finally crumpled and she fell to Vlad Deferens?

That cannot be allowed, she thought, coldly. *I cannot let my knowledge fall into his hands – or go to the Witch-King.*

It was an odd thought. She had assumed, given his history, that the Witch-King knew everything she knew and more. And yet, he'd made at least two attempts to obtain Elaine for himself, maybe three, if one counted Hawthorne's mad rampage. Was there knowledge in the Black Vault that the Witch-King didn't know? It seemed absurd, yet she was starting to think it was possible. She had cheated, after all, to reach such levels of knowledge. No other magicians knew as much as she did.

The Witch-King had to be behind everything, she was sure. Vlad Deferens would never have sat on the Golden Throne unless he'd *known* it was safe – and only the Witch-King could have ensured he knew. And then, Deferens hadn't surrounded himself with naked and submissive women, in the belief that it was all they were good for, but had put them to work. Elaine had never thought she would see the day when *not* acting like a misogynist would seem a bad sign, yet it was now. It spoke of someone else pulling the strings, keeping his eye on the prize. And who knew what the Witch-King really wanted ...?

How does he do it? she asked herself, not for the first time. *How does he influence so many at such a distance?*

The thought had nagged at her mind ever since she'd first deduced his existence. There was no shortage of compulsion spells; some blunt tools that could be resisted, while others were so subtle that few could realise they had ever been influenced at all. And yet, they all required someone to either cast the spell directly or leave the spell hidden for the victim to find and activate. The idea of long-range control was unthinkable ... and if it was some form of long-distance control, the Witch-King should have won by now. There was something about the method that made it work, but added limits. But what was it?

He left a book for some of his slaves to find, she thought. Some of the spells in it had been nasty, others might have tilted the user towards insanity, weakening their defences. *But how did he get it into their hands?*

She sensed the spell holding her rubbing against her defences, just long enough to bring her mind back to the here and now. Cursing mentally, she tightened her defences once again, then opened her eyes and looked around the chamber. There was nothing she could use, either to escape or to kill herself. The only option for the latter was a spell that caused instant brain death, leaving her thoughts so fragmented that no one, not even a necromancer, could summon her ghost back from the realm of the dead. But would she be able to shape and cast it before the compulsion spell overwhelmed her? The timing would be very fraught. She couldn't afford even the smallest mistake.

Despair threatened to overwhelm her as she stood and started to pace, testing the limits of her bonds again and again. There was no hope of escape unless she broke the spell, yet the mere act of *trying* to break the spell was dangerous in itself ... her thoughts raced around, time and time again, going back to the simple point that there was no other way out. But would she have the time to break the spell?

And then she felt a presence pushing up against her mind. No, *inside* her mind. She almost panicked, then reached out, understanding in sudden wonder that the apprenticeship bond was finally working. Johan's mind was touching hers, a level of intimacy she hadn't enjoyed with anyone, even her first lover. The mere touch sent her reeling; hastily, she checked and rechecked her defences, then tried to send a thought back down the link. But there was no sense Johan had heard her.

Concentrate, she told herself, firmly. It had been years since she'd had any classes in mental communication – the bond should have formed naturally, if it had been normal – but she knew the basics. *Focus your mind.*

She gritted her teeth. Johan hadn't broken her defences. The bond was already present within her mind, allowing Johan to contact her. All she had to do – *all* – was make contact in return. She held her defences in place with part of her mind, then reached through the bond with the rest of her attention. There was a flurry of confusing images – Daria in wolf form, Daria naked as the day she was born, a blonde-haired girl who looked oddly familiar – and then an overwhelming sense of him pressing his mind against hers. She shrank back from the contact – it wasn't painful, but it was powerful – and tried to warn him to moderate his voice. The barrage of thoughts were coming at her so fast she couldn't separate them out into individual, understandable concepts.

"Slow down," she said, or thought. She honestly wasn't sure. Some of the books in her head insisted that some mentalists preferred to vocalise their thoughts, but she was all-too-aware that someone might be spying on the holding cell. "I can't understand you."

The jabbering grew louder for a long moment, then faded. "Elaine," Johan said. She heard his voice in her mind. "Where are you?"

"In the Imperial Palace, a prisoner," Elaine muttered, too low for anyone to overhear. It was important to get that piece of information out first, although she wasn't sure what Johan could do with it. At least he would know to remain hidden. "How did you make contact with me?"

"There's an Inquisitor – ex-Inquisitor – here," Johan said. "She boosted the link."

Elaine felt a sudden flush of overwhelming *pride*. She had never thought of asking another magician to help, if only because it would have exposed her thoughts – and Johan's – to outside scrutiny. Her mental privacy had been important to her even before she'd absorbed the contents of the Great Library. It had been the only privacy she'd enjoyed at the orphanage, then at the Peerless School. The idea of private rooms had been laughable.

But Johan, who had been abused far worse than her, had opened his mind to another, just to contact Elaine.

"Then you need to listen," Elaine said. She briefly outlined the spell holding her and what she'd done to hold it back. "You have to break the link completely."

"No," Johan said. "I won't."

There was a sudden sense of ... *expansion*, as a third person joined the conversation. "I know the spell," Cass said. The sense of her identity flooded through Elaine's mind as she spoke, bringing with it an awareness of power and confidence that left her feeling envious and afraid at the same time. "It's astonishing you've held out as long as you have."

Johan coughed. "Why?"

"The spell is known only to Inquisitors," Cass explained. "Unlike most compulsion spells, it absorbs magic and strengthens itself by attacking the target's defences. The standard response to any compulsion spell will merely make the spell stronger, while it burns through the victim's mind. It isn't used unless you don't care about your target walking away with real damage. Even the merest use of the spell can leave someone in deep trouble."

She paused. "Elaine has held out very well."

"Not well enough," Elaine said. She knew something about escaping ordinary compulsion spells – Millicent had given her more than enough practice, while they'd been at school together – but this was different. "My body is under their control."

"That sounds like a bad romance novel," Cass observed flippantly. "Or a line from a worse play."

Elaine tried to bite down on the anger surging through her mind. Emotion, no matter the cause, would only weaken her defences. Cass was right; there were no shortage of plays about women – and sometimes men – who had married someone they hated, merely to carry on the family line. The heroines always talked about surrendering their bodies, but never their minds. Elaine had always hated those plays with a white-hot passion.

Johan tried to pour oil on troubled waters. "Can you break the spell?"

"Not from here," Cass said. "I'd have to do it in person

and ... and there would be no guarantee it wouldn't leave traces in her mind."

Elaine shuddered, knowing that both of them would feel her horror. There was no shortage of people who took damage from using the wrong kind of spell. Light Spinner, as horrific as it seemed, had maintained her sanity. Others had gone mad, or lost their confidence, or simply killed themselves as soon as they could. Who knew what *this* spell would do to her if it had enough time to leave its hooks in her mind?

"Then we have to rescue her," Johan said. "Is there a way into the Imperial Palace?"

"A couple," Cass said. "But we shouldn't be talking about them through the bond."

"She needs to know we're coming for her," Johan said. "We should tell her ..."

"No," Elaine said. She was touched – more than touched – by Johan's loyalty. Even if she had been the first person to treat him with a modicum of human decency, his loyalty was still astonishing. Or perhaps it was a function of their bond. "What I know, they can make me tell."

"She's right," Cass said. "The more that damned spell tightens its grip on her mind, the more they can control her and force her to talk."

Johan's horror was easy to feel through the link, but he held his peace.

"We will come," Cass said. "I promise. The city may be under occupation, but we will have a way through if we're careful."

"I may have to try to remove the spell earlier," Elaine warned. "If it starts to break through my innermost defences, I won't have a choice."

"I understand," Cass said. "Just be careful."

The link broke. Elaine staggered as the presences withdrew from her mind, leaving her completely alone. For a moment, she almost started to cry, knowing that they were gone. And then she gathered herself and held back the tidal wave of despair. She wasn't alone, not really. Her friends were on their way.

But it might be a trap ...

She cursed herself for not considering the possibility while she was in contact with Johan and Cass. Light Spinner had told the Privy Council that Johan was dead, but Dread might well know better. Elaine had lied to his face, but Dread was good at sniffing out lies ... and he was an Inquisitor, his loyalty sworn to the Golden Throne. If Deferens asked, Dread would have no choice but to admit that Johan was still alive. And then Deferens would set a trap.

Had Deferens thought to ask? There was no way to know. She hastily reviewed all the knowledge in her head on Inquisitor oaths, but it wasn't clear if Dread would feel compelled to volunteer the information or not. They were sworn to uphold the Throne, she knew, yet Dread had never liked Deferens. He could do precisely as he was told, without volunteering any information he wasn't specifically asked to volunteer. She knew Dread well enough to know he might well try to keep it to himself ...

... And yet, there was still no way to know.

She cursed under her breath, then closed her eyes and started to concentrate on strengthening her defences once again. The spell hadn't remained dormant; it had taken advantage of her distraction to start breaking through wards that should have stopped any normal spell in its tracks. Elaine shuddered in horror, then rebuilt her defences once again, knowing she was fast running out of magic. Indeed, if she hadn't known how to angle her defences just right, she would be overwhelmed by now. But it was only a matter of time.

No wonder Deferens didn't bother to try to force me to swear an oath, she thought, savagely. He – and his master – had been stung by Elaine before. They probably preferred her to be a useless vegetable, a repository of knowledge, rather than a thinking human being. She would be so useful to them, without the intelligence or willpower to seek loopholes in their command and use them as a weapon, or just a way to escape. *The bastard wants me ruined completely.*

She opened her eyes, then started to pace the room again. Cass wouldn't have hesitated, she was sure; Cass would have jumped right into the spell, counting on her prowess with magic to ensure that nothing went seriously wrong. *Elaine* knew she was skilled, yet she also knew just how many things could go wrong. She cursed the spell's inventor, once again, as she stopped in front of the mirror and eyed her reflection. There was no disputing the fact she looked a mess. Her hair was sweaty and damp, while her face was pale and her eyes were sleepless. The glamour that concealed her eyes had vanished, leaving red light glaring out of her face. She yawned, as if the sight had reminded her that she really needed some sleep, but she knew she couldn't allow herself to rest. When she opened her eyes, her free will would be gone.

There's no more time to waste, she thought, as she walked back to the sofa, stopping just before she sat down. Instead, she knelt down on the floor, feeling her body ache in protest as she rocked back on her haunches. It was uncomfortable, which would keep her from falling asleep before she had finished, one way or the other. *I have to get rid of the spell now.*

She focused her mind, pushing aside all thoughts of Johan, Daria or any of the handful of other friends she had made along the way. There weren't many; she had never been a sociable person, and the isolation had only been made worse by her being Millicent's favourite victim at the Peerless School. It was funny, she reflected savagely, just how many of her old acquaintances had come crawling out of the woodwork when she'd been appointed to the Privy Council. They had all believed she could help their careers with a single word. And instead, she'd told them to go away.

But now ... she half-wished she'd done more with her life. Daria had tried to take her out dancing – and she had met a few men – but none of them had stayed. Perhaps there was something wrong with her; Daria had a different man every day, while Elaine had half-hoped for a true love she suspected she wasn't going to find. The red light in her eyes would see to that, she knew all too well. Even a mundane would find them more than a little creepy.

You're not going to die, she told herself firmly, as she gathered what remained of her strength. *You're going to live.*

And then she closed her eyes, undid her defences and plunged into the maelstrom surrounding her mind.

Chapter Eleven

"You actually have a way into the Imperial Palace?"

"Several, actually," Cass answered. "Unfortunately, most of them require an Inquisitor's Ring."

Johan rubbed his forehead. His head was pounding and he wanted nothing more than to go and lie down, but Elaine needed him. "And is there a way in we can use?"

"Of course," Cass said. "You just need to be careful."

Daria leant forward. "And you know where to find it?"

"Yes," Cass said.

Johan sighed inwardly as the two women started to argue, as if they had taken an instant dislike to one another. It had been strange and wonderful to finally have the bond work properly, but he'd picked up enough of Elaine's emotions to know she was in very real danger. His every instinct called for him to run out of the building and straight to her side, but cold logic told him that would merely be a good way to get killed. They needed a plan, a way into the Imperial Palace and a distraction.

"Enough," he said. His father had been able to command respect with a single word. No one had ever respected him, even when they'd discovered he actually had magic. "We need to move."

"We need to wait for darkness to fall completely," Cass said, shortly. She paced over to the covered window and peered outside. "We won't be any help to her if we get caught on the way."

"I thought Inquisitors were good at sneaking around," Daria jibed. "You should be brilliant at it."

"They will have dogs and wolves out watching the streets," Cass countered. "We don't want to be tracked on our way to the palace."

She turned and looked at Johan. "I'm going to check upstairs to see if there's anything we can use," she said.

"Finish eating as much as you can, then stick the rest back in my pouch and seal it. I don't think we'll be coming back here."

Johan nodded. If Cass could track them down, someone else could too. He knew, all too well, just how easy it was to trace someone with magic; his father had done it to him often enough. Even now, with his ties to his family broken, someone could still use their blood to find him. And how many people knew he was still alive?

He watched Cass stepping out of the door with an easy grace, then turned to Daria. "Why don't you like her?"

Daria flushed. "Is it that obvious?"

"Yes," Johan said. "I grew up with sisters."

"A fate I would wish on no man," Daria said, dryly. "Among my immediate family, I am a beta female. Do you know what that means?"

Johan shook his head.

"I'm the oldest of my sisters," Daria explained. "I am meant to be in charge – beta, because the alpha female is my mother. When I encounter another alpha or beta female, the wolf in me insists on a struggle for dominance over the newcomer. Cass is a powerful woman, so the wolf sees her as a rival, someone to be brought to heel under my paws. And I know she isn't a werewolf, but I still feel that way."

"How very human," Johan said. He might not have grown up in a pack, but he understood the constant struggle for power. "And I assume there's always someone at the bottom?"

"Unfortunately," Daria said. "But they don't get mistreated, otherwise they might leave the pack."

Johan understood. Why would anyone want to stay when they were permanently on the bottom rung? *He'd* been in that position and had spent most of his time planning to leave, when he finally gained his father's blessing. And then power had found him ...

"How would you know," he asked, "if they were happy?"

Daria wrinkled her nose. "You can't hide what you're feeling from another werewolf," she reminded him. "Someone who was truly unhappy would be very obvious to us."

"Oh," Johan said. "How did you manage to cope with Elaine?"

"She doesn't trigger the beta female instincts," Daria said. "I don't see her as a threat to my dominance. It would be different, I suspect, if she worked with me or I worked with her."

"You'd be struggling for supremacy," Johan realised. It didn't seem to make much sense, but werewolves were influenced by their inner wolves. "Are we lucky it isn't the full moon?"

Daria gave him a sharp look. "Very lucky," she said. "Because that's when the wolf runs free."

Cass returned before Johan could think of something – anything – to say. "There wasn't much of use on the upper floor," she said. "Just hints of writing in a foreign script on the walls."

"I saw," Daria said. "What writing *is* it?"

"I don't recognise the script," Cass said. She sounded perturbed by the discovery. "But it wasn't magically-active, so it shouldn't be a problem."

"Elaine would probably know," Johan mused, as he stuffed the remaining food back into the pouch. "Why would people use it here?"

"Wild magic," Cass said. "It does strange and unpredictable things."

She walked back over to the door, opened it and peered outside. A gust of cold air slapped at Johan's face, a moment before she closed the door and turned to face him. Johan was almost relieved; he'd grown up, like most children, fearing the dark. According to legend, the night was the domain of creatures that were very far from human. Anything could be hiding in the shadows, anything at all. And even the Golden City, the very heart of human society, could have dangers lurking in the shadows.

"Put out the fire," Cass ordered. "It's time to go."

She looked at Daria. "You should go in wolf form," she said. "It will help you to remain unnoticed, if we run into trouble."

"I won't be able to talk to you," Daria pointed out, snidely. "And any fool can recognise a werewolf."

"Not in the darkness," Cass assured her.

Johan cleared his throat. "How are we going to pass muster if we *do* get caught?"

"We'll have to improvise," Cass said, with a shrug. "It would depend on who caught us."

"You're an Inquisitor," Daria said. "Can't you just order them to let us go?"

Cass took a harsh breath. "I *was* an Inquisitor," she said. "Do you know what the penalty is for claiming to be an Inquisitor?"

"You could actually fake it convincingly," Daria reminded her. "I'd bet most frauds didn't actually do the job."

"I don't have a ring any longer," Cass snapped. The sudden anger in her voice was shocking. "And if we ran into another Inquisitor, he would take me for a fake, even though he would know me personally. We would be very lucky merely to be dragged to the Watchtower in chains and made to walk the plank. There is no way I could fool someone into believing that I was still on active service."

"The soldiers wouldn't be able to tell," Daria said. "I ..."

"The soldiers would look for a ring," Cass said. "I cannot wear one without taking – retaking – the oaths, which would bind me to the Emperor. Nor can I fake a ring without risking everything. You have no idea just how many protections are bound up in those rings."

Elaine probably knows, Johan thought. *And she might be able to fake one too.*

He held up a hand, realising that Cass was skirting the edge of breaking point. She had loved her career, he suspected, and giving it up *hurt*. He understood how that had to feel; he'd wanted things too, in his life, only to lose them to his lack of power. And Daria, prodded by her inner wolf, was being bitchy for the sake of being bitchy.

"We have to go," he said, sharply. Both women glared at him, rather than each other. It struck him, suddenly, that he was the least experienced of the three. "Let me put out the fire, then we can go."

Cass muttered a spell, just loudly enough to be heard. The fire emitted a hissing sound, then died, leaving steam billowing up from the grate. Johan inspected it quickly, realised that Cass had cast a powerful cooling charm, then stood up and reached for his coat. It smelt faintly of smoke and fire, but he didn't care. All that mattered was staying warm in the darkness – and remaining unseen by prowling eyes.

"I'm going to cast a pair of concealment spells on you," Cass said, once they were ready to go. "You should remain unnoticed, as long as no magicians are actively searching for you."

Daria frowned. "And what if we run into an Inquisitor?"

"Then you run while I distract him," Cass said, sharply. "And you'd better pray to whatever gods you worship that we don't, because one of them could easily call others."

She cast the spells – Johan heard Daria growl, very quietly, as Cass moved her wand over her body – and then opened the door. Cold air lashed at them, but the snowstorm had faded into the darkness. Outside, there was almost no light to be seen, not even the glow that shimmered over the Golden City from the streetlamps that illuminated the better-kept streets and allowed the population to remain awake and active after dark. It was easy to convince himself, suddenly, that they were the only people left alive in the city, perhaps the world.

"The city never sleeps," Daria muttered. "But it's sleeping now."

"Most people are weak," Cass scoffed. "When faced with uncertainty, their first instinct is to bar the doors and pray that whatever is outside passes them by. By the time the sun rises, the Emperor will be solidly in control of the city. And then he will take the world."

Daria snorted as she stepped out into the snow. "You've seen this happen before?"

"I've been in places where martial law has been declared," Cass countered. "And yes, most people try to hide, if only to avoid being noticed."

Daria shrank. Moments later, a small wolf crawled out from under her robe and looked at Johan meaningfully. Johan nodded, then picked up the robe and cradled it under one arm, wrapping it tightly to keep it dry. He couldn't help noticing that Daria wore nothing, apart from the robe; she didn't even wear undergarments. The thought caused a flush of excitement, which he swiftly suppressed. Daria would probably be able to sense it, no matter how quickly he pushed it aside. He flushed, then followed Cass as she started to walk down the street.

"Stay as quiet as you can," she hissed. "There's almost no background noise."

The Golden City felt eerie, Johan realised, as they walked through the snow. Normally, it was always awake, even at the dead of night; the shops and cafes were open, serving their customers at every hour of the day. It was the heart of a giant empire, after all, and people were often at work during daylight hours. People invested in silencing charms, his father had once commented, because the city was always buzzing. But now it was quiet.

Cass had been right, he realised as they left the former Blight. Shops that should have been open were barred and shuttered, with warning signs plastered over their doors. Even Johan, with his strictly-limited education in all things magic, could tell they were warning would-be thieves that the owners had invested in *nasty* defensive hexes for their shops. Anyone who tried to break in without permission would be lucky to escape without being branded, although most such hexes were designed to hold a thief long enough for the City Guard to catch him. A handful of dark shops had no obvious warning signs, but only a fool would try to break in. They were owned by magicians.

And a magician can do whatever he likes to anyone who tries to break in, Johan thought, grimly. *They'd be lucky not to be enslaved on the spot.*

Cass held up a hand, then motioned for him to slip into the shadows. Moments later, another line of patrolling soldiers appeared from a side street and marched past where they were hiding, wrapped in eerie silence. They had to be using charms to smother their footsteps, Johan thought, allowing them to sneak through the streets. If Cass hadn't heard them, he had the sense he would have walked right into their path and been arrested.

Daria slipped over to the footsteps the soldiers had left in the snow and sniffed once, then returned to Johan's side. Cass gave the werewolf a sharp look, then started to walk back down the street, away from the soldiers. Johan followed her, wondering just what the soldiers were trying to do – and where they had come from. He tried to reach out to Elaine, but all he sensed was a flurry of confusing mental pictures that made absolutely no sense. Without Cass's support, the link had returned to its normal state.

He frowned, suddenly, as he realised they were approaching the Peerless School. It was the largest building in the Golden City, a towering dark shape wrapped in protective magic to keep the students safe ... and shield the general population from their mistakes. The building was far larger on the inside than the outside, according to Charity; there was something about the magic surrounding the school that made it impossible to see its true shape. Johan stared, forgetting – for a moment – where they had to go, but no matter how hard he stared it was impossible to see anything fixed and solid. The school's appearance changed every time he blinked.

Cass slipped back to him. "Too many guards surrounding the walls," she said. "The students must be held inside."

Johan frowned. His siblings had slept at the school, even when they'd moved to the Golden City and they could have slept in their own bedrooms. Boarding at the school was meant to help young sorcerers network, his father had explained once, when Charity had complained about having to leave home. She wouldn't amount to anything, he'd insisted, if she didn't know anyone. Charity had pointed out, in return, that her father was planning to marry her off as soon as she was old enough, so it didn't actually matter what she knew. Their father had not been pleased.

"What's going to happen to them?" he asked. "My brothers and sisters are in there."

"Probably nothing," Cass said. "The Emperor wouldn't seek to piss off everyone with magic by closing the place down."

Johan frowned, looking up at the school. The Emperor, it seemed, had *already* pissed everyone off by assuming the Golden Throne. Surely he wouldn't think twice about using the children as hostages ... or worse. The school itself was dark and silent, without a single light breaking the darkness.

Normally, it would be glowing with light as the wards caught and absorbed waves of magic from the children. Now ...

"Don't worry about it," Cass said, shortly. "Follow me."

Johan obeyed, following Cass through a maze of side-streets that seemed to hold dozens of largely-unmarked shops. One of them was decorated with the outline of a naked woman, suggesting it was a brothel. Johan sighed, remembering some of Jamal's tales, then reminded himself that his brother had been an incurable braggart. Most of his stories had probably been nothing more than outright lies.

But not all of them were, he thought. *Some of Jamal's attempts at courtship required father to spend a vast amount of money to cover them up.*

He pushed the memory aside, bitterly, as they turned the corner and found themselves looking at a very familiar building. The Great Library was as dark and silent as the Peerless School, but it seemed to have fewer guards. A small bunch of soldiers were positioned in front of the entrance, blocking all access. Johan couldn't help wondering what had happened to Vane and the rest of the staff. Had they been told to go home for the night or had they simply been placed under arrest? There was no way to know.

"Guards on the front entrance," Cass muttered. "But they're not guarding the side."

She led them forward, up to a brick wall. It shimmered as they approached, revealing a stone door built into the brick. Daria ran forward and sniffed at the door suspiciously, then tilted her head, somehow managing to convey doubt and scepticism in her disturbingly-human eyes. Johan wondered, in sudden horror, if her wolfish instincts were stronger in wolf form and if she was going to try to bite Cass. It wouldn't be long before the guards saw them, if they patrolled the streets ...

"Open the door," Cass ordered.

Johan gave her a sharp look, then pressed his hand against the stone. He expected resistance, but instead the door opened silently, allowing them into the darkened building. As soon as they were inside, it closed behind them, completely soundlessly. Cass chuckled to herself, then cast a light spell. An eerie radiance started to shimmer through the air.

"Well," she said. "I wasn't sure that would work."

Daria swelled back into her human form. "You weren't sure that would *work*?"

"You were the Head Librarian's apprentice," Cass said, nodding to Johan. "She would have keyed you into the wards. Hell, merely being her apprentice would have allowed you access to her wards."

"And you didn't know this would work before you tried it?" Daria demanded. She snatched her robe out of Johan's hands and pulled it over her head, her voice becoming slightly muffled as she ranted on. "You could have gotten us all killed!"

"This is the easiest passage to reach," Cass said. She smirked at Daria, then turned to lead the way up the passageway. "And, as there is no one in the building, we can make as much noise as we like."

She looked back at Johan and winked. "Shall we go?"

Chapter Twelve

It had been centuries since anyone had used the Parade Grounds for their proper purpose, Charity knew, as a grim-faced servitor showed her into the review box. Successive Grand Sorcerers hadn't needed armies, not when they had powerful magic and the Inquisitors to maintain their rule. They'd chosen to allow the Parade Grounds to host graduation ceremonies for sorcerers from the Peerless School instead, which had at least kept the grounds looking nice. And they'd warded it carefully against the weather, even though the Golden City was almost always temperate. The snow was brushed away by the wards, allowing the soldiers to march freely, illuminated by glowing balls of light that floated in the air.

The Emperor was seated in his chair, watching the lines of soldiers forming up and marching out onto the streets. Charity honestly couldn't imagine how he'd managed to smuggle so many men into the city before making his bid for the Golden Throne, although the planned conference had probably made it easier. A number of sorcerers stood nearby, wearing the red and gold colours of the Emperor's homeland. Maybe they'd turned the soldiers into small objects and simply *carried* them into the city. It was a very old dodge and hellishly difficult to guard against.

"Your Majesty," Charity said, as she went down on her knees. "The Great Houses have agreed to provide hostages."

"Good, good," the Emperor said. He sounded distracted, as if he was listening to a voice only he could hear. "Have them moved to proper holding chambers when they arrive, then keep them there."

"Yes, Your Majesty," Charity said. "Should I be providing for their education as well?"

The Emperor looked up at her. "Why?"

Charity hesitated, feeling a sudden flicker of terror.

"Because ... because we are responsible for them while they remain as hostages," she said. "We have to see to their schooling as well as keeping them alive."

"No need to worry about that," the Emperor said, dismissively. "They will not remain hostages for long."

He turned his attention back to the marching soldiers, leaving Charity to worry. She knew the conventions as well as anyone else, thanks to her father. Hostages effectively became part of the family holding them, at least until they were returned to their true families. It often led to friendships ... and heartbreak, if there was a pressing need to actually *kill* the hostage. She knew boys at the Peerless School who had been regular semi-willing guests of some of the Great House and had made friends with their captor's children. But the Emperor was practically talking as though *his* hostages wouldn't be hostages for more than a few days.

"Their families will be concerned," she warned. "The children require schooling ..."

"Their families will do as they are told," the Emperor said, without looking away from the soldiers. "And so will you."

He waved a hand towards the marching men. "What do you think of them?"

Charity looked at the men, puzzled. They didn't *look* very impressive, not to her. The armour they wore would stave off swords and spears, but a child with a single spell could turn the soldiers into toads or freeze them in their tracks. There were limits to just how many protections could be layered over a single mundane, no matter how many sorcerers were involved. And what use was a sword against a fireball or a lightning strike?

"They're *men*, doing what men should," the Emperor said. "They're preparing themselves to confront the enemy, to place their lives on the line to win glory and fame everlasting."

"And death," Charity said, before she could stop herself.

"To die gloriously is the highest of all aspirations," the Emperor said. "They are *men*."

He smiled as he turned to face her. "Or perhaps you do not agree?"

"They will still be dead," Charity said. "I know a hundred

spells that could kill them, directly or indirectly, without letting them lay a finger on me. Their deaths would be utterly pointless."

The Emperor smirked. "And yet you're the slave," he said. "Are you better off than a dead man?"

Charity felt herself flush, then spoke before she could think better of it. "Are you saying I should have died?"

"A man would have told me to go to one of the many hells rather than accept my binding willingly," the Emperor said. He leered at her, sending chills running down her spine. "But you ... you took my binding, rather than forcing me to break your mind or simply to kill you outright. You live now in a world where you are my puppet. Would you not sooner have died?"

"It wasn't like that," Charity said. "I ... I needed to stay alive."

"And that's the difference between a man and a woman," the Emperor said. "A true man will accept death with a smile on his face, while a woman will do whatever it takes to stay alive."

Charity shuddered. "The Head Librarian defied you to your face," she risked reminding him. "She won't break."

"Like you?" The Emperor asked. "She will be broken soon enough, once the spell has finished burning through her mind. I doubt she has the nerve to kill herself."

"It wasn't like that," Charity repeated. "Without me, the family crumbles into dust."

"But with you here," the Emperor said, "what happens to your family?"

He smirked, again. "You're making excuses to cover up the fact you were prepared to abandon your chance of dying bravely, or at least forcing me to bind you against your will," he told her. "Come up with all the excuses you like, my dear. It won't make any difference to the final outcome."

"No," Charity agreed, mournfully. He was right. Maybe he was wrong about women in general – the Head Librarian was definitely a woman, and she *had* resisted – but he wasn't too far wrong about Charity herself. She had submitted to him willingly and now she was his slave. "It won't."

The Emperor turned back to the soldiers. "These men will

fight a war for me," he said. "And many of them will die, but they will die bravely."

"A war," Charity repeated. "A war against whom?"

"There are states in our little empire that harbour dreams of independence," the Emperor reminded her. "Their Court Wizards, alas, have been failing in their duties. Even now, they are mustering their troops for the coming struggle."

"But surely you have done the same, Your Majesty?" Charity asked. "This army wasn't built from nothing."

The Emperor smiled. "I had a feeling it might come in handy," he said. "And with the limitless manpower resources of the Empire at my disposal, who knows what will happen?"

Charity knew next to nothing about fighting a war, but she had a sudden vision of just what the Emperor's philosophy of warfare *meant* in the real world. His troops would fight to the bitter end, disdaining retreat as unmanly, only to be slaughtered for nothing. He would spend their lives freely, replenishing the dead troops with men from the rest of the Empire, then go on and on until he won the war or ran out of soldiers. And such men would be brutal, when they occupied rebellious states. The first rebellion's repression would lead inevitably to the next.

But was that what he wanted, she asked herself. Whatever else could be said about the Grand Sorcerers, they had kept the peace for over a thousand years. Until Kane had threatened the Golden City itself, the only real threat had been Dark Wizards causing havoc in the outskirts of the Empire. There had been no fighting and no glory ... but who had *wanted* glory when the human cost was so high? She glanced at the Emperor and knew the answer.

"Tomorrow, we will continue preparations for the Conference," the Emperor informed her. "You will handle it personally."

"Yes, Your Majesty," Charity said. Light Spinner had been planning to discuss reforms in the Empire with the Court Wizards, but she dreaded to think what the Emperor would have to say to them. "Can I see the agenda?"

"It will be made available in due course," the Emperor said. "Have them assemble in the Arena, as planned. I will address them there."

"Yes, Your Majesty," Charity said. "What else would you have me do?"

"I could come up with a list, but perhaps later," the Emperor said. He tossed her a smirk, then returned his gaze to the soldiers. "We will need to start recruiting more soldiers soon enough, I think. The men of the Golden City are weak, used to being ruled by a woman, but we will toughen them up. Organise a conscription drive for unemployed men in the right age bracket. Make sure they know that the first to qualify as soldiers will receive all kinds of perks. Your brother would be so jealous."

He snickered. Charity shuddered. She knew more than she cared to know about Jamal's activities, including advances on women that might as well be rape. It was quite possible, she had thought, that Jamal might have killed himself since losing his powers ... or that he had been hunted down and killed by one of his former victims. But if the Emperor was planning to use Jamal's idea of fun as a reward ... she shuddered again, helplessly. What sort of men would he unleash on the Empire?

"Yes, Your Majesty," she said, helplessly. "When do you want the drive to start?"

"Tomorrow will be fine," the Emperor said, casually. "I will provide training officers, of course."

Charity sighed, inwardly. She now had *two* tasks for the following day. And, thanks to her oaths, she couldn't skip either of them. The oaths would force her to work indefinitely until they were both completed. Unless, of course, she could convince herself that the oaths were better served by delay ... she felt another flicker of sympathy for the maids in her house, back home. She had never really understood how they must feel, when they were at the mercy of anyone who wished to issue orders.

She turned as she heard someone hurrying into the review box. "Your Majesty," one of the red-coated soldiers said. "The hostages have begun to arrive."

"I will escort them to their chambers," Charity said, quickly. It might just get her away from the Emperor, at least for a few hours. "They'll be expecting an aristocratic escort."

"Of course, of course," the Emperor said. "Get some sleep afterwards, my dear. You'll need your rest before you start work tomorrow."

Charity felt her cheeks heat again as she rose, then walked back towards the antechamber. It had been a long time since she'd studied the different states in the Empire, but from what she recalled the Emperor's homeland expected men to take care of women, as well as leading them. He wasn't being considerate to her, not really; he was merely doing what he thought was expected of him, treating her as if she were a pet. How could anyone endure such treatment indefinitely? Perhaps his viewpoints made sense, at least to him. He poured on the bad treatment and his women *still* stayed with him.

But they don't have a choice, Charity thought, bitterly. *The local law won't allow them to leave their husbands.*

It wasn't something that had ever occurred to her before. She had known her marriage would be arranged for her, but she had also known that her husband wouldn't be able to hurt her. The marriage contract would include terms of protection ... and besides, she had her magic. A man who laid a finger on her against her will would lose everything, even if he *was* her husband. But how could she fight a man without magic? She had never been taught to fight without magic – it was seen as unseemly for magicians to learn hand-to-hand combat – and she doubted she could fend off a man. Men were generally stronger than women ...

She gritted her teeth. Maybe it *had* been a mistake to bow the knee to the Emperor. If he had forced her to submit, there would be hope of breaking free, but accepting the oaths willingly rendered that impossible. Her only hope would be being freed by him, yet why would he let her go? She was far too useful to him as a slave.

The antechamber was crammed with children and their guardians, mostly weeping mothers and a handful of older sisters. They knew, of course, that swapping hostages wasn't uncommon, but it *was* rare not to have someone in exchange. The Emperor could kill the hostages and their families would have no one to retaliate against. Forcing the Great Houses to give up hostages was a way of forcing them to submit, although – she noted as her cynical eye matched names to faces – none of the hostages were first or second-born children. Their families could lose them without seriously risking their power and influence.

And how long would it be, she asked herself, *before the Emperor demands more hostages?*

She shrugged, then tapped her lips, using a spell to boost her words. "The hostages are to prepare themselves to go to their chambers," she said. Thankfully, the building's staff had already prepared a series of rooms for the children. "Everyone else is to leave as soon as possible."

The mothers surrounded Charity, bombarding her with questions about what their children could expect and shoving pieces of paper at her, marked with their dietary requirements, demands for various forms of special treatment and far too much else. She winced at the thought of tending to all of the demands – one child apparently refused to eat mushrooms, while another expected to have a bedtime story read to her every night – and then passed them on to the staff. It had been centuries since the palace staff had catered for children – very few Grand Sorcerers had had young children – but she was sure they could handle it. If not, more help could be drafted in from the outside.

"Sonia needs to have a special potion each night," one of the women said, pushing a bottle into Charity's hand. "Make sure she takes it with her food."

Charity eyed the bottle suspiciously, then nodded and passed it to one of the staff. There would be time to sort out who Sonia was later, when the parents were gone and the hostages were on their way to their rooms. She collected four more bottles, several food parcels and a small pile of books, almost all designed to entertain and educate young magical children. She found herself praying that the children wouldn't torment the staff as she chased the parents out of the chamber, then turned to look at the hostages. They looked ... scared, apart from a couple of boys who looked excited. No doubt they'd heard tales of how great it was to be a hostage ...

... And it could be great, if they weren't killed.

"All right," she said. "You will be shown to your rooms

now. You will stay in your rooms until we come to fetch you tomorrow morning, so get as much sleep as you can."

She sighed, wondering why the Emperor had been so insistent on getting the hostages as soon as possible. The palace was nowhere near ready for thirty small children – the oldest was twelve – and entire levels would have to be warded against them, if only to keep the children from poking their noses into places where they didn't belong. If they were anything like she'd been at that age – she still cringed at the memory of the hundreds of times she'd tried to sneak into her father's study – they were going to be *everywhere*. Her father's wards had kept her out without hurting her, but she knew that wouldn't be true of the Emperor's wards ...

"This building isn't safe," she added. "You could get seriously hurt if you go into the wrong building or touch the wrong object. Stay in your rooms until we have parts of the building cleared for your use."

Two of the boys exchanged grins at her words, causing her to swear under her breath and resolve to cast sleep spells on them as soon as they were in their beds. Her mother had admitted she'd done that once or twice with her own children, back when they'd been screaming half the night. It wasn't advised to make a habit of it, though. The children soon developed a resistance to the spell that would haunt them in later life.

"Follow me," she ordered, and led the way down the corridor until they reached the holding chambers. She glanced at the one she knew to hold the Head Librarian, guarded by a single soldier wearing armour, then walked past it and opened the first door. "These rooms are all the same, so take any room you like."

She heard the soldier yelp as one of the little monsters cast a hex on him. Charity cancelled it, then plucked the boy out of the group and pushed him into his room, closing the door as soon as he was inside. The boy started to shout childish insults at her through the door, which she ignored. He didn't know how lucky he was, she told herself, as she resisted the urge to do something unpleasant to him. *Her* parents would have turned her into a toad for such insolence.

Once the rest of the children were in their rooms, Charity closed and warded the doors, then headed back to her own quarters. The Emperor had been right about one thing – she would need her sleep. She stood in front of the guarded door for a long moment, wondering if she should talk to the Head Librarian, then stopped herself. There was no point. What could they possibly say to one another?

Instead, she turned and kept walking back to her rooms.

Chapter Thirteen

Elaine held herself together by sheer force of will as the spell howled and reached for her, attempting to overwhelm her mind. She already knew it was more than just a simple compulsion spell, but she hadn't realised just how powerful it was until she dropped her defences and embraced the maelstrom. It had absorbed her own defences, her first set of protections, and turned them into weapons against her mind. In a very real sense, she was grimly aware she was fighting herself.

The chain of incantations unravelled themselves under her mental gaze, even as the spell tried to embrace the core of her mind. It had already mutated, adapting itself to her mind with terrifying speed, sending tendrils deep into her thoughts. Normally, mental influence could be countered by a mind-healer, but few healers would know her mind so intimately that they could remove the contamination without doing colossal damage. The fragments of the spell were practically part of her, impossible for an outsider to separate from her true thoughts. And given enough time, they *would* be her true thoughts.

SURRENDER, the spell thundered, as it raged against her thoughts. *RESISTANCE IS FUTILE. SURRENDER AND SUBMIT.*

Elaine wanted to cover her ears, but it was pointless. The sound was inside her head. Instead, she gathered her thoughts and plunged down until she was slamming right into the spell, examining the mutating incantations that swarmed and multiplied until they threatened to push her true thoughts out of her own mind. It was an impressive piece of work, part of her mind noted, a thing of deadly beauty. And it was so dangerous that she understood *precisely* why successive Grand Sorcerers had banned knowledge of the spell, at least outside the Inquisition. The only real question was why they had thought the Inquisitors needed to know how to use it.

They would have found it an effective weapon against a Dark Wizard, she thought, as the howling grew louder. The spell twisted uncomfortably under her gaze, then tried to fade away into the background. *No normal wizard could have held it off for more than a few minutes ...*

She gritted her teeth as she reached out and pulled the spell back into view, then lashed out with all the force she could gather at the incantations holding it together. Pain seared through her head as the spell fought back, trying to escape her wrath; it mutated again and again, trying to evolve defences against her. It was like playing chess against herself, Elaine realised; white knew what black was planning and vice versa. But the battle wouldn't stalemate, she knew, or at least not for very long. Eventually, she would run out of magic ...

... Angrily, she pushed the thought aside. Even considering the possibility of defeat would bring defeat closer. The spell howled, then whispered, alternatively gloating over her certain failure and then promising joy in submission. Elaine gritted her teeth and held on desperately, even when the spell started to dig up her old memories and throw them at her, one by one. It knew precisely which memories to use, but how could it *not*? The spell was effectively part of her mind.

... She is sitting on a chair at the back of a meeting room, while two parents are explaining to the Orphan Mother that no, they do not want to take Elaine home with them. The Orphan Mother is angry, all the more so because they cannot put their reasons into words. When the parents are gone, she pulls Elaine's ears and sends her to the punishment room ...

... She is staring at the Orphan Mother as Rose explains, untruthfully, that Elaine stole some candy from her drawer. Elaine tries to tell the older woman that it wasn't her, that Rose is lying through her teeth, but the Orphan Mother doesn't listen. Rose is young and pretty and someone will take her home the very next week. Elaine ... is just a plain girl with an introverted nature. It isn't hard for the Orphan Mother to believe Rose and send Elaine to the punishment room ...

... She is standing in the punishment room, trying not to

cry. They don't shout at her or beat her, even though either one would be preferable. Instead, they just make her stand up for hours on end, waiting in the darkness. By the time she is finally released, she is a nervous wreck ...

... She is entering the Peerless School for the first time, awed at the opportunity that has been dropped into her lap, when she sees Millicent for the first time. The girl takes an instant dislike to Elaine, turning her into a toad on her very first day ...

... She is walking up to one of the form mistresses, obeying a compulsion she knows she should be able to resist. As soon as she is in front of the older woman, she opens her mouth and emits a stream of horrific insults. She knows she is lucky, when the enchantment lets her go, that she isn't expelled on the spot ...

... She is leaving the Peerless School as a graduated magician when the ink on the scroll starts to run and fade. It isn't real ...

"It didn't happen like that," she said, out loud. "That's one of my nightmares."

She heard the spell laughing at her, as if it was an intelligent being. It had dragged up her memories, then started to improvise newer and darker thoughts to wear down her resolve to fight. Elaine braced herself, then shoved hard against the spell. It recoiled from her touch, then returned to the fight. It was drawing on her magic, her memories and everything else just to grind her down. But she felt a wave of cold anger that suddenly made it easier to focus her mind.

"It didn't happen like that," she said, forcing herself to remember the good days in her life. Meeting Daria for the first time, entering the Great Library as a staff member, meeting Johan ... she might have been a weak magician, but she was far from powerless. "And I will be rid of you."

She plunged into the fight with renewed determination. This time, the spell seemed to cower back from her touch, then started to shatter under her pressure. It mutated, again and again, each fragment growing into something new, but it could no longer draw on her power. She probed at its innermost structure, located the weak spots and pushed, hard. Piece by piece, the spell started to come apart ...

... And then it lashed back at her, a final desperate attempt to overwhelm her mind. She staggered mentally, realising just how deeply it had embedded itself in her very soul, but she held herself together and *pushed*. The spell fell backwards, into a locked corner of her mind, and held itself there. Elaine staggered, then opened her eyes and stood. Her limbs felt wobbly, and she could hear the spell howling in her mind, but she could walk to the door without impediment. She was *free*!

And drained, she realised, slowly. She was used to running out of power, used to watching as more powerful witches and wizards cast spells while she caught her breath, but she had never truly felt so drained in her life. What remained of her power was being used to hold the spell in check ... and when she lost it, the spell would flower through her mind and overwhelm her once and for all. It didn't seem *fair*, part of her mind told her, that she should have to keep using her magic to keep her body free. But the spell was nothing if not persistent.

You need to get rid of it, she told herself, *but how*?

Holding it at bay with her mind, she considered what she knew. The spell was dangerous because it fed on people, real people. It wasn't just powered by magic, like every other spell she knew. In some ways, it was as much an oddity as Johan's magic. But ... she gritted her teeth, then stumbled towards the door. There had been a guard outside, if she recalled correctly, hopefully not an Inquisitor in civilian clothes. She banged on the door as hard as she could, then leant against the wall. Moments later, the door opened and a man wearing a bright red uniform looked in at her.

"Please," Elaine said. She made a show of stumbling to the floor. "I need help."

The guard caught her, instinctively. Elaine gathered herself, clutching his hand as though it was holding her back from falling, then concentrated on the spell and shoved it into his hand, knowing it would rapidly infest the rest of his body. The guard let out a yelp and shoved her to the floor, but it was already too late. His face went blank and his arms dropped to his side, leaving him helpless. Elaine pulled herself to her feet, then closed the door. Hopefully, no one would notice that the guard was missing for a few hours.

"All right," she said, studying the guard through tired eyes. "What's your name?"

"Talbot," the guard said.

Elaine frowned. It was a typical name from Vlad Deferens' homeland, although *that* shouldn't have been a surprise. Very little remained secret in the Golden City; no one, not even a Privy Councillor, would have been able to recruit more than a few personal guardsmen without hard questions being asked. On the other hand, Deferens was a powerful figure in his homeland. He could muster an army without having to worry about someone noticing what he was doing, then smuggle it into the Golden City.

We must have been asleep, she thought, numbly. Even after everything that had happened to her, she still found it hard to believe that Deferens had managed to take over so quickly. In hindsight, it was an obvious weakness ... but she knew that there were people who lived next to volcanoes, always believing there wouldn't be an eruption during their lifetimes. And sometimes they were right ... and sometimes they weren't so lucky.

She looked up at the guard. "And where are you from?"

"Kurii," Talbot said.

It meant nothing to Elaine. "How did you get here?"

"We were in our barracks, then we were in the warehouse," Talbot said. "Then we were here."

Elaine frowned. Talbot couldn't lie to her, but he wouldn't volunteer information and, if she didn't ask the right questions, he might not understand what she meant. Maybe Deferens had outsmarted himself after all; the spell would have eventually overcome Elaine herself, but he would have had to ask careful questions to get what he wanted out of the affair. Unless he'd been planning to remove the spell himself, at some later date ...

But Talbot's description suggested that they had been transfigured, then transported to the Golden City.

She shook her head. "How many of you are there?"

"Forty thousand," Talbot said.

Elaine blanched. Forty thousand soldiers – and the Inquisitors – would be enough to keep the Golden City under control. But it seemed too many to be real. Forty thousand newcomers to the Golden City? The city council had been having enough trouble finding living space for the Court Wizards and their hangers on ... and there were only a few hundred of them. Forty thousand newcomers would be impossible to house.

She cleared her throat. "How many soldiers are in the Golden City?"

"Three thousand," Talbot said.

That sounded more reasonable, Elaine decided. She bounced a handful of other questions off him, but Talbot simply didn't know very much. He'd been a farmhand who had seen the advantages in becoming a soldier, done well in his basic training and then been assigned to a barracks along the edge of the wildlands. And then there had been a request for some volunteers ... and then, the next thing he recalled was being in the warehouse. One of the big shipping warehouses on the edge of the city, Elaine guessed. They were used to house goods brought in and out of the city. Given enough time, someone could probably house an army there without being detected, at least until it was too late.

They were building up stockpiles of food for the Conference, she told herself, grimly. She'd attended the Privy Council meeting – her *last* council meeting – when they'd agreed to spend extra monies on procuring food for the Court Wizards. *All they had to do was transfigure the soldiers into something harmless and bring them in with the wagons, then store the poor bastards in the warehouse until the time came to return them to normal.*

"Talbot," she said, "what orders do your people have for the city?"

"I don't know," Talbot said.

Elaine glared at him. "Why not?"

"I am only told what I need to know," Talbot said, in a monotone. "What I do not need to know, I do not know."

"Because you might be forced to talk," Elaine muttered. "What do you normally do when you occupy a city?"

"The old sweats say we patrol streets, keep the population respectful and hit anyone who even looks at us funny," Talbot informed her. "The women are to be ravished so they learn their place, while their menfolk are to be broken. What we want, we take."

Elaine felt sick. How could Deferens have brought such monsters into the Golden City? She knew there were truly evil people out there – Hawthorne had planned to take her and make her his wife – but this was different. She thought of the people she knew being chased by such monsters and shivered in horror. This was ... this was awful.

She changed the subject, quickly. "Do you know what the passwords are to enter or leave this building?"

"No," Talbot said. "I have orders not to leave my guardpost until I am relieved."

Elaine cursed herself under her breath. She hadn't thought about that, even though she should have realised that Talbot wouldn't be expected to stay there all night. What time was it, anyway? They'd taken her clockwork watch along with her wand and everything else she'd been carrying at the time. She thought it was late at night, but she honestly wasn't sure. It felt like hours since she'd thrown caution to the winds and attacked the curse with everything she had.

"I see," she said. "And when will you be relieved?"

"I don't know," Talbot said.

He didn't have a watch or any other way to tell the time, Elaine noted. She briefly considered trying to swap clothes with him, but the thought of anyone being fooled if she wore the red uniform was ludicrous. The other option was to take him with her, yet she knew it would be dangerous. Anyone could shout 'STOP' and Talbot would obey. The state he was in, he would do anything for anyone. It crossed her mind that she should kill him, or order him to kill himself, but she couldn't bring herself to take that step. The mere thought was horrific.

"Do you know," she asked, "where they put my wand?"

"No," Talbot said.

Elaine sighed, then ordered him to turn out his pockets and drop everything he was carrying on the floor, while she washed her face in cold water. His pockets were largely empty, save for a dagger, which she took, and a pendant that – she suspected, was designed to allow him to pass through some of the palace's wards. She pocketed the pendant, making a mental note to study it later, then looked up at Talbot. The guard's eyes looked back at her, glassily. She shuddered. Deferens would probably have been happy to leave her in a similar state indefinitely.

A thought struck her and she leant forward. "Are there any other prisoners here?"

"Children," Talbot said. "The Emperor's servants said they were to be treated with respect."

Elaine blinked. *Children*? As far as she knew, Deferens was unmarried; she'd assumed he was hoping for a marriage into one of the Great Houses, linking his status as a Privy Councillor with the wealth and magical heritage of the aristocracy. It was possible – even probable – that he had a run of bastards, but would he bring them to the Golden City? There were Great Houses that wouldn't give a damn, yet it was odd. He'd want his heir, assuming he had one, kept well away from anything that could blow up in his face.

"Children," she mused. "Whose children?"

"I don't know," Talbot said.

Elaine sighed. "Did you see them do anything that might show who they were?"

"One of them hexed me," Talbot said. "He cast a spell on me."

"I understand the impulse," Elaine said. A magical child ... he had to be from one of the Great Houses. And that meant ... what? Hostages? Or something worse? There were quite a number of spells that could be worked with the blood of innocent children. "But there's no time to worry about it now."

She took a breath. "Here are your orders. You are to carry them out as soon as I leave the room. You will use wet cloth to block up your ears, then hold yourself in readiness. Once someone comes into the room, you will ... you will knock them out, then make a break for it and run as far as you can."

She felt a twinge of guilt as Talbot nodded in understanding, then violently pushed it to one side. He might be an automaton now, but he would have gleefully raped and looted his way through the city if Deferens had given the word. And his comrades might do the same, if they managed to tighten their grip on power.

Gritting her teeth, she glanced out of the room, checked that the passageway was empty and then closed the door firmly behind her. And then she started to run.

133

Chapter Fourteen

In Johan's experience, the Great Library had always been crammed with students. There wasn't an hour of the day when there weren't at least fifty students and older researchers making their way through the library, studying books in between snatching catnaps at their desks. He knew that Elaine hadn't really minded, as long as they didn't drool on the books. She'd been a student herself, only a few short years ago.

But now the building was dark, and as silent as the grave. The librarians were gone, hastened out to their staff accommodation or wherever they lived in the city, while the handful of guest visitors had been ordered to stay elsewhere. Lights that should have been burning indefinitely, powered by the wards, were no longer lit, leaving the entire building shrouded in darkness. Even Cass's light spells couldn't push the darkness back more than a few metres, as if it were a physical thing. Johan couldn't help seeing *things* in the darkness, right at the corner of his eye. He wasn't sure if they were real or just tricks of the light.

"The Golden City has always been restricted in its growth," Cass commented, as they made their way down a long book-lined corridor. Titles glimmered at them and then faded into the darkness. "The mountains saw to that, really."

"Everyone knows that," Daria pointed out. She sounded unhappy to be in the darkness, even though she could probably see better than either of the two humans. Werewolf eyes were sharper too. "The Emperors didn't want too many people infesting their city."

"And so they placed their capital within the heart of a mountain range," Cass said. "But they rapidly found themselves running out of space. There was just no room to expand."

"I know all that," Johan said, tartly. "My father certainly

bitched about it often enough."

Cass turned and half-smiled at him. "And did your father ever grumble about why he wasn't allowed to dig underground?"

Johan frowned. "I don't recall him saying anything of the sort," he said, finally. "But he might not have wanted to grumble like that in front of me."

"There are passages below the city," Daria said, suddenly. "And people aren't allowed to burrow underground because they might stumble across those passageways."

"You used them," Cass said. She sounded irked that Daria had known her secret, although Johan wasn't too surprised. Even he had heard rumours of a secret tunnel network linking the important buildings together. "I had forgotten."

There was a hint of a chuckle from Daria. "But I thought all of those tunnels would be ... protected and guarded," she said. "The Great Houses wouldn't want just *anyone* sneaking into their homes."

"They wouldn't," Cass agreed. "But there are some passageways that are known only to the Inquisitors and certain members of the Privy Council. One of them leads from the Great Library to the Imperial Palace."

Daria turned to look at Johan. "Did Elaine ever mention a secret passageway to you?"

"The building is riddled with secret passageways," Johan said. Whoever had designed the Great Library had rapidly run out of space, so he'd used magic to extend the space he had until the building was far larger on the inside than the outside. "But I didn't know there was one leading to the Imperial Palace."

"She might not have mentioned it to you," Cass said. "Knowledge like that is rarely passed on unless there is a pressing need for it."

"Which is why many of those passageways have been forgotten," Daria commented, snidely. "How many are rediscovered every year?"

"Kids sometimes find entrances and go exploring," Cass said, curtly. "Some of them never return."

She led the way through a door into a large chamber, then paused for a moment. It took Johan several seconds to realise that they'd entered one of the reading rooms, if only because it looked so different in the darkness. The desks, normally occupied by students, were cold and empty, while the bookshelves on the walls looked untouched. Something *moved* high above him, but when he looked up he saw nothing but shadows. He kept a wary eye on the darkness as Cass moved forward, then opened a door leading into a private reading room. It was large enough to house a dozen students without serious problems.

"There's nothing here," he said, puzzled. Elaine had let him explore the library, once she'd explained to the staff that he was a guest. "Why are we coming here?"

"There's an inner room here," Cass said, pressing her hand against the far wall. It opened with an audible click, revealing a second smaller compartment. "I believe it was originally intended for the Emperor, then the Grand Sorcerers."

Daria bit off a laugh. "The Grand Sorceress came to the Great Library to study?"

"She doesn't know everything," Cass said. "If she's still alive."

Johan shivered. The Grand Sorceress was the most powerful magician in the world, as far as anyone knew. If she'd been killed, or captured, it suggested that the Emperor was more powerful than her by far. Johan wasn't quite sure of the limits of his own power, but he knew his weaknesses. A traditional duel was out of the question. He felt for Elaine's presence in his mind, seeking reassurance, but only felt the faintest of shimmers in return. It didn't feel good.

He forced himself to look around the hidden compartment instead, fighting down his fears for his mistress. The room was smaller than he'd expected, but luxurious beyond belief. Each of the walls were covered in gilt-edged bookshelves – a handful of texts sat on the shelves – while the table was made of the finest wood and the chair was sinfully comfortable. A large cabinet sat in the far corner, surrounded by a handful of preservation runes. Johan guessed that the rules against eating and drinking in the Great Library didn't apply to the Grand Sorceress and her predecessors. He wouldn't have cared to be the library attendant who tried to explain the rules to Lady Light Spinner. Anyone who tried was likely to wind up as a frog for a few hours.

"She was looking at ancient history books," Daria said, with some surprise. She had walked over to look at the bookshelves. "Was there a reason for that?"

"We have an enemy," Cass said. She drew her wand and started to poke and prod at the walls. "One who comes to us out of the shadows of the past."

"How very dramatic," Daria sneered.

"I believe Elaine intended to explain everything, once we were out of the city," Johan said, before the two women could start arguing again. "There are too many listening ears here."

"I'll wait," Daria said, although she didn't sound happy about it. "And you're poking and prodding the wrong part of the wall."

Cass turned to stare at her. "How do you know?"

Daria smirked. "Only one person has been in this room over the past month, apart from us," she said. "Their scent is strongest in the chair, but she paced a lot and came in and out of the room there."

She jabbed a finger at the closest bookshelf. "You'll find the passageway there."

Johan stared at her. "You can tell everything so perfectly?"

"Everyone has their own unique scent," Daria said. "And a born werewolf can track a single person through a morass of different scents, if necessary. This" – she waved her hand to indicate the room – "isn't very hard at all."

"Oh," Johan said. "And what do I smell of?"

"Slugs and snails and puppy dog tails," Daria said, mischievously.

Cass laughed, not unkindly. "You walked right into that one," she said, as she started to wave her wand at the bookshelf. "But I wouldn't take it too seriously, if I were you."

"But you're not me," Daria said. "You smell differently."

There was a click from the bookshelf, followed by a low whine as it moved to one side, revealing a darkened passageway leading down into the bowels of the earth. Cass held up a hand in warning, then stepped forward, wand raised. There was a flash of light, then a sense of sudden emptiness and despair that was almost overwhelming. If Johan hadn't struggled with feelings of worthlessness for his entire life, it might have killed him. Daria snapped back into wolf form and howled, mournfully. Johan hesitated, then knelt beside the small wolf and wrapped his arms around her.

"Careful she doesn't bite you," Cass warned, as she snapped the final ward. "Being a made werewolf isn't much fun, I'm afraid. Most of the horror stories about werewolves come from made werewolves who go mad after the change."

Johan shivered. "How bad is it?"

"Some go feral and bite as many others as possible," Cass said. "Some kill themselves, or are driven away by their families; some just try to live a normal life, hiding in iron cages when the full moon rises. The lucky ones are adopted by a werewolf pack, but their lives will never be the same. And almost none of them will manage to climb the ladder and become one of the alpha pair."

Daria shivered again, then snapped back into human form. Johan let go of her hastily, then looked away as she adjusted her robe. It was the closest he'd ever been to a naked girl ... he felt his cheeks flame as he rose to his feet, knowing she would pick up on the changes in his scent. He would be lucky if she didn't rip his throat out.

"A nasty little protective hex," Cass said. She shot Johan an unreadable look. "I'm surprised you weren't badly affected."

"I've felt worthless for most of my life," Johan snarled. He scowled as he rose and peered into the darkened corridor. "What does another bout of worthlessness matter to me?"

"I've often felt that people like you were treated poorly," Cass commented. She turned and started to step into the passageway. "You deserved better."

Johan glared at her back. "Then where were you?"

"It is never easy to take a child from his parents," Cass said. There was a dark note in her voice. "I've seen parents who used dark magic as a lazy way to discipline their children, or to teach them obedience. But bloodlines are sacred and parents have ultimate authority over their children. We can only ever intervene in the worst possible cases."

"And by that point, the child might be dead," Johan said, bitterly. "I think I hate the system."

"Most people do, when they think about it," Cass said, evenly. "But the alternative is total chaos. We learn to live with it."

Johan made a disgusted face, then stepped back to walk close to Daria. The werewolf looked uneasy, her teeth bared in a permanent scowl, her hands flexing as if they were claws. Johan had felt worthless enough in the past, but what did it mean for a werewolf to feel worthless, particularly one who had been raised by a pack? Had Daria felt completely alone ... or worse? There was no way to know ... and no way he dared ask. She might be furious at him for daring to open his mouth.

"Thank you," Daria said, quietly. "I wasn't expecting a hex."

"You're welcome," Johan said. He reached out, greatly daring, and took her hand. Her fingers felt cold and clammy in his, despite the thin line of hair. "I felt bad too."

He looked up at the walls as they walked further into the darkness. They were carved stone, marked with runes and symbols he barely recognised. A handful were jokes, if his father had been telling the truth, puns that could only be expressed in the runic alphabet. Others were written in a language he could read, calling on the blessings of the gods. The workmen had clearly had fun, he decided. Leaving hidden jokes and snide asides carved into the stonework was an ancient tradition.

They stopped as they reached a crossroads, then Cass led them forward through another tunnel. Johan glanced down both sides of the crossroad, but saw nothing, apart from darkness. He couldn't help wondering where the tunnels went ... the Peerless School? The Watchtower? Or, for that matter, who used them? He listened carefully, but all he could hear were his footsteps as he made his way up the tunnel. There was no hint that anyone else was using the tunnel network at the moment.

"You said kids got into the network," he said, suddenly. "What happens to them?"

"Some are never seen again," Cass said. "Some are pulled out by us, soundly smacked and then sent home. Some plot out enough of the tunnels to use them to get from place to place without being seen. And some find work living down in the tunnel network. There's quite a few things under the city that are never seen by anyone on the surface."

"There are legends of children living under the city," Daria said, suddenly. Her voice was stronger now. "They ran from workhouses and orphanages and built their own little community."

"It would be nice if that were true," Cass said. "But runaways rarely find happiness at the end of their journey."

Johan swallowed. His father had told him all sorts of horror stories about the world outside his walls, in the hopes of convincing Johan to stay inside, out of sight and out of mind. There were predators out there, men and women who preyed on the Powerless, who would do worse than kill him if he fell into their hands. The stories hadn't made him want to stay, if only because his family had treated him poorly, but had there been some basis in truth?

Daria squeezed his hand, then let go of him. "How much further," she asked, "do we have to walk?"

"Not much further," Cass said. "We're underneath the Imperial Palace now."

Johan glanced up, but saw nothing apart from bare stone.

"I thought the Imperial Palace was the most heavily warded building in the city," Daria said, suspiciously. "How can you just take us through the wards?"

"The wardcrafters didn't include the secret passageways in their protections," Cass explained, "although we may have to break another ward or two when we enter the palace itself. They were never told the passageways existed, you see. A chink in the building's defences known only to the Grand Sorcerers and their most trusted allies. And even if someone has taken the Golden Throne, they won't know about the passageways."

"You make it sound as though someone was planning to overthrow the Emperor right from the start," Daria observed.

Cass shrugged. "I believe there were times, back then, when everyone knew there were quite a few potential heirs to the Golden Throne," she said. "And I believe the Grand Sorcerers of that time weren't too keen on the idea of handing power to someone who just walked in and sat down on the Throne. They would have taken precautions, relying on the newcomer being largely ignorant of how the protections actually *worked*."

She shrugged, again. "But as time went by," she added, "the threat of a newcomer taking power receded almost to nothingness."

Johan felt a sudden glimmer of sympathy for the long-gone heirs, deprived of their birthright by a simple accident of fate, then shook his head savagely. The new Emperor, whoever he was, had arrested and tortured Johan's mistress, then threatened her with a fate worse than death ...

"Ah," Cass said. The passageway twisted, then came to a dead end. "There's a vision spell here."

She poked it. Part of the wall suddenly turned transparent, revealing a line of occupied beds and mattresses on the floor. They were crammed with soldiers wearing light armour, catching up on their sleep ... Johan felt his blood run cold as he looked at them, counting nearly a hundred crammed into the small room alone. The coup – and coup it was – had been planned for a very long time.

"That room normally houses the maids," Cass said. She sounded more than a little disturbed by the sight. "Did the Grand Sorcerers of the past spy on the maids as they undressed and prepared for bed?"

"Why not?" Johan asked, more savagely than he'd intended. "Jamal certainly spied on them whenever he could."

Daria had a more practical question. "Can they hear us?"

"I doubt it," Cass said. She waved her wand, casting a handful of spells into the air. "No, the entire passageway is heavily warded. They can't hear a word we say."

"Lucky," Johan muttered. He winced as he felt a sudden burst of ... *something* coming down the link from Elaine, but the feeling faded before he could get a grip on it. "Very lucky."

Daria caught his arm. "What are you feeling?"

"I'm not sure," Johan confessed. "But I think we should

hurry."

Cass nodded. "Follow me," she ordered. "And run."

The passageway twisted twice, then stopped dead. Johan stared at the stone, then cursed himself for a fool. There had to be a way through, perhaps hidden by magic. Cass poked and prodded at it for a long moment, then swore out loud, just before a flare of magic lashed out at them. Johan responded instinctively and told the magic to go away. There was a flash of light, then the magic was gone.

"Well," Cass said. "You got rid of the ward."

"Good," Johan said.

"But you probably set off all the alarms too," Cass added, as a dull gonging echoed through the palace. "They might not understand *what* happened, but they will know that *something* did. I think we had definitely better hurry."

Daria snapped into wolf form, moved out of her robe and sniffed the air. "This way," she said, as she shifted back into human form. "I can smell her!"

"Then lead us there," Cass ordered, as Daria became a wolf again. Johan scooped up the robe and tucked it under his arm. "Hurry!"

Chapter Fifteen

The first door she came to was locked, but not warded. Elaine frowned, then used a simple spell to unlock the door, and peered inside. It was a smaller room than the one they'd given her, with a comfortable bed, a nightlight and a small table and chair. A child was sleeping in the room, lying so still that she knew he was under the influence of a spell. Elaine knew little about children, but she thought he was about seven years old.

A hostage, she thought. There were definite traces of protective magic surrounding him, although clearly not enough to fight off even a simple sleep charm. *But why would Deferens want hostages*?

She considered the possibilities, none of them good, as she closed the door and then looked up and down the corridor. Deferens was the Emperor and, more importantly, he had the servitude of the Inquisitors. He could easily have maintained the *status quo*, at least for the time being, without alienating the Great Houses by demanding hostages. But he'd felt it was nevertheless important to bring the children into the Imperial Palace.

There were at least thirty such rooms in the corridor – and perhaps more, elsewhere in the palace. If they each held a child, she calculated, it meant that Deferens had secured thirty children from the Great Houses – and probably from the traders and other wealthy mundanes as well. It would give him clout, she suspected, at the risk of making new enemies. He didn't have hostages to offer *them*, after all. And probably wouldn't, even if he had had them to offer. She gritted her teeth, wondering if there was a way she could get the children out of the palace without being detected, but she couldn't think of one. It would be hard enough to get herself out of the building.

She slipped down the corridor, trying desperately to

summon the strength for a single spell or two, but nothing worked. Her magic was so badly depleted she could barely sense the flickers of magic moving through the air, let alone actually *do* anything. It wouldn't be long, she suspected, before she simply collapsed of exhaustion. If Deferens and his men found her while she was helpless, it would be the end.

Need to keep moving, she told herself. She reached out to Johan, but even after their first successful link she couldn't even get a hint of his presence. *I have to keep moving ...*

She paused as she heard people moving ahead of her and ducked into a sideroom before they came into view. They had once been servants and maids, she realised, as they walked past the room, but now they were slaves. Collars sat on their necks, glimmering with magic, rendering them hopelessly obedient to their new master. Elaine had worn one once, after depleting the magic, and it had nearly overwhelmed her. A handful of mundanes didn't stand a chance. They would be slaves for the rest of their lives, unless their master chose to liberate them. And Deferens would no more do that than Elaine would burn the Great Library to the ground.

Poor bastards, she thought. But there was nothing she could do for them.

She braced herself, then ran out of the room and down the corridor as soon as the servants were out of sight. One room held a couple of men sitting at desks, but neither of them looked up and saw her as she ran past; another held a handful of guards, playing cards or trying to catch up on their sleep. Elaine felt a sudden flicker of magic running through the palace, followed by a series of dongs. The palace was under attack! She tried to slip into the nearest room as she heard the soldiers snap to their feet, but the door was locked. And, before she could summon the strength to open it, the soldiers saw her.

"Stop," one of them shouted. "Stop now!"

Elaine turned and fled down the stairs. The soldiers gave chase, one of them chanting a spell out loud as he ran. Elaine could have deflected it, if she'd had her magic, but right now she couldn't have cast even the simplest of spells. The tripping jinx struck her and sent her cart-wheeling to the floor; she barely managed to get her hands out to break her fall before she banged her nose into the ground. One of the soldiers ran up behind her and pressed his foot on her back, trapping her as soundly as any spell, while his companions surrounded her, laughing nastily. They didn't know who she was, Elaine realised through a haze of pain, but they did know she was female. They were going to have some fun.

A low growl echoed through the corridor. Elaine looked up, just in time to see a small wolf streak out of the shadows and lash into the men with teeth and claw. It had always surprised her, once she'd actually learnt the truth, that Daria made such a small werewolf, but size didn't matter. Daria's teeth and claws tore through the men as if they were made of paper, killing the magic user before he could cast a single spell. Behind her, a blonde-haired woman carrying a wand ran up to Elaine and helped her to her feet. Elaine leant against her gratefully, then blinked in surprise as she recognised Cass. It had been months since she'd last seen the young Inquisitor ...

"Don't worry," Cass said. "We'll get you out of here."

A shout echoed down from the edge of the corridor. A small army of soldiers had arrived, led by a pair of men in red robes. Cass lifted her wand and cast a spell, sending a wave of fire washing up the corridor towards them, then followed up with a handful of lighter prank jinxes. Elaine stared at her, puzzled, then slowly worked out that the pranks would be harder for the magicians to handle when they would be expecting lethal spells. She heard two of the soldiers screaming in pain as the fire burned through their armour, then Cass cast another spell, levitating Elaine into the air.

"I can walk," Elaine protested.

"No, you can't," Cass said. She waved her wand, sending Elaine floating off down the corridor. "You're right on the edge of collapsing into a useless heap."

Elaine had no time to argue. Johan waved to her as the spell carried her towards a gaping hole in the wall, then turned his attention towards the guards. Cass ran back, waving her wand over her shoulder and casting spell after spell into the inferno. Flashes of light were coming back at her, then there was a low *thump* and the fires evaporated into nothingness.

Cass swore out loud. "You!"

"You're trespassing, girlie," a male voice said. It sounded oddly familiar to Elaine, but not *that* familiar. It wasn't Dread. "And you deserted your post."

"The Emperor is mad," Cass said. "He's ... oh, what's the use?"

Elaine turned her head, just in time to see a dark-skinned man wearing Inquisitor robes lift a wand and cast a spell towards Cass. The younger Inquisitor blocked it, but was sent stumbling back by the sheer force of the impact. Daria roared and lunged, only to be picked up by a wave of magic and hurled right into a wall. Elaine stared in horror as blood leaked from Daria's haunches, staining her fur. Werewolves healed quickly, but it was quite possible the Inquisitor wouldn't give her time to heal. Cass hurled another spell and then another, but both of them were blocked effortlessly. The Inquisitor was advancing forward ...

Johan stepped forward, raising his arm. A fireball of staggering power appeared between him and his target, then flew forward, aimed right at the Inquisitor. The man lifted a shield, then yelped as the flames burned right through his protections. Elaine had a momentary vision of him engulfed by fire, then closed her eyes as the levitation spell carried her into the darkened passageway. Behind her, Cass scooped up Daria and ran after them, closing the passage as she moved. It wouldn't be long before the other Inquisitors caught up with them ...

"Don't pass out," Cass ordered, as she propelled Elaine down the corridor. "Whatever you do, don't pass out."

"I'm trying," Elaine muttered. Her body wasn't sore, but it was *tired.* Every muscle in her flesh was calling out for immediate rest. "What ... what happened to him?"

"Dead, I think," Johan said. There was a savage note to his voice she hoped never to hear again. "He was trying to kill us."

"He was bound by his oaths," Cass said, tartly. "But yes, he would have killed us if he could."

"It's Deferens's fault," Elaine said, through the haze that threatened to overwhelm her mind. "He stoned Light Spinner, took the Golden Throne."

Cass leant down. "Keep talking," she urged. "Talk about ... talk about something we don't know."

Elaine snickered, tiredly, but she understood what Cass wanted. "No one really knows if the gods exist," she said. It was one question that she hadn't been able to answer, despite having all the knowledge of the Great Library dumped into her head. "But there are hundreds of spells that call on them and some of them actually work. They *only* work if you call on the gods."

"Better not say that too loudly," Cass advised. "You'll be stoned to death merely for suggesting there are no gods."

She was right, Elaine knew. There were hundreds of thousands of gods, ranging from simple household gods to giant figures with millions of worshippers. And yet, were they real or figments of human imagination? Elaine had seen enough of the history of magic to know that the early magicians might easily have served as the catalyst for human belief in gods. But there was no point in casting a spell that called on other magicians, at least not without that magician's consent. The gods were different.

No one denies that the gods exist, she thought. *They merely don't worship all of them.*

She shuddered at the memory. The orphanage had always been short of food, but – every day – she'd been forced to place a small offering in the shrine as a gift to the gods. Between them, the orphan children had given away enough food to feed a dozen more orphans. She'd thought the god ate the food, but one day two boys had been expelled for sneaking down at night and stealing the food from the shrine. Gods or no gods, it had been very hard to blame them.

"The spells that work are the ones that call on the embodiment of various concepts," she said, wearily. It was growing harder to focus. "Random gods don't seem to grant wishes, but embodiments do. You can call on the God of Love to cast a love spell, or the God of Justice if you wish for true justice. Why do those spells work?"

"Because the gods are real?" Johan asked. "People ask

them for favours and they are granted?"

"Or because the spells are calling on the concept, rather than any god," Elaine said. "A balancing spell calls on the God of Justice, but can only ever be applied to a living person, rather than an object. It is a poor thinker who blames the weapon rather than the person who wields it."

"There are weapons that contaminate the mind of anyone fool enough to carry them," Cass pointed out.

"And spells calling on the God of Justice would show it," Elaine said, through her tiredness. "The user would not be held to account for what he did, if he picked the weapon up in true innocence. But someone who made a deliberate decision to use a cursed blade would be held accountable for his sins, even though the blade might have made them worse."

She coughed, then cleared her throat. "I don't know what it proves, but it proves *something*."

"That you should keep your mouth shut," Cass said, dryly. "Denying the gods will get you in hot water."

"There are too many," Johan said.

"Doesn't mean they don't exist," Cass said. She paused, then propelled Elaine through the hatch and into the Great Library. "Can you still touch the wards?"

Elaine concentrated. The Great Library might be quiet, but it was very far from dead. Magic surged through her, allowing her to focus her mind on the wards and tighten them against all intruders. A quick scan of the building revealed that there were a handful of guards outside, but no one actually inside, apart from her and her party. She locked the doors, warded them firmly and, as an afterthought, sealed up the secret passageway as well. It hadn't been part of the protective wards earlier, she saw. They'd been programmed to ignore the passageway unless their mistress knew it existed.

"I never knew about the passageway," she muttered, as she forced herself to sit up. She was drawing power from the wards, but it wouldn't last for long, unless she wished to permanently bind herself to the library. "And because I didn't know, I never warded it against intruders."

"Lucky you didn't, really," Cass said. "You got the spell

out of your mind?"

"I think so," Elaine said. "I gave it to a guard."

Cass snickered. "And what did he manage to do for you?"

"There's three thousand soldiers in the city," Elaine said. She yawned, suddenly. "And I really need to sleep."

"Good idea," Cass said. "Is the building secure?"

"It's as secure as I can make it," Elaine said. "Are there any other secret passageways?"

"None that I know about," Cass said. "But I was never told everything."

Elaine muttered a tired curse. There was no point in trying to scan the building for more secret passageways. The wards wouldn't show them to her, let alone block them, unless she already knew they existed. She considered several options for trying to block hypothetical passageways anyway, but they would all do significant damage to the wards. And to think, she told herself, that she had thought she was the absolute mistress of the Great Library.

"I've done my best," she said. Her entire body sagged. "Can you help me to my chambers?"

"You might be better sleeping here," Cass said. "But I can levitate you to the reading room, if you think that will help."

"Please," Elaine said.

Cass cast a spell, levitating Elaine into the air. The magic of the Great Library fluttered around them doubtfully, then allowed Cass to move Elaine through the door and into the giant reading room. Elaine smiled at seeing the room dark and empty – she could have kept the library in perfect order if it wasn't for those pesky users – and then sighed as Cass lowered her to the ground. Johan gave her a concerned look, then knelt down beside her. Behind her, Daria slowly returned to human form and stretched her bruised body. Her chest and lower thighs were black and blue.

"I'm healing quickly," she said, when Elaine looked at her. "Don't worry about me."

Cass squatted on her haunches next to Elaine. "Are you sure you got rid of the spell?"

"I don't know," Elaine admitted. She had destroyed or evicted the active parts of the spell, but it had left traces within her mind. A few hours of sleep might give it time to damage her ... or perhaps the damage would come later, once she lowered her guard. She needed a mind healer or someone else experienced in repairing spell damage, but she knew she would find neither. "I need to sleep and I don't want to sleep."

"There are potions you could take," Johan offered. "The ones that keep the students awake while they're cramming for a test ..."

"They also tend to catch up with you," Cass pointed out, sharply. "The only way to be sure would be to scan Elaine's mind for damage, but the mere act of scanning might invigorate the spell."

She reached out and rested a hand on Elaine's shoulder. "We'll take care of you, I promise," she said. "And we won't let you go."

"Thank you for coming," Elaine said, softly. She closed her eyes, feeling the wards brushing against her mind. It was going to be a problem when she left the city, she knew; she'd intended to pass them to Vane before she joined Johan and Daria with the Travellers. Instead, she might have to carry them indefinitely or risk the library falling into Deferens's hands. "How ... how did Light Spinner know?"

"I think she merely wanted you to have an escort," Cass said. Her voice seemed to be coming from a far distance. "I would have had to bring Johan in for study, if I had still been bound by my oaths when I discovered he was still alive. Instead, I get to help the pair of you."

"And thank you," Elaine said, now utterly exhausted. "I know it wasn't easy for you."

Cass grunted. Elaine winced in sympathy. Cass had trained for years to be an Inquisitor, to wear the skull-ring. Light Spinner had made her throw it away, even if there was a prospect of returning to the ranks at a later date. And there weren't that many Inquisitors. Cass would have known the one they'd faced, the one Johan might have killed; she would have known and respected the older man, even if she didn't *like* him. She would certainly mourn his death.

"There's a temple on the lower levels, if you wish to pray," Elaine offered. "I ..."

"Thank you," Cass said. "But I will be fine."

Elaine sighed, then nodded. The wards billowed around her protectively, offering support. She drew on it gratefully, then felt herself fall into darkness. She almost caught herself, fearing the consequences of going to sleep, but exhaustion overwhelmed her.

The darkness absorbed her moments later ...

And then she was asleep.

Chapter Sixteen

Charity snapped awake as she heard alarms echoing through the Imperial Palace. For a long moment she was helplessly confused, unsure of what was going on. Had the Grand Sorceress recovered and attacked the Emperor, the Great Houses mounted an offensive or ... she pulled herself out of bed, silently grateful she hadn't bothered to undress, then padded over to the door. It was locked and warded, keeping her prisoner.

The Emperor doesn't trust me, she thought, rolling her eyes in a manner she hadn't dared do to her father for years. *And yet I gave him my oaths.*

She sat down on the bed and looked around. There hadn't been much time to inspect the rooms before she'd collapsed into the bed, but now she had all the time in the world to see what sort of quarters she'd been given. Judging from the pink decor and a handful of paintings featuring horses and unicorns, it had probably been intended for a very young girl, maybe someone below ten years old. She couldn't decide if the room had been given to her as an oversight or an unsubtle insult. The Emperor's homeland certainly regarded grown women as little better than children, unable to think for themselves or do anything without male permission and supervision.

Idiots, she thought, savagely. It was a weakness, she told herself, a flaw in their armour someone could exploit. But the oaths she'd sworn ensured *she* could never exploit the weakness for herself. Someone else would have to deduce its existence and use it for themselves. *And all the while, I'm trapped here like a fool.*

She paced the room restlessly, checking out the bathroom – it would have been spectacular, to a ten-year-old girl – and the tiny cabinet crammed with food. There were layers of protective spells everywhere, designed to ensure a safe environment for a child. Charity was sure that if she tried to drown herself in the baths, the spells would sound the alarm and prevent her from dying. A child, of course, might be drowned by accident. But the spells seemed to be designed to ensure the child's safety without actually requiring anyone to interact with the poor child.

I think she would have been lonely, Charity thought, wondering just who the child had been, before she'd presumably grown up. To the best of her knowledge, none of the Grand Sorcerers of recent times had had children. But if they'd had a child that they'd wanted to keep hidden, they could hardly have done better than craft the room for the child and leave her there. *I wonder if Johan felt the same way.*

She shuddered as she inspected the knives and forks. It was a dining set, like the one she'd been given when her mother had deemed her old enough to start practicing for the day she would have to host dinners, but everything was enchanted. A knife wouldn't cut living flesh, the spells blunting it beyond use every time the child might have cut herself. The forks too were charmed, as if the child had been at risk of stabbing herself in the eye. Charity had grown up in a Great House and yet she had been exposed to more risk, largely thanks to her brother. What manner of child had grown up in these rooms?

A small cupboard revealed a cradle, a bassinet and a pram, all locked and warded against human contact. Charity shook her head, then closed the door and walked back to the bed, turning the mystery over and over in her head. It provided a distraction, at least, from her worries about what was going on outside. She sat down and tried to meditate, knowing she would not be able to go back to sleep. It was nearly an hour before the door opened, revealing a grey-haired Inquisitor. She couldn't help the flash of guilt that rushed through her mind, remembering the last time she had met an Inquisitor. He had had some very sharp things to say about how she'd treated her Powerless brother.

"My Lady," the Inquisitor said. He was oddly familiar, although she couldn't place him. "You will accompany me."

Charity nodded, then stood and allowed the older man to

lead her out of the room and down the long corridor. Hundreds of soldiers ran everywhere, carrying weapons and looking alert ... although, if they had been alert, perhaps there wouldn't have been a security breach in the first place. Behind them, a number of men in red robes paced from place to place, waving wands in the air and chanting loudly. They were sorcerers, Charity could tell, but they didn't seem to have been trained at the Peerless School. But they shouldn't have been trained anywhere else.

She puzzled over it as she followed the Inquisitor around a corner ... and stopped dead. The walls were blackened and burnt, although the Imperial Palace would hardly be without the standard fire-prevention charms. A handful of charred bodies lay on the ground ... she took a breath in shock, then gagged at the stench. Burning humans smelt like pork ... Heaving, she turned to one side and retched, silently grateful that she hadn't eaten anything before she went to bed. It would have come out of her ...

The Inquisitor waited for her to finish retching, then picked his way through the scene and down towards a hole in the stone wall. Charity followed, breathing through her mouth, and saw the Emperor standing there, beside a pair of Inquisitors and a red-robed man. The Emperor looked furious, yet calculating. Her father had often shown the same expression, when he'd been preparing for a counterstroke against his enemies. The results had not been pleasant for his victims.

A man popped out of the hatch and prostrated himself in front of the Emperor. "Your Majesty," he said, as he rubbed his head against the ground, "the building is sealed. We cannot break into the Great Library."

"I see," the Emperor said. His voice was very cold. "Summon all the wardcrafters you can find in the city and assemble them in the Peerless School. They will have the task of breaking down the wards from the outside."

The man looked surprised at not having been ordered to attend his own execution. "Your Majesty," he said, "those wards are some of the strongest in the Empire."

"I imagine they are," the Emperor said. "But any ward can be broken."

He turned to look at Charity, then the grey-haired Inquisitor. "Follow me."

Charity hastened to obey, trailing behind the two men as they walked back up the corridor and into one of the conference rooms. Light Spinner might have ruled the Empire, her father had remarked more than once, but it was the bureaucracy that made it work, the hordes of men and women who did the actual paperwork. He'd noted that it was surprisingly easy to subvert the clerks, even if they *had* sworn oaths of loyalty. With the proper incentive, a bureaucrat would sell his mother for a handful of bronze coins.

"The wards should not have been broken," the Emperor hissed. "No normal magician could have broken them. Nor could one have killed a dozen soldiers on the streets."

"Yes, Your Majesty," the Inquisitor said.

"But there was one magician who *could*," the Emperor added, turning to face Charity. "Is your brother alive?"

"I was told he was dead," Charity said, truthfully. After the ... incident at House Conidian, Johan had been declared dead. It was why the headship had fallen to Charity. "Lady Light Spinner herself told me he was dead."

The Emperor glared at her. "And you believe everything you are told?"

He turned back to the Inquisitor before Charity could muster a response. "Dread, do you know if Johan Conidian is alive or dead?"

"I was informed he was dead," the Inquisitor said, stiffly.

Charity studied him for a long moment. Her father had been good at hiding his feelings, but Dread was in a class of his own. His face was stony, betraying no hint of any feelings at all, while his body was perfectly relaxed. In a way, she decided, he was attractive, even though he would never be considered handsome.

"But someone broke through the wards in a very strange manner," the Emperor said. "Do you think he may still be alive?"

"I have no proof of his continued survival," the Inquisitor said. "I was informed that he was dead."

But the Head Librarian could have lied, Charity thought.

And Dread could only tell what he believes to be the truth.

She looked at the Emperor. "Why not ask the Head Librarian?"

"The bitch has made her escape," the Emperor hissed, angrily. "She has fled the room, after leaving one of my servants tainted with her curse."

Charity blinked. "Tainted with her curse?"

"She passed the compulsion spell to him," the Emperor said. "I would not have believed it possible."

He swung back to face Dread. "Did *you* know it was possible?"

"No one has been able to hold out for more than an hour before," Dread said. His voice was still stiff, but Charity thought she detected a hint of amusement in his tone. "The long-term effects of fighting such a spell for so long have never been studied."

"Then it *will* be studied," the Emperor snarled. "Round up a few test subjects from the Watchtower and cast the spell on them."

"As you command, Your Majesty," Dread said.

He turned and marched out of the room, leaving Charity alone with the Emperor. She found herself watching the retreating back wistfully, even though she knew Dread couldn't have protected her if the Emperor had decided to take his anger out on her. Her father never had, but then her father hadn't been spited so badly until Johan had developed his powers. And there had just been too many other problems for him to focus on his oldest daughter.

And if he had paid more attention to me, Charity thought, *Jamal's problems would only have got worse.*

"The Head Librarian has fled back to her library," the Emperor observed. Surprisingly, he seemed calmer now that Dread had left the room. "And she has barricaded herself behind the wards. But she is also caught like a rat in a trap."

Charity shuddered. The Great Library had powerful wards, but the Emperor's forces could surround the building and wait for the fugitives to starve to death. She had no idea how much food and drink was stored within the building, yet she doubted they could hold out for more than a few days. The librarians had always reacted badly to *anyone* who brought food into the building. They wouldn't store more than the bare necessities themselves ...

But they were preparing for the Conference, she thought, glumly. *They might have stockpiled enough for a hundred guests.*

There was a tap on the door. A tall man, wearing yet another red uniform – this one covered in gold braid and a handful of medals – bowed to her, then prostrated himself in front of the Emperor. Charity stepped backwards, wondering just why the Emperor encouraged such submission. Even the Grand Sorceress had never demanded that people prostrate themselves in front of her, unless they were slaves. But slaves prostrated themselves in front of everyone.

"Your Majesty," the man said. He sat upright, but remained on his knees. "I have surrounded the Great Library with troops and combat sorcerers. They will be unable to make a move without being caught."

Unless there's another secret passageway, Charity thought. She kept that insight to herself. *There might be another way out.*

"Just like a woman," the Emperor sneered. He aimed his words at Charity. "She has run to a place she considers safe, without any idea of how to escape afterwards."

"She has managed to save herself, for the moment," Charity pointed out, stung. "And it will take weeks to bring down the wards."

"It doesn't matter," the Emperor said. "She cannot escape, so all we have to do is wait for her to die, or the wards to fall, whichever comes first."

Charity said nothing. She had the horrible feeling that he was right.

But the Great Library is full of knowledge, she thought, slowly. *There might be a spell in there the Head Librarian can use to escape.*

The Emperor kept speaking, addressing his subordinate. "You will take command of the troops personally, General Vetch," he said. "I will not tolerate failure."

"Yes, Your Majesty," General Vetch said. He prostrated himself once again, then rose to his feet and backed out of the room. "I will not fail you."

Charity frowned after him, then looked at the Emperor. "Why do they all prostrate themselves in front of you?"

The Emperor smirked. "It is good that you're asking such questions," he said. "It shows you are learning your place in the new order."

And that I want you bragging instead of thinking, Charity thought.

"Our society is based on the strong ruling over the weak," the Emperor said. "It is a strong man who can protect his women and his servants, while a weak man will lose his wives and daughters to the strong. A strong man thus demands respect from the weaker men surrounding him, or they will start to think of themselves as his equals and consider how best to overthrow him. Prostrating themselves in front of me helps to keep them humble."

He leered at her. "Not that I need that with you, my pretty."

Charity flushed, darkly. The Emperor hadn't *hurt* her, or forced himself on her, but he seemed to take an unholy delight in constantly reminding her that she had submitted herself to him. Perhaps it was that which had saved her from warming his bed, she considered, although she knew she didn't dare ask out loud. Her submission marked her as weak and, as such, useless to bear the strong children he wanted.

But if they're breeding their women into helpless docility, she asked herself, *what is that doing to the male children*?

Magicians could determine the sex of their children, but – apart from the firstborn child – rarely bothered to make sure they had a male or female child. Mundanes preferred male children, yet could rarely afford the potions to ensure they birthed a boy. There was no real difference between male and female when it came to magic and a daughter could be just as useful as a son. And yet ... she had the feeling that the Emperor's homeland had been specifically selecting male children, at least among magicians.

"A true man is constantly rebellious, constantly looking for a way to turn the tables on anyone who holds him down," the Emperor added, breaking into her thoughts. "I have to watch my subordinates carefully, knowing that one of them will eventually try to put a knife in my back."

"You don't seem too worried about the possibility," Charity observed.

"If I am overthrown and killed," the Emperor said, "I will be replaced by someone stronger, because he was able to kill me. The prize, as always, goes to the strong."

Charity shuddered. "Your son might kill you," she said. "Or even a random slave."

"I killed my father," the Emperor said, almost casually. "Did your brother never consider killing *your* father?"

"I do not know," Charity said. "I hope not."

She scowled at the thought. Jamal ... Jamal *might* well have considered killing his father, but the Inquisitors would definitely have investigated. If caught and convicted, Jamal would have been executed, rather than been allowed to assume the headship. And Johan ... Johan *had* rendered both his father and Jamal powerless. Had he wanted to subject his tormentors to a fate worse than death?

But father could cow Jamal, Charity reminded herself. *He only did it once or twice, but he could.*

The Emperor smirked. "Do *you* think your brother is still alive?"

"I do not think Johan would stay in the Golden City," Charity said. "All he wanted to do was leave."

"I see," the Emperor said. "But he was apprenticed to the Head Librarian, right? He would have had to stay with her?"

Charity pursed her lips. It was ... *improper* for a young man to be apprenticed to a woman, even if there were only four years between them. No, that made it worse, because it was certain that their hormones would push them into bed together. As far as she knew, Johan was still a virgin ... he wouldn't be able to understand or resist the impulses coming down the link. If he had had to bond with a woman, it should have been with one at least old enough to be his mother ...

"I suppose," she said, finally. "But he did not seek my approval for the bond."

The Emperor scowled. "A male submitting to a woman," he said. "It is never a good sign."

"The Empire itself submitted to a woman," Charity pointed out, before she could stop herself. "Light Spinner was very definitely a lady – a Lady."

"And her power fell when I challenged her," the Emperor said. "And so will the rest of the Empire."

He smiled at her, coldly. "Go organise the wardcrafters," he said. "I want to be in the Great Library as soon as possible."

Charity paled. "And what about the hostages? Or my other tasks?"

"Forget them," the Emperor ordered. There was no give in his voice at all. "Just break into the Great Library as quickly as possible. I will not be denied my prize."

"I will have to organise someone else to look after the children," Charity said. The thought of young children starving in their rooms, or running around the palace looking for food, drink and fun, was horrific. "I ..."

"Go," the Emperor thundered. "The children can wait!"

Charity bowed her head, then obeyed.

Chapter Seventeen

"Is she going to be all right?"

"I think so, Johan," Cass said. "But these spells are always chancy."

Johan scowled as he looked down at Elaine's sleeping form. She looked smaller, somehow, when she was asleep, her chest rising and falling as she breathed in and out. He felt a sudden surge of protectiveness that stunned him, then silently promised himself he would do whatever it took to protect her from the world. And yet, she was the one protecting him ...

"The wards," he said, as he straightened up. "How long will they last?"

"Long enough," Cass said. "Do you know where we can find showers?"

Johan gaped at her. "You're in the middle of a library and you want a shower?"

"You need to wash the blood off too," Daria said. She was still naked, looking down at the bruises covering her body. "There's stuff in my bloodstream you really don't want in yours."

Johan flushed, then forced himself to look away. "There are sleeping quarters on the upper levels," he said, after a moment's thought. "You should be able to wash there. I don't know if there will be any spare clothes, though."

"I can clean them," Cass assured him, dryly. "What about yourself?"

"I should stay with her," Johan said. He looked down at his stained tunic and sighed. "But I'll go for a shower once you're back."

He watched the two women leave the room, then turned his attention back to Elaine. Her presence in his mind was clearer now, as if Cass boosting the link had strengthened it permanently. Johan settled down next to her and tried to clear his mind, calling on exercises Elaine had taught him when he had started to use his magic for the first time. But nothing seemed to work for more than a few seconds. His thoughts kept twitching all over the place.

"We have guests," Cass said, as she strode back into the room. "There's a small army outside our walls."

"Crap," Johan said. He wished he was surprised. "Can they break in?"

"Not for a while, I think," Cass said. She leant against the bookshelves, clearly thinking hard. "They would need to break through the wards, young man, and the wards protecting this building are some of the strongest in the world. I don't think they'll be breaking through the protections in a hurry."

She paused, as if waiting for him to comment. Johan hesitated, then took the plunge.

"We have no way out," he said. "Do we?"

"Not unless there's another secret tunnel," Cass said. "They'd see us coming out and snatch us before we could make our escape."

Johan stood up and started to pace. "So we're trapped here?"

"For the moment," Cass said. She didn't seem that worried about it. "There are worse places to be, I assure you."

"I believe you," Johan said. He looked back down at Elaine. "Might she know a way out?"

"Let us hope so," Cass said. "And then, of course, where do we go from there?"

Johan considered it. "They'll have blocked the tunnels under the mountains," he said. "What about climbing the mountains and escaping that way?"

"Only if we want to commit suicide the hard way," Cass said. "There's enough wild magic flaring around the peaks to make trying to climb over them suicidal. Whoever designed the weather manipulation spells surrounding the city never expected them to be so badly disrupted, I imagine. We can't drain the reserves until they dampen down of their own accord."

She shrugged. "There are easier ways to commit suicide," she added, darkly. "You don't want to try climbing the mountains these days."

Johan gave her a sharp look. "The Watchtower is up there," he pointed out. "And it's safe."

"The Watchtower is heavily warded," Cass reminded him. She sighed. "And we have seriously considered evacuating it for a few years, until the magic calms down. If it ever does. The spells manipulating the weather are so old that disrupting them had a whole series of unexpected side effects."

"Snow, for one," Johan said. He'd seen snow, outside the Golden City, but the residents weren't used to anything more than a temperate summer day. Legend had it that it was permanently sunny in the Golden City, reflecting off the gilded buildings that made up the heart of the Empire. It was how the city had got its name. "And colder weather."

"Yeah," Cass said. "I don't know how many people are going to survive the coming winter."

"I don't understand," Johan said. "Why ..."

"Because hardly anyone would have anything suitable for winter wear," Cass pointed out, sharply. "Why would they stockpile clothes for colder weather when few people even bother to leave the city for a holiday? But, right now, it's getting colder and colder and it's only going to get worse."

Johan swallowed. "They could ward the buildings," he said, slowly. "Or import clothes."

"I doubt the Emperor will give a shit," Cass said. "And warding every building in the city would be an impossible task. The poor will freeze to death if the weather gets much colder."

She shrugged. "But I doubt you understand that, really. You were born to a Great House."

"I know what it's like to be deprived," Johan countered.

"Do you?" Cass asked. "I fancy you never really lacked for anything you needed to keep you alive."

"Except respect," Daria said, as she entered the room. She had a towel wrapped around her chest, much to Johan's relief. "And without respect, you have nothing."

Johan shrugged. "I'll go wash myself now," he said. At least *he* had a couple of changes of clothes in his quarters, even if they had been planning to abandon them. "You two keep an eye on Elaine and try not to kill each other."

Daria made a rude gesture; Cass merely snorted. Johan laughed to himself, then walked out the door and down the long corridor, past an endless series of portraits of library staff through the ages. Elaine's portrait sat at the end of the corridor, but if her name hadn't been written below the painting, Johan wouldn't have known it was her. The painting looked so prim and proper that Elaine looked a great deal older, as well as cleaner. She'd never had such an air of authority in her life.

"They're meant to imply that we were all the same, really," Elaine had said, when he'd first found the paintings and asked who they were. "Look at the expressions."

Johan nodded to himself. The library staff had come in all shapes and colours, but their paintings showed them with the same cold expressions, the same unspoken warning that anyone who dared desecrate the books would suffer torments beyond imagination. It was a warning people would do well to heed, Johan knew, as he turned and walked the rest of the way to his quarters. There were books in the Great Library that were literally irreplaceable.

It felt warmer now that Elaine had returned, he noted; the lights had come on, allowing him to pick his way through the building without risking using his magic to light his path. But it still felt eerie, as though the library had been permanently abandoned. It was a relief to enter his quarters, glance at the bed and then start to undress. His clothes were right where he'd left them, in compartments under the bed.

Good thing Elaine insisted I buy more, Johan thought. He'd dreaded the thought of spending hours picking through clothing stores with her – Charity had loved spending days shopping – but Elaine had been almost brutally efficient. *I ended up with more than I could take with me.*

He dug out a change of clothing, then stepped into the shower and sighed in relief as the warm water washed over his body. It was tempting to stay in the water – he knew the Great Library had an unlimited supply of spell-cleaned and warmed water – but there was no time to waste. Instead, he stopped the water, towelled himself dry and stepped back into his room, where he pulled his shirt and trousers on. Once he was dressed, he looked at his desk – a handful of letters still sat there, where he'd left them – and then reached out and picked them up. Most of them, sent before his supposed death, were useless – or worrying. The Great Houses had moved from being completely unaware of his existence to trying to court him into their ranks.

And to think I could have been something better, if my powers had developed earlier, Johan thought, as he picked up an envelope and opened it carefully. *But I had soured on my family by the time my powers emerged into the light.*

He glanced down at the contents, then shook his head in disbelief. It was yet another offer from his father, written before their final meeting; yet another attempt to lure him back into the fold. Angrily, Johan tore it into scraps of paper and dropped them on the desk, then turned and strode out of the room. Magic flickered around him – the lights dimmed for a long moment – as he walked, leaving him puzzled and alarmed. Was it his fault?

"Cass went to watch our enemies," Daria said, as Johan entered the reading room. "They're trying to break the wards."

"Let us hope they hold out," Johan muttered, as he knelt down next to Elaine. His mistress was still fast asleep, so deeply asleep she wasn't even dreaming. "Has she moved?"

"She's just been lying there," Daria said. "But her scent doesn't indicate she's in trouble."

Johan looked back at her, realising – once again – just how *open* the werewolf packs had to be with one another. There was no point in trying to hide one's feelings, not when no one could control or even deaden their scents. Daria would know if one of her brothers had had an intimate moment with his girlfriend, or ... Johan shook his head, grimly. He knew more than he wanted to know about Jamal's activities and *he* had no inhuman sense of smell. But, for the werewolves, it was natural and right.

Perhaps that makes them the better people, he thought, dryly. *They would know if their words were causing distress.*

"Good," he said, dully.

"Cass left a potion for you on the desk," Daria said, indicating a small bottle. "It should give you enough energy to remain awake for a few more hours, if you need it."

"But then it all catches up with you," Johan said, softly. He'd used such potions before, only to find that they worked well ... until tiredness came crashing down like a hammer. "I might not wake up in time to help, if they broke down the wards."

"Then take a nap over there," Daria said, pointing to the corner. "I think we should be fine, for a while. The Great Library is protecting its mistress from all harm."

Johan looked over at the corner. It didn't look very comfortable, but it probably looked better to a werewolf. He thought about going back to his own bed, then dismissed the thought. It would be better if they stayed together, he told himself, no matter what else happened. The Great Library was too large for them to risk being separated, if the wards fell.

"I'll read for a while," he said, instead. He walked over to the bookshelves, selected a book at random, then sat down at one of the desks. "I don't want to fall asleep."

He looked at the book, then started to flick through the pages, taking in nothing. It was so hard to concentrate on the written word when Elaine was in trouble and they were under siege, even if they were relatively safe for the moment. There were ample stocks of food in the basements, he knew; Elaine had supervised the purchases personally, just to make sure she could feed the Court Wizards who had reserved quarters in the Great Library. They could survive for years, if necessary, without having to leave the building. But the Emperor would never leave them alone.

"If nothing else, he wouldn't be able to leave us here without admitting he'd lost control of the Great Library," he muttered to himself. "And the Court Wizards would take note."

Daria looked up. "We can't stay here indefinitely," she agreed. "But where can we go?"

Johan closed the book and looked at her. "House Conidian," he said. "It's the last place they would look for us."

Cass swept into the room, looking disgustingly alert. "They're struggling with the outer wards," she said, shortly. Her blonde hair gleamed under the light as she sat on one of the desks and crossed her long legs. "I think we have days, at least, before they start posing a real threat."

"But we will have to leave eventually," Johan pointed out. "House Conidian would be a good place to hide, at least until we can leave the city."

"They'll start searching the city as soon as they discover we're not in the Great Library," Cass pointed out, sweetly. "Why would they leave House Conidian out of the search?"

"Because they wouldn't expect us to go there," Johan said. "We'd want to hide among the poor, or perhaps back in the Blight. House Conidian would be practically hiding in plain sight."

"Might be worth trying," Cass said. She shrugged, expressively. "But we have to get out of the current trap first."

She studied Johan through bright blue eyes. "Tell me about your powers," she said. It wasn't a request. "How do they actually work?"

"I make things happen," Johan said. "That's the best I can say."

Daria snorted. "*How* do you make things happen?"

"I don't know," Johan said. "I can do some things, but not others."

"I see," Cass said. "What *can't* you do?"

"I can't brew potions," Johan said. "And I can't use magic on myself, I think."

"That isn't always a bad thing," Cass pointed out. "People who use magic on themselves tend to come to sticky ends."

She frowned. "To make a potion, you need to use your magic to unlock the magic within the ingredients," she mused. "But it's a gradual process. If things aren't done in precisely the right order, you end up with sludge."

"There are magicians who have problems manipulating their own magic to make potions," Daria said, slowly. "Johan could merely be having the same problem."

"No," Johan said. "Elaine was very clear that I wasn't manipulating the potion at all. My results were no better than a mundane trying to make a potion like one would cook a stew."

He paused. "I can cast a spell, if I know what the spell is

meant to do," he added, "and I can make things happen if I know what I want to do ... but I don't know if I am really casting a spell."

"Interesting," Cass mused. "Intent is important, naturally, but so is following the steps to channel one's magic. Yet you seem to bypass the steps and jump immediately to the final outcome. There's quite a puzzle there, Johan."

She frowned. "Do you get tired?"

"No," Johan said. "I don't get tired at all."

"Even the strongest magicians get tired," Cass said, thinking out loud. "Or have you merely not discovered your limits?"

"I don't know," Johan said. "Do you have a plan for using my magic?"

"I would prefer to know what I was dealing with before I tried to use it," Cass said. "So far, your powers seem dangerously unpredictable. Have you ever had any problems?"

"I smashed a table," Johan said. "I was trying to levitate the table and it just shot upwards and slammed into the ceiling. There was no fine control at all."

"But you did have fine control when you were removing a person's magic," Cass said, darkly. "Or did you just *wish* for the final outcome?"

Johan shifted, uncomfortably. "I wanted them to suffer," he admitted. "And nothing would hurt worse than losing their powers."

"I imagine so," Daria said, briskly. She stood up in one smooth motion. "Why don't you show me where the kitchens are? We're all going to need something to eat."

"Of course," Johan said. He couldn't help feeling relieved. Daria had probably picked up on his unease and stopped the questioning. "But I should warn you my cooking skills are not good."

"Werewolves can eat anything," Daria said, as she opened the door. "So can Inquisitors."

"I'm not an Inquisitor any longer," Cass reminded her, dryly. "Maybe it's time to start developing a few expensive tastes."

Daria laughed, then pulled Johan out the door and down the

corridor.

"Thank you," Johan said, once they were out of earshot. "I was starting to feel like she would never stop asking questions I couldn't answer."

"It's always annoying when someone does that," Daria agreed. "My older cousin really hated it when I badgered him about his wife. Why did he marry her? I asked. Because she smelled right, he said. But why does she smell right? I asked. Because she does, he said. And eventually he raged to my parents about my questions."

"Oh," Johan said. He hated to imagine what his father would have said if his cousin had reported him for pestering her. "And what did they do?"

"Told me I'd understand when I was a little bit older," Daria said. "I was just a kid."

Johan smiled, remembering some of his father's comments, before he'd realised that Johan would never amount to anything. They'd always ended with a note that he would understand once he was a grown man. And, even now, Johan wasn't sure he *did* understand. Perhaps he'd been spared some horrors by being born without magic.

He stopped dead as a new sensation echoed down the link. Elaine was waking up.

Chapter Eighteen

Elaine's eyes snapped open.

For a few moments, she honestly wasn't sure where she was. Her memories were a blur; she recalled Deferens, and Charity Conidian, and then ... and then everything was blurred until she opened her eyes, back in the Great Library. The wards touched her mind seconds later, before she could start to panic. She knew where she was ... and she knew she was safe. And that was all that mattered.

Alarms echoed through the wards as she sat upright. There were people outside, people trying to break through the protections surrounding the library. Elaine tested the wards quickly, one by one, and discovered they were still holding firm. It would take days, perhaps weeks, for the wardcrafters to shatter the wards, or even force them to allow a handful of magicians to enter the building. And even if they did, the Great Library wouldn't be defenceless. Corridors would lead to nowhere, entire subsections of the library would vanish, taking unwanted intruders with them ... and, at worst, the knowledge within the Black Vault could be turned against the enemy.

"Better stay still for the moment," a voice advised. It took Elaine a moment to recognise Cass, kneeling beside her. "You've had a nasty shock."

"I know," Elaine said. Her mind *hurt*. She might have freed herself from the spell, but there was no way to know if she'd eradicated all of its traces. "What's the situation?"

"The Great Library is surrounded," Cass said. "Johan and Daria have gone to make breakfast. Other than that, I think I need to ask you."

Elaine rubbed her forehead, then forced herself to stand. Cass caught her arm and steadied her as she rose to her feet. Her limbs felt weak, as if she'd been very ill, but she was growing stronger as she moved. The wards helped, allowing her to draw on a little of their power, even though it risked draining them at the worst possible moment. Elaine placed her hands on the nearest table and rested for a long second, then stood on her own. There was a chilling moment when she thought she was going to faint, then the sensation faded away into nothingness. She was alive and well.

"Thank you for your help," she said. "But you're going to have to tell me what happened in the palace. My mind's a blur."

She listened to Cass's words, allowing them to unlock the blurred parts of her memory. "He had children," she said, suddenly. "Children from the Great Houses. But why?"

"Hostages, perhaps," Cass said, darkly. "Or worse."

"Vlad Deferens is the Emperor," Elaine said, shaking her head in disbelief. It sounded like a bad joke; she'd known that Deferens had been a contender for the post of Grand Sorcerer, but having him become the Emperor ... the Witch-King had certainly laid his plots very well. "And he's taking hostages. Why?"

"The Great Houses won't be happy about an Emperor," Cass observed. "But I doubt they gave him anyone really important."

Elaine nodded, slowly. The Great Houses were utterly ruthless at times. Johan's father had been quite willing to do whatever it took to lure him back to the family, destroying a budding romance along the way. If the Family Heads had sent hostages, she would have bet half her salary that the hostages were the youngest children, the ones who were suitable only as pawns in the endless struggle for good marriages. Deferens might discover that he'd lulled himself into a false sense of security.

"I suppose," she said, finally. "What do we do now?"

"Get out of this building," Cass said. "We may be safe, for the moment, but we can't do anything to help Light Spinner or stop the Emperor."

She paused. "You were going to find the Witch-King," she said. "Did it occur to you that he might be buried below the Golden City?"

Elaine shook her head. "I thought about it," she answered, "but there are thousands of magicians in the city. Having his body hidden here would be an unacceptable risk."

"But the Golden City was the capital of the Empire even back then," Cass pointed out. "He might not have had a choice."

Elaine closed her eyes, remembering the stories that had been decanted into her head. The Witch-King had been the hero of the First Necromantic War, then the villain of the Second. He had killed most of the Imperial Bloodline personally, perhaps in a desperate attempt to take power, then created great and terrifying armies to sweep across the land. And then he had been defeated, but his body had never been found. Could it have been slipped back to the Golden City? She doubted it; back then, there had been far more sorcerers with experience in dealing with the darkest of forbidden magics. They would have found the lich and destroyed it before the Witch-King could recover his strength.

And even if he had somehow evaded their watchful gaze, Elaine was sure, he would have had to hide from successive Grand Sorcerers and the Inquisitors too. She knew how thoroughly the Golden City was monitored for unexpected and unexplained bursts of magic, particularly after the Blight had been created. The Witch-King would have been taking a ghastly risk if he had kept his body in the city, assuming – of course – that he'd been able to leave. A lich wasn't always mobile. It would depend, the knowledge in her head told her, on just what condition the body had been in, at the moment it had been frozen in mortal stasis. And there was no way she could answer that question until they found the body.

"It would be an insane risk," she said, slowly. "And he would have had to make his way back to the city in any case."

"Yeah," Cass said. "So where did he fall?"

"Beyond the Garston Mountains," Elaine said, flatly. "We were planning to go there when Deferens took the Golden Throne."

She looked up as Johan and Daria entered the room, Johan carrying a large plate of bacon sandwiches and Daria carrying a tray with several mugs of hot tannin. Johan put his plate down on the nearest table, then leant forward and gave Elaine a hug. She hugged him back, then gently let go of the younger man. Johan reached for the plate and held it under her nose. Elaine took one of the sandwiches, then motioned for him to share them out. After so long without food, it tasted heavenly.

"It's good to see you again," Daria said, sitting next to Elaine as she munched her sandwich. "I was so worried."

"Me too," Elaine admitted. She took a breath, then filled them in on everything that had happened since she had been taken out of the Great Library. "He's got control of everything."

"Almost everything," Cass corrected. "He doesn't control the Great Library."

Johan had a more immediate point. "He's using my sister as ... as what?"

"An assistant, for the moment," Elaine said. She knew what he was thinking. "She swore her oaths to him when he took the Golden Throne."

"She actually gave him her oaths?" Cass said, in disbelief. "What a stupid bitch."

"I imagine she wasn't given a choice," Elaine said, before Johan could explode with rage. He might have largely discarded his family, but Charity was the only one who had been good to him, from time to time. "Deferens had just taken the Throne and stoned Light Spinner. Charity probably thought it was a choice between offering her oaths or being killed outright."

"She still shouldn't have given him her oaths," Cass said. "There will be no breaking them now, will there?"

Johan looked at her hopefully, but Elaine shook her head. Forcing someone into submission through a compulsion spell could be unreliable, if someone had the mental fortitude to fight back and break the spell, yet they who submitted willingly placed themselves completely at the mercy of their master. Charity could not hope to free herself, Elaine knew; her only hope was Deferens choosing to let her go. And that wasn't likely to happen. What did she have to offer him, in exchange for her freedom, that he couldn't simply order her to bring to him, if he wanted it?

But there is something Deferens might want, Elaine thought. *Johan. Johan and me.*

She kept that thought to herself. Instead, she turned to Cass. "How many Inquisitors are left?"

Cass hesitated for a long moment before answering. "Not counting me," she said carefully, "twenty-four. Twenty-three now, assuming Akron didn't survive the flames."

Daria's mouth fell open, revealing inhumanly sharp teeth. "Twenty-three Inquisitors for the entire world?"

"It isn't something we normally tell people," Cass said. "And I should bind you all to secrecy."

Elaine wasn't sure if she should be relieved or furious. She'd known the Inquisitors had taken heavy losses in the fight with Kane, but she hadn't realised just how few remained. No one had known, apart from Light Spinner ... and she hadn't been able to launch a recruiting drive for fear of tipping off her enemies. Twenty-three Inquisitors ... they would be a formidable force, particularly with a Grand Sorceress at their head, but hardly enough to stand off the massed power of the Great Houses. Light Spinner's rule, the shortest in recorded history, had been weaker than anyone had dared suppose.

"They belong to Deferens now," Daria said, sharply. "Would he choose to discard the women?"

"Perhaps," Cass said. "But that would leave nineteen alive and well. And fifteen of them are in the city now."

Elaine understood, suddenly, why Deferens had taken hostages. The Great Houses had never been able to challenge the Grand Sorcerers, but now ... now Deferens was Emperor, rather than claiming the title of Grand Sorcerer in his own right. He might look weak, even if he *did* have the Inquisitors on his side. If someone chose to challenge him openly, the whole edifice might come crumbling down.

But the Witch-King is still out there, she thought, grimly. *I assume he must have a plan to handle dissent.*

"There were those other magicians," Daria said. "The ones in red robes. Who are they?"

"I don't know," Cass said. "But there's quite a few of them outside our wards."

"Deferens probably trained up a force of private combat sorcerers," Elaine commented, thinking hard. Deferens probably hadn't ... but the Witch-King had. And then he'd given the sorcerers to the new Emperor, strengthening his hand against the Great Houses. "They might be Inquisitor-grade."

"And even if they're not," Cass sneered, "they could just wear black robes and everyone would mistake them for Inquisitors."

"As long as no one asked to see their rings," Johan pointed out, snidely.

Elaine finished her sandwich, then stood up and started to pace. "Tell me if this makes sense," she said. "We can't hope to beat Deferens alone, right?"

"Right," Cass agreed, glumly. "He has the red-robes and the Inquisitors."

"And the Golden Throne," Elaine added. "Our only hope, therefore, is to continue the original mission, hunting down and destroying the Witch-King. We cannot stay in the city and hope for the best."

"I wish I disagreed with you," Cass said.

Elaine understood. As an Inquisitor, Cass had been taught to go straight for the threat and remove it, whatever the cost. Dark Wizards could not be allowed chances to recover, for fear they would return and pose much greater threats in future. Leaving Deferens in possession of the Golden City practically guaranteed a civil war, with or without the Witch-King. It could tear the Empire apart.

But any attempt to remove Deferens would prove fatal – and futile.

"There are assassins, right?" Johan said. He sounded unsure of his own words. "My father used to have a few hired killers on his payroll. We could find one and pay him to kill Deferens ..."

"Deferens will be extremely well protected, by both his own magic and the Imperial Palace," Cass pointed out, rudely. "I doubt any assassin would take the hit for any amount of money, Johan, and he would be *very* unlikely to succeed. There hasn't been a successful assassination attempt on a Grand Sorcerer for over seven hundred years."

Johan looked up. "What happened to him?"

"He trusted the wrong woman and she killed him with the Death in Joy one night," Cass said, with some amusement. "I believe he died happy."

"I'm sure he did," Daria said.

Elaine smiled. Johan threw her a questioning glance, but she wasn't about to explain. The Death in Joy was a sex magic rite, used for draining someone's life force when they were caught in orgasm, all defences down. Female assassins were very fond of it, if only because it required nothing beyond a limited magical talent and bad intentions. And their victims often died with a smile on their faces, without leaving any signs of a struggle.

"You're a Privy Councillor," Johan said, instead. "Couldn't you convince the Great Houses to stand against him?"

"I doubt it," Elaine said. "I was never a popular councillor."

It was worse than that, she knew. She had never liked attending council meetings and had skipped out of them, where possible. Lady Light Spinner had even threatened to stick her to her chair, once upon a time. The other councillors had built networks of patronage and influence, boosting the careers of their friends and families in exchange for loyalty, but Elaine had never cared for power. In hindsight, allowing her crippling shyness to rule her mind might have been a mistake.

There's nothing you can do about past mistakes, she thought, recalling the advice of one of her tutors. He'd been one of the few she'd actually liked. *Bad rolls of the dice are inevitable, young lady. All you can do is roll with the mistake, learn from it and move on.*

"And they will worry about the hostages," Cass offered. "Even if they are the youngest and most expendable members of their families, they will worry. I would have to think hard about whom to approach, if we tried to start an uprising."

"My father wouldn't give a damn if he'd sent me as the hostage," Johan said, darkly. "Or even Chime. Her only value to him was who she married."

"She would still have magic," Cass pointed out. "Giving her up for nothing might rebound against him. The family magic ..."

"The family magic did nothing for me," Johan hissed. "It

wouldn't do anything for Chime, either."

"You don't know that," Cass said. "Powerless are rare ... and one of the reasons they're rare is because their families kill them. But you remained alive."

"Not by choice," Johan snapped. "I would have gone if they'd let me!"

Elaine winced as she turned and stared at the bookshelves. If she had been on her own, she might have seriously considered just sealing the wards and remaining trapped in the building, alone and untouchable. There were no shortage of books to read and she would die of old age long before she ate her way through the food supplies. But she couldn't do that, she knew, no matter how tempting it was. Johan, Daria and Cass wouldn't want to stay with her for the rest of their lives ... and the Witch-King, once he rose again, would eventually shatter the wards protecting her. And then the world would fall into darkness.

But what does he want? she asked herself. *And what would it cost us to give it to him?*

She shuddered. There were so many different stories in the history books, even the ones that had been officially forbidden, that it was impossible to know for sure. She could imagine him wanting his living flesh and blood back, if only to enjoy life as a human again, and then wanting to rule the world ... what had he wanted, back then? But the history books vacillated between dismissing the whole thing as a bid for power and a desperate attempt to deliver the entire world to the dark gods. Clearly, *something* had gone very badly wrong with the great hero of the First Necromantic War. Had he looked into the darkness long enough for it to look back?

Dark thoughts dripped through Elaine's mind. No one else, not even Light Spinner, knew just how many forbidden and forgotten spells were stored in the Black Vault. Elaine knew, all too well; there were spells she could use, if she wanted, to boost her meagre power reserves, but they all came with a terrifying price. Sanity, for starters ...

There were spells so powerful that to attempt to cast them on one's own risked death, spells that released so much magic that they could have unpredictable side effects, spells so nasty that even being caught in the backwash could have disastrous results, spells that invoked the darkest of the dark gods ... and spells that risked ending everything, if cast with the right preparations. Elaine sometimes wondered if a god had been playing with her life, dangling power in front of her with one hand and keeping her away from it with the other. It would have been nice to have extra power at the Peerless School, but now ... if she wanted to try some of the more dangerous spells in her mind, she would have had to boost her power first, destroying her mind in the process.

It just isn't fair, she thought, with a flash of self pity. *If they catch me, they can use me as a mobile library of deadly spells. But I can't use the spells for myself.*

Life isn't fair, her mind responded, dryly. *And would you want to destroy the entire world anyway? Even the Witch-King isn't that insane ...*

Daria cleared her throat. "Are you all right?"

"I've been better," Elaine said. A plan was already forming in her mind. "Here's what we're going to do."

Chapter Nineteen

The streets surrounding the Imperial Palace, the Great Library and the Peerless School were deserted, save for the soldiers, combat sorcerers and a pair of Inquisitors. Charity, who had attended the Peerless School as a younger girl, had been used to seeing the streets filled with students and those who served them; now, she couldn't help feeling, as the sun slowly rose in the sky, that something was dreadfully wrong. It just felt odd.

She turned her attention towards the Peerless School and sighed. The school had been placed into lockdown by the new Administrator, Light Spinner's personal appointee to the building, while he waited to see what happened. He would have no choice, Charity was sure, but to swear loyalty to the Emperor soon enough. The Peerless School had served the Imperial Bloodline long before the first Grand Sorcerer had taken up the post and it was still reflected in the oaths.

Light flared around the Great Library as the wardcrafters kept pounding on the wards, poking and prodding at defences that had been old when the first Grand Sorcerer took power. The wards were tough, the sorcerers had noted, but nothing lasted forever. Charity smiled to herself as she sensed the magic crackling through the air, only to fade back into the wards surrounding the building. It looked as though the Head Librarian would remain trapped indefinitely, along with her companions.

A grim-faced Inquisitor eyed her darkly as she stepped up to stand beside him, then turned his attention back to the wards. Charity took the hint and kept her mouth shut, merely watching as the wards shimmered in and out of visibility. She was no expert, but it looked as though the wards were resisting everything the wardcrafters did to weaken them before attempting to break the protections down. They were definitely much more complex than the wards she'd had to take over, when she'd become the Family Head. Her father hadn't been capable of producing anything as powerful and complex as the wards surrounding the Great Library.

She cursed inwardly, wishing she'd been smart enough to flee the city, just like Jamal and her father. The Emperor owned her now, body and soul, and she had no choice but to obey his orders. And he'd ordered her to stay with the men until they broke though the wards. She shivered – sun or no sun, it was still cold and snow was lying on the ground – then cast a warming charm around herself. All she could do was follow orders and hope the Emperor didn't recall her to the palace. If nothing else, she had more latitude when she was away from his presence.

There was a sudden flicker of light around the building, followed by a flare of magic. The wards shimmered into view, then started to shatter. Charity blinked in disbelief – the wards shouldn't have fallen so quickly – then stared as the sorcerers started to run forward. The Inquisitor caught her arm before she could join them, clearly suspecting trouble. But it was too late. There was a brilliant flash of light – Charity covered her eyes, too late to do any good – and then darkness descended like a thunderbolt. Panic gibbered at the corner of her mind as she sank to the pavement, one hand grasping desperately for her wand. She'd been blinded and was effectively helpless. Anything could be out there in the darkness, anything at all.

"Stay still," a harsh voice snapped. The Inquisitor, she assumed. "Don't move, whatever you do."

Charity obeyed, helplessly. Magic spiked around her – she could still sense magic, thankfully – and then it faded away. But she couldn't see anything but darkness.

***

It was odd, but true that most magical protections were geared to resist magical threats. Any sorcerer worthy of the name knew a hundred wards capable of stopping a punch or a thrown rock, yet few would admit to using them. Sorcerers never brawled with their fists, while their power kept mundanes from being willing to challenge them to fights. It was a poor sorcerer, Elaine had been taught, who could be killed by a mere powerless mundane. His death would serve to improve the breed.

She plunged her mind into the wards, then generated a powerful flash of light, bright enough to do real damage to anyone watching without custom protections. The view through the wards showed the wardcrafters and some of the red-robed men stumbling backwards in disarray, suggesting that they hadn't been smart enough to include protections against blindness. She smirked to herself, then thrust out a wave of raw magic that disrupted or destroyed the spells they were using to try to crack the wards. They'd been primed for limited feedback, not a shockwave that overfilled their reservoirs and shattered the containment fields. It struck her, suddenly, that she could keep doing it indefinitely, if she didn't mind risking cracks in the wards. But with a team of skilled wardcrafters on the other side, there was too great a chance of disaster.

Instead, she focused her mind on something else. The stone surrounding the Great Library was already charmed, serving as part of the building's defences. She churned it up with the wards, then forced it outwards as a wave of dust, propelled by the wards themselves. Anyone smart enough to protect themselves against flashes of light would find themselves blinded by the dust, forcing them to concentrate hard on saving themselves from breathing in all kinds of poison. The stone alone would be hazardous to their health. She grinned unpleasantly, then turned to run, resetting the wards as she moved. It was time to leave the Great Library for good.

She couldn't help feeling a pang as she ran down into the entrance hall, where Cass and Daria were already pushing the moving statues out into the streets. They'd been glamoured to look like escaping fugitives, something that would hopefully cause more confusion as the forces outside gathered themselves and started banishing the dust. Cass winked at her, then tapped the first statue with her wand. It broke into a run and headed towards where the largest group of sorcerers had been standing, before the first flash of light. The others followed, one by one.

"Come on," Cass snapped. "They won't stay shocked for

long."

Elaine nodded, glancing back into the Great Library. She had known she would have to leave, but not like this, not leaving the building open to her prospective enemies. Part of her wanted to tell them to leave her and make their escape ... she shook her head, then sent one final command to the wards. She might not be able to lockdown the library completely, not from the outside, but she could make sure that no one got their hands on the Black Vault without her assistance. The wards responded, perhaps sensing her urgency, although she hadn't *thought* they could think for themselves. One by one, powerful wards dropped into place, hiding the Black Vault. Even Vane would be unable to find it without Elaine's presence.

Good luck, she thought.

The dust was still billowing outside, held up by hundreds of light charms that would have to be cancelled, one by one, if someone wanted to get rid of the dust. Cass caught her arm and pulled her onwards as the dust swarmed closer, threatening to blind her too. Elaine hastily checked the protective charms she had cast around her face, then followed as the dust started to blow around them. It wouldn't be long before the charms started to fail ...

***

Charity flinched as she felt a wand touching the spot between her eyes, feeling old memories bubbling up inside her. The last person who had touched her with a wand had been her father, casting the charm she'd asked – demanded – that he cast on her. Because she'd been young and foolish and ... there was a flash of magic and she could suddenly see again. But there was still something wrong with her eyesight. She – and the Inquisitor – were surrounded by a protective bubble ... and, beyond the bubble, there was a growing storm of grey dust. It was so thick she couldn't see anything beyond the bubble.

She gripped her wand tightly in one hand, unsure what to do. A banishing charm should have been sufficient to get rid of the dust – it smelled funny, part of her mind noted absently – but the Inquisitor could have done it himself, if he'd thought it was a good idea. Her skin crawled as the dust pressed closer, right up against the bubble of air. It seemed somehow uncanny to her gaze, as if it wasn't quite *right*. But there was nothing right about a storm of dust blocking her view.

"Idiots are multiplying the cloud," the Inquisitor muttered, as magic rippled through the air around them. "The charms holding it in the air are sucking material from the pavement below our feet."

Charity looked down. The Golden City's streets weren't paved with gold – rumour to the contrary – but they were among the best-kept in the Empire. A thousand cleaners brushed them every day, according to her father, scooping up everything from waste paper to human litter and the occasional sleeping drunk. It was considered a major scandal to have even a single paving stone out of place. But now, the stones looked decayed and rotting. As she watched, a line of dust broke free and drifted into the swarm surrounding them.

She gulped as the implications struck her. "What's to stop them sucking material from us?"

The Inquisitor gave her a sharp look. "They used modified prank spells," he said. "I don't *think* they left out the safety precautions."

Charity gulped again. What sorcerers considered a prank was considered a nightmare by anyone else. Prank spells might prevent permanent physical harm, but they did nothing to stop the mental trauma suffered by the victim. Jamal had used similar spells on her, more than once, but Johan – the only one who couldn't fight back – had been his main target. And Johan had spent most of his time plotting to leave home for good. It was hard to blame him, really.

And if he's still alive, she thought, *what is he doing?*

A shape loomed out of the dust and came right at them. Charity had only a moment to cast a protective spell to shield her eyes, nose and mouth as the bubble snapped, then stared in horror as the Head Librarian walked right into her. The impact threw her to the ground, hard enough to make her cry out in pain. Moments later, the Head Librarian also fell, her hands and feet bound by a powerful spell. Charity pulled herself to her feet, giving silent thanks to the household gods that Jamal had never learnt *that* charm, then peered down at the stricken girl. Elaine No-Kin looked different, somehow. There was something odd about her face ...

The Inquisitor bit off a curse. Moments later, the face snapped out of existence, revealing an angelic stone face that smiled at them both beneficently. Charity stared, then shuddered – she'd heard stories of stone angels that moved when no one was looking – as the Inquisitor straightened up. Despite the howling of the storm, growing stronger and stronger, she could still hear people shouting and cursing. Everyone caught out in the open, it seemed, thought they'd captured the fugitives. Instead, they seemed to have caught more damned statues.

"They're the ones from just inside the library," the Inquisitor said. "Crafty bastards, definitely."

He waved his wand and cast a series of cancelling charms, one after the other. Charity hesitated, then joined him. The dust might not be so easy to remove, but the charms that kept it in the air – and sucked more material out of the ground – were easier to banish. Slowly, the dust started to fall back, then drop to the ground as the sorcerers cast more and more spells to rid themselves of the nuisance. And Charity found herself looking out on a scene from any of the innumerable hells.

The pavement looked rotten, as if a team of workmen had dug up hundreds of randomly-selected paving stones and discarded them somewhere out of sight. Indeed, it had been totally destroyed in places. Water was spurting up from burst pipes and mixing with the dust to produce a form of mud that seemed suspiciously sticky, clinging to clothes and starting to set. A careful glance revealed a handful of very tiny spells, each one largely harmless in and of itself, but working together to produce a very odd effect. Charity would have been impressed if she hadn't been sure, as the last of the dust faded away, that the Head Librarian and her friends had made their escape.

"I caught her," a voice shouted, in a thick accent that reminded her vaguely of the Emperor. "She's here ..."

"She's another statue," the Inquisitor snarled, looking down at the prone girl. He waved his wand and the illusion shattered, revealing a stone face. "They've got clean away, you moron."

The sorcerer gritted his teeth. "You don't get to talk to me like that," he snapped. "I am a trusted servant of the Emperor ..."

Charity turned away, leaving them to their argument. She shook her head in disbelief as the wardcrafters pulled themselves up from the ground, some rubbing at their eyes and cursing as the mud started to set around their clothing. Giving the cursing men a wide berth, she walked towards the Great Library, up to the doors she'd once entered every day of her student life. A ward should have blocked her access, but there was nothing. She pushed at the stone door and forced it open, stumbling into the building. It was as dark and silent as the grave.

They're gone, she thought. The lights were out, the magic that should have protected the building against cheaters and thieves alike had faded ... although she knew better than to try to take something out of the building, even if the magic seemed weaker than before. *They've left this place for good.*

She stopped in the centre of the entrance lobby as the Inquisitor followed her in, ordering the wardcrafters and the combat sorcerers to remain outside. Charity was almost relieved. The Emperor had given her no orders concerning the stockpile of knowledge in the Great Library, but she was sure he wouldn't want just *anyone* walking in off the streets and taking a few irreplaceable books. Sorcerers who hadn't gone to the Peerless School – and she was sure they hadn't, because some of them were young enough to have shared classes with her if they had – would want the books, very badly.

"They're gone," she said. "But where?"

"We will find them," the Inquisitor said.

Charity swallowed. It would be *her* task to bring the news to the Emperor. Her father had never taken bad news very well, even if it had been something as minor as her marks not being as high as he'd expected. Unless it had been Jamal bringing it, of course. His marks had never been as high as hers, but he'd somehow managed to avoid the lectures and humiliating punishments that had been piled on her. Not for the first time, she cursed her wretched brother under her breath. If her father had held him to account for his misbehaviour, he might not have grown into such a monster.

"Summon the Deputy Librarian," she said, carefully. "I will have some good news, at least, to present to the Emperor."

She found a chair, then sat down and waited. It was nearly thirty minutes before the Deputy Librarian – a woman she recalled seeing behind the desk, when she'd been a student – was escorted into the lobby by two uniformed guards. She looked strong and confident, very much the opposite of her superior, and yet there was something about her that indicated she was nervous. But it was hard for anyone to blame her, Charity reminded herself. The Golden City had been turned upside down.

"You will swear loyalty to the Emperor, then assume control of the wards," she said, once the woman was sitting facing her. "Or you will never work in the library again."

Vane eyed her for a long moment, then closed her eyes in surrender. Charity listened, without pleasure, as Vane submitted herself to the Emperor, then reached out with her mind to the wards. Magic flickered and flared through the building, but the lights refused to come on. After a long moment, Vane opened her eyes and peered fearfully at Charity. It took Charity several seconds to realise that Vane was actually afraid of her.

Or what I represent, she thought, grimly. *The Emperor who claimed the Golden Throne.*

"The wards have been altered," she said. "I can't take control."

Charity blanched. "*You* can't? Or *anyone* can't?"

"I think they've been programmed to reject anyone assuming ultimate control," Vane said, quickly. "It wasn't my fault!"

"I'm sure it wasn't," Charity said. She wasn't blaming Vane for anything, but she was uneasily aware that the Emperor might think differently. "What sort of link do you have?"

"I had a limited link from the Head Librarian," Vane said. Her voice turned pleading as she willed Charity to understand. "That link is still there, but it won't expand into a full merge without her permission."

Charity cringed, her mouth suddenly dry. The Emperor was *not* going to be happy.

"Work out what you can and cannot do," she said. At least they could give the Emperor a full report. Maybe that would please him enough to spare their lives. "And then we will take it to the Imperial Palace."

And continue the search for the Head Librarian, she thought, bitterly. *Because, without her, the Great Library is useless.*

Chapter Twenty

"This is where you grew up?"

"We only moved here seven months ago," Johan said, as House Conidian came into view. "I used to live on an estate a few hundred miles from the Golden City."

He couldn't help a little wistfulness sinking into his voice. The estate hadn't been completely isolated, but his father had been less strict about keeping Johan in his room, out of sight of anyone who might use him against the family. There had been horse-riding and swimming and even a chance to spend a few nights in a tent, away from his siblings. In hindsight, he should have enjoyed it more than he had.

"It looks impressive," Daria added. She gave him a droll look. "No wonder you're such a spoilt brat."

"The last house was bigger," Johan said. "And cheaper too."

Beside him, Elaine rolled her eyes. Housing costs in the Golden City were astronomical. The house his father had purchased, then warded heavily, had cost him half of his savings ... and it was small, compared to some of the other buildings. But it was a status symbol he hadn't been able to decline. A house on the other side of the mountains would have been half the price, yet wouldn't have carried the social cachet.

"No doubt," Cass agreed. "Are you sure you can get into the house?"

"I think so," Johan said. He stepped up to the door and pressed his hand against the warding crystal. "My father keyed me into the wards when I developed power. My ... my sister thinks I'm dead. She wouldn't have bothered to remove me from the list of people permitted to open the door."

A faint tingle ran through his hand, then the door unlocked, allowing him to lead the way into the building. He was expecting a mess, after his last visit to the house, but Charity had evidently paid through the nose to have the damage repaired within a couple of days. The paintings had been changed – a large painting of the entire family, including Johan, now dominated the hallway – but there were no other signs that anything had changed. Johan snorted to himself, then stepped aside to allow the others to enter the building. As long as they were with him, the wards wouldn't think they were intruders and attack.

"Well protected, but lacking any flair," Cass announced, waving her wand in the air. "Your sister is evidently not a wardcrafter."

"My father never had time to specialise in anything, but running the family," Johan said. Charity would merely have inherited his work. "He used to encourage the younger children to study the more specialised branches of magic, just so the family would have experts it could actually trust."

Elaine smiled. "And did they?"

"They haven't reached the point in their schooling when they can choose a specific path," Johan said, feeling a twinge of the old pain. He'd once thought he would go to the Peerless School, just like his older brother. But, as time wore on, it had become an unattainable dream. "But now ...I don't know what Charity would urge them to do."

Daria sniffed the air, suddenly. "We're not alone," she said, sharply. There was a flurry as Elaine and Cass lifted their wands. "Three people in the house; all young girls."

"No servants?" Johan asked. "I don't think Charity would have dismissed them."

"Just three girls," Daria said. Her nose wrinkled, slowly. "The other scents aren't fresh."

There was a clatter from up the stairs, then a young girl came into view, clutching a wand so tightly that her knuckles were white. Johan sucked in his breath as he recognised Jolie, his fourteen-year-old sister, looking strikingly like a younger version of their mother. Behind her, Chime and Chanel were holding their own wands, their eyes wide with fear. Johan was surprised to see them, as surprised as they were to see him. They should all have been at the Peerless School.

He felt a sudden mix of emotions as his younger siblings stared down at him. Fear, because they'd often used him as a plaything; glee, because he could now pay them back in their own coin ... and shame, for thinking about tormenting them as they had tormented him. It hadn't been fair when they'd done it to him and it wouldn't be fair if he did it to them. He started as he felt someone slip a hand into his and turned to see Daria, looking up at him with worried eyes. She had to have picked up on his emotions as he stared at his younger siblings.

"Johan?" Jolie asked, nervously. "What are *you* doing here?"

Johan grunted. "What are *you* doing here? You should be at school."

"Charity brought us home to help with the repairs," Jolie said. "You made quite a mess of the house."

"I wanted to burn it down," Johan said. "What happened to the servants?"

"They fled," Jolie said. "And Charity hasn't come home. And we're starving ..."

"Charity has other problems," Johan said, flatly. Naturally, there had been no suggestion that the magical children could learn to cook. His father had had servants to do the hard work of actually keeping everyone fed. "Go back to your rooms and stay there."

"They do need to be fed," Daria said, quietly.

"I know," Johan muttered. He cursed his siblings under his breath. Why couldn't they have stayed at the Peerless School? It was unlikely they'd be harmed by the Emperor, not when Charity was already his devoted slave. The Great Houses would never stand for it. "And now I don't know if we can stay here after all."

"Take me to the kitchens," Cass ordered, firmly. "We'll see what there is in the way of food."

"Of course," Johan said. He opened the door to the visitor's room, then peered inside. It hadn't been touched when he'd smashed his way into the house, he decided, because hardly anything had been moved from where his father had put it. "Elaine and Daria can wait here for us. Don't let the kids bully you into doing anything."

Elaine gave him a sharp look. "Are they that bad?"

"They're little monsters," Johan said. "Maybe not as bad as Jamal, but still pretty awful."

"They're kids," Daria protested.

"They're kids who were allowed – nay, encouraged – to pick on the powerless from the moment they could wield a wand," Johan snapped. "I don't think a term or two at the Peerless School will have cured them of that ... bad habit."

He turned and marched out of the room, through a long corridor and down a flight of stairs into the servants rooms. Jamal had once thought it a great joke, he recalled sourly, to turn Johan into something immobile and leave him in their rooms, just because he thought a Powerless would never amount to anything more than a servant. His father had not been amused, but he had never properly punished Jamal. The older boy had been the apple of his father's eye.

Cass followed him, her footsteps so quiet that Johan could barely hear them. He hardly heeded her as he stepped through the door and into the kitchen, then looked around. The servants had clearly fled in a hurry; they'd left a colossal mess behind them. Johan sighed to himself, then peered into the preservation chamber. Thankfully, the spells keeping the food fresh had remained intact.

"Get the bread from the breadbox," he ordered, as he pulled a large chunk of cheese out of the chamber. "I'll make them bloody cheese sandwiches. There's no time to make anything more complex."

"Understood," Cass said. If she picked up on his innermost thoughts – that he didn't want to waste effort making anything better than sandwiches for the brats – she didn't comment on it. "I can boil some water too, if you would like."

"They'll turn their noses up at adult drinks," Johan said. "Pour them each a glass of water, then place the glasses on a tray."

He finished slicing the bread and cheese, then rapidly prepared the sandwiches as Cass poured water into glasses. "I'll take half of these for us," he said, "and take the other half up to the brats. You can carry the water."

"I could," Cass agreed, dryly. "You don't want to help

them, do you?"

Johan turned to face her. "Do you have siblings?"

"Not any longer," Cass said. "Inquisitors tend to snap family ties once they don the skull rings. If anyone stays in touch with their families, they don't make a big issue of it."

"My siblings were my tormenters," Johan said. "I ... I find it hard to forgive them, even after the family has been shattered."

He shook his head. It was wrong to hate his younger siblings – Chime was only eleven years old – but the memories kept tormenting him. All of them had developed magic at a very young age, save for Johan himself, and they hadn't hesitated to use it. Their father had cooed over their success at mastering complex charms and ignored the fact that they'd tended to test those spells on Johan. And Johan knew, even if his father had chosen to forget it, that so much magic used on a single person could have disastrous long-term effects. His father might have quietly hoped, even if he had been unwilling to admit it to himself, that Johan would expire before he should have attended the Peerless School. It would have hidden the fact his family had produced a Powerless.

Picking up the tray, he marched back up the stairs and gave Elaine and Daria some sandwiches, then walked up a second flight, up to the floor put aside for the younger children. The three girls seemed to have gathered in Jolie's room, having dragged blankets and stuffed toys in from their own room. Johan shivered, remembering hours of torment, then put the tray of food down on the desk. The three girls were so hungry that they didn't even bother to complain about the food before tucking in.

Jolie looked up at him, between taking bites out of her sandwich. "What are we going to do now?"

"You ... *children* are going to wait here," Johan said, firmly. "We will decide what to do and then we will *tell* you what to do."

Chime's hand twitched towards her wand, then stopped. Johan wondered, absently, just what Charity had told the younger children about what had happened to the family. Might she have told them the truth, that Johan had ripped the magic from their father and their elder brother, or had she told them a comforting lie. Jamal would have told them the truth, he was sure, and laughed at their horror, but Charity was made from different stuff.

Turning, he walked out of the room, closing the door behind them, then looked towards his old room. The door had been closed and warded, judging by the rune someone had carved into the wood, but he knew he could open it, if he wished. But there was nothing in the room that he wanted, nothing apart from bad memories. Beyond it, Jamal's room lay open, as if someone had gone inside and ransacked the place. Curious, Johan stepped up to the door and peered inside. Jamal had always been a bit of a clotheshorse – he'd purchased hundreds of outfits every year – but now half of them were scattered on the floor, while a dozen books on magic lay on the bed. And a mirror that Johan knew had been hanging from the wall lay on the ground, in pieces.

"Someone wanted to leave in a hurry," Cass said, following him into the room. "The signs are quite obvious, if you know where to look."

Johan shrugged. Jamal had had to leave the city in a hurry before his enemies caught up with him and took revenge for years of slights, bullying and worse. Charity would probably have lived up to her name and allowed him to take some of his possessions with him .... Johan looked around, trying to decide what Jamal had taken, but couldn't tell what was missing. A few sets of clothes would have brought in some cash, if he'd sold them to his former cronies ...

"Let the bastard rot," he said. He picked up the books from the bed – Elaine would want a look at them, if nothing else – and led the way back out of the room. "I don't want to see him again, ever."

"You will probably get your wish," Cass said. The former Inquisitor closed the door behind her, then followed him down the stairs. "I doubt he will show his face again."

Johan nodded as he stepped into the visiting room and placed the books on the table. Elaine was sitting on the sofa, looking tired and utterly out of place in the room's splendour. Daria was back in wolf form, curled up on the armchair and snoring loudly. Johan had to struggle to conceal his amusement at the sight, knowing precisely what his father would have said if he'd seen a werewolf sleeping on his chair. There had been no tolerance for mess – or dog hairs – anywhere his guests might have noticed.

"We left you some of the sandwiches," Elaine said. She met his eyes. "Are you all right?"

"I think so," Johan said. "Is it my fault that I feel unenthusiastic about helping the little brats?"

"I never had siblings," Elaine said, "so I won't pretend to be able to understand what you're feeling right now. But I do know that they're kids, unable to fend for themselves ..."

"They should have grown up with the Travellers," Johan said. "I don't think they could even make sandwiches for themselves."

He shook his head. "I assumed they would be at the Peerless School," he added. "But if they're here, Charity might come home at any moment."

"Then we grab her," Cass said, sitting down in one of the comfortable chairs. "Can you alter the wards enough to catch her when she arrives?"

Johan shook his head. "My power doesn't work like that," he said. "I can't reprogram the wards."

Elaine cleared her throat, loudly. "Their upbringing certainly lacked ... *something*," she said, tartly. "I don't blame you for wanting nothing to do with them. But do you really want to be the bully now?"

"What would you do," Johan asked, "if one of your tormentors from the orphanage suddenly fell into your power?"

"I like to think I wouldn't take revenge," Elaine said. Her face reddened. "Although I might have accidentally on purpose turned one of my old tormentors into a statue."

"I heard," Cass said.

"So what do we do with them?" Johan asked. "I don't know how to care for them for more than a few days. There wasn't *that* much food in the kitchen."

"So we go buy more," Cass said, practically. "The kids might be able to do that for us. Or maybe they will come in handy for something."

Elaine shrugged. "Until then, Johan," she said, "you and I

need to meditate. Is there a private room we can use?"

"No shortage of them," Johan muttered. He took a swift drink of water, then stepped over to the door. "I can't guarantee that the wards will let us know when someone arrives."

"I'll add a few of my own," Cass said. "Good luck."

Johan sighed, then led the way down the corridor and into his father's outer study. His father had hosted private meetings there, with his most trusted allies. But there were no family secrets within view, nothing that might end up being used against him. The walls were lined with bookshelves, but none of them were anything special. Johan had still been forbidden to read them, back when everyone had thought he was Powerless.

"Not a pleasant room," Elaine commented.

"My father liked to create an impression," Johan said. There was something cold and sterile about the study, nothing like the reading rooms in the Great Library. "And he didn't like wasting time in boring meetings."

He pushed the chairs to one side, then sat down cross-legged on the floor. Elaine sat facing him, her brown eyes worried. Johan silently marvelled at the skill she'd shown in crafting her glamour; her eyes might not show the right colour, but they showed her emotions perfectly. Charity had never been able to manage anything so creditable.

"I know coming here wasn't easy for you," Elaine said, as she took his hand. "And I thank you for the courage you have shown."

"You're the one who broke an unbreakable spell," Johan said, softly. Elaine's hand felt warm against his bare skin. "All I did was break a few wards."

"I'm proud of you," Elaine said.

Johan felt a sudden rush of pride. He would have loved his father to say that, just once, and actually *mean* it. But his father had seen him as an embarrassment ... he looked up at Elaine and smiled at her, then looked down at the carpeted floor. There were so many things he wanted to say, but he couldn't find the words.

"Thank you," he said, finally.

"You're welcome," Elaine said. "Now, we actually did

manage to make a connection in the Imperial Palace.”

Johan nodded. Skin-to-skin, the sense of her presence was much stronger.

“I want to concentrate on trying to open the connection on our own,” Elaine said, as she met his eyes again. “So concentrate, right here and now, on me.”

Johan closed his eyes and tried, hard, to focus his mind. Elaine was right in front of him, her presence seemingly split between the girl before him and her presence at the back of his mind. He took a deep breath, then another, trying to reach out to her. But the awareness of her existence didn’t grow any stronger.

“It’s not working,” he said, frustrated. “Why isn’t it working?”

“I don’t know,” Elaine said. “And that’s what bothers me.”

Chapter Twenty-One

Charity had always hated having to face her father with bad news. Sometimes, he took it gently and merely lectured her on her failings; sometimes, he went through the roof and shouted at her for hours. Facing the Administrator of the Peerless School had been easier, but she had a feeling that facing the Emperor would be much harder. He could order her beheaded on a whim ... or even order her to cut off her own head, if he felt like it. But there was no way she could hide the truth from him.

She stepped into the Throne Room, followed by Vane, and prostrated herself in front of the Golden Throne. The Emperor was talking to two of his military officers, speaking in a language she didn't understand; he spared her a glance, then ignored her. Charity felt her muscles aching after several minutes in full prostration, but she knew better than to try to stand up. The protocol for facing the Emperor had been firmly drummed into her mind.

Beside her, Vane shifted uncomfortably. She was a scion of the Great Houses, like Charity herself, and she wouldn't be used to anything other than curtseys. Charity hoped she would have the sense to remain prostrate, no matter how uncomfortable or humiliating it was; the last thing either of them wanted, right now, was to upset the Emperor. Thankfully, Vane stayed quiet until the Emperor dismissed his officials and turned his attention to the newcomers.

"Rise," he ordered. "What news do you bring?"

Charity swallowed, nervously. "The Great Library has been largely opened, Your Majesty," she said, carefully. "But the fugitives are gone."

"They made their escape," the Emperor said. "And do you know *where* they have gone?"

"No, Your Majesty," Charity said.

"Of course not," the Emperor said. "But you do have

control of the Great Library?"

"We do not have control of the wards," Vane said, too quickly for Charity to try to stop her. "I cannot take full control without the Head Librarian."

The Emperor glowered down at her. "But you can get into the library?"

"I can get into the public levels, yes," Vane said. "But I can't open the Black Vault."

Charity shivered as the Emperor's eyes blazed with a sudden fury. His face shifted so rapidly that, for a moment, she thought she saw someone else looking out through his eyes. And then his face returned to normal, his dark eyes boring into her very soul. For once, he wasn't smiling or smirking at her.

"You can't open the Black Vault," he said. He turned his gaze to Vane, who froze like a thief caught in a capture ward. "Why not?"

"The wards are still sealed, Your Majesty," Vane stammered. "I ... the Black Vault is a pocket dimension, wrapped within the protective wards. It can't be opened without the Head Librarian's presence. She didn't have time to pass the wards to me before she ... ah, was taken from the library."

Charity felt a flicker of amusement, which she rapidly suppressed. If the Head Librarian's arrest had been delayed, even by as a little as ten minutes, the wards would have been passed to her successor and there would have been no hope of escape. Instead, the arrest had – perversely – allowed the Head Librarian to not only escape, but impede the Emperor's long-term plans. It would take years, she'd been told, for the wardcrafters to break through the protective wards without accidentally destroying everything in the vault. No one had ever managed to *steal* from the Black Vault.

"Then we must find her," the Emperor snarled.

"If I may," Vane said, "the Grand Sorceress might also be able to open the ..."

Her words trailed off as the Emperor glowered down at her. "The Grand Sorceress is no longer available," he hissed. "And you will be punished for your failure."

Vane stared at him. "But I ..."

"Silence," the Emperor said. He must have sent a command through the wards, for a pair of guards stepped through one of the side doors without warning. "You will be taken to the kitchens, where you will spend the next few hours washing up. Manually."

He snickered at the horrified expression on Vane's face. Scions of Great Houses did *not* do anything as menial as washing up. There were servants – or spells – to do it for them. It wasn't a bad punishment, not compared to some of the rumours Charity had heard while she'd been a student, but it would be humiliating. Charity just hoped she had the sense to keep her mouth shut and do as she was told. The punishment could easily be a great deal worse.

The guards caught Vane's arms and escorted her out the door, which closed behind them with a solid thud. Charity half-wished she was going with them too; it would have been humiliating to have to work with the servants, but at least she would have been away from the Emperor. The moment when she thought she'd seen someone else behind his eyes ...

"You are surprised, of course," the Emperor said.

"Yes, Your Majesty," Charity said. There was no point in trying to deny it. "She was not to blame for the failure."

"The punishment was quite mild," the Emperor said. "Or do you think it should have been worse?"

"No, Your Majesty," Charity said.

She grimaced at the thought. She'd heard students – mainly boys – claiming that their parents had punished them in all kinds of ways, but most of them had to be exaggerated. There was no way anyone would survive some of the punishments, even with magical healing. And yet ... she went cold when she remembered just how much her father had allowed her siblings to torment Johan. Perhaps the students hadn't been exaggerating after all.

"So," the Emperor said. "Where do you think they're hiding?"

Charity considered it. She'd never actually had to hide herself, not outside playing hide and seek at the Peerless School. The thought of being on the run, cut off from friends and family, was more than a little disquieting. But if she had to hide ...

"Somewhere she wouldn't be recognised," she said, finally. "I think she'd go to the poorest parts of the city."

The Emperor smiled at her. "And why do you think that?"

"The Head Librarian is known to the Great Houses and the rest of the magical community," Charity said. "If she tried to hide among them, they would know it – and one of them might betray her to you. She has few friends and fewer allies among the aristocracy. But in the slums, she could pass for a native."

"Risky," the Emperor observed. "A young girl, all alone, in a world where anything can happen to young women. But is she really alone?"

"I don't know, Your Majesty," Charity said.

"Someone broke into the Imperial Palace," the Emperor reminded her, sarcastically. "But who? Who might still be alive ... and willing to help her? And who could do such strange tricks to my wards?"

"You think my brother is still alive," Charity said, flatly.

"I believe it should be considered," the Emperor said. There was a long pause as he stroked his beard, meditatively. "Who else could produce such strange magical tricks?"

He smirked. "And to track one's prey," he added, "one must know it. The Hexane Beast can never go too far from water, so a skilled hunter would know to set an ambush there. Where would your brother go?"

"Away," Charity said. "He would be trying to get out of the city."

"We have the tunnels heavily guarded," the Emperor said. "Where else might he go?"

Charity shook her head. She knew Johan had tried to explore parts of the city, but he'd never spent a night somewhere – anywhere – outside the house. He could have found a hostel, if he'd gone looking or perhaps a ticket to leave the city, if their father's magic had eventually started to drag him back. It was quite possible that Johan wouldn't *know* where to go, now he was on the run. But if he wasn't alone, someone else might know where to go.

"I don't know," she admitted. "We didn't really talk."

"How frustrating it must have been for your father," the Emperor sneered. "To have the prospect of such power in his family and then lose it, because of his own cruelty and shame."

"Yes, Your Majesty," Charity said.

"And what," the Emperor asked, "might your brother *want*?"

"Freedom," Charity said, simply. "I don't think he wanted anything else."

The Emperor looked disappointed. "Nothing else? Wine? Women? Song?"

Charity felt her face heat. "I think he was interested in a girl," she said, "but my father managed to ruin it. He wanted to arrange their marriage, but the girl broke it off with him instead. Apart from that ..."

She shrugged. Johan, unlike Jamal, had never played any games with the female servants, let alone lured them into his bed. Unless he'd had a relationship that had remained well hidden ... no, it wasn't too likely. Johan had been under their father's supervision; he wouldn't have tolerated anything that might bring the house into further disrepute. And besides, the maids hadn't been as respectful of Johan as they'd been of his elder brother. They might not have let him touch their breasts, let alone open their legs for him.

"No vices," the Emperor mused. "What a *pure* young man."

"I don't think he ever had the chance to develop any," Charity said.

"I suppose not," the Emperor said.

He stood and started to pace the room. "There will be a grand search of the entire city, starting with the poorer regions," he said. "Every rock will be lifted and inspected for the missing fugitives. Wherever they are trying to hide, young lady, we will find them."

Charity frowned. The poorer regions had no political power to object to a total search, but it would still cause massive disruption. And it would require thousands of soldiers to be put on the streets, ready to catch and identify anyone trying to leave the area. It would be an absolute nightmare, particularly with the city already flooded with visitors for the Conference.

"It will be difficult," she said.

"The rats will have gone to ground," the Emperor said. "I want to flush them out."

"Yes, Your Majesty," Charity said. There was no point in arguing with him when she'd just wind up being ordered to carry out the search anyway. "But it could take some time to organise."

"You will remain here until the search begins," the Emperor said.

Charity bit down on her anger and fear. Her younger siblings were at the house, probably scared out of their minds. But she didn't dare protest out loud. The last thing she wanted the Emperor to do was remember that she had younger siblings. Whatever he wanted with the hostages – and she had a feeling it was nothing good – she didn't want her siblings to be added to the group.

"I will do as you command," she said. "And what about the hostages?"

"They're being fed," the Emperor said, dismissively. "Once the search is organised, I have another task for you."

Charity groaned inwardly, but tried to look attentive.

"You will go to the Peerless School," the Emperor said. "Once you are there, you will consult their records and identify the youngest thirty-three newborn magicians. *Not* children from a Great House, or even a known magical bloodline; children without any magicians in the family. I want those children brought to the barracks in the Imperial Palace and held there, under guard."

"More children?" Charity asked. "Why?"

"Because I want them here," the Emperor said, tartly. "And you will do as you are told."

"Yes, Your Majesty," Charity said, thinking hard. Thirty-three was a strongly magical number – and requesting newborn magicians, without family who could or would object, struck her as worrying. Very worrying. "The youngest in the school?"

"Yes," the Emperor said. "The youngest you can find."

Charity tried to think of a reason, but drew a blank. The Great Houses had long since learnt the folly of trying to exclude newborn magicians, even though their families might be dung-gatherers or sheep farmers. They brought in new blood from the gods, strengthening the gift of magic that her ancestors had once been given, centuries ago. But the Emperor couldn't want to add their bloodlines to his own, could he? It would be years before they were mature enough to bear children.

And he didn't specify girls, she thought. *Boys can't bear children.*

She shuddered. His motive had to be sinister ... but what?

"Yes, Your Majesty," she said. "May I ask why you require such young magicians?"

"You may ask," the Emperor said, "but I choose not to answer."

Charity bowed her head, trying to keep her feelings under control. The Emperor would probably be sadistically delighted if he realised she was having problems coping with his orders, or suffering even as she carried them out. The children ... what did he want them *for?*

"Yes, Your Majesty," she said, bitterly.

The Emperor leered. "You may go organise the search," he said. Clearly, he *did* understand that he was causing her pain. "And then you will return to me before you carry out your next set of orders."

Charity bowed, then backed out of the Throne Room. A handful of red-robed men were standing outside, talking to one another in low voices. The looks they shot Charity were far from friendly, suggesting that they weren't remotely pleased to see her. Charity gazed back evenly, refusing to admit to the fear she felt running through her veins. Whatever they wanted, whatever they were doing in the Golden City, she wasn't *theirs*.

A pair of Inquisitors had already set up a map of the city in the War Room. Charity took a moment to admire the level of detail someone had worked into the map, then started to explain what the Emperor wanted. The Inquisitors didn't seem surprised; they merely started to make notations on the map, then organise the search itself. Charity rapidly found herself out of her depth, so she just sat back and watched as the planning came together. The poorest regions of the city would be isolated, then the soldiers would go in and start turning the place upside down. If the fugitives were there, the Inquisitors were sure, they would be found.

"But the locals won't know them," Charity protested. "Nor will the searchers."

"The object of the search will be advertised," one of the Inquisitors said. "I believe we can count on the local criminal masterminds to hand the fugitives over to us, rather than risk us making all sorts of discoveries when we search their premises. *We* may not know who has moved into the vicinity, but rest assured *they* know."

He looked down at the map, marking out places to set up roadblocks. "It won't be as bad as it was in Yukon," he added. "There, the city sprawled out for miles."

Charity nodded. The Golden City might be inconveniently small, but – for once – that smallness worked in their favour. There were simply fewer places to hide, while there were also more magicians and soldiers on hand to do the searching.

"Good," she said. "When can we begin the search?"

"I would prefer to have the troops in place this evening," the Inquisitor said. "There will be too much disruption otherwise."

"Very well," Charity said. She hesitated, then took a gamble. "What would you need thirty-three magical children for?"

The Inquisitor frowned. "Black magic," he said. "There isn't much else that requires children. Even sexual predators would be wise to stay away from magical children."

Charity nodded. Children with magic, when frightened or angry, could produce blasts of raw power that had random effects on their tormentors. Even the most perverted monster would stay away from magical children, knowing that the child might accidentally kill the attacker or the child's parents would track him down and subject the bastard to a fate worse than death. And besides, even the Emperor couldn't afford to do the one thing that would unite most of the world against him. Unless he intended to provoke an uprising that he could then crush ...

But black magic?

The thought was appalling. She knew little about black magic, save for the fact it was considered evil beyond all hopes of redemption. Only Inquisitors and Healers were allowed to study it in the Peerless School ... and only so they could detect and counter its effects. She couldn't even *begin* to imagine what required thirty-three children, save for the darkest of spells. But what did the spells actually do?

"Why do you ask?" The Inquisitor said. "And who do you know who might be practicing black magic?"

"I don't think my oaths will let me tell you," Charity said. And even if she did, what good would it do? The Inquisitors, sworn to wipe out black magic, would still help the Emperor if he wanted to slaughter half the city for a dark ritual. "I'm sorry."

Shaking her head in bitter guilt, she turned and walked back to the Throne Room. This time, the Emperor was alone, reading a long scroll of parchment. He looked up when he saw her, then smiled brightly.

"Is the search underway?"

"It will start later this afternoon, once the soldiers are in place," Charity said. "There's no point in starting earlier."

"Good," the Emperor said. "Off you go to the Peerless School, then. Oh, and Charity?"

"Yes, Your Majesty?"

"You are not to tell the children – or anyone else – anything, apart from the fact they have been selected to receive lessons from me personally," he added. "I don't want you to alarm them."

Charity felt her heart break under his words, but resistance was futile.

"Yes, Your Majesty," she said. "I will do as you command."

Chapter Twenty-Two

"So," Daria said. "No luck?"

Elaine shook her head. She and Johan had meditated for hours, ignoring the muted protests from the upper floors, but they'd managed to do nothing more than make themselves sleepy, no matter how hard they tried. Elaine had resisted the temptation to go for a nap; Johan, who had barely slept since they'd fled the Imperial Palace, was currently lying on the sofa in the next room, snoring loudly.

"It doesn't work," she said. "He has a sense of my presence, but I don't have anything from him unless someone else is boosting the link."

"He has a sense of *my* presence," Daria said, evilly. "Poor guy doesn't know where to put his eyes."

"It's a fairly common problem," Elaine pointed out. "It's your fault for running up and down in front of everyone wearing nothing."

Daria smirked. "Is it *my* fault that human society is so dreadfully repressed?"

"Johan is a virgin, I believe," Elaine said. "And I don't think he actually managed to get that far with Jayne before his father managed to ruin it. You're probably the first near-naked lady he's seen."

"Poor guy," Daria said. "It's so much easier being a werewolf."

"Because you don't think of sex and a relationship as being the same thing," Elaine said, dryly. "Johan probably doesn't have the slightest idea how to handle his feelings."

"I noticed," Daria said. She sniffed, loudly. "Do you think I should let him take matters into his own hands or give him some assistance."

Elaine coloured. "I don't think you should do anything," she began. "I ..."

"I'm sure he'll get matters in hand eventually," Daria said.

"It's practically genetic ..."

"Enough," Elaine said, feeling her blush deepen. "I think he probably feels all hopelessly confused and embarrassed already."

"That's why werewolves have the advantage," Daria said. "We don't lie to ourselves, not like you humans. Nor do we bother to hide our feelings."

"You *can't* hide your feelings," Elaine said. She took a breath. "How many boyfriends have you had since we first knew one another?"

Daria made a show of counting, first on her fingers and then on her bare toes. "Um," she said, finally. "A lot?"

"A lot," Elaine agreed. "And how many of them were boys from the Golden City? You know, the ones who weren't interested in anything more than a quick fuck?"

"You've been listening to me," Daria said, amused. "Most of them weren't interested in seeing me the following morning, let alone the rest of the week."

Elaine felt her cheeks grow hot. She'd known – it had been impossible to miss – just how many times Daria had brought someone back to the apartment they'd shared. Thankfully, Elaine had rarely actually *seen* the men – Daria didn't like keeping them overnight – but the sounds they'd made had echoed through the thin walls. She'd wanted to complain ... and, at the same time, she'd envied her friend the freedom to hunt for pleasure in her own way.

She pushed the thought out of her mind and leant forward. "Are you interested in Johan?"

"He's nice-looking," Daria said. "And interested in me. And not stupid enough to think he knows everything. And young enough not to make a fuss when I dump him."

"I think he's been very isolated for most of his life," Elaine said. "You cannot expect him to have the normal reaction of a magic-born child. Sex was not a normal part of his life, not like the boys we knew from the Peerless School. He might well become far too attached to you ... or he might lash out when you leave him. I don't think it would be healthy for either of you."

"He wants me," Daria said.

"Sometimes what we want isn't something good for us,"

Elaine countered. "Johan is in a mess, no matter how hard he fights to repress it. That's going to explode one day and I don't think I want you anywhere near it."

"You make it sound like he's going to turn into a monster," Daria said. "I thought *I* was the one who turned into a monster."

Elaine sighed. "Johan has spent the past sixteen years of his life being told that he's useless," she snapped. "He has been made to feel a cripple in his family, the butt of every single joke, the victim of charms and hexes you and I could just shrug off. I don't think he ever threw a tantrum like Millicent did, back in Year Two; I think he repressed everything as far as he could, burying it deep within his mind. And even crushing his father and brother didn't do anything to help his repression. His anger issues could easily become terrifying."

"Like Jared," Daria said.

"Exactly like Jared," Elaine agreed. Their classmate had been incredibly unpopular; he'd thrown tantrums when he didn't get his way, hit out at his schoolmates and generally shown no concern for anyone, even himself. And then he'd collapsed, six months after they'd entered the Peerless School. Whatever his parents had done to him, the class had found out later, had permanently damaged his magic. "Only with a great deal more power."

"I see," Daria said. "And what do you intend to do about it?"

"I was planning to live somewhere well away from the rest of society and use the bond to help him work through his issues," Elaine said. "But the bond isn't forming properly, so I don't even know if it will work."

"Good luck," Daria said. "And you should probably be careful not to fall in love yourself."

Elaine glowered at her. "I haven't found anyone during your absence," she said. "And I could hardly go clubbing ..."

"Use a glamour," Daria suggested. "You don't have to *look* too different to avoid being recognised."

Elaine snorted. One of the cases that had come up before the Privy Council had been of a sorcerer who had glamoured himself to look like someone famous, wealthy and powerful, then lured a succession of young witches into bed. It might have lasted indefinitely if he hadn't managed to get two of the girls pregnant, who had then applied to the *real* person for marital rights. A glamour might have worked for Elaine, if she had been interested in a single-night stand, but it still smacked of deceptiveness. Besides, she wanted more than just a partner for the night.

"I think that would be dishonest," she said. "And why am I talking to you about this anyway?"

"Because you want something and you're asking your friend for advice," Daria said. "I do read your emotions too, you know."

"I read yours," Elaine said. "Lust, hunger, lust, hunger, lust ..."

Daria made a rude gesture. "What else do I need?"

She shrugged. "None of the lads I meet on the town are interested in a long-term relationship with a werewolf," she said. "One day, I will go to the Pack Meet and see if I find anyone who smells right. Until then ... I will just enjoy myself. And you should do the same."

Elaine opened her mouth to reply, but stopped when she heard Cass coming down the stairs and into the room. "The kids are asleep," she said. "I had to tell them a whole series of very boring stories until they finally closed their eyes."

"Probably best to keep them away from Johan," Daria said, curtly. "He had a remarkably wide range of emotions when he saw the little brats."

Elaine eyed her. "You picked up on the subtle points there and not earlier?"

"There's nothing subtle about a man in lust," Daria said. "Or a woman, for that matter."

Cass cleared her throat. "I should imagine that it doesn't really matter," she said. "They're scared of him too."

"Good," Elaine said. She knew enough about Johan's home life to know the orphanage had been preferable. The Orphan Mother might have been a pain, but she hadn't been abusive. "I wonder what Charity told them about him."

"Just that he had powers now ... and that he was mad at them," Cass said. "They heard far too many rumours at the school and they now think he's a minor god."

She closed the door, then sat down on one of the hard chairs. "So," she said. "What do we do now?"

"Good question," Elaine said. "Does the Emperor know you're with us?"

"I don't know, but the Inquisitors will certainly suspect something," Cass said. "It isn't exactly common for an Inquisitor to be released from her oaths. They will probably decide your planned departure and mine were linked. Even if the Emperor hadn't shown himself, they would still be irked with me."

"You deserted them," Daria said, quietly.

"That's what they would think," Cass agreed. "We're not trained to rely on anyone outside the Inquisitors."

She sucked in a long breath. "We need information," she said. "One of us needs to go out of the house and ... well, I'm the best choice."

"The kids might be better," Daria pointed out. "One of them could get the information we want without being detected ..."

"The oldest is fourteen," Cass sneered. "She wasn't raised in the packs, either. I doubt she could ask anything without tipping off the information brokers."

She shrugged. "And it might be dangerous to put her on the streets, anyway," she added. "I think those soldiers are from Deferens's homeland. An unescorted woman on the streets would be considered fair game."

Elaine shuddered. "How can they live like that?"

"It's astonishing what someone can get used to if they don't realise they have a choice," Cass said, coldly. "Sometimes, very rarely, we get fugitives coming out of his homeland. The remainder are trapped."

"Should turn them all into werewolves," Daria snarled. "No werewolf husband would dare treat his wife with anything other than respect."

"It might be a workable idea," Cass agreed. She waved a hand over her face, casting a glamour. "How does this look?"

"Very attractive," Daria said.

Elaine rolled her eyes. Cass now looked like a weather-beaten man, around thirty years old if she was any judge. His brown hair was already thinning, indicating weak magic, but his body looked muscular and solid. Not the type of man to pose a threat, she decided, yet also not the type of man to seem an automatic victim. And older than the boys Daria normally brought home to the apartment.

"Thank you," Cass said. Even her voice had changed. "It will be my pleasure to escort you, my fair lady."

Daria snickered. "And what would you do when you got me home?"

"I'd think of something," Cass said. She returned to her normal appearance, then brushed her blonde hair back out of her face. "While I'm gone, I want you to think about options. There has to be a way out of the city we haven't considered."

"Maybe Johan could burn us a private tunnel through the mountains," Daria suggested. "Or ... if he's as powerful as you say, maybe we should just point him at the Emperor and watch the chaos from a safe distance."

"He's not invincible," Elaine said, quietly. "His powers don't seem to follow the normal rules, I will concede, but he does have limits. Deferens is smart enough to take precautions against Johan, if he knows Johan is still alive."

"He might," Cass said. "Johan turned those men into statues."

"And Dread may suspect something," Elaine added. "I lied to his face."

Cass whistled softly. "Either you're a better liar than I thought," she said, "or he chose not to challenge you. There's very little that gets past him."

Elaine sighed. "I still feel bad about it," she confessed. "Is that wrong?"

"Well, lying to an Inquisitor can earn you a public flogging," Cass said. "So yes, I would say it was wrong. But ... if the Grand Sorceress ordered you to lie, it will probably be blamed on her. And as she's the one who issues orders to the government, you're probably in the clear."

"I know," Elaine said. "But I still feel bad."

She sighed, remembering her first meeting with Dread ... and those that had followed. He'd seemed the embodiment of power at the time, but he'd given her a considerable amount of latitude when he'd caught her in Ida. And then, they'd become friends, of a sort. It was easy to think that he wouldn't want to see her again, at least personally, after she'd lied to him.

I will tell him when this is over, she told herself. *And then he will say whatever he says.*

"Then we can't use Johan as a secret weapon," Daria said. She sounded disappointed. "What can we find outside these walls?"

"Food and information," Cass said, primly. "There are people I can visit, who will happily trade information for money. I have enough, if necessary, to pay my way. Once we know what's going on, we can start making some proper plans."

"Just don't get caught," Elaine said. She hesitated, then started to root through her pockets for a knife. But she'd had it taken from her while she'd been a prisoner. "Do you have a knife? We can set up a blood-bond, if you wish. We'd know if something happened to you."

Cass's eyebrows rose. "And where did you ... never mind, silly question," she said. She dug into her pockets until she found and produced a ritual blade. "Can you craft one safely?"

"Yes," Elaine said. "It's not actually a dangerous art, I think."

"And yet it's forbidden," Cass mused. She didn't sound convinced. "Why is it forbidden if it isn't dangerous?"

"Because it can allow two magicians to share thoughts and impressions without being detected," Elaine said. "There's no need for crystal balls if two magicians can talk mind-to-mind. But the link is also harder to separate, once formed."

"It strikes me you should be trying this with Johan," Cass said. "Why doesn't your bond with him work?"

"I wish I knew," Elaine said, allowing a hint of frustration to enter her voice. "It should work, everything I know says it should work, but it doesn't. I honestly don't know why it worked to the point you were able to boost it ..."

"Maybe you're not merging your magics properly," Cass said. "Your magic is conventional, right? His is not."

Elaine thought about it while she drew a rune on a piece of parchment, then carefully cut her palm and allowed a droplet of blood to drip down. Cass held out her hand, then slapped it down on the parchment, muttering the first stage of the charm as her hand hit the blood. It flared with magic, just briefly, but long enough for Elaine to mutter the second stage of the charm. The link flared to light, then dimmed sharply. Moments later, it was gone.

Cass stared. "What in the name of all the gods *happened*?"

"I don't know," Elaine said. The blood-bond was simple magic. Even a complete novice could have forged one, if he'd had the inclination to try. And she was a trained magician with years of experience ... and a unique understanding of how magic actually worked. "It should have worked perfectly."

She stared down at the parchment. The blood was already turning black, then decaying into dust. There was no way she'd made a mistake, not with something so simple. And Cass's protections wouldn't have stopped the bond if she'd wanted it to form. It should have formed quickly and easily, not ... died.

"You have a bond with Johan," Cass said, quietly. "Could that have impeded your efforts to forge a bond with me?"

Elaine frowned. It shouldn't have ... but then, the bond she shared with Johan wasn't normal in the first place. In fact, there were so many issues with it ... she stopped as a thought occurred to her. If Johan's magic wasn't supporting the bond, which seemed likely, it was *her* magic that was doing all the work. She might be expending so much effort on holding the bond in place that she couldn't form a separate link with Cass. And that meant ...

"I think we were going about it the wrong way," she said, slowly. "I'll have to give it some thought."

"Do so," Cass ordered. She rose and replaced her glamour. "If Charity comes home, I suggest you stun her before she realises you're here. These wards will probably tell her she has intruders once she enters the house."

"Understood," Elaine said.

She watched Cass slip out of the door, then looked down at her hands. The bond hadn't formed properly, which meant they would have to snap and redo it. But what would that do to their relationship? Maybe there were ways to push magic in and out of the bond without actually breaking the link. And yet ...

I've been thinking of Johan as a magician, she thought. There were ways to forge a similar bond with a mundane, but she hadn't used them. *Maybe I should have thought of him as someone without magic, only power.*

"I know that look," Daria said. "You're thinking, aren't you?"

"I suppose you wouldn't recognise the process," Elaine jibed, deadpan. She rose, then headed for the door. Johan's father had set up a workshop next to his study, crammed with magical tools. It was quite possible he hadn't used any of them for himself – magical research won respect, even if it was just amateurish fiddling – but they would be serviceable. "I'm going to try something. When Johan wakes, send him to see me."

"As you wish," Daria said. She sniffed the air. "But you should know he's having nightmares."

"I've had them too," Elaine said. It was true. Every two or three days, she woke up screaming. "But there's nothing to be done about them."

Chapter Twenty-Three

Charity hadn't expected to return to the Peerless School. Most students only returned if they chose to become teachers – and only after ten years of experience teaching or tutoring outside the school. There was so much competition for each place at the school that only an experienced magician had a hope of gaining a job.

She remembered the first day she'd walked through the giant doors and into the entrance hall when she'd been a mere eleven years old. The hall had seemed massive at the time, easily capable of holding the two thousand students who had gathered to watch the new bugs enter the building. They had been addressed by the Administrator personally, before they were divided up between the dormitories and sent to their first classes. The old man – he'd seemed ancient at the time – had been reassuring to the young children, convincing them that they would soon grow used to living away from their families. And he'd been right.

The thought made her wince as she stepped into the deserted entrance hall and waited. Only the Grand Sorcerer had full and free access to the school; the wards would already have notified the Administrator of her presence and summoned him to greet her. She waited, looking around the room at the paintings hanging from the walls. One of them showed a man carrying a wand in one hand and a staff in the other, his face too handsome to be real. A note at the bottom identified him as Valiant, one of the great heroes of the First Necromantic War and the founder of modern magical theory. He'd died sometime between the two Necromantic Wars, having set the stage for the Peerless School.

It wasn't long – only five minutes – before the Administrator made his appearance. Charity couldn't help a twinge of disappointment as she saw the man, even though she knew that *her* Administrator had died during the struggle to select the next Grand Sorcerer. He'd been a power in the city, she recalled; the new Administrator was nothing more than a puppet, selected by Light Spinner personally. Given time, he might become a power, but for the moment he was nothing more than her servant. Charity scowled, inwardly, as the Administrator made his approach. It just felt wrong to see someone else wearing the black and gold robes of the Administrator.

"My Lady," the Administrator said. "You graduated a year ago, as I recall."

"Yes," Charity said. "I'm surprised you recall me."

"I recall all of my students," the Administrator said. "You were the one who put frogspawn in Yasmin's potion during her half-term tests."

Charity flushed at the memory. "I was an immature little brat at the time," she said. "The weeks of detention taught me a lesson."

"They're very effective," the Administrator said. He gave her a thin smile. "And I understand that you're working for the Emperor now?"

"Yes," Charity said. She wasn't surprised he knew. The only thing that moved faster than thoughts exchanged between master and apprentice were rumours in the Golden City, where everyone who wanted to be someone had sources in all kinds of places. "I am his assistant."

"An interesting post to have," the Administrator mused. He looked at her, his green eyes bright with amusement. "Do you offer suggestions, from time to time, or do you merely do as you are told?"

"Both," Charity said. "I'm afraid I didn't come to bandy words with you."

"They never do," the Administrator said, mournfully. "Everyone who comes to see me wants something."

Charity shrugged. "It's the price of your job," she said. "But it's also the chance to build your own web of power within the city."

"And you will be doing the same, of course," the Administrator agreed. "And you seem to have an unfair advantage."

"Maybe," Charity said. The Administrator could act

against the Emperor. She couldn't do anything that knowingly opposed her master. "The Emperor sent me here with a request."

The Administrator lifted one eyebrow. "He did? It will be our pleasure to serve."

That, Charity knew, was what she was afraid of. "He wants thirty-three young students, the youngest you have, all born of mundanes," she said. "I am to take them back to the palace."

She hoped – prayed – that the Administrator would refuse to grant her request. There weren't any *good* uses for young students, unless one happened to be a Sixth Year looking for a servant. The Emperor couldn't want them for anything good, particularly not children from families that enjoyed no power or influence. But would the Administrator have the backbone to order her to go back to the Emperor and tell him to go to hell? It had only been six months since he'd assumed his role, hardly long enough to build up a power base among the school's staff. They might support him ... or they might seek to curry favour with the Emperor instead. There was no way to know.

Short of actually doing it, she thought. *And then it might be too late.*

"Thirty-three newborn students," the Administrator mused. "Did he say why?"

"He wants them to learn from him personally," Charity lied. She couldn't tell him anything else, not when it would spite the Emperor. "He is a powerful sorcerer, after all. They could learn a great deal from him."

"I'm sure they could," the Administrator said. "But learning to use magic too quickly can have unpleasant side effects."

"I know," Charity said. Her early struggles with magic hadn't been fun, even though her father had paid for private tutors from a very early age. The students often became impatient at their slow progress from tiny little spells to the ones that really impressed people, but they had to learn to walk before they could run. "The Emperor is determined, though."

The Administrator eyed her for a long moment, then bowed

his head. "I will have the children assembled," he said. "And you may take them back to the palace."

He turned, leaving Charity to stare at his back in despair. How could he simply give up the children he had sworn to protect? It was horrific. And yet she thought she understood the mark of a small mind. He would do as he was told, for the alternative – losing his power and place – was unthinkable. Why, he would fall from being one of the most respected magicians in the city to being one of the least. The luxury of his quarters would be replaced by a garret on the edge of town, if he was lucky. But at least he would have been able to keep his soul.

And what, a voice in her head asked her, *of yours*?

It isn't my fault, Charity thought back. *I didn't know he was a monster ...*

Quickly – too quickly – the children assembled in the hall. They all looked young, wearing the same basic uniform – black trousers for the boys, long black skirts for the girls – and looking at her with disturbingly trusting eyes. Charity could see the subtle signs that none of them had been raised in magical households, although it was clear that they had taken to magic like ducks to water. No one would pick on them for being born into non-magical families, she knew. The Great Houses had long since learnt the folly of trying to exclude new blood from their family trees. Her younger siblings, if her father had still been in charge, would probably have found themselves married to newborn magicians. The gift of the gods could not be allowed to fade away into nothingness.

And besides, she reminded herself darkly, it was always safer to pick on the magicians with limited power. And, whatever else could be said of new magicians, they rarely lacked raw power.

"Please take care of them," the Administrator said. Charity wanted to curse him into next week ... or something else foolishly destructive that would bring the school's wards down on her like a hammer on a nail. "They are young and, as yet, unaware of etiquette."

Charity sighed, inwardly. She'd had ruthless etiquette lessons from the moment she'd first manifested her magic, until she knew precisely how deep a curtsey she should offer to anyone in power. But newborn magicians wouldn't have any such training until they reached the Peerless School. They hadn't just been taught how to use magic, she knew. They'd been taught how to fit in with the rest of their peers.

And who to know, she thought, remembering just how many magicians had flocked around her during her final year. *The school makes sure we all know each other, even if we can't stand to see the other's face.*

She looked at the children and shivered, inwardly. They all looked so young – the youngest was nine, a freak whose powers had developed earlier than expected – and they appeared completely innocent, as if butter wouldn't melt in their mouths. Charity knew better – her first year had been spent establishing her place in the pecking order, exchanging pranks and hexes with her fellow classmates – and she had no doubt that the innocent faces before her were capable of the same level of bloody-minded malice. If they hadn't been accustomed to struggling to hold themselves ahead of the others when they arrived, they sure as hell were now.

Her gaze lighted on a girl who couldn't have been any older than Chime – who might well share classes with Charity's youngest sister – and she shuddered, again. The Emperor wanted children ... and he couldn't want them for anything good, not if he was selecting children without relatives who might make a fuss. But there was nothing she could do to stop him.

"Follow me," she ordered. She hesitated, then felt compelled to cast the standard child-protection spells her tutors had once used, when they'd taken the children out into the Golden City. None of the kids would be able to wander very far without her noticing ... if, of course, they dared. The Golden City wasn't always a safe place for children. "And don't lose sight of me."

Outside, the sun was already starting to set. The streets were almost deserted, save for the ever-present soldiers and a handful of patrolling magicians. Charity felt another pang of guilt and grief as she nodded to the magicians, then led the children past the Great Library – carefully skirting the damaged road – and down towards the Imperial Palace.

Many new soldiers had appeared outside it and were being reviewed by officers wearing dark red uniforms and supervised by red-robed magicians. The children had been talking quietly amongst themselves, but they stilled when they saw the small army. There couldn't have been more than a hundred soldiers in the area, yet it looked like an invincible force.

A child with a wand and a couple of spells could stop them all in their tracks, she thought, darkly. Mundanes couldn't beat magicians who knew to expect them. But the magicians supporting the soldiers – and the protective amulets they wore – would help shield them from magic before it was too late. *And most of the city's population doesn't have magic.*

She kept her face impassive as she led her charges past the soldiers, who stared at her with dark calculating eyes. Charity was used to being ogled – she knew, without false modesty, that her face was beautiful – but there was something different about the stares. It wasn't lust, it wasn't a desire powerful enough to overwhelm common sense; it was something different, something darker. And then it struck her. Jamal had looked at their family's maids in the exact same way. They hadn't been *people*, not to him. They'd been *things*, things he could use. Charity shuddered at the memory, then forced herself to keep walking normally, rather than either breaking into a run or drawing her wand and firing off hexes at the men. The Emperor would not have been pleased.

A handful of slaves carrying heavy boxes walked past her as she entered the building, leading the children down towards the Throne Room. Charity glanced at the label on one of the boxes and almost froze with shock. Crystals could store magic, she knew, but why would the Emperor want so many perfectly-cut crystals. The guilds who controlled the crystal trade kept the prices high, even for the Grand Sorceress ... or the Emperor. How much of the city's budget had the Emperor just spent on crystals? There were more in a single box than the Peerless School used in a year!

But there was no point in asking the slaves. She stepped to one side and motioned for the children to follow her, to allow the slaves to walk past, and then led the children into the

Throne Room. The Emperor was alone, thankfully, reading a book that fairly reeked of dark magic. Charity shivered, unable even to *look* at the book without feeling sick, then hastily prostrated herself in front of the Emperor. The children seemed confused – she heard a couple giggle quietly – then copied her. There was a long pause, then the Emperor looked up and cast his gaze over the children.

"You have done well," he said, firmly. "And I welcome these children to my home."

Charity cringed, inwardly. The children had been brought to the palace like lambs to the slaughter ... and *she* was their betrayer, the traitor who'd bought them there. There was no hope for forgiveness from the household gods, not now. She was damned beyond any hope of redemption for what she had done. And yet, she knew she couldn't leave. There wasn't even the option of surrendering her magic in breaking the oaths. She'd sworn to him willingly, after all. All she could do was pray he would free her, one day.

But he won't, she thought. *Why should he?*

The Emperor clapped his hands. There was a low rustle, then the curtains behind the Golden Throne parted, revealing a number of young women wearing gauzy outfits that made Charity think of dancers in the night. The outfits concealed nothing; she found herself staring at one young woman in particular, her breasts clearly visible despite the material covering them. Behind her, the children tittered as the newcomers dropped to their knees, staring down at the marble floor as if they were unworthy to gaze upon the Emperor. It would have been comical, part of her mind noted, if it hadn't been so serious.

They're slaves, she realised, numbly. She looked at the women closely and realised what was missing. *But they're not bound by magic. They're willing slaves.*

The Emperor smirked. "You will take these children to their rooms and you will prepare them," he ordered. "They are to be treated well, but kept safe and secure."

He looked at the children. "Place your wands on the ground, then go with my ... servants," he said. "This is not a place for you to practice your magic."

One of the boys, braver or stupider than the others, was

moved to protest. "We were told never to let go of our wands ..."

The Emperor's face darkened. He snapped his fingers, without bothering with further argument, and the boy became a tiny statue of himself, his wand clattering down to the marble floor. One of the servant women stepped forward, picked up the statue and carried it out of the room. The other children stared in horror, then dropped their own wands practically in unison. Charity watched, helpless, as they were escorted away by the servant women.

"I wonder what they're teaching students these days," the Emperor mused. "Clearly, obedience wasn't on the syllabus for the year."

"I was taught never to be without my wand," Charity offered, as she straightened up. "They must have been told the same thing."

"That was at school, where anyone could prank you at any moment," the Emperor reminded her, dryly. "Or were you in the habit of practicing magic without a wand?"

Charity shook her head. The wand she carried had been specifically chosen for her by her father, who had had it made specially. She would sooner have cut off her own arm than surrender her wand, even though her father had tried to insist that she learnt to use magic without it. The wand was practically *part* of her. But then, the Emperor was right. Anyone could prank a fellow student at any time and, without a wand, cancelling the prank might be difficult.

And if you were late to class because someone had turned you into a toad or fixed your feet to the spot, she thought, *it was always your fault.*

"I thank you for your service," the Emperor added. "Pick up their wands, then take them down to the ritual chamber. The masters will be glad of them."

Charity hesitated, then did as she was told. None of the wands were anything more than pieces of wood, probably crafted by woodcarvers rather than magicians. Not that it really mattered, her tutors had told her. The wands served as focus tools for magicians; they weren't magic in their own right. As long as there was no iron in the wands, anything would serve. But it still felt strange to be holding someone else's wand.

Because there are few taboos as strong as those against destroying a wand, she thought, morbidly. You could practice nasty pranks on a younger student and no one would care, but break a wand and the tutors would have you in detention for the rest of the year.

A nasty thought struck her. The Emperor had mentioned a ritual ... and masters, who had to be ritual masters. Rituals were common, but if they involved wands and children ...

"Your Majesty," she said, as she picked up the last wand, "what are you going to do with the children?"

"Wait and see," the Emperor said. He smirked, again. "Wait and see."

Chapter Twenty-Four

"I made some food," Johan said, as he stepped into the workroom. "Are you coming to eat?"

"Cass isn't back yet," Elaine said. She turned to look at her apprentice. "I thought I told Daria to send you to me when you awoke."

"The brats needed something to eat," Johan said. "I'm sorry."

"Good thing you're not working for Miss Prim," Elaine said. "She would have sent you to be flogged for daring to be late."

Johan smiled. "And will you have me flogged?"

Elaine shook her head. "Not unless you burned the food," she said. "What did you make?"

"I'm afraid it's only cold chicken, bread and butter," Johan said. "I don't think the servants will be back anytime soon."

Elaine shrugged. She didn't blame the servants for fleeing, after Johan had attacked Conidian House. The only real question was how Charity Conidian had managed to keep her siblings fed, at the same time as handling the affairs of the house and trying to salvage something – anything – from the disaster. Maybe the servants had left some food in storage before leaving ... or, more likely, she'd hired workers who couldn't come back to the house after Deferens had ordered a curfew.

"We can't stay here indefinitely in any case," she said. "Did your father ever let you spend time in his workshop?"

"More time than I wanted," Johan said. "They used to do all kinds of tests on me."

Elaine shuddered. Johan probably viewed the workroom as a place of horror, just as she viewed the isolation box from the orphanage. Bringing him back here had been unkind, yet she knew there was no choice. Half of the tools in the room were charmed to prevent them being taken *out* of the room, save by the master of the house. The remainder were so commonplace they could have been purchased anywhere, with enough gold.

"Your father had quite an impressive collection," she said, waving her hand at the iron workbench, the tools placed in wooden cupboards and the small collection of potions' ingredients in a large cabinet. "But I don't think he ever did much with it."

Johan snorted, rudely. "Father liked to think of himself as a tinkerer, but all he ever really did was play politics," he said. "I don't think he cared enough to try to carry out research of his own, even on me. The only person I ever saw use this place was that rat-arsed druid."

"Not everyone has the inclination to do research," Elaine said. *She* was honest enough to admit she wouldn't have known what half the tools were, without the knowledge decanted into her head. "Can we do one final experiment?"

Johan eyed her, doubtfully. "Is it important?"

"I believe so," Elaine said.

She took a long breath. "The bond that formed between us only worked properly when boosted by another magician," she said. "But we did the ritual correctly, so it should have worked perfectly. Why didn't it?"

"I don't know," Johan said. "Why didn't it?"

"Your magic seems to be ... well, tamed wild magic," Elaine said. "Children having their first bouts of accidental magic can produce stunning effects, which they can't always duplicate until much later. We teach children to channel their magic properly to avoid causing mental problems as their magic sparks and flickers. You, on the other hand, don't seem to need to channel your magic to keep doing interesting feats."

Johan frowned. "So what does that mean?"

"My scans show that you have a flicker of magic, nothing more," Elaine said. "You shouldn't be able to do half the things you do. But if you're ... well, using accidental magic all the time, you can do astonishing things."

"Except it isn't an accident," Johan said, slowly. "I can make things happen by wanting them to happen."

"I think you produce the same effect," Elaine said. "There

are some other tests we can run – and we will, once we're out of the city – but I think that explains your manifold oddities. You keep keying into the level of power that caused accidental flashes of magic; indeed, to some extent, you have learnt to master it deliberately."

"I see," Johan said. "I think ... is this dangerous?"

"I'm not sure," Elaine admitted.

She shrugged. "But I think that explains why the bond refused to form properly," she added. "Your magic isn't tamed to the point where it can hold up its side of the bond, so my magic has been doing all the work. And mine isn't strong enough to maintain the bond indefinitely, hence my inability to sense you. I should have reworked the ritual to channel additional magic into the bond, rather than relying on the standard form. But we did need a legal claim to being mistress and apprentice."

"Or my father might have challenged it," Johan said. He looked up at her, alarmed. "But what does this actually *mean*? Can we fix the bond?"

"I believe so," Elaine said. "Are you willing to work with me to repair it?"

Johan had another question. "And the other Powerless? Are they simply denied access to their powers?"

"I don't know," Elaine said. "It's possible that you were merely intended to develop powers later in life and your father's ... treatments actually buried the magic deeper. Or ..."

"Or I'm a freak accident," Johan said. "Why wasn't I born into a normal family?"

"You should have grown up in an orphanage," Elaine said, quietly. "I would have *killed* to have the advantages you and your siblings were offered."

"It couldn't have been that bad," Johan said. "Really. It couldn't have been as bad as having Jamal as an older brother."

"Being alone is unpleasant enough," Elaine said. "And there were worse things out there than merely being alone."

She shook her head. "I think I know how to rework the ritual," she said, as she motioned for him to sit down on one side of a small table. "Are you ready to allow the link to reform?"

"Yes," Johan said. "Are you sure this will work?"

"Nothing in life is certain," Elaine said. She sat down facing him, placing a silver knife in the middle of the table. "But I think this will work."

She took a long breath. The ritual for bonding a magician to a mundane carried dangerous implications ... and reworking the ritual so those implications were minimised or removed altogether had been difficult, almost impossible. Indeed, she was fairly sure that no one else would have been able to rework the ritual without access to the Great Library and a number of unwilling test subjects. But she thought she had something that would either work perfectly or fail completely, depending on just what happened.

"Hold out your hand," she said. "I need to make a cut in your left palm. Once you've been cut, take the knife from me in your right hand and make a similar cut in *my* left palm. Do you understand me?"

Johan winced – Powerless or not, he'd grown up in a household where everyone knew to make sure that no one managed to steal a sample of their blood – then he nodded, tersely. Elaine winced inwardly, remembering the first days at the Peerless School, then reached out and cut his palm as lightly as she could. The blade was charmed to minimise the pain, but Johan still grimaced in agony, then took the blade and sliced into Elaine's palm. Being inexperienced, he cut deep enough to do real damage. She had to fight down the urge to cast a healing spell at once; instead, she gripped his left hand with her left hand and allowed their blood to mingle, then chanted the bonding spell under her breath. There was a sudden stab of pain, then disorientation ... and then she was suddenly looking at her own body from the outside. No, she realised slowly. She was peering through Johan's eyes.

His memories rose up around her, a blur of nightmare and horror, of abuse and bullying and desperate attempts to coax even a flicker of magic from him. She blushed furiously as she realised *he* would be seeing *her* memories, then forced the thought to one side. There were secrets she wished to keep from him, from anyone, but there was no point in trying to hide them. He was her apprentice, bonded to her. Whatever her personal feelings, he had a right to know what she was and what she'd done. The bond would ensure he kept those memories to himself.

She snapped back into her own body and stared at him, feeling her entire body trembling as sweat trickled down her back. His hand was squeezing hers so hard it hurt ... no, she was feeling his pain as well as her own. Her eyesight seemed to flicker; for a moment, she was looking at herself again, then snapped back to normal. Carefully, thinking through every step, she released his hand and waited for him to let go of hers. As soon as he did, she pulled back her palm, now covered in their mingled blood, and cast a healing spell.

Johan coughed. "What ... what is that?"

Elaine stared down at her palm. The cut was gone, although she knew from experience her palm would ache for days. But now, instead of bare skin, there was a single rune carved into her flesh. It wasn't included in the textbooks she'd seen at the Peerless School, but she knew what it meant. *Partner*. It was far more than just a simple apprenticeship rune. Slowly, she reached for Johan's left hand, already knowing what she would see. The blood was gone, leaving the same rune marked on his flesh.

"It means we're partners," Elaine said. She hadn't expected *that*. Most apprenticeships didn't bother with runes, but when they did the master always manifested the master rune while his apprentice manifested the apprentice rune. To be partners ... what did it mean? For once, there was nothing in her stockpiled knowledge to tell her. "I think."

Johan stared at her. "I can feel you now," he said. "Can you feel me?"

Elaine closed her eyes. Johan's presence was there, shimmering at the back of her mind. She understood, now, why it wasn't considered remotely proper for a female to apprentice to a male and vice versa. It had been written in the books, but she hadn't really comprehended what it meant, not really. No one could unless they underwent it for themselves. She was so close to him, so intimate, that it would be easy to take the final step forward and invite him into her bed. Indeed, they shared an intimacy well beyond anything she'd shared with Bee.

"Yes," she said, irked. She'd have to do something about the bond ... but she already knew she wouldn't be doing anything of the sort. The whole idea of giving up the bond, even moderating it, was unthinkable. "We'll have to move out of the building and separate, just to check it works properly. We should be able to talk together at any distance."

"It feels different," Johan said. "Firmer too."

He paused. "What was that dark room?"

Elaine cringed, mentally. "When children were naughty at the orphanage," she said, trying hard to keep her tone light, "the Orphan Mother would put the brat in the dark box, leaving him completely alone."

Johan winced. "I'm sorry," he said. He would have picked up on her horror ... and her memories of being in the box herself. "But at least you weren't being starved to death."

Elaine shook her head. "Being sent to bed without supper was another regular punishment," she said. "And sometimes, we wondered what we'd done wrong."

"I don't understand," Johan said.

"You never had to hunt for food," Elaine said. "There were days when the orphanage simply didn't have enough food to feed us all. So we went to bed hungry, wondering what we'd done to be denied food. Some of us even begged to be beaten instead because we were so hungry. But it never worked. None of us understood until we were much older."

"But you went to the Peerless School," Johan said. "You were fed there?"

"I was," Elaine said. "And I ended up working over the holidays, just to stay away from the orphanage. The first time I went back there, no one was pleased to see me."

She wondered if he would understand. The orphans had watched her leave, wearing new clothes, to a school where she would be safe, warm and well-fed. She'd come back, having put on weight, and started to eat from their communal supplies again. It was hard to blame them for resenting her, even though they'd largely left her alone. She'd been a magician, after all, with a wand at her side.

"No one was pleased to see me either," Johan said. "And

to think I thought my dad was bad, when he was angry at us."

He looked down at the blood on his hand. "What do I do about this?"

"Allow me," Elaine said, brandishing her wand. A simple charm and the blood was gone, leaving only the rune standing out against Johan's pale skin. "And we should probably meditate until we know just how deeply the bond runs between us."

Johan frowned. "It seems pretty deep," he said. "Is this remotely normal?"

"I don't know," Elaine said. She looked down at the rune on her palm, feeling – for the first time in months – as ignorant as a new student. "There haven't been bonds like this for a very long time."

She hesitated. "You may dream of my life," she warned, "and I may dream of yours. Just remember ... that not everything may be in context when you see it."

"I'll try," Johan said.

Elaine followed him out of the door and down towards the dining room. It was as spotlessly elegant as she'd expected, but Johan's family would probably not have approved of Daria, or Elaine herself, let alone the decidedly plebeian food on the table. Elaine had to smile at the thought as Johan started passing out sandwiches, wondering just what his father would make of him serving the food. Even as a Powerless, menial work was below a Conidian.

"Your scents have changed," Daria said, sharply. "What have you done to yourselves?"

"Bonded," Johan said. He held up his palm. "What does this smell like?"

"Elaine," Daria said. She sniffed Johan's palm, then smiled. "Concentrated Essence of Elaine."

Elaine blushed. "It's just a bonding rune ..."

"You might want to glamour it," Cass said. Elaine jumped, one hand reaching for her wand, as the former Inquisitor stepped into the room. "Any magician worth his wand who sees it will know there's something odd about it."

Johan found his voice. "Where the hell have you been?"

"I just got back," Cass said. "The poorer parts of the city are being searched, ruthlessly. I think thousands of people have already been displaced by the soldiers."

"They're searching for us, I presume," Elaine said.

Cass nodded. "The people there can't really make a fuss," she said, darkly. "I imagine the search will continue until they're *sure* we're not hiding there."

"That's a good thing, isn't it?" Johan asked. "If they're searching there, they won't be searching here."

"On the face of it, yes," Cass said. "But the search will upset the criminal element, who will then have an incentive to look for us, just to end the search before the searches stumble upon something they can't ignore. And there are other problems."

She sighed. "The soldiers are not being very nice to the population," she added. "There will be riots, soon enough. And then all hell will break loose."

"We can't do anything about it, though," Daria said. "Can we?"

Cass gave her an odd little smile. "Not unless you want us to surrender to the Emperor," she said. "Our best bet would be to get out of the city, then let the Emperor know we've made it out."

"Which we will, if we can," Elaine said. "Did you hear anything else?"

"Just that the Emperor has been taking students from the Peerless School," Cass said. "My source was quite certain that all of the children came from mundane families."

Elaine rubbed her eyes in confusion. She hated politics, but the more she thought about it, the more it puzzled her. Hostages made sense, but children from mundane families were useless as hostages. Their families could neither cause trouble for the Emperor nor offer him anything worth taking, if he wished it. And that suggested he had something else in mind ...

She swore. "A ritual," she said. "He's planning a dark ritual."

"It certainly seems that way," Cass said. "There's nothing else he could do with the children."

"Unless he wants to train them as his personal assistants," Johan offered, hopefully. "He would want more sorcerers loyal to him, wouldn't he?"

"Yes, but half of the children he took are girls," Cass said. "And even if he was able to overcome his revulsion at the thought of teaching a girl how to use magic, it would still be years before they could do anything useful. Why not take students from their sixth year instead?"

Elaine shuddered. "We have to stop him."

Cass tilted her head. "How?"

"I ... I don't know," Elaine admitted. "But there has to be something we can do."

"He will carry out the ritual under heavy security," Cass said, tightly. "There will be layer upon layer of protection surrounding him. We could not do anything to stop him."

"There are Inquisitors there," Johan said. "Wouldn't *they* stop him?"

"The Grand Sorcerer can do no wrong," Cass said. "Anything they do is legal by definition. I think that will be true of an Emperor too."

She shook her head. "They won't try to stop him," she added. "And they may even find themselves helping! And there's nothing *we* can do to stop him."

Chapter Twenty-Five

"Ah, Charity," the Emperor said, as she prostrated herself before him. "I trust that you are ready to witness my work?"

"Yes, Your Majesty," Charity said. She had hoped the Emperor would allow her to remain in her rooms or even go back home to check on her siblings, but instead he had kept her busy until the moon had risen high above the city. "I am ready."

"Then follow me," the Emperor said, picking up a long, iron-tipped staff. "Time waits for no man, not even an Emperor."

Charity shivered as she rose from the floor and followed. The timing of rituals rarely mattered, she'd been told at school, unless the rituals involved sacrifice. A lunar ritual tended to mean ... what? She was sure she'd been taught something, once upon a time, that suggested just what the Emperor was planning, but she couldn't recall what she'd learnt. The Peerless School had only taught them the warning signs, nothing actually useful ...

The Emperor walked through the darkened corridors, ignoring the soldiers who saluted – banging their fists against their chests – and the slaves who prostrated themselves in front of him until he had walked past them. Charity followed, wondering absently what would happen to a child who grew up with everyone automatically bending the knee to him. It had been hard enough dealing with Jamal ... but then, whatever his faults, Jamal had been a powerful magician. What would happen to a child who was raised to practically expect worship and yet lacked the power to make it happen?

She pushed the thought aside as the Emperor led the way into the ritual chamber and looked around, sighing with heavy satisfaction. A large containment circle had been drawn on the ground, surrounding a complicated network of lines, runes and carefully-placed crystals; the edge of the circle was surrounded by smaller circles, each one large enough to take a small child. Charity was no expert, but judging by the lines, the children were expected to voluntarily offer their power to the man in the centre of the ritual.

The Emperor turned to face her. "Do you recognise the runes?"

"Some of them, Your Majesty," Charity said. She'd been taught a few Runes of Protection, back at the Peerless School, and a dozen of them had been drawn around the circle. "But others are new to me."

"The Peerless School has buried entire fields of knowledge," the Emperor said, as he produced a silver knife and looked down at it contemplatively. "Our ancestors knew secrets that are completely unknown today, save for the books stored in the Black Vault."

"Our ancestors also fought endless wars," Charity said. "Over magic ... and power ... and who had the right to learn and use both."

The Emperor looked up at her. For a long moment, she was uneasily convinced that someone else was peering out through his eyes. "And do you believe those questions are immaterial?"

Charity swallowed. Her mouth was suddenly dry.

"I don't think we should be killing ourselves over them," she said. Sweat was trickling down the back of her neck. "The wars did nothing but render a quarter of the world uninhabitable for centuries."

The Emperor closed his eyes. When he opened them, he looked himself again.

"The Peerless School saw fit to bury secrets, rather than allow the strongest to survive," he said. "But the secrets came out, as secrets have a way of doing, and I will use them to cement my rule."

He turned and peered towards the door, just as the first of the children entered the chamber and stumbled towards the circle, escorted by one of the serving girls. She was drugged, Charity was sure, or under a spell, for she just kept moving forward without even hesitating when she saw the ritual.

Children *were* taught some of the warning signs, after all, and the circle itself should have set off alarm bells in her mind. Behind her, the other children appeared, led to the ritual like lambs to the slaughter. Charity wanted to shout at them, to tell them to run, but her lips refused to open. She could do nothing to prevent the Emperor from going ahead with his spell.

"A child is completely helpless before a normal compulsion spell," the Emperor observed, "although even short-term usage on a child's mind can cause all sorts of long-term problems for the brat. But the magic can also interfere with the ritual, which makes it inconvenient to use any such spells."

"I suppose they wouldn't offer themselves willingly," Charity sniped.

Surprisingly, the Emperor took it in good humour. "Of course not," he said. "So we drugged them with something purely mundane. There will be no interference with the ritual from compulsion spells."

He smirked, then gave her a long considering look. "You are to stand over there and watch calmly," he ordered. "Whatever happens, you are not to move from that spot until I give you leave."

"Yes, Your Majesty," Charity said, defeated.

She walked into the corner and turned to face the ritual circle, wishing she could close her eyes. The red-robed magicians had appeared out of nowhere and were marking the outer edge of the circle with blood, sealing in the magic. But the Emperor's orders wouldn't let her do anything but watch helplessly. The children looked sweet and innocent as they waited, dressed in white robes that glittered in the candlelight. Maybe they weren't as innocent as they looked, but it hardly mattered. Compared to the sins of adulthood, childhood was an innocent time.

"We begin," the Emperor said, as he stepped into the circle and walked to the centre, careful not to step on any of the lines or runes. "Let us commence the ritual."

The red-robed magicians started to chant, rapping out words in a harsh-sounding language that echoed with magic. Charity shivered as she felt the magic – cold, unfamiliar magic – drifting into existence, shimmering around the chamber. The chanting grew louder, including a handful of names she knew to belong to long-forgotten gods. Light flared around the circle, brilliant blue-white light, while shadows built up at the edge of the room. And ... *something* started to manifest in the chamber, as if it were slowly imprinting itself into the human world.

She should be panicking, she knew, but the Emperor's orders had cast an inhuman calm over her as she watched. The chanting reached a crescendo, then stopped; silence hit like a thunderbolt, broken only by faint sounds of breathing from the magicians. Charity watched, helplessly, as the shadows grew stronger, as faint *things* moved in the darkness. If it hadn't been for the light of the ritual, she was suddenly sure, they would all be dead by now. There was something out there, just watching them ...

"This is our time," the Emperor said. She wasn't sure if he was speaking in the standard tongue for her benefit or for the children, but it hardly mattered. "The wheel has spun once and we are now free to walk the world once again. And soon, he who is gone will return."

Magic surged around him, then the crystals lit up with blinding light. Charity half-covered her eyes as the light grew brighter, then she heard the children start to scream. The drug, whatever it was, had been cancelled by the spell. She stared as the children withered away in front of her, their bodies collapsing into dust. Magic pooled around them, then snapped away as soon as their bodies were completely gone. The crystals flared one final time, then faded to a dull white glow.

"They come," the Emperor shouted. "They come!"

Charity saw ... *something* form out of the darkness, then vanish before she could get a proper look at it. Another followed and another, until there was a whole stream of ... *things* appearing out of the shadows. Some seemed tiny, barely larger than a cat or dog; some appeared so vast that the entire chamber seemed unable to hold them. She had to remind herself, as she tried to get a better look, that creatures of pure magic might not be comprehensible to human eyes. There was something about them that made it impossible to get more than a vague impression of their shape and form, if indeed they had either. The entities were so completely inhuman that, in comparison, werewolves and vampires were practically human.

There was a final flare of light, so bright that she had to cover her eyes despite the Emperor's orders, then the room plunged into darkness. No, she realised slowly; the candles were still burning. And yet, the room felt dark. She blinked, several times, then rubbed her eyes until tears started to form. The ritual had finally come to an end.

She looked towards the centre of the circle and stared. The Emperor was lying on the ground, his red outfit torn to shreds. For a long moment, she thought – prayed – that the forces he'd been manipulating had killed him ... and then he slowly, casually, rose to his feet and looked around. Charity had to fight back a gasp. His face was covered in tiny scratches, each of which had drawn blood. His bare muscular legs were also scratched, so deeply that blood was trickling down his skin and pooling on the floor. The gods alone knew what it would do when it interacted with the remaining magic in the chamber.

The Emperor muttered something, too tired to be loud. There was a flicker of magic, then the scratches healed and his blood vanished. Charity hoped he'd lost enough to make him ill, or careless, but as he made his way out of the circle a young girl appeared, carrying a gourd of potion. A blood potion, she guessed, as the Emperor took it and drank in one smooth motion, then handed the gourd back to the slave. If he'd practiced such rituals before, a long way from the Inquisition, he would have known to take precautions against accidentally hurting himself.

"Take the dust," the Emperor said, to his sorcerers. "Place it in storage for later use."

Charity felt sick. Only the vilest of arts used human remains; she'd been told, years ago, that anyone trying to practice such arts had to be stopped as quickly as possible. But the Emperor *was* the highest authority in the land, while the Inquisitors were his slaves. Who could stop him? Certainly not a foolish girl who had managed to swear unwavering obedience before considering *all* of the possible consequences. With each passing day, death, or forced enslavement, or even permanent transfiguration seemed a far better option.

The Emperor walked over to her, holding his head high. "You will accompany me," he said. "Come."

Charity bowed her head, realising – for the first time – just how rapidly the air had cleared after the ritual. The sense of ... *presence* had faded, although she still had the jumpy sensation she was being watched. She glanced around, noting how the sorcerers were taking both the dust and the glowing crystals from the circle, then followed the Emperor through a side door and into a hidden passageway that led up a long flight of narrow stairs, all the way to the Emperor's private quarters. The Emperor sagged as soon as the hidden entrance was sealed, stumbling on suddenly weak legs. Charity remembered the first time Jamal had drunk too much and – somehow – managed to keep her mouth closed. The Emperor would not have wanted to show weakness in front of his subordinates.

"Help me into a chair," the Emperor ordered. "And then fetch water."

"Yes, Your Majesty," Charity said. The Emperor had a whole *collection* of chairs, some of them worth more than an alchemist's takings for a year. Charity picked one that looked sturdy, then helped the Emperor to sit down. "Please stay still. I'll find you some water."

The Emperor's bathroom was larger than her entire apartment back home, she discovered, as she looked inside. Powerful wards and protective charms stirred uneasily as she looked around, then took a glass of water from the sink. It would be safe to drink, she was sure, thanks to the magic running through the room. Nothing remotely dangerous would be allowed to enter without the Emperor's specific permission. She carried the glass back to the Emperor, then helped him to drink it. Up close, she was far too aware of a faintly-unpleasant smell surrounding him.

"You're a good nursemaid," the Emperor said. "I chose well."

Charity flushed, angrily. "I'm only doing what seems right," she said. She briefly considered poison, but the wards would stop her if she somehow managed to break her oaths and survive. "I don't know many healing charms."

"They shouldn't be necessary," the Emperor assured her. He leant forward, resting his powerful hands in his lap. "Using the knife, cut off my jacket and leave it lying on the floor."

"Yes, Your Majesty," Charity said. She didn't want to do it, but she had no choice. "Hold still, please."

The Emperor snorted as she cut away his jacket, then stared down at his chest. There were scratches everywhere ... and, under a chest of grey hair, a series of nasty scars that didn't seem to have healed properly. Compared to the glossy black hair on his head, it was a striking sight. She had to fight to conceal a sudden bout of amusement; did Vlad Deferens, the ultimate macho man, dye his hair?

She sobered as she studied the sight. There were blood clots on his chest that didn't seem to have been removed by the spell he'd used in the chamber, something that struck her as odd, while some of the scars looked to have been made by creatures rather than by human swords or spells. She hesitated, then walked back to the bathroom to get a cloth and a bucket of warm water, which she carried back to his side. And then, carefully, she started to wipe the blood away from his body.

"You would definitely make a good nurse," the Emperor said, snidely. "Such a gentle touch. You must have practiced."

Charity coloured. There were few rules concerning how magicians could have relationships with other magicians – or even mundanes – as long as they were discreet and careful. Her father wouldn't have been too pleased if she had managed to get pregnant, or had the entire city branding her a slut. Indeed, apart from a handful of kisses she'd exchanged with a boyfriend during her final year at the Peerless School, she hadn't been intimate with anyone until now. Wiping the blood away from the Emperor's body was the closest she'd been to a near-naked man.

She looked down at him, silently measuring his looks. A handful of girls would probably consider his rugged features to be attractive, although she knew enough about his politics to know better than to willingly form a relationship with him. Maybe he was vain enough to dye his hair, but there was nothing fake about the muscles on his arms and legs. She'd thought her father was strong, yet the Emperor was unquestionably stronger. It was rare for a magician to put so much effort into developing his muscles.

"Magic is one form of strength," the Emperor said, as if he'd read her mind. "Muscles, knowledge, discipline ... a cool head in a crisis ... they are all alternate forms of strength, young lady. You can go quite some distance merely by keeping your head when everyone else is panicking."

"Yes, Your Majesty," Charity said. She took a breath. "How old are you? Really?"

"Thirty-three," the Emperor said.

Charity wasn't sure if she believed him or not. She was no expert, but her father had been in his fifties and *he* barely had the first hints of grey hair in his temple. Maybe *he'd* been dyeing it too, or using a glamour to hide the first signs of old age. And yet ... if someone had spent half of their life experimenting with dangerous or forbidden magics, maybe it would give them grey hair ahead of time too. It wasn't something she had been encouraged to explore at the Peerless School.

"I see," she said. "And why do you develop your muscles so well?"

The Emperor snorted. "Didn't I tell you that life in my homeland is a constant struggle for supremacy?" he asked. "What sort of fool would I be if I drained my magic, without something else to fall back on?"

Charity considered it. She had never really thought about fighting without magic ... or done more than practice duelling, at the Peerless School. But she could see some advantages to being physically strong as well as skilled in magic. The opponent might not have thought to ward himself against a punch to the face.

"Thank you for your touch," the Emperor said. He pushed himself to his feet, then walked unsteadily towards the bedroom. "I will sleep until I wake. You will go to the Throne Room and handle all business, in my absence, aside from that which touches on the ritual. If any of the sorcerers ask to see me, you will tell them to wait unless it is truly urgent."

"Yes, Your Majesty," Charity said. She sighed under her breath – she would need an energy potion to remain awake, although at least she would be spared nightmares – but she rose to do as she was told. "How long will you sleep?"

"As long as necessary," the Emperor said. "You will have sole charge of the city, in my absence. Don't do anything that might make it harder for me to regain control."

"I couldn't, anyway," Charity said, unable to keep the bitterness from her voice. "I have to serve you."

"You made your choices," the Emperor said, coolly. "You have only yourself to blame."

Chapter Twenty-Six

It hadn't been a pleasant night. Johan had thought he was used to Elaine's presence in his head, but he hadn't really tasted a proper apprenticeship bond. Strange dreams tormented him; some erotic, yet horrific; others nightmarish, yet strangely attractive. By the time he finally gave up on sleep as a lost cause and stumbled into the shower, he felt a curious mixture of refreshed and utterly exhausted. Offhand, he couldn't recall any of the apprentices he'd read about having the same problem.

But they were partnered with men, he thought. *Or women, if they happened to be women.*

He shuddered as he stared at his face in the mirror, feeling oddly as though he were looking at a stranger. It felt almost as though he should be looking at a feminine face, framed by long brown hair. Elaine's face. Was that normal, he asked himself, or had they managed to mess up the bond still further? He dressed quickly, then walked down to the dining room, where Elaine, Daria and Cass were seated around the table. None of them looked as if they had had very much sleep.

"Something happened last night," Elaine said, by way of greeting. "Something bad."

"Black magic," Cass said. "I think the whole city could feel it."

Johan frowned. "Was that why I couldn't sleep last night?"

"Probably," Cass said. "Even people with a tiny sensitivity to magic, no real gift to speak of, would have felt *something*. I dare say the whole city will be on edge."

"More than before, you mean," Daria said, dryly. "I mean ... we're only occupied by a few million soldiers and a bunch of strange magicians."

Elaine snorted, rudely. "I think most people will try to get on with their own lives," she said, "because it doesn't really make much difference to them if we have an Emperor or not. But black magic ...? The entire city is going to be worried."

Johan met her eyes. "What did he do?"

"Something big," Elaine said. "I think he sacrificed the children. There are rituals that could boost his power, or do all sorts of other things, if he offered magical children in return."

"Shit," Johan said.

He shivered at the thought. Magicians were ruthless, he knew; his father certainly hadn't shirked from doing whatever was necessary to expand his power base. And Jamal ... Johan had always thought his father was simply too indulgent towards his eldest son, but it was quite possible that his father had seen it as training for the day Jamal took over as the head of the family. A softie wouldn't last long in the dog-eat-dog world of the Great Houses, let alone in the endless struggle for power in the Golden City. Indeed, it was a surprise that his father hadn't arranged an accident for Johan himself. No one would have questioned his word if his son had accidentally cut his own head off while shaving.

Elaine gave him a sympathetic look. It struck him, suddenly, that she had to be feeling the same way too, only worse. He, at least, was used to having her at the back of his mind; she had to be struggling to control her own reactions, having no time to rest and meditate. And the black magic hadn't made things easier. Perhaps she was so tired because she had had no real chance to sleep.

"Whatever he did is immaterial," Cass said, into the silence. "The important issue remains getting out of the city."

Daria scowled at her. "And how do you plan to do that, oh great and powerful Inquisitor?"

Cass scowled back. Johan felt a flicker of tired amusement that, he realised in shock, came from Elaine. She was ... *amused* ... by the verbal bickering? It surprised him, until he realised that Elaine liked and trusted both of the other girls. And, deep inside, she didn't expect either of them to betray him. He couldn't help feeling envious at the thought; she might have grown up in a hellish orphanage, but she had friends. *He'd* never had anyone he could trust until he'd met

Elaine.

"I don't know," Cass said. "The tunnels are heavily guarded, both by the soldiers and sorcerers. Should we try to break through one, the guards will be on us like flies on shit."

Elaine leant forward. "How are people getting in and out of the city?"

"People are walking in as normal," Cass said. "But no one is being allowed out of the city."

Johan thought about it as he poured himself a cup of tannin. It tasted foul – everything seemed to taste foul, as if there were something unpleasant hanging in the air – but it helped jerk him awake. The Golden City produced nothing, apart from orders from the Imperial Palace and magical artefacts, put together by the alchemists and enchanters. Everything the city would need to eat or drink had to be brought in through the tunnels, which meant ... he tried to work out how much food the city would need, each day, and gave up in annoyance. It didn't seem likely the blockade could be maintained for long before food prices started to rise.

He frowned. "Wouldn't we starve sooner rather than later if they're not letting anyone out of the city?"

"Eventually," Cass said. "The city has thousands of tons of food delivered each day. Some of it gets preserved, just in case of a transport shortage, but most of it is eaten within the first few days. I don't know what will happen once people start to starve ..."

"Riots," Daria said. "The city's population will have nothing left to lose, if they're faced with starvation."

"I thought there was an emergency food supply," Elaine said, in surprise. "Something we could use to save the city if necessary."

"They earmarked most of it for the Conference," Cass said. "I have a feeling they didn't really *plan* on having the tunnels barricaded while the Court Wizards are here."

"They must be worried stiff," Daria observed. "Elaine, do you know any of them? Personally?"

Elaine shook her head. "Most of them wouldn't have come to the city for years," she said, dryly. "They'd know Miss Prim as the Head Librarian, if they bothered to take note of whoever was in that post. The only person I know from outside the city is Bee" – Johan flushed as he sensed a wash of emotions shadowing her words – "and I don't think he would accompany the Court Wizard."

Daria's lips quirked. "Not even to see you again?"

"He took one look at my eyes and fled," Elaine growled. There was something in her voice that made Johan want to kill Bee, wherever he was. The bastard had hurt Elaine! "I don't think he will ever show himself in the city again."

"Probably not," Daria agreed. "I think you should have spent more time building up your power base."

Elaine lowered her eyes. Johan tasted her emotions and felt a flicker of sympathy. Elaine didn't have the cutthroat determination to succeed that his father had developed, nor did she have the bloody-minded unpleasantness of Jamal that could sometimes pass for determination. It didn't strike him as a weakness to enjoy books more than the company of other people, but it had rendered Elaine largely ineffective as a power in the city. Perhaps, the cynical side of his mind wondered, Light Spinner had counted on it. Elaine would cast a vote in the Privy Council and not much else, rather than trying to undermine the Grand Sorceress or position herself for the inevitable struggle when the Grand Sorceress passed on.

"I think it wouldn't have mattered in any case," Cass said, briskly. She tapped the table with one pale hand. "The real question is just how we get out of the city."

Johan looked from Elaine to Daria and realised they were both out of ideas. Short of climbing the mountains, there was no way out that wasn't heavily guarded. Perhaps, with his magic, they could punch their way through one of the barricades, but the tunnels would simply be collapsed on top of them ... or they would be intercepted as they left the tunnels at the far end. And there was no way they could sneak through the tunnels either. If no one was being allowed to leave, there was no point in trying to forge papers or use glamours to get past the guards.

"Perhaps we should try to escape over the mountains," Daria mused.

"Perhaps you should swallow molten silver," Cass snapped. "It would be quicker and more amusing."

Johan looked down at his hands. Something was nagging at the back of his mind, something so obvious he should have seen it at once. And yet it wasn't coming into view.

"We could try to convince him we were dead," Elaine said, hesitatingly. "There are spells to fake our deaths."

"You'd be trying to fool Inquisitors," Cass pointed out. "We've had people trying to fake their deaths before, you know. Even had someone who took a long-term poison to escape prison. It didn't work."

"I could force-grow blood," Elaine said. "With some effort, we could make it look like a teleport spell that went badly wrong."

"They'd know that no one in their right mind would *try* a teleport spell," Cass said. "I would be suspicious, if I had been asked to investigate, and Dread would be even more so. He knows you."

"I thought we agreed we were trapped," Elaine said. "We might be desperate enough to try."

Johan cleared his throat. "Perhaps we're approaching this from the wrong angle," he said, slowly. The vague idea at the back of his mind had finally come into the light. "There are other ways to look at the world."

Elaine turned to look at him, encouragingly. "What do you have in mind?"

"Ask the Levellers," Johan said, simply. "There isn't anyone else with experience in thwarting the Inquisitors without magic."

Cass barked off a laugh. "Are you joking?"

"I'm quite serious," Johan said. "They're still intact, despite having magicians searching for their heads. Even the Inquisition hasn't managed to destroy them."

"They were never considered a serious threat," Cass sneered. "What's the point of claiming that ... that I am equal to a fishwife from Tyre, when I can snap my fingers and turn that fishwife into a haddock? Or my adoring slave? No one was really concerned about them, save for a handful of weak magicians who lacked confidence in their own powers."

"Then they exist under the range of any scanning spells," Johan said. "I *was* without magic, Inquisitor. It doesn't make you helpless."

"You were *practically* helpless," Cass said. "Or did you believe that you could one day use your mind to kill your family?"

"Even the greatest of magicians can become careless and eat a poisoned meal," Johan pointed out, sweetly. There had been times when he'd seriously considered dropping something nasty into Jamal's food and watching him die. The wards might have saved his life ... or they might not. "And even a flea can be dangerous, if it happened to bite the right place."

"Or merely distract the wizard from looking in the right direction," Daria said. "It seems like the best idea we have, Blondie."

Cass shook her head. "Do you think we could rely on them to help us?"

"I think we don't have any better ideas," Elaine said. "There's no one else in the Golden City who might have an interest in helping us. The Great Houses gave up hostages to the Emperor ... and even if they are prepared to let those hostages die, they might not want to face the Inquisitors and the small army of sorcerers Deferens brought with him."

She shrugged. "The other option is waiting here until the Emperor gets tired of blockading the city and gives up."

"Or the searchers start poking through this part of the city instead," Daria said. "They'll know we're not in the poorer parts of the city soon enough, if they don't already."

"I dare say the crime lords will have done their best to convince the searchers that we're not there," Cass mused, reluctantly. "You can't rely on anyone these days."

"How true," Elaine agreed, dryly.

Johan picked up a flicker of amusement from her and smiled back. She was pretty, really, prettier than he'd ever realised ... or was that the bond, pushing them together? Elaine lacked the rough-edged attractiveness of Daria, or the glowing blonde hair that enshrouded Cass's face, but she was still attractive. Or was the feeling caused by the bond? There was no way to know.

"We do have another problem," Cass said. "The children."

"Leave them here," Johan said. Cold hatred boiled at the back of his mind, mixed with a certain kind of shame. A brother should not hate his younger sisters so much he wished for their deaths. "Wipe their memories and abandon them. They'll be fine."

Elaine reached out and squeezed his hand. "They can't stay here indefinitely," she said, flatly. "Charity will be back soon, just to check they're fine."

"Probably," Johan conceded, reluctantly. So far, Charity *hadn't* come ... had she known the servants had fled? Stupid question, he told himself; of course she knew. "Perhaps we could send them back to the Peerless School."

"And then they'd tell everyone about us," Cass said. "I'd prefer not to use memory-altering spells on young children, if it can be avoided."

"You wouldn't show so much consideration if the children were mundanes," Johan pointed out, snidely. "Who *cares* if a mundane shows up with memory loss? Or mental problems caused by losing part of his mind?"

Elaine cleared her throat. "We can take the children to Lady Lakeside," she said. "I think she would take care of them, if asked."

"And what," Cass asked, "is to stop Lady Lakeside from telling the Emperor that we gave her the children?"

"I could threaten her," Johan said, reluctantly. "Let her know that I will take her magic, if she tells the Emperor anything."

"The children can tell her that they walked to her house," Elaine said. "We can use a simple spell to make sure they stick to that story, no matter what she does. They'd know the truth, of course, but they wouldn't be able to tell."

"I suppose," Cass said, reluctantly.

Johan felt his stomach growl. He rose, then stalked through to the kitchen and hunted for bacon and eggs. The preservation spells were starting to flicker, something that bothered him more than he cared to admit. Had he damaged them when he'd attacked the house – had it really been only a week ago? – or had Charity not managed to take them over properly after their father had been rendered powerless? He retrieved the bacon carefully, eyed it sharply, then decided it was probably safe to eat. Placing it on the pan, he lit a match and started to cook.

"That smells divine," Daria said, as she stepped into the kitchen. "Do you need any help?"

"Just get the last of the bread out of the breadbox," Johan said. "I thought you were arguing with Cass."

"We hashed out a plan," Daria said. She opened the breadbox, then pulled out the bread and dropped it on a plate. "Are you making enough for all of us?"

"I'm cooking the last of the food," Johan said. "Elaine would probably be furious if I refused to feed the brats, wouldn't she?"

"I wouldn't get her angry," Daria agreed. "You do realise she still has problems with darkness? I recall she used to use a nightlight when she was in the Peerless School. The little bitches used to make fun of her for not embracing the shadows."

It took Johan a moment to realise what she meant. "And to think I thought my father was bad," he muttered. "But I would have happily traded places."

"So would she, I think," Daria said. She gave him a reproving look. "And while the children might have been brats to you, they remain children."

"I know," Johan muttered. He eyed the frying pan, doubtfully. There were only twelve strips of bacon left in the house, as far as he'd been able to tell. Charity hadn't thought about replenishing their food supplies since becoming the house's mistress. "I think we would have enough for one plate each, but there won't be seconds."

He cracked open the first egg, then let it drop into the pan and watched as it started to fry. "Is it wrong of me to dwell so much on the past?"

Daria shrugged. "Werewolves – born werewolves – grow up in a pack," she said. "I can't say there was anything particularly bad about my childhood, save for discovering that we were often feared and hated by particularly stupid people. But then, they did have problems with made werewolves, so it was quite hard to blame them."

Johan cracked the second egg. "Really?"

"My parents were strict, but fair," Daria added. "Your parents, from what you say, played favourites, while Elaine grew up without parents. Both of you are pretty screwed up by your experiences.”

“Maybe I should just ask to be bitten,” Johan muttered. He scraped the eggs out of the pan and dropped them on a plate, then added bread and bacon. “I could join the packs and ...”

“And lose much of your connection to human civilisation,” Daria said, sharply. “There’s always a price tag.”

“Always,” Johan echoed. “But isn’t that always the case?”

He shoved the plate at her. “Take this to the brats, then come down; I should have your eggs and bacon ready by then. Unless they turn you into something, of course.”

“I think Cass had a few words with them,” Daria said. “They’ll behave themselves.”

Johan shrugged, but held his tongue.

Chapter Twenty-Seven

Elaine eyed herself doubtfully in the mirror, then cast the spell. Her hair turned black, her face paled and her shirt and trousers became a long black dress, matching her dark eyes, but slit down the side to expose her long legs. After a moment, her breasts grew out, straining against her dress.

"Oh, very sweet," Cass said, clapping her hands. "I like it!"

"I look awful," Elaine said. "This ... *this* ... is what passes for fashion in the Golden City these days?"

"The Secret Grand Masters of Fashion decree it to be so," Cass said. "This style only came in a week or so ago."

"These Secret Grand Masters are all men, aren't they?" Elaine asked. She looked down at the glamour, then shook her head in bitter amusement. "And is it wise to be walking around wearing this when the city is occupied by women-hating soldiers?"

"As long as I am with you, it should be safe," Cass said, briskly. "I'm disguised as a Great Lady, after all."

Elaine sighed, then carefully anchored the glamour in place. It had taken her half an hour to craft the spell, ensuring that any sorcerer who happened to check the glamour would conclude that it was nothing more than a cosmetic spell designed to make her eyes look inhumanly large and dark. No one should look at it and be able to tell that it was actually a full-body disguise, at least not without cancelling the spell completely. And if that happened, she would have more problems to worry about than her appearance.

She checked the spell one final time, then strode out of the door and into the living room and placed her hands on her hips. Daria snickered, rudely; Johan stared, then looked away, clearly embarrassed. Elaine tasted the confusing mix of emotions running through his mind and shivered, inwardly. Johan knew she was using a glamour to hide her face, that there was nothing real in the glamour at all, and yet he was still attracted to it. She kept her own expression under tight control as she placed a similar although masculine glamour on him, then Daria. No one would be able to recognise either of them under the spell.

"Just remember you're my bratty teenage children," Cass said, as she entered the room. Her appearance had changed too; her hair was still blonde, but her face was clearly older and wiser ... and gave off a very definite impression, to Elaine's eyes, that she was definitely not someone to mess with. "But do try to behave yourselves."

Elaine shivered as she looked away. Cass reminded her, far too much, of some of the aristocratic or wealthy women who would come to the orphanage, looking – shopping – for children to take home. They'd all had the same air of arrogance, of knowing that their money could get them whatever they wanted, whenever they wanted it. She knew, now, that most of them had little real power, but it didn't make the memories any easier to bear. If one of them had chosen her, she could have grown up somewhere – anywhere – other than the orphanage.

"I'll be a terrible brat," Daria said. She reached out and elbowed Elaine, then grinned at her mischievously. "Mum! My sister just elbowed me!"

"Do that in public and everyone will laugh at you," Cass said, darkly. "And we really don't want people paying too much attention to us."

She turned, then motioned for the three children to enter the room. The girls looked nervous, understandably so. Elaine drew her wand, carefully ran through the spell in her head, then cast it before any of the children could object. Their eyes glazed over, for a long moment, then returned to normal. None of them looked happy, but it was hard to feel sorry for them after her nightmares. She'd seen far too much of how Johan had been treated as a child.

And what would you have been like, she asked herself guiltily, *if you had had your magic when you were a young child?*

"Gather round, children," Cass ordered. "Stay behind me,

don't call attention to yourselves and don't talk to anyone, unless addressed first. Refer any questions you might get to me. Do not try to lie unless pushed – and then stick only to the basics. Don't give them anything they can use to hang you."

Elaine had to fight to conceal her amusement. Cass knew a great deal about being lied to – and she'd given them a long lecture on how best to conceal the truth. It was best, she'd explained, to stick to a simple story ... and to say nothing more than the bare minimum, when asked a question. The more someone said, she'd warned, the easier it was for an outsider to pick the story apart, piece by piece. One flaw would be enough to tear the whole edifice of lies apart, revealing the truth.

Cass gave the children a long look, then nodded to Jolie. The oldest girl unfurled a note and passed it to Cass, who read it quickly and then placed it on the table. It would tell Charity where to find her siblings, when – if – she came home. Elaine had never had sisters, as far as she knew, but she was surprised that Charity hadn't shown more concern for her younger siblings. Maybe the oaths Deferens had made her swear had forced her to put him before everything else ...

Or maybe she's scared of attracting his attention to the girls, she thought, as Cass opened the door. *Deferens would not treat them very kindly.*

She pushed the thought aside as she stepped out into the open air. It was bitterly cold, with a faint stench of bad magic – very bad magic – hanging in the air. There was no point in trying to cast a spell to ward it off, she knew; the stench was so pervasive that even mundanes could probably sense it. Snow lay on the ground, making her smile; in the distance, she could see children throwing snowballs at one another, laughing and cheering despite the shadow that had fallen over the city. They were probably wealthy or magical children, she decided; their parents wouldn't be afraid of a few soldiers. Even Deferens would think twice before making enemies of every magician in the city.

"It's cold," Johan muttered. He wrapped his arms around himself and shivered. "Can you use a heating spell?"

"Done," Elaine said, casting the charm. "Did you ever play in the snow as a child?"

"Not here," Johan said. "And I stopped when Jamal started enchanting snowmen to chase us around the house."

Elaine shook her head, then looked at the houses as Cass led them down the street. They were made of stone, quarried from the mountains, but would they stand up to the cold when the snow fell deeper and deeper? Or what about the poorer houses in the city? Could the families who lived there afford to warm themselves? She had a sudden mental vision of the entire city buried beneath the snow, if only because it didn't seem to be melting very quickly, if at all. They might wake up one day and discover they were trapped under the snow.

"We were planning to start bringing in emergency supplies," she muttered. "But I don't think Deferens will give a damn."

"Probably not," Johan agreed. He would have seen her memories of Deferens, even if he'd never met the man face-to-face. "What did you have in mind?"

A handful of older boys, all in their late teens, ran past, a couple wolf-whistling at Elaine and Daria. Cass lifted her wand and fired a handful of itching curses after them, while Daria snorted and Elaine blushed. It was the first time in her life anyone had ever wolf-whistled at her, even though it was just a glamour. But at least it proved that the glamour was working.

They stopped outside House Lakeside and inspected it, for a long moment. The building was old enough to date back to the first Grand Sorcerer, warded with enough protections to stave off the wardcrafters for several days. It definitely looked inhabited, Elaine decided, although she wasn't entirely sure. In hindsight, perhaps it *had* been a mistake not to build up a power base of her own. She could have met Lady Lakeside socially, perhaps even made a genuine friendship. But she'd been too shy and intimidated to try.

"Good luck, brats," Johan growled.

Elaine elbowed him, sharply, as the children ran up the steps, triggering the wards that would alert the occupants that they had guests. Cass led them all out of sight, then waited;

moments later, Elaine heard the door open and a brief snatch of conversation, mercifully incoherent at her distance. The door closed; Cass walked back to check, then returned to tell them that the girls were safe. Lady Lakeside wouldn't mistreat them, not when they were too young to be anything other than chips in the eternal game of power. Besides, with Charity at the Emperor's right hand, it would be dangerous. It was far more likely that Lady Lakeside would return them to their sister, then claim a favour in return.

Johan strode onwards, his thoughts dark and contemplative. Elaine wondered, absently, if something was wrong with all three of the older Conidian children. Jamal had been a bullying bastard – she knew the type all too well – while both Johan and Charity showed a striking lack of concern for their younger siblings. Johan, at least, was understandable; he'd been mistreated, to the point where it would be hard to blame him for not wanting to have anything to do with them. But Charity ... she must have sworn oaths that put her new master ahead of her family. It was the only explanation that made sense.

Unless she's interested in nothing more than power, Elaine thought. *That makes sense too.*

The streets began to get more crowded as they walked back towards the Peerless School, although she couldn't help noticing that most of the people on the streets were either men or heavily-escorted women. There were almost no young girls at all, save for a handful of five or six-year-old children, wearing male clothes. Elaine winced inwardly, then said a silent prayer that the soldiers never realised the children were actually girls. The wearing of men's clothes by women was utterly forbidden in their homeland. It tipped the natural order of the world upside down.

Or so they say, Elaine thought. *And how much of that owes something to the Witch-King?*

She slowed as they entered the market street, then frowned as she saw the lines of people gathered in front of the handful of opened stalls. It looked like a budding riot was well underway, she thought, as she heard a handful of men shouting at the stall-keeper. The man, it seemed, had taken advantage of the food shortage to jack up his prices, charging easily two or three times the standard price for everything from eggs to fresh fruit and vegetables. Cass led them past the stall hastily, then past a line of closed stalls, still covered in snow. Behind her, she heard the sounds of a fight breaking out. She glanced back, just in time to see the stall-keeper knocked to the ground, blood staining the snow where he fell. His assailants ravaged the stall of everything edible, then marched off, dividing it up amongst themselves as they left.

"The shortage of food will only make tempers flare," Cass said, quietly. "And they say civilisation is only one or two missed meals from collapse."

Elaine shuddered. It had been bad enough going hungry at the orphanage – but it would be worse, she was sure, if she had a husband and children to feed. If she hadn't had magic, she knew, she would have been kicked out of the orphanage at sixteen, perhaps with a useful skill like sewing or knitting. Maybe she would have married, maybe she would have had children ... only to be forced to watch them starve, as the first snowfall in centuries drifted over the Golden City. How long would it have been before she started thinking about stealing, just to feed her brood?

"Come on," Cass said. "We don't want to be here when the soldiers arrive."

She led them down a side-street, past a bookstore that was also under siege. This time, the crowd wanted books. Elaine stared in disbelief, then realised, to her horror, that they were planning to *burn* the books to keep themselves warm. The thought was utterly horrific; thankfully, the shopkeeper was a magician and had used wards to keep his merchandise safe from harm. Elaine breathed a silent sigh of relief, then followed Cass out of the end of the alleyway and into the next street. It was almost deserted, which puzzled her until she saw the soldiers approaching. She heard Cass mutter a curse, just loudly enough to be heard. It was too late to duck back into the alleyway to escape.

"Papers," the lead soldier said, curtly. His subordinates didn't bother to hide the fact they were staring at Elaine and Daria. "Papers, now."

Cass drew herself up to her full height, magic sparkling

around her eyes. "Are you daring to suggest, young man, that I, a granddaughter of the Great Bartholomew, should show *you* my papers?"

She continued before the soldier could say a word. "My family has produced five Grand Sorcerers and over a hundred magicians, warlocks and alchemists who have gone down in history," she thundered. "The Emperor will be hearing of this, you may be sure. My great niece, his *personal* assistant, will take the word to him *personally*. You, a man of no birth and no magic, daring to ask *me* for my papers? The very thought!"

Elaine blinked. Cass was related to Johan? Or was she lying?

"And to think that your ill-brought-up young men should stare at my granddaughters," Cass stormed. "What cheek to think that they might have a hope of marrying into *my* family! What impudence to think that such stares will not go unpunished! What foolishness to endure the risk of spending the rest of one's life crouching on a lily pad, snapping at flies, for a brief gaze at an unattainable beauty! What ..."

"I beg your pardon, Great Lady," the soldier said. "We all humbly beg your pardon."

Elaine thought, for a moment, that he was being sarcastic. But he bowed low, then led the soldiers – their gazes locked firmly away from the girls – down the street, leaving them behind. Johan snickered, then managed to turn it into a cough, as Cass motioned for them to start walking in the opposite direction.

"I cannot believe that worked," Daria said, eying Cass with new respect. "Do you think he actually believed you?"

"I didn't actually lie to him," Cass said. She shrugged. "And I thought you would know all about Alpha Bitches."

"I don't understand," Elaine said, before Daria could come up with a crushing insult. "How did that work?"

Cass smirked. "I've known far too many men like him," she said, simply. "If you show them a hint of weakness, they will take it as an invitation and you'll find yourself pressed against the wall or bent over the table. They pride themselves on seeing weakness and exploiting it. But if you show them strength and firmness, they will genuflect to you instead.

"And besides, Deferens isn't a complete idiot. He wouldn't have picked men for his invasion force who are likely to provoke the Great Houses into starting an uprising against him."

Elaine looked back at the soldiers, then followed Cass as she made her way down the street and round the corner, into a line of pubs. Half of them were closed; the remainder were guarded by men carrying clubs, who glared ominously at passers-by. A handful of sorcerers stood at one end of the street, ignoring everyone. Elaine eyed them suspiciously, wondering just what they were doing. Keeping an eye on the area, for the Emperor, or laying a trap for someone? Would the Emperor have guessed where they might go?

"In here," Cass said, as they reached the Waving Wand. "And remember not to cast any offensive spells in this building."

"I've been here," Johan said. "I know the rules."

Inside, it was warm, thanks to a roaring fire in the grate. A handful of men sat around the fire, drinking beer and muttering to one another; in the corner, a pair of students from the Peerless School were sharing a large glass of wine, looking around nervously for either proctors or tutors. They were playing truant, Elaine guessed, savouring the spice of having escaped the school while it was under lockdown. She hoped their families were powerful enough to keep them from being expelled – or used as a sacrifice – if they were caught. It was harder to get into the school than out of it.

"Johan Conidian," the bartender said, as he looked at Johan. "I was told you were dead."

Elaine stared at him. "You can see through the glamour?"

"I can see many things," the bartender said. "What can I do for you?"

Cass cleared her throat. "We want to meet with Hawke," she said. "Can you arrange it?"

"He has rooms nearby," the bartender said. "I will send for him, if you are prepared to pay."

"We will," Cass said. "Two gold coins?"

"Ten," the bartender said. They haggled back and forth until they settled on five. "Take a seat in the booth and order drinks. I will send him a message. If he comes or not is up to him."

"Understood," Cass said. She led the way over to the booth, then sat down. "We can wait."

"And see," Elaine muttered. "And if this goes wrong ..."

"We will have to think of something else," Cass said. "But I honestly don't know what."

Chapter Twenty-Eight

"I need to see the Emperor," Lord Regan said. "At once."

Charity sucked in her breath. Lord Regan was an overweight man with a receding hairline, who couldn't be bothered to use a charm to freshen the air around him. Merely looking at him made her feel sick. Charity, who had known his daughter while she'd been at school, disliked him on sight. The girl had been a spoilt brat, she'd thought, but she'd clearly been doing very well, given what sort of father she had.

"The Emperor is currently resting," she said, pasting a sweet smile on her face. "May I ask why you wish to speak with him?"

"My daughter's marriage contract has been finalised," Lord Regan said. "The Emperor needs to stamp his approval over the match before we can proceed."

"I see," Charity said. She had a feeling that Lord Regan was trying to pull a fast one. There was no legal obligation for a marriage contract to require the Emperor's approval – although, she had to admit, it had been so long since there had *been* an Emperor that it was possible there *was* such an obligation and everyone had forgotten it. "The Emperor will handle the matter once he wakes and deals with more immediate problems."

"This is important," Lord Regan insisted. "The Emperor must sign the contract!"

"Why?" Charity asked. "May *I* see the contract?"

Lord Regan hesitated, then pulled a long scroll of parchment from his robes and passed it to her. Charity took the scroll, opened it up and read it, carefully. It was the most one-sided marriage contract she'd seen since the one her father had tried to organise for Johan, when he had thought his son could be bribed back into the family. Lord Regan might be giving away his daughter, a girl Charity's age, but he was claiming most of the assets from her would-be husband's family. It puzzled her for a long moment – there was no logical reason for the contract to require the Emperor's blessing – until she realised that the other parties might want to bow out. But if the Emperor had blessed the contract, bowing out might be considered treasonous.

Poor girl, Charity thought. She hadn't *liked* Donne Regan very much, but there was no need to shackle the young girl to a man twice her age, just so her father could get richer. *What did she do to deserve this*?

"I'm afraid the Emperor will consider it a low priority," she said, picking up her notebook. "I can offer you an appointment in five days, at sunset ... but it might have to be cancelled on short notice. The Emperor is a very busy man."

Lord Regan glared at her. "Now, *listen here*," he snapped. "I am a very important man ..."

"And you're not as important as the Emperor," Charity said, cutting him off. Spiting him was fun ... and besides, she was sure she was right. "I can book you an appointment at the specified time or not, as you choose. There is no legal obligation to get his blessing, so you can just proceed with the marriage now, if you wish."

And Donne will have her chance to flee, Charity thought, as Lord Regan clenched his fists threateningly. The contract was notable for lacking his daughter's signature. No doubt her father planned to trick her into signing it. *At least she will have a chance to escape.*

"The Emperor will hear of this," Lord Regan said. He turned and stamped out of the room, pausing just before he stepped out of the door. "This is a disgrace! A member of a respected Great House denied access to the Emperor! A disgrace!"

Charity watched him go, then sat back in her chair and giggled. A respected Great House? Everyone knew that House Regan was short on money, trained magicians and common sense ... and that Lord Regan had a habit of spending money like water. Even the most optimistic bankers had long since stopped loaning him anything, knowing that he would never be able to repay his debts. If his home hadn't been legally secured, he would probably have lost that by now too.

A thought occurred to her and she smirked, then reached for a sheet of paper and began to scribble a note. If Donne had any sense, she would stay somewhere well away from House Regan, even though she was Lord Regan's only child. *Charity* wouldn't have felt safe anywhere near him and *she'd* grown up with brothers and sisters. She wrote out a brief warning about the marriage contract, then placed it in an envelope and muttered a spell over it. Only Donne would be able to read it. And, if she wanted to escape, she could vanish before her father badgered her into signing the contract.

Poor girl, she thought, again. *But at least she has a chance.*

Shaking her head, she returned to the colossal pile of paperwork and cursed under her breath. She hadn't realised just how many papers were placed in front of her father every day, let alone the Grand Sorceress. It seemed like there wasn't a single bureaucrat in the building who could make a decision without having the Emperor sign a piece of paper ... she rolled her eyes, wondering if it was a form of passive resistance, then started to read through the papers one by one. Her father had drummed it into her head, time and time again, that she should never sign something until she had read it. Who knew *what* sort of magic would be worked into the paper?

She was still reading paperwork when a shadow fell over her.

"Good morning, Lady Conidian," Dread said. She started – a man that old shouldn't be able to sneak up on her – then looked at him. "I trust you had a pleasant evening?"

"No, I didn't," Charity snarled. "And I haven't slept a wink either."

It was such a stupid question that, as her brain caught up with her words, she realised that it had been designed to elicit an unthinking response. Of *course* Dread would have known that *something* very bad had happened. The entire city knew. She'd had several people asking to see the Emperor, each one making subtle and not so subtle enquires as to what had actually taken place. She was pretty sure the rumours were already bad and growing worse ... if the snow hadn't started to fall again, the Great Houses might be having private meetings to discuss taking steps. But what could they do?

"I'm sorry," she said, softly. "I'm just exhausted."

"I wouldn't drink *too* much of that stuff," Dread said, eying the bottle on her desk. "It always catches up with you, in the end."

Charity nodded. "I feel tired already," she said. The energy potion had done its work, but the more she took, the weaker the effects. "But the Emperor won't let me leave."

Dread leant forward. "What happened last night?"

"I can't tell you," Charity said. Not because the Emperor had issued specific orders, but because her oaths told her that betraying the Emperor was a very bad idea. Maybe there would be no harm done, if she told the truth, yet she wasn't *sure*. "I really can't say a word."

"Something bad," Dread said. His grey eyes were watching her closely, as a master brewer might scrutinise a slowly-bubbling potion. "Something involving children. A *summoning*, perhaps, or a *channelling*. Or both."

He already knew, Charity realised. Not everything, but enough.

"He killed them all," she said, feeling tears dripping down her face. "Turned their bodies to dust as ... as *things* came out of the shadows. He killed them all."

She buried her head in her hands and wept, bitterly. It was her fault, no matter how much she tried to tell herself otherwise. She'd taken the children from the school, she'd brought them to the Imperial Palace and she'd given them to a madman. And the Emperor had used them, killed them, for a dark rite she didn't even *begin* to understand.

"Stop him," she pleaded. Her oaths tightened around her, cutting off her words. It was suddenly very hard to speak. "Please."

"I can't," Dread said. "The oaths won't let me stop him."

Charity forced herself to calm down, with an effort. "Why?"

"The oaths were designed to ensure the Inquisitors could never turn on their master," Dread said. His voice was flat, too flat. "We are not allowed to remove him, no matter what he does. Our oaths forbid it. The person who holds the power may do as he pleases."

"No," Charity said. "Why ...?"

But she already knew the answer. The Emperors and the Grand Sorcerers wouldn't have wanted to allow any limits to their power. Maybe they hadn't wanted to use any form of dark magic, but they had known they might need to use it in the future. And so they'd crafted themselves a loophole, a statement that anything they did was legal by definition. The Emperor could sacrifice the entire city to the dark gods and the Inquisitors couldn't do anything to stop him.

"I'm sorry," she said, although she wasn't sure if she was talking to Dread or the murdered children. "I'm so sorry."

She found herself trying to think of ways to escape, with or without her powers, but nothing came to mind. Even suicide was forbidden ... as was anything that might lead to her death, even if she didn't specifically *intend* to die. She couldn't even walk up to one of the darker champion duellists and call him a filthy name, knowing he would hex her into the next world. It would be considered a form of suicide ...

"I know," Dread said. His face, as always, was impassive. "I'm sorry too."

Charity forced herself to wipe her eyes, then look at the scrolls he was carrying under his arm. "What are those?"

"Maps," Dread said. "He plans to deal with a problem the Grand Sorceress saw fit to put off, in the hopes it would resolve itself. He's going to invade Ida."

"I've never heard of it," Charity said. It was part of the Empire, she assumed, but there were hundreds of little kingdoms within the Empire. "Is it important?"

"There was an outbreak of dark magic there, six months ago," Dread said. "I dare say the Emperor doesn't want competition."

Charity laughed, bitterly. "I dare say he doesn't," she said. "It might make life difficult."

She looked up as one of the slave girls entered the room and prostrated herself in front of Dread. Charity looked at the girl's bottom, sticking up in the air, and wondered if she looked as big an idiot when she prostrated herself before the

Emperor ... and, if she did, just how the observers had resisted the temptation to kick her. But, even in full submission, the girls were stunningly beautiful. They reminded her of the girls in school who used glamours, but hadn't realised that making themselves look too pretty only made them seem uncanny. And yet, they were real. There wasn't a hint of magic surrounding any of them.

"Rise," Dread ordered, in clear irritation. "Speak your message."

"Most Noble Inquisitor," the girl said, as she sat back on her haunches, "the Emperor has awakened and desires your presence. And yours, Lady Charity."

"Then we shall attend upon him," Dread said, gravely. "Take us to him."

The serving girl bowed low, exposing the tops of her breasts, then turned and sashayed off, swinging her hips in time to a beat only she could hear. Charity felt instantly jealous, then looked at Dread and realised he wasn't impressed. Most of the men who saw the girls fell in lust instantly, but Dread wasn't affected. Perhaps it was true, part of her mind noted, that Inquisitors were *fixed*. They had nothing to distract them from their duty.

They walked through the long corridor and into the Emperor's morning room, which didn't seem to be part of the complex she'd seen the previous night. The Emperor himself was sitting at a table, eating breakfast; Charity gritted her teeth as her body automatically fell into yet another prostration. Beside her, Dread merely nodded, holding his hands behind his back.

"Rise," the Emperor ordered. "What news do you bring me?"

"I have reviewed the plans for Ida that were drawn up in the wake of the attack on the Golden City," Dread said. "They called for additional regiments of troops and at least a dozen Inquisitors, none of which could be spared. The Grand Sorceress, therefore, decided to leave the kingdom under Queen Sacharissa, in the hopes she could root out the dark influence within her realm."

The Emperor snorted. "And she *trusted* this Queen?"

"There was no reason to suspect Sacharissa of anything

other than an unfortunate choice of parents," Dread said. "The Inquisition kept a careful eye on Ida and concluded there was no reason to worry, now King Hildebrand and Prince Hilarion are both dead."

"I remember Hilarion," the Emperor said. His lip curved with disgust. "He thought he could become Grand Sorcerer, did he not? And now he is dead?"

"Yes, Your Majesty," Dread said. "The entire family is dead, save for Sacharissa."

The Emperor tittered. "She will have to choose her consort carefully," he said. "Or maybe I will choose one for her, should Ida be free of dark magic."

He looked up at Dread. "How quickly could the invasion be launched?"

Dread didn't hesitate. "We would need at least two weeks to get troops into position, then assault up the mountains, if we didn't manage to trick the Queen into just letting us get our troops right into the city. I assume, if she knew we had bad intentions, we would have to force our way into the capital or lay siege to the city until the population starts to starve. But if she is using dark magic, that estimate may be very badly wrong."

"It would be possible, I suppose," the Emperor said. He sounded oddly irked by what Dread had said, although Charity couldn't see why. "How quickly could we overwhelm the city?"

"It would depend on too many factors," Dread said. "If the Queen happened to be alert, we would have to fight our way up the mountainside, which would be hideously costly. Ida is a small state, but its geography means that even a tiny handful of defenders can put up a real fight. I think we might be looking at several weeks, at the very least; months, if they have defences lined up, ready and waiting for us. It could go very badly."

"Then we will need more troops," the Emperor said. He looked at Charity. "How are we proceeding with recruitment?"

Charity blinked, tiredly. That was one of *her* responsibilities?

"We have started to recruit hundreds of young men," she

said, remembering what had been written on a piece of paper in the vast pile. The Emperor, perhaps wisely, had turned recruiting duties over to a bunch of officers from his homeland. "But there is little enthusiasm for joining the army among mundanes, sire. They are ... concerned that there is no honour in serving in the ranks."

The Emperor spat. "What a spineless bunch of ninnies inhabit the Golden City," he sneered. "Small wonder that the last five Grand Sorcerers all came from outside the city limits."

He didn't mention Light Spinner, Charity noted. But she rather doubted he counted the petrified woman as anything other than a bump in the road to success.

Or maybe he thinks she proves his point, she thought, morbidly. *She was born in the Golden City, after all.*

"You will start conscripting from second sons, if they will not come voluntarily," the Emperor ordered. "Once the barricades are lifted, it will be time to start moving my armies to Ida."

Dread cleared his throat. "Your Majesty," he said. "There are other problems that deserve your attention."

"Ida can serve as a demonstration of both my power and my will," the Emperor said. "The destruction of the state will break all those who question my right to the throne."

Charity scowled, inwardly. If she'd never heard of Ida before now, it was unlikely to be as important as any of the larger kingdoms. Destroying Ida might serve as a warning from the Emperor, without risking the already-fragile united economy. Or maybe the Emperor was just acting out of spite. If Prince Hilarion had truly opposed the Emperor, before he'd taken the throne, destroying his homeland could be seen as delayed revenge. Petty and pointless, but perfectly understandable. Hilarion had broken more than a few taboos when he'd stepped up and put his hat in the ring.

"As you command, Your Majesty," Dread said.

"I will start conscripting," Charity said. She'd have to tell the recruiting officers to do it, she knew. "But I ..."

She yawned, suddenly, and staggered as her legs suddenly threatened to give out.

"Go take a nap," the Emperor said, as if he'd given her a

great boon. His voice turned sickly-sweet. "Dread can handle the recruiting sergeants, can't you?"

Dread didn't look best pleased, but he nodded.

"Thank you, Your Majesty," Charity said, as she yawned again. She wasn't blind to the smirk on his face, or the certainty that he was being kind to someone he considered little better than a pet dog. "I ..."

She yawned. This time, she thought she saw something vast and horrific leaning over the Emperor, something that didn't seem to quite come into focus. A spider's web, perhaps, or something stranger. She blinked ...

... And it was gone.

"Go rest," the Emperor said. "Now."

Charity obeyed, thinking hard. What *was* that thing? Something real, something the Emperor had summoned, or something else? Dread clearly hadn't seen anything ... or, if he had, he hadn't said a word.

And, when she finally reached her rooms and fell asleep, her sleep was plagued by nightmares.

Chapter Twenty-Nine

"This is a waste of time," Cass grumbled, after twenty minutes had passed. "We're out here, exposed and helpless ..."

"Wait," Daria urged. "The Levellers wouldn't show themselves so openly."

Johan shrugged, keeping his thoughts to himself. Hawke had approached him ... but that had been before his supposed death. Now, Hawke thought Johan was dead, while two of his companions were a Privy Councillor – assuming that Deferens hadn't already fired Elaine – and a former Inquisitor. He didn't blame Hawke for being careful, not when his entire organisation was at stake. Deferens was unlikely to live and let live when he felt his power was being challenged.

The waiter came up to them, carrying a tray of drinks. Johan looked up – the waiter looked utterly unremarkable – and took his drink, then frowned as he saw a flicker of amusement on the waiter's face. There was no glamour, no attempt to magically hide his features, yet he was sure the man was wearing a disguise. The waiter placed the last two mugs on the table, then smiled at them.

Johan took a gamble. "Hawke?"

"Johan," Hawke said. "The boss has organised the back room for you and your friends. If you would like to come with me ...?"

Johan exchanged glances with Elaine, then picked up his mug of hot chocolate and rose, following Hawke through a back door and up a cramped flight of stairs. The compartment smelt unpleasant, a mixture of beer, urine and something he didn't want to identify, but somehow he managed to breathe through his mouth until they reached the top floor. A woman – barely older than himself – stood outside a wooden door, smoking. The outfit she wore left absolutely nothing to the imagination. Hawke nodded to her and she stepped to one side, allowing them to pass. Inside, it was a simple business room, complete with table, chairs and a small drinks cabinet. If it hadn't been for the aroma, and the mundane candles hanging from the walls, it could have passed for one of his father's meeting rooms.

"Well," Daria said. She sounded edgy. If the room smelt bad to him, Johan realised, it had to be far worse for a werewolf. "I never knew this was here."

"This pub is neutral ground," Cass pointed out. "Having a place for people to meet runs with the territory."

"You're very welcome," Hawke said, putting the tray down on the table. "I should warn you that this place has a strict no fighting policy. Unless you want to take a round or two in the pit downstairs. It's quite spectacular and people will bet on you."

"Bare knuckle fighting isn't my thing," Cass said. "And I doubt this place could handle a wizard duel."

"It couldn't," Hawke confirmed. "But most magicians who come here don't want to fight. They want to get drunk, to feel they're doing something naughty, and then spend the rest of the night with a whore."

Johan sensed Elaine's embarrassment at Hawke's words. He couldn't help feeling a little embarrassed too, as well as amused. Was that what Jamal had been doing when he'd been away at the Peerless School? Maybe there was something to be said for not going to the school, after all. But then, he would have happily worked at the Waving Wand if it had meant getting out of the house for a few hours.

"Please, sit," Hawke said. He sat down at the end of the table, shedding the last fragments of the waiter persona, and gave Johan a friendly smile. "I thought you were dead?"

"The reports of my death were a little inaccurate," Johan said, as he sat down. "It was decided, by various people, that the city would be happier if it had a report of my death, so one was written and distributed. I thought they could have exaggerated the report a little, maybe come up with an exciting story, but no one would have believed it."

Hawke smiled, again. "And you're here now," he said. His eyes suddenly sharpened. "Why?"

Cass stood behind her chair and leant on it, as if she was unwilling to sit down. "Why a waiter?"

"A waiter hears much and sees all," Hawke said, dryly. "And no one ever pays attention to the staff."

He was right, Johan knew. His family certainly hadn't paid much attention, at least until the staff had taken advantage of his father's ... indisposition to flee. Jamal had always been more interested in using the maids for sexual pleasure, rather than regarding them as living beings in their own right. Johan wondered, suddenly, what Jamal might have told the maids while they were sharing his bed, then dismissed the thought. It was impossible to imagine Jamal knowing anything useful that he could babble to his unwilling partner.

"Point," Cass said. "But what about loyalty spells?"

"Not here," Hawke said. He rested his hands on the table in front of him, then smiled. "And then, I don't always work as a waiter."

"True," Cass said. "I should have recognised you from the start."

Elaine cleared her throat. "Why ...?"

Hawke rose and gave her a sweeping bow. "Robert Hawke, at your service," he said. "You may have heard of me."

Johan felt Elaine's astonishment. "You're a merchant!"

"And as powerless as a Powerless," Hawke said. He sat down, his eyes hooded. "And what could I do if some magician decides he wants my property – or my wife and daughters?"

"So you joined the Levellers," Cass said, softly. "Why?"

"He had cause," Johan said, quietly. Hawke's daughter had been cursed by a magician, one of Jamal's friends. Johan had broken the spell ... had that really only been ten days ago? It felt like years. "Believe me, he had cause."

"Very well," Cass said. "What's happening out there?"

"Nothing good," Hawke said. "Homes are being ransacked, hostages are being taken, daughters have been ravished, a handful of people have been enslaved for daring to protest ... and soldiers are being recruited for the Emperor's armies. I believe they will even start to conscript young men soon enough, as they haven't had many volunteers."

Johan blinked. "Why not?"

"Few people would willingly join the army," Cass said. "It would be one thing if you got to stand around in a fancy uniform all day, but most soldiers either find themselves chasing bandits or serving as targets for mad magicians. There's just no one to fight."

"There might be," Elaine said, quietly. "Not everyone in the Empire is going to be happy about having an Emperor again."

"Yes," Daria agreed. "The events of the last six months weakened the Grand Sorcerer's grip on power. There are quite a few kingdoms that might declare independence if they thought they could get away with it. Deferens would have to fight a long civil war to put the Empire back together or accept a sundering of his power."

"He wouldn't," Elaine said. "He's the kind of person who wants it all."

"Worse than that," Cass said. "He was raised in a society where endless competition is the order of the day. To beat someone is to claim all they owned, from wives and children to goods and obligations. He won't allow a state to declare independence; he'll just see it as another challenge to his power. Civil war will result."

"Unless the revolts come right up to the mountains," Daria pointed out. "The Golden City can't beat the rest of the world on its own, can it?"

"Maybe," Cass said. "We still don't know what Deferens was *doing* last night."

"I was hoping you could shed some light on it," Hawke said. "Our best guess is that he killed a great many people."

"Children," Elaine said. "But we don't know why."

"All that matters is that he has to be stopped before things fall apart completely," Cass said, firmly. "He has to be stopped."

"True, true," Hawke said. His eyes moved from face to face. "In short, things are going to the nine hells. And, with that in mind, what can I do for you?"

Elaine shook her head. "How could things have fallen apart so quickly?"

Cass snorted, rudely. "The Empire was never based on anything but the iron fist in the iron glove," she said. "It was built on the strong oppressing the weak. The thin veneer of decency you saw was all there was to it."

"We need to flee the city," Elaine said. "Can you show us how to escape?"

"The tunnels are heavily guarded," Hawke said, slowly. "And while bribery might work, some of the soldiers are spellbound. Try to bribe one of those and they'll cut off your balls."

Johan winced. His father had once said that everyone had a price ... but someone who was spellbound couldn't be bribed, or pushed into doing something against the interests of his masters. And there would be no way to know who was spellbound and who wasn't until it was far too late.

"Then we need a distraction," Cass said. "Something that will get them away from the tunnels."

"There are fewer guards on the Iron Dragon tunnels," Hawke pointed out. "If they happened to be reduced still further, you could probably get out that way."

Elaine scowled. "I don't know how to operate an Iron Dragon," she said. "Do you?"

"Yes, as it happens," Hawke said. "But why don't you just walk?"

"Oh," Elaine said.

Johan felt her embarrassment and cringed, mentally. The Iron Dragons might be out of commission, but the tunnels were ... well, tunnels. There was nothing to stop them from just walking through, unless they happened to encounter an Iron Dragon coming the opposite way. He'd read an article in the broadsheets about a handful of kids stupid enough to do just that, a year ago. They'd been smashed to paste, of course. No one had really given a damn.

"We would still need a diversion," Cass said, tightly. "Even if they're not used to thinking of the Iron Dragon tunnels as a way to leave the city, they will still have them guarded."

"I think I can give you one," Hawke said. He reached into his pocket and produced a green crystal, which he dropped firmly on the table. "But I would need your oaths, first."

Cass's eyes narrowed. "Mundanes are forbidden to use those," she snapped.

Hawke looked at her, evenly. "And are you going to arrest me for possessing an oathbinder?"

"I should," Cass said. "Those things can be very dangerous."

"I need your oaths that you will not betray my confidence," Hawke said, firmly. "This oathbinder is preset. What we speak of in this room, past this point, will be unspeakable in public, at least until I tell you otherwise."

"You have some magicians on your side," Daria said, as Cass picked up the oathbinder and examined it, carefully. "Don't you?"

Hawke nodded. Johan felt a strange mixture of emotions from Elaine; shock, perhaps, that a magician would betray his own kind, then a grim realisation that she might have done the same thing, if she'd been a different person. She was barely magical enough to go to the Peerless School ... and if she'd been forced to work as a low-power magician instead, she would probably have resented the stronger magicians as much as Hawke did. And she might have aided his plans instead of reporting them.

"I have a question," Johan said. "What's to stop Deferens trying to force the information out of us anyway?"

"It would have the Great Houses rising up against him," Elaine said, quietly. "Oaths are the foundations of our society. To force someone to break one's oath would outrage every magician with half a brain. They'd all see their own oaths at stake."

"And crossing that line would mean no going back," Cass added. She put the crystal down on the table, then sat down and nodded. "We won't speak your words to anyone outside the group."

Hawke nodded and tapped the crystal. There was a flash of green light, which faded so rapidly Johan wasn't sure if it had been real or if he'd imagined it. He felt magic shimmer around him for a second, then fade away. Elaine coughed, then looked at the crystal thoughtfully. It was now cracked and broken.

"Shoddy work," Cass commented.

"There's a shortage of carved crystals just now," Hawke said. "The Emperor has been buying up every box he can find. Prices have been going through the roof and past the mountain peaks."

"That bad, huh?" Daria asked. "What do you want to tell us?"

Hawke leant forward, his eyes darting from face to face. "We're planning an uprising," he said. "But it was always chancy."

Cass spluttered. "You must be joking!"

"I'm not," Hawke said, quietly. "The ... problems we faced six months ago convinced many of us that we could no longer endure our lives in the Empire. We started to plan for something more than just pointless protests."

"You'll be slaughtered," Cass said, flatly. "One wave of my hand and you would be my obedient slave! You couldn't hope to get close enough to me to kill me with a sword before I killed you, or transfigured you, or enslaved you, or merely knocked you into a wall. This plan is madness."

"There are ways around your spells," Hawke said.

"None of which would last long enough to save you from an entire city of magicians," Cass said. She rose to her feet. "This is a waste of time."

"Sit down," Hawke snapped, with sudden authority. "How much magic is in the Iron Dragons?"

Elaine frowned. "None," she said. "They're purely mechanical."

"Quite," Hawke said. "You understand, of course, the problems with using magic for everything?"

"You need a magician to make it work," Elaine said.

"Exactly," Hawke said. "In fact, given the tales of great feats performed by magicians in the past, it is actually possible that magic is leeching out of the world. Where are the teleport gates, or the flying castles, or the great beasts that once darkened our skies. Is the magic fading or are our magicians merely forgetting what they could do?"

"Interesting point," Elaine said. Johan had the sense she wasn't being quite honest. "But most of those stories grew in the telling."

Hawke shrugged. "Regardless, there are people who were

looking at ways to do things without magic," he said. "The Iron Dragons are one such example. They may be crude, they may be dependent on iron rails, but they need no magic. And ... well, once they had one success, they just kept looking for more. You should see some of the wonders we created in our workshops."

"Wonders?" Cass sneered. "I could use magic to make an Iron Dragon."

"But would it work without draining your magic?" Hawke asked. He reached into his pocket and produced a small vial of grey powder. "Is there any magic in this substance?"

Elaine took the vial, ran her wand over it, then shook her head.

"One of the problems with potions is that they need a magician to make them work," Hawke said, as he took back the vial and stood. "You need to use your magic to force the magic inherent in the ingredients to actually blend together. That's problematic if you don't have any magic. So people started looking at ways to get potions without using magic, drawing on natural ingredients. Eventually, they discovered this."

He placed a metal tray on the table, then poured a little powder on the tray and then placed a tiny piece of paper beside it. "Watch carefully," he said, as he took one of the candles from the wall and carried it back to the table. "This is always interesting."

Johan watched, puzzled, as he used the candle to light the piece of paper. The flames spread rapidly towards the grey powder and ... the powder exploded. He rubbed his ears as the noise faded away, then stared at the tray. There was a nasty black mark where the powder had been, but the powder itself was gone.

Somehow, he found his voice. "What the hell was that?"

"We call it Firepowder," Hawke said. "I won't tell you how many people were killed or injured in accidents before we finally managed to get a working formula that wasn't dangerously unstable. What I will tell you is that, if emplaced properly, it will make one hell of an explosion."

"And you plan to use it to kill the Emperor," Cass said. "Getting it close to the Imperial Palace will be difficult."

"There are too many guards there," Hawke said. "We've been looking for ways to do it, but we couldn't find one we were sure would work. We were going to use it against the Watchtower instead."

Cass stared at him. "You ..."

She broke off. Johan was sure he knew what she was thinking. The Watchtower was warded against all manner of magical threats, but no one had anticipated a non-magical threat. If the Firepowder was completely devoid of magic, it wouldn't set off any alarms when it crossed the wards. The Levellers could leave their device in plain sight and no one would even notice until it was too late.

"There are quite a few tunnels below the Watchtower," Hawke said. "We've been moving Firepowder there for quite a few months now. And when the Emperor is attending the Conference, we would be able to assassinate him too."

"Maybe," Elaine said, reluctantly.

"There would certainly be chaos," Daria agreed. "We could slip out of the city while everyone was panicking."

"Yeah," Cass said, "but you would need to be damn sure you got rid of the Emperor."

"I know," Hawke said. "That's the chancy aspect."

"Then I'll go with you," Cass decided. "Daria, Elaine and Johan can flee the city."

Chapter Thirty

"So tell me," the Emperor said. "How are you feeling?"

"Wretched," Charity said. She had slept, as he'd told her to sleep, but her sleep had been disturbed by vile nightmares. In the end, she'd given in and downed a potion designed to ensure a peaceful night. It hadn't worked. "I feel like I haven't slept at all."

"You can go to bed at a more reasonable hour tonight," the Emperor said. "Would you like to go to bed at sundown, perhaps?"

Charity felt her cheeks heat. She hadn't had a set bedtime since she'd gone to the Peerless School, where magicians were expected to develop their own discipline. Her father certainly hadn't told her when to go to bed when she'd moved back home. But at least it wasn't an order. She took comfort in that, if nothing else.

"The Conference is due to start tomorrow," the Emperor reminded her. "I want you to make a *personal* inspection of the Arena."

"Yes, Your Majesty," Charity said. Thankfully, most of the preparations had been made before the Emperor had revealed himself. "Is there anything in particular you wish me to do?"

"Take the statue with you," the Emperor said, waving towards the petrified Light Spinner. "I want her in the exact centre of the Arena."

"Yes, Your Majesty," Charity said. "Do you want to gloat?"

"I want to make a show of what happens to all who dare to oppose me," the Emperor said. "Take the statue and go."

Charity lifted her wand, telling herself that at least she would be away from the Emperor for a few hours, then levitated the statue out of the Throne Room. Magic crackled over the stone, a clear indicator that it wasn't a normal statue, but there didn't seem to be any hope of Light Spinner reversing the curse any time soon. Was she even awake and aware in there? Charity hoped she wasn't, even though it would have kept her trapped indefinitely. Being a statue for the rest of her life would be bad enough, but it would be far worse if she knew what had happened and couldn't do anything about it.

"I'm sorry," she muttered, as she lowered the statue to the ground and called for a pair of burly servants. "You deserved better."

The servants appeared and prostrated themselves in front of her. Charity shuddered, then told them to get up and carry the statue down to the Arena. The servants rose, bowed and obeyed, grunting and groaning as they carried the statue out of the palace. Charity hesitated, long enough to feel the weight of her oaths pushing at her, then strode out of the palace herself and paused to take a breath. The air was cold, but the stench of dark magic still hung around the palace, warning everyone that the Emperor had gone mad. Charity wondered why none of the Great Houses had started planning a coup ... but then, they wouldn't have told her, would they? She was Deferens's slave.

Gritting her teeth, she started to walk towards the Arena as snow started to fall. It wasn't the largest building in the city, but it provided seating for over twenty thousand spectators, most of whom came to watch the gladiators bleed out and die on the sands or magicians duelling with their rivals. It was said – untruthfully, she knew – that the spectators were just as much at risk as the duellists, as their spells might be reflected into the audience. Her father, in one of his kinder moods, had pointed out that the audience *liked* the hint of danger. But it wasn't real.

She paused outside the gates, then stepped up and through the ward keeping members of the public out of the building. A small army of slaves, mainly gamblers convicted of trying to cheat their partners, were sweeping snow out of the Arena, while a team of wardcrafters were erecting wards that would divert the snow away from the sands. Someone had cast hundreds of heating spells, she realised, as she walked further into the building. The snow was actually dripping, producing a muddy carpet for the Emperor. She hoped, silently, that they actually managed to clear up the mess before the Emperor arrived. He was not going to be pleased if he saw *that* as his podium.

It wasn't the only problem, she knew. The seats weren't comfortable, nothing more than bare stone; there were charms that could probably help, but there was a marked absence of luxury or anything else that might allow the Court Wizards a chance to show off their power and prestige. On the other hand, she told herself, at least it wouldn't grow into a competition between them. The last time such a conference had been held, the Court Wizards had competed savagely to see who could produce the most tacky displays of luxury. She honestly didn't know why the Grand Sorcerer hadn't put a stop to it.

Probably wanted them to waste their time rather than plotting against him, she thought, as she walked over to the Royal Box. A harassed-looking woman sat there, issuing orders. *It would have kept them busy and he wouldn't have had to lift a finger.*

"Lady Conidian," the woman said, turning to face her. "Welcome to the Arena."

"Thank you," Charity said. Lady Aisling wasn't grovelling before her, which was something of a relief. It had been easier to accept grovelling when she hadn't been forced to grovel herself. "Are we ready for the speech tomorrow?"

"More or less," Lady Aisling said. "We're just sweeping out the snow now, then we'll dry the seats and sands. The Emperor himself will be speaking from a podium in the centre of the Arena, but we'll have to keep that dismantled until just before we open the doors."

"Very good," Charity said. She turned as she saw the two servants enter the Arena. "The Emperor wants ... *that* ... in the middle of the sands."

"I can put it near the Emperor's podium," Lady Aisling said. "But it won't go on the podium itself, unless he wants it to be moved at the last possible moment. The whole thing isn't designed to carry much weight."

Charity frowned. "Can't you use spells to hold it in place?"

"Not without risking some of the other spells," Lady Aisling admitted. "There are quite a few subtle protections built into the podium."

"The Emperor will probably accept it," Charity said. "And what about the tickets?"

Lady Aisling grinned. "Not counting the Court Wizards, who will be coming anyway, we've sold three quarters of the tickets to various people," she said. "Most of them are magicians, but mundane society has requested quite a few too. They want to see the Emperor in all his glory."

"And so they shall," Charity said, with the private thought that they would see more than they wanted to if the Emperor wore his kilt. "Will they all be able to hear?"

"The spells on the Arena take care of that," Lady Aisling said. "Every last grunt or groan – or scream – from the gladiators is captured by the wards and rebroadcast to the watching crowds. I don't think the Emperor's speech will be any different."

"I'm sure it won't," Charity said. "And the food?"

"Being prepared in the canteens now," Lady Aisling said. "Once the speech is concluded, I understand the Emperor and the Court Wizards will return to the Imperial Palace, while everyone else will be fed here. I didn't organise specific food for the Emperor and his guests."

"He's definitely planning to host a dinner at the Imperial Palace," Charity said. There seemed to be a striking lack of preparations, but the Emperor didn't seem inclined – thankfully – to burden her with everything. He'd brought a huge staff into the palace almost as soon as he'd taken over. "The Senior Magicians will be fed there."

"Good," Lady Aisling said. She smiled, weakly. "I don't mind telling you that catering for so many people is quite hard."

She reached out and took Charity's hand, then led her through a set of doors into a grey stone corridor. "And I wanted to ask someone quite senior," she added. "What are *those*?"

Charity followed her pointing finger. A crystal was firmly embedded in the stone wall, glowing faintly with white light. It was one of the crystals from the rite, she realised after a moment of confusion, carried down and placed within the arena by ... whom? But she knew she couldn't answer the question. All she could do was lie.

"They're part of the Emperor's personal security wards," she said. "He prefers to use them rather than the standard precautions."

Lady Aisling snorted. "No one is going to try to assassinate him in the midst of the Arena," she said. "This may not be the Peerless School, young lady, but we have a *lot* of protective wards to prevent the audience from doing anything stupid."

Charity hesitated. "And how often do they try?"

"Every damn day," Lady Aisling said. "I don't see why the Emperor ordered those things brought down here. There's over fifty of them in various places. I don't like it."

"I can take your complaints to the Emperor, if you wish," Charity said. She didn't blame Lady Aisling for being doubtful. Even if she hadn't seen the rite, she would have known that *something* was fishy. "But I don't think he will be inclined to listen. He's not in a good mood right now."

"So I've heard," Lady Aisling said. "I don't suppose you can tell me why, can you?"

Charity shook her head. "I have to inspect the entire building," she said, instead. "Can you show me round?"

It took nearly two hours to cover the entire building, Charity discovered, after poking through each and every room. Most of them were empty – the gladiators had been sent elsewhere for the week – but a handful held sporting gear, weapons and various devices she didn't recognise. A couple held statues of naked men and women, which made her blush in shock; Lady Aisling, when asked, refused to tell her why they were in the Arena, leaving it to Charity's imagination. But none of her ideas made very much sense.

"We're going to be bringing in extra servants tomorrow," Lady Aisling concluded, after they returned to the sands. Light Spinner was now placed on the sands, her twisted face looking shocked. Charity felt another bitter stab of guilt and sympathy, which she clamped down on savagely. There was nothing she could do for the former Grand Sorceress. "But they will all be spellbound."

"Glad to hear it," Charity said, softly. Once, it wouldn't have seemed a hard thing to her; now, she understood just how the spellbound must feel. "And then you will discharge them, afterwards?"

"Of course," Lady Aisling said. "But there is another issue to raise."

Charity turned to face her, then nodded.

"I've been involved in placing the Court Wizards in accommodation," Lady Aisling said. "It wasn't an easy task, because far too many of the Great Houses refused to open their doors."

Charity flushed. House Conidian had few allies among the Court Wizards and she knew better than to invite magicians she didn't trust into her home. Besides, she had been too busy trying to clean up the mess her father and Jamal had left behind to give the matter any thought. It had been too likely that someone would have taken advantage of her if she'd allowed them anywhere near the house.

But in the Golden City, where accommodation was always at a premium, it couldn't have been easy to find places for each and every Court Wizard.

"We did find them all places, eventually," Lady Aisling said. "But the search for the fugitives is turning their arrangements upside down. Please will you speak to the Emperor for us and inform him that the search is causing us considerable problems."

"It isn't just you," Charity said. "And the search has to be carried out until completion."

She shivered. She'd heard a whole series of complaints as she waited for the Emperor to wake up, all from mundanes or very poor magicians. The soldiers had gone through their homes, ransacked their possessions and generally caused trouble. At least one soldier had been turned into a toad for trying to molest a magician's daughter, who had proven perfectly capable of defending herself. But she had a feeling that the Emperor wouldn't be pleased, when he finally heard about it. A girl using magic on a man? Unthinkable!

"The search is causing too many problems," Lady Aisling snapped. "And I need you to impress that on the Emperor. The Court Wizards are getting restless."

Charity rather understood how they felt. First, Light Spinner had ordered them to undertake the journey from their bailiwick to the Golden City, journeys that could be long and arduous in many cases. Then they'd discovered that the city was on edge, the accommodation was very poor and snow was falling for the first time in centuries. And then the Grand Sorceress had been replaced by an Emperor, who was a complete stranger to them. At least Light Spinner had been a known factor.

And they can't even politick because they're trapped inside the houses, she thought. *Or because they don't know where all the pieces are going to fall, since the Grand Sorceress fell.*

"I will bring it to the Emperor's attention," she said. "But there are other concerns here."

"He should be heeding you," Lady Aisling said, sharply. "You are his assistant, are you not?"

"I don't think he takes my opinions seriously," Charity said, fighting down the urge to start crying. She'd seen too much, too quickly, to believe that the Emperor gave a damn about her thoughts and feelings. Everything he did was for his best advantage, not hers. "And all I can do is what I am told."

Lady Aisling took a step forward and peered into Charity's eyes. "He's got you spellbound, hasn't he?" she said. "The Great Houses will crucify him for this."

"You can't tell them," Charity pleaded. "You mustn't tell them!"

"I should," Lady Aisling said. "Or do you want to remain his slave for the rest of your life?"

Charity shook her head. "Don't tell anyone," she said. She had no idea how the Emperor would react when he found out that someone knew what he'd done to her, but she doubted it would be pleasant. "Please."

But it wouldn't stop there, she knew. If it became public knowledge that she was spellbound, her place as House Conidian's mistress would be called into question. Johan was either dead or missing, while Jay and Jolie were both two years below the age of maturity. House Conidian would be leaderless when it needed a leader the most. The other

Great Houses, scenting blood, would converge on the family and rip it apart. And she was sure the Emperor would do nothing to stop it.

"Tell me," Lady Aisling said. "Is that what *you* want or what the *Emperor* wants?"

"Both," Charity said. "I ..."

She forced herself to stand tall. "Have everything completed in time for the speech tomorrow," she ordered. "The Emperor will not be pleased if it has to be cancelled."

"I understand," Lady Aisling said. "And I won't let either of you down."

Charity nodded, then strode out of the Arena and back onto the streets. The snow was falling faster now, making it harder for her to see as she walked into the park. A number of couples were sitting or walking within the foliage, using magic to protect themselves from the cold and snow. She felt a sudden stab of envy as she saw them, wondering if she should have indulged herself more at the Peerless School ... but her exams had always seemed important, even if her father had probably intended to marry her off to someone he chose. No magician would want an ignorant wife.

They're happy, she thought, bitterly. *It's cold, the city is occupied and they're at risk, but they're happy.*

She forced herself to look away, then start walking back towards the palace. The snow seemed to grow stronger for a second as she reached the outer edge of the wards, then stopped altogether as she walked through them. They'd finally finished modifying the wards, she deduced, as she entered the palace itself. The guards, hanging back inside the building, merely nodded as they saw her pass.

"My Lady," an unfamiliar voice called. "I have a message for you."

Charity looked up. A young man – he couldn't be more than fifteen – was standing there, holding a scroll of parchment in one hand and a wand in the other. Charity frowned, then took the parchment and broke the seal on it with a practiced motion. It was from Lady Lakeside, informing her that her younger sisters had moved into House Lakeside until Charity came to collect them.

"Thank you," she said, as she folded the parchment and

stuffed it into a pocket in her dress. "And thank your mistress too."

"I shall," the messenger said. She guessed he was from a cadet branch of the Lakeside Family, close enough to be trusted to run messages, too distant to be granted any real power or influence. "Will there be a reply?"

Charity considered it, then shook her head. The last thing she wanted was the Emperor asking who had sent her a messenger. She didn't know what he would do with her younger siblings, if they fell into his hands, but she didn't want to find out. Instead, she watched the messenger go, then walked further into the palace, pausing only to drop the parchment in the nearest fire. It flickered once, burst into flames and then crumpled into dust.

And may he never ask, Charity prayed, silently. *Because as long as they are safe, there's hope for us yet.*

Chapter Thirty-One

"I wish we were back in our old apartment," Daria said. "This place is the *pits*!"

"You know," Cass said, from where she was sitting. "You sound like a teenager."

"I'm only twenty-three, or thereabouts," Daria said. "I'm not *that* old."

Elaine snorted. It was clear, at least to her, that Daria and Cass liked each other, at least enough to be comfortable bickering like an old married couple. It wasn't romantic, she suspected, given how many men Daria had chased, but it was a form of true friendship, even companionship. She felt a brief stab of envy that she forced to one side. Daria had always found it easier to make friends than Elaine and had always been a social animal, while Elaine ... had preferred the company of her books to other people. But then, books couldn't reject her.

She sighed, then turned her attention back to the paper in front of her. There were spells Cass could use, if she was determined to go ahead with the assassination attempt, and she wanted to get them out on paper before it got too late. She barely heard Daria's announcement that she was going out for some fresh air, or Cass's reminder to stay in wolf form for the entire walk. All that mattered was writing down the spells.

"I know that one," Cass said, after pacing up and down the room like a caged animal. "You don't need to tell me it twice."

Elaine frowned. "Just how many spells on the forbidden list are taught to Inquisitors?"

"More than you want to know," Cass said. She paced away from Elaine, and then back again. "How many spells on the forbidden list are crammed into your head?"

"All of them," Elaine said, flatly. "Unless one or two were deemed too dangerous to write down and died with their creator."

"We should be so lucky," Cass said. "*Everyone* writes down their spells. Tradition."

"Tradition," Elaine echoed, with a sigh. "One that we might want to change."

She paused. "Is there something you want to talk about?"

Cass scowled at her. "What makes you think I want to talk about anything?"

"You're stamping around the room like a wild bull," Elaine said. "What's bothering you?"

"Do you know," Cass said, "just how many plots there are, each year, against the Watchtower?"

"No," Elaine said. "But I can't see there being many."

Cass gave her a wintery smile. "Try thousands," she said. "They range from idiot young sorcerers who think they can climb up the mountains, to dark wizards and outright thieves who want to steal something from us. We've had family members plotting to liberate their relatives from our cells, junior dark wizards looking for our books and idiots who hate us all looking for a little revenge. And most of those plots don't get very far before we stop them, if they even get moving in the first place. After a thousand years, you'd think we'd have plugged all the holes in our defences, wouldn't you?"

"Yes," Elaine said.

"And now there's a great gaping hole in the Watchtower's wards that none of us ever considered," Cass snapped. "We thought we were safe from lunatics with swords, or spears, or even hurling knives. And now the entire building is about to come crashing down!"

Elaine looked down at the table. "Is that a bad thing?"

Cass whirled around to face her. "Would you say the same if someone destroyed the Great Library?"

Elaine flinched back, then caught herself. "A year ago, I would have been horrified at the thought," she said. "Now ... now I'm not so sure."

"How lucky you are to be so certain," Cass sneered. "A year ago, I was an Inquisitor. Now, I'm conspiring against the rightful ruler of the world and plotting the destruction of my former comrades. And my family. I'm guilty of so many crimes that it would be hard for them to decide which one they're going to hang me for, if they don't burn out my brain and put my body in a cheap whorehouse. I don't think *anyone* has ever committed so many crimes in so short a space of time."

"Valiant did," Elaine said, quietly. Very few people knew the truth behind the great hero of the First Necromantic War. "He became the Witch-King."

She stared down at her hands, feeling her heartbeat racing inside her chest. "You can't blame yourself," she said. "What you're doing ... is what you need to do."

Cass glowered at her, then paced over to the bed and sat down on it, hard. "My family wanted me to be like Charity," she said, angrily. "Gorgeously beautiful, without a single brain cell between my ears. I think they had ideas of marrying me off to the Grand Sorcerer or perhaps the Administrator, both men in their nineties. Or someone wealthy and powerful enough to deserve their daughter. They didn't even insist on me studying household charms at the Peerless School. I was bored out of my mind when I heard an Inquisitor speak about the job and I knew what I wanted to do.

"My parents were furious when I changed my major, but by then it was too late. I'd studied everything I could and practiced duelling with the older boys until I could fight with and without a wand. The Inquisitors accepted me for training, which was so hard I nearly quit five or six times before I finally passed through all the hoops. And then I spent a year apprenticed to Dread before I earned the ring. Do you know how many people he's failed since he earned his own ring? Do you know that someone can be denied a chance to retry if a senior fails him? I did not fail! They put me on the streets and I did well.

"And now look what I have to do," she said. "My mentor will kill me, if he gets a chance, while I will either kill the Emperor or die trying. It won't look very good. My parents would disown me if I hadn't already cut all ties to them."

"As part of the price of being an Inquisitor," Elaine recalled. "You never had a boyfriend?"

Cass snorted. "You try telling the boys you're an Inquisitor and see how quickly they jump out of your bed," she said. "The only people who might really understand the job are your comrades and you're not actually allowed to sleep with them. And most of my childhood friends abandoned me when they realised that I was actually planning to *study*."

"I'm sorry," Elaine said, tiredly. "And I wish I could do something to help."

"I know you can't," Cass said. "And I don't blame you for it."

"Thanks," Elaine said, dryly. She paused, then leant forward. "Are you actually related to Johan?"

"Fifth or sixth cousins, I think," Cass said. She smirked. "I was playing an older woman, so I lied about the precise relationship."

She sighed. "Not that it really matters. I broke my family ties a long time before I knew he existed."

"My ties are worse," Elaine said.

"I know," Cass said. "I read your modified file. And that got me thinking. What happened to your mother?"

Elaine frowned. "I don't know," she said. "All I know from the orphanage was that I was left on the step one morning, in a cheap basket. The Orphan Mother never told me anything else, even when I was an adult. I used to wonder ... well, I had all sorts of fantasies about who my parents might have been. But when I found out, I wished I'd just been the daughter of a maid or someone who absolutely could not tell her parents she was pregnant."

"It happens," Cass said. She rolled her eyes. "And to think any alchemist shop would stock a potion to prevent any little mishaps."

"The parents probably don't help," Elaine said. The Orphan Mother's only pieces of advice on growing up and having sex had been rather less than informative. It hadn't been until she'd gone to the Peerless School that she'd understood why she bled each month. "If they don't tell their little darlings the facts of life, they get surprised when their little darlings run into trouble."

"True," Cass agreed. "Would you like to know how many

times I've dragged a bratty teenage child home, only to have the parents insist that it was someone else's fault?"

She sighed. "But really, what happened to your mother?"

"I don't know," Elaine repeated. "Did the Inquisition turn up anything?"

"Nothing," Cass said. "But all we could really do was compare you to the register. If your mother was ever a magician, she never studied at the Peerless School."

"I don't think I want to know who she was," Elaine said. "After my father ... no, I don't think I want to know."

"You might *want* to worry," Cass said. "What happened when your father got his hands on you?"

Elaine shivered. Her father had used their relationship to copy the knowledge from her head into his own, then use it to nearly claim the post of Grand Sorcerer. It wasn't something she cared to think about, not really. Discovering that her father had been a *real* prince – or at least a king's son – had come with a nasty sting in the tail. But Cass was right. There was a very real chance her mother was still alive.

"We know the Witch-King goes in for long plots," Cass said. "You might have a sister or two out there as well. Or a brother. You may have been the only one who threaded the needle and went to the Peerless School."

"I will see what happens when it happens," Elaine said, tiredly. "But ... but I don't want to think about it now."

"I don't blame you," Cass said. She walked over to the bed, then started to undress. "I don't want to think about tomorrow either."

She paused. "When's Johan due back?"

"He's got the next room," Elaine said. "Hawke was going to show him a few things, then bring him back here. I could call him now, if you like."

"Don't bother," Cass said, as she finished undressing. "Just remember to make sure you and he both get plenty of sleep before tomorrow comes."

Elaine nodded. "I will."

***

"Mildred is far better now," Hawke said, as they sat together in a secluded booth. "I thank you."

"You're welcome," Johan said. It was odd, but he felt more comfortable with Hawke than with any of the magicians. "Did you get her out of the city?"

"She and her mother are currently staying somewhere safe, yes," Hawke said. "I understand your brother fled the city."

"He did," Johan confirmed. "Are you planning to go hunting for him?"

"I could," Hawke said. "Should I?"

"No," Johan said. "Having to live without power is punishment enough."

Hawke lifted his eyebrows. "Are you sure of that?"

Johan smiled. "Jamal could wave his hand and everyone would jump to make sure he got whatever he wanted," he said. "Now, no one is going to give a shit about him. If he wants food, he will have to work for it; if he wants a bed, he is going to have to earn enough money to rent it. All his life, he's been using magic to manipulate the world around him. Now, he no longer has any power. I think he will have a whole series of unpleasant surprises until one of them finally breaks and kills him."

"I've heard too much about his antics," Hawke agreed. "You want to place a bet on how he dies?"

"Too many possibilities," Johan said. "All I want is never to see him again."

"Amen," Hawke said. He lifted his glass of beer and took a long swig. "You like this place?"

"The pub?" Johan asked. "It's ... different."

"Where many different worlds meet," Hawke agreed. He nodded towards a cluster of men sitting in the far corner. "Court Wizards, from a handful of kingdoms. They're not sure what's happening here, but they're not planning to leave until they find a way to take advantage of it for themselves. Behind them, the girl sitting there and looking vapid is a sneak for one of the major broadsheets. There will be some interesting headlines in the papers tomorrow."

Johan smirked. "Why don't they just use privacy spells?"

"I think they don't really realise that mundane people have ears," Hawke commented. "The idiots don't take anyone without power seriously."

He nodded towards another table. "They're local

merchants," he added. "They want to keep moving goods out of the city, and bring in raw materials, but the blockade is making it harder for them to earn money. Chances are, the banks will foreclose on their loans soon enough and ... well, they won't be able to put food on the table any longer."

"I know," Johan said. "It isn't easy out here, is it?"

"Your words betray your birth," Hawke said. "It was never easy out here."

Johan took a long breath. "I'm sorry," he said. "I ... I used to want to be out here, riding the Iron Dragons. They were magic enough for me."

"You may get your chance," Hawke said. "The future is never written down."

He sighed, then looked up at Johan. "Have you ever slept with a girl?"

"... No," Johan said, shocked. "Never."

Hawke met his eyes. "Do you want to?"

Johan started to sputter. "You ... you can't just ask like that!"

"Why not?" Hawke asked. "You think you're the only student who comes here hoping to pick up a girl? There are girls there" – he nodded towards a handful standing at the end of the bar – "who would be happy to tend to your needs. There would be no obligation, no long-term consequences ..."

"No babies?" Johan asked. "Or would they consider it a honour to bear a magical child?"

"They would use protection," Hawke said. "Or I could find you a boy, if you were interested ..."

"I like girls," Johan said, quickly. "But ..."

He swallowed, staring at the girls. They looked attractive although, given how few girls he'd seen before he'd left his family, he knew that was meaningless. None of them looked more than a year or two older than him ... he wanted them, he knew he wanted them. And yet, he knew that Elaine would know what he'd done. Would she say anything to him about it? The thought made his face heat in embarrassment. What if she scolded him for enjoying himself when he should be sleeping? Or what if ... she was jealous?

No, he told himself firmly. *That's absurd.*

But was it? They shared an intimate bond. Logically,

there would be some resentment if one or both of them found intimacy elsewhere ... but magic so rarely responded to logic. If he slept with one of the girls, or if she slept with a boy ... what would it do to them?

"They're safe," Hawke said, quietly. "And I owe you more than just a night of pleasure."

"I think it would be better if I didn't", Johan said, softly. Clearly, the risk of ending up in bed together wasn't the only danger posed by the bond. She would experience his strong emotions and vice versa. "But I thank you for the offer."

"It's the least I could do," Hawke said. He reached into his pocket and produced a folded sheet of paper, which he passed to Johan. "There's an address on the front which belongs to one of my business partners, in Knawel Haldane. Take it to him after you leave the city and he will help you on the way. Wherever you're going, I wish you good luck."

"Thank you," Johan said, automatically. "Why are you giving this to me?"

"I trust you more than any born magician," Hawke said. "And one of you has to know where to go."

"Elaine is a good person," Johan said. "I like her ..."

Hawke sighed. "But what has she done, in six months on the council, to keep rogue magicians under control? People like her think of us mundanes as *pets*. They don't consider us real people. Maybe she isn't as powerful as the former Inquisitor up there, but she still has magic and that sets her apart from the common herd. And besides ... your friends were horrified when they saw the Firepowder. You were the only one who saw the possibilities."

"Of using it to level the balance of power," Johan said. Something clicked at the back of his mind. "You had a workshop in the Western Hills, didn't you?"

"It was attacked by a Dark Wizard," Hawke confirmed, "along with most of the city. We didn't know if it was coincidence or something worse."

Johan thought about Jamal and his future – or lack of a future – and nodded. The prospect of Firepowder – and whatever else came out of the fertile minds of researchers – reshaping the balance of power was attractive to him, but he could see why Cass and Elaine would be horrified. Their magic might not give them any advantages in a world where *anyone* could make stuff blow up.

But it will be a long time before they manage to duplicate everything we do with magic, he thought. *A very long time indeed.*

He drained the last of his beer, then rose. "I'll go to bed now, if you don't mind," he said, quietly. "Alone."

"I understand," Hawke said. He rose, taking one last look at the girls as he moved. "And good luck. I doubt we will see each other again past tomorrow."

Johan stuck out a hand. "Good luck to you too," he said. "And good night."

Chapter Thirty-Two

Charity entered the Emperor's dressing room and stopped, dead. The Emperor stood in the centre of the room, stark naked, while a set of naked serving girls washed his body with warm, sweet-smelling water. She hastily looked away, blushing bright red, and then prostrated herself in front of him. The Emperor laughed, then ordered her to rise to her knees, forcing her to watch. Charity wanted to look somewhere – anywhere – else, but the orders were specific.

"I trust that all the preparations have been made," the Emperor said, as the girls washed a *very* intimate spot. "And everything is in place?"

"Yes, Your Majesty," Charity said. "Lady Aisling sent a note in which she confirms that the Arena is ready for your speech."

"How good to know that someone can actually do their job," the Emperor mused. "It's *such* a pleasant change."

Charity kept her face impassive with an effort, but suspected it was a waste of time. Lady Aisling and her family had been charged with operating the Arena since time out of mind, as they were politically neutral, while also not being powerful enough a bloodline to produce a Grand Sorcerer of their own. They knew how to handle everything from the acclamation of the next Grand Sorcerer, to the gladiator or beast fights that kept the plebs amused. It might have been short notice, but they'd definitely been able to prepare the Arena for the Emperor.

"But enough of such sweet thoughts," the Emperor said. He struck a pose as the girls pulled back, allowing her to see everything. "What do you think of me?"

"Very ... masculine," Charity said, embarrassed. She'd never known a magician to show off his body before, even the teenage boys she'd met at the Peerless School. A magician could be short and fat, yet – with enough magic –

he would still have no trouble finding a girlfriend or a wife. "And very wet."

The girls returned, carrying towels. Charity watched, unable to tear her eyes away, as they dried the Emperor, then left him standing in the middle of the room as they reached for his clothes. She'd honestly never heard of someone hiring maids to help them dress, unless they were old and frail or badly injured. The Emperor was certainly fit enough to don his own clothes and yet ... there was something about the whole affair that struck her as almost ritualistic. Piece by piece, the maids placed items of clothing on his body and then withdrew to pick up the next piece of clothing.

"These undergarments are designed for protection," the Emperor informed her. "We wouldn't want anyone harming the family jewels."

He snickered, as if he'd made a funny joke, while Charity stared at him, perplexed. His chuckles grew louder, then sobered as the girls returned with the outer layers. A Grand Sorcerer would wear black and gold robes, but an Emperor, it seemed, wore only gold. By the time the girls were finished, the Emperor was decked out in gold thread from head to toe, covering every last piece of his body below the neck. Even his hands were hidden behind golden gloves.

"Excellent," the Emperor said, as he looked at himself in the mirror. "Do I look impressive?"

"You look blinding," Charity said. "Everyone who looks at you will be very impressed."

"Good," the Emperor said. "Let them be blinded with my magnificence."

He stalked forward, heading for the door. "Follow me," he ordered. "We're going for breakfast."

There was no breakfast provided for her, Charity discovered, as they entered the Emperor's private dining room. She wasn't too surprised, but she *was* a little relieved. The entire city – or at least the politically powerful sections of the city – would be attending the speech and all of them would, she knew, see her as the Emperor's assistant. But would they realise she was his slave? He would probably find it amusing to make her prostrate herself when everyone was watching, even though it would destroy House Conidian.

She said a silent prayer for the children, then forced herself to look around the chamber. Private dining room or not, it was large enough for a small army of diners.

The door swung open, revealing Dread. "Ah, Dread," the Emperor said, wiping his mouth on a golden tissue. "I trust security is in place?"

"No one can enter the Arena without being checked," Dread informed him, stiffly. "I have seen to it personally."

"How good to know," the Emperor said. "And are there any threats?"

"I do not believe so," Dread said. "The Great Houses are still trying to decide what it means to have an Emperor instead of a Grand Sorcerer, while the others pose no threat."

"And what do you think it means," the Emperor said, "to have an Emperor instead of a Grand Sorcerer?"

"More instability," Dread said. "I do not think it means we will have a peaceful future."

Charity's mouth dropped open. She would never have dared say *that* to the Emperor ... but then, Dread's oaths probably didn't prevent him from offering good, if unwanted, advice to his superiors. Indeed, she could see some advantages on *insisting* that the Inquisitors could give good advice. Their oaths already prevented them from becoming a major threat to the Grand Sorcerer – or the Emperor.

The Emperor's eyes narrowed. "And why do you think we won't have a peaceful future under my rule?"

"You have seven sons," Dread said. "Fourteen children, if you count daughters. Which one of your children will inherit the Golden Throne?"

Fourteen children? Charity stared; her father had been older than the Emperor and he'd only ever had seven children. But the Emperor came from a culture where men were permitted multiple wives. It was quite possible that he'd had several wives pregnant at once ... and, given that he was a wealthy man, he could certainly have afforded all the help they'd needed to bring up the children.

"It is a contest, as always, among the heirs of my blood," the Emperor said, darkly.

"Which will plunge the Empire into instability," Dread said. "You have fourteen children who can inherit the

Throne. Each of them will become the centre of a faction dedicated to placing *them* on the Throne while advancing the interests of their supporters. And, as your culture insists on testing strength against strength, the children you don't select as your heirs will attempt to overthrow the one you do. The end result will be civil war throughout the Empire."

The Emperor leant forward, angrily. "Who are you to say such things?"

"I am charged with offering good advice to the monarch, should he or she ask for it," Dread said. There was a very faint hint of amusement in his voice. "You are quite within your rights to refuse to accept it."

For a terrifying moment, Charity was sure the Emperor was about to throw a spell at Dread, or simply order him to kill himself. And then he calmed down, so quickly that she would have suspected a spell if she hadn't been sure his protections would have prevented anyone casting a charm on him. Maybe he'd faked his anger. Her father had once told her that faking anger before one actually became angry wasn't always a bad idea.

"I thank you for your advice," the Emperor said, "but the entire Empire was – is – based on the rule of the strong. Choosing the strongest of my heirs to succeed me will be simple."

"I highly doubt it," Dread said.

"Then leave the issue to me," the Emperor ordered. "We will be at the Arena in two hours from now."

"The crowds will be waiting," Dread said.

"Let them wait," the Emperor said. "Charity?"

"Yes, Your Majesty?"

"Make the arrangements for us to arrive twenty minutes late," the Emperor ordered. "We don't want to arrive *too* early."

Charity was tempted to point out that the Great Houses valued precision and timekeeping, even in minor matters. Her mother and father had often told her off, when she was a little girl, for showing up to meals more than five minutes late. It had helped to prepare her for the Peerless School, she realised in hindsight, but at the time she had screamed and thrown tantrums, like any young girl threatened with going to bed without supper.

But instead she merely nodded. "Yes, Your Majesty."

***

Johan hadn't slept well. Part of him had been dimly aware that the Waving Wand was still buzzing with life, even after the curfew; part of him kept thinking that he should have taken Hawke up on his offer. It was frustrating, immensely so, to know he could have a girl ... and yet know his mistress would *also* know. He couldn't help wondering what would have happened if he'd actually developed a proper relationship with Jayne, if his father hadn't tried to meddle. Would Elaine have felt their kisses and lovemaking through the link?

Of course she would have known what we were doing, he thought, as he pulled himself out of bed and peered out of the grimy window. Dawn was just breaking over the city, greeted by chanted prayers from a hundred temples, but hardly anyone was visible in the street below, apart from a handful of marching patrols. *She would have known what we were feeling, when we were together.*

He shuddered at the thought, then undressed and stepped into the shower. Unlike the magically-powered showers in the Great Library, it was cold and weak; by the time he had washed himself, he was shivering from head to toe. Cursing under his breath, wishing his magic was reliable enough to heat the water for himself, he towelled himself off and dressed again, then took one last look around the room. Somehow, it didn't quite match the descriptions Jamal had given him, back when he'd been bragging about having a different whore each night. Jamal had talked about fancy rooms, where the girls had worn nothing; the room Johan had been given, for himself, was small, dark and smelly. Perhaps he'd gone to a different place ...

Or perhaps he was lying, Johan thought, as he picked up his bag and stepped out of the door, closing it firmly behind him. *He certainly loved to lie through his teeth, every damn day.*

He tapped on Elaine's door, then stepped back sharply as it opened to reveal Daria, wearing absolutely nothing. Johan looked away hastily – the last thing he wanted was for Elaine to realise he was attracted to her best friend – and then stepped into the room. Elaine was dressed, thankfully, wearing a long brown dress that matched her hair. Cass was nowhere to be seen.

"Good morning," Elaine said, from where she was brushing her hair. "Are you ready to eat?"

"Yep," Johan said, trying to keep his gaze fixed on the wall. "And you?"

"Make sure you have everything," Daria said. A rustle behind him suggested that she was pulling her robe over her head. "We won't be coming back to the rooms."

"I've got my bag," Johan said. "And you?"

"I have everything I need," Daria said. "You can turn around now. I'm decent."

Johan flushed. Behind him, he heard Daria snicker.

"That's good to hear," he said, in his most dignified voice. "But I don't think you're ever decent."

Elaine laughed. "He's got you there," she said. "I remember you bringing two boys home at once."

Johan was still bright red as they walked down a single flight of creaky stairs and entered a small dining room. Cass was sitting at a window table, staring out at the nearly-deserted streets. Her blonde hair was glimmering in the light; somehow, she looked years younger and softer. Johan knew she was an Inquisitor, but anyone who saw her without actually *knowing* her would think she was nothing more than a teenage girl, probably from a middle-class family. The act was really quite remarkable.

"Sometimes, people see what they expect to see," Cass commented, as they sat down at the table. "And no," she added, as Johan gaped at her, "I didn't read your mind. I've just had that reaction before."

"You look like a student," Daria said. "But you smell too good to be a student. No sweat, no fear, no panic in the face of oncoming exams."

"Luckily, most people won't notice my smell," Cass said. "There's always been a ban on recruiting werewolves into the Inquisition."

Johan blinked. "Why?"

"We're meant to be controlled at all times," Cass said, darkly. "I've yet to meet a werewolf who could keep his temper during the full moon."

"I can," Daria protested. "I go out and find a man instead."

"That isn't an option for most Inquisitors," Cass pointed out. "Do you know how many crazies there are, running around on the full moon?"

The waitress, a pink-cheeked girl who couldn't be older than fourteen, marched over to the table and held out a set of menus. "What can I get you?"

"Toast," Cass said, before anyone else could say a word. "Toast and hot tannin and nothing else."

Johan sensed a flicker of astonishment from Elaine; beside her, Daria twitched in annoyance.

"You don't want to eat anything else in a place like this," Cass informed them. "Trust me on that, really. You'd wind up spending the rest of the day on the toilet."

"I wouldn't," Daria protested.

"Everyone else would," Cass said.

Johan looked at Elaine, who shrugged. She hadn't been out of the city very often, Johan knew, and probably had very little experience staying in hotels. When they'd stayed in the Western Hills together, Elaine had done most of the cooking herself. He was tempted to protest, to demand bacon, sausages and eggs for himself, but when he looked towards another early-riser, he saw the man had a plate of foul-looking meats in front of him. His appetite faded very quickly.

"I'll take your word for it," he said.

"Maybe you should," Elaine agreed.

Cass smiled at the serving girl as she returned with a large pot of tannin, then waved her wand in the air, casting a light privacy spell. Johan frowned, then decided that everyone with anything even remotely private to say would use such spells. They weren't too difficult to cast, he'd been told, and while they could be broken it was immensely difficult to break one without the caster knowing what had happened.

"I'm leaving immediately after breakfast," Cass said. "I suggest you depart at the same time and head straight for the tunnels. Don't look back."

"Understood," Elaine said. "And you?"

"I'll see what happens," Cass said. It dawned on Johan, suddenly, that she wasn't expecting to return. "Don't worry about me."

The serving girl returned with a large plate of toast, a small knob of butter and a large pot of jam. Cass eyed it doubtfully, then sniffed it and shook her head. Johan sniffed it too and winced at the smell. It wasn't *bad*, but it was far too strong to be anything other than a cover, meant to conceal something else. Instead, he took a piece of dry toast and nibbled on it thoughtfully, wincing slightly at the taste. Elaine did the same, but Daria ate her way through several pieces in quick succession. A werewolf could probably cope with something bad better than any normal human.

"Time to go," Cass said, once they had finished. "Just try to stay well out of sight."

"We'll be behind a glamour," Elaine said.

"Inquisitors can see through glamours," Cass reminded her, dryly. "Better not to use anything magical, if it can be avoided."

She rose, then waved to the serving girl. When the girl appeared, Cass pressed two silver coins into her hand, then winked. The girl winked back, then dropped the coins into her pocket and smiled at Cass. Johan frowned as the girl walked away, not understanding the byplay.

"She will probably be expected to share her tips with the staff," Daria muttered, in his ear. "But if they don't know she's been tipped, they can't demand their share."

"I see," Johan said. "Is that fair?"

Daria shrugged. "She won't have had a proper education," she said. "That poor girl will have been pushed into the family business as soon as she was old enough to walk, I imagine, just because it is cheaper to use your own family than hiring someone from the outside. And even the toughest of men has a soft spot for a sweet little girl. I'd be surprised if she wasn't the person who got the biggest of tips."

"But ..." Johan remembered all the horror stories about life outside House Conidian and shuddered. "But anything could happen to her."

"That's life here for you," Cass said, as they started to walk down the stairs. "Nasty, brutish and short."

She smiled as they stepped outside, breathing in the air. It smelled of horses and too many people in close proximity, but she seemed to find it wonderful. Johan watched as she pulled Elaine away, then passed her a pair of small envelopes. Elaine nodded, dropped them into her pocket, then gave the older woman a hug. Moments later, Cass hugged Daria too, then reached for Johan and pulled him into a tight embrace.

"Take care of Elaine," she said. "Do you understand me?"

"I will try," Johan said. The feel of her body pressing against his was hellishly distracting, if only because no one had ever hugged him so tightly before. Her breasts felt hard, yet soft against his chest. "I promise."

"Good," Cass said. She kissed him lightly on the forehead, then winked as he stared at her in shock. "Have a safe trip – and good hunting."

She nodded to Elaine and Daria, then turned and strode off into the distance.

"Come on," Elaine said, urgently. "It's time to go."

Chapter Thirty-Three

The streets slowly came to life as they hurried towards the edge of the city, where the Iron Dragons were kept. Elaine was almost relieved as more and more people appeared, knowing it would be easier to hide amongst the crowds. With everyone who was anyone – or who thought they were anyone – going to the Arena, it was unlikely the Inquisitors would have time to search the city for a person using glamours. And she knew she could get past any number of soldiers who had no magic.

Unless they're using protective charms, she reminded herself. *You might have to trick them on short notice.*

Johan caught her arm as they walked. "What did she give you?"

"Tell you later," Elaine said. Cass had made her promise to forge a life-charm, then keep the envelopes until she knew, beyond a shadow of a doubt, that Cass was dead. "Cass wanted me to hang on to them until she rejoined us or she died."

Johan gave her a sharp look, but said nothing as they moved into the industrial estates. There were fewer people around, Elaine noted; it was easy to deduce that they were either Levellers involved in Hawke's plan or engineers who had come to hide from the authorities, now that the Emperor had placed the entire city into lockdown. The ruling class had never been entirely convinced of the benefits of Iron Dragons, after all, and had always been doubtful about allowing them to be built. In hindsight, Elaine suspected they might have had a point.

"I used to want to drive one of those," Johan said, as they walked past the oldest, the original Iron Dragon. It was mounted on a stone plinth and surrounded by protective spells, allowing people to look, but not to touch. "It was a dream of mine."

"Not an uncommon dream," Elaine agreed, as they paused long enough to stare. The Iron Dragon was small and simple compared to its successors, but it was still impressive. There was no magic in its construction at all. "The orphans were equally fond of it. I think the guilds had hundreds of applications for workers as soon as they started hiring recruits."

"The future," Johan agreed.

"But there will still be a place for magic," Daria said quietly, as they walked down to the rails. "The world will not change."

Johan looked doubtful. "Elaine," he said, "is the magic going away?"

Elaine blinked in surprise. "I don't think so," she said. "Why?"

"Hawke said that the magic seemed to be fading," he said. "That magicians of our time can't do the impressive feats of magicians from a thousand years ago. That magic itself might be going away, leaving the world dependent on raw muscle and non-magical ingenuity. Is this true?"

"I don't think so," Elaine said, slowly. "But ..."

She considered it for a long moment. It was true that magicians had performed great feats during the Necromantic Wars, but many of those feats had been powered by human sacrifice or other, darker, rituals. No single magician could channel enough power to lay waste to a country, not if he wanted to survive the attempt. And such rites and rituals had been banned, then forgotten. The magic taught at the Peerless School drew on a magician's natural resources, not on outside sources of magic. And she knew, better than anyone, that even it was inefficient. There was no shortage of magicians who might be able to make something of themselves, if they were taught spells that didn't rely so much on raw inherent power.

"I don't think the magicians of a thousand years ago hesitated before throwing people under the blade to be sacrificed," she said, finally. "These days, human sacrifice is taboo – and with very good reason."

"The Emperor killed children," Johan reminded her.

Elaine nodded. Feeling the rite, even at long distance, had

been horrific. She didn't *know* what the Emperor had had in mind, but she knew she wouldn't like it when she found out. It was why, she admitted to herself, she hadn't tried harder to talk Cass out of her suicide mission. The former Inquisitor was the only one of them who might have a chance at killing the Emperor ... and, if he was prepared to dig up rites from a thousand years ago, the Emperor had to be stopped. No one knew better than Elaine just how close the human race had come to destroying itself.

"Yes," she said. "He did."

She wondered, suddenly, what a world without magic would be like. No Witch-King, true; magic, powerful magic, was all that kept him alive. But there would be no werewolves, no vampires, no dragons ... even though no one had seen a dragon in centuries, there were still legends of good and evil dragons that echoed down the ages. And for the wizards who considered their destruction a good thing, there would be no spells, no wands, no Peerless School. Everyone would be equal ...

But we wouldn't be equal, she thought, sourly. *We'd just move to different ways of measuring strength.*

It was a bitter thought. She knew she wasn't strong or pretty ... all she really had on her side was intelligence and magic. It had been enough to pluck her out of the orphanage and give her a job, but without it ... she knew she would have been lucky to find work in the Golden City. Johan would be able to beat up his brother, without worrying about being turned into a toad, yet what would that do to him? How long would it be, she asked herself, before the aristocracy of magic was replaced by the aristocracy of violence?

She jumped as she felt someone prod her arm. "Elaine?"

"I'm sorry," she said, as she looked up at Johan. "I was just drifting away."

"We should be waiting here," Daria said, as she nodded towards the rails on the ground. "I think the barricade is just up ahead."

"Over there," Johan said, pointing to a small workshop. "We can wait there."

Elaine nodded, then looked towards the Watchtower, looming over the city. It was an ancient building, old enough to predate the Inquisition itself, and heavily protected. No one had managed to slip in or out of the Watchtower without permission; no prisoner, no matter how skilled, had managed to escape the cells below the brooding fortress. Cass had been right, Elaine knew; a thousand years of magicians testing and retesting the defences had sealed all the cracks. The Watchtower was as close to invulnerable as any non-personalised fortress could become.

And Hawke had come up with a daringly simple scheme that would bring it crashing down in flames.

She honestly wasn't sure if she should be pleased or horrified. On the one hand, she knew it had to be done; on the other, the Watchtower was the symbol of magical supremacy. If the Levellers managed to destroy it ... what would it mean for the future?

And what, she asked herself, *if it kills Dread?*

But there was nothing she could do, but wait.

"Don't worry," Daria said, as they settled down. "Either it works or it doesn't."

"How very precise," Johan muttered, with heavy irony.

***

Cass had known there was no point in trying to use any form of magical glamour as she approached the Arena. Elsewhere, it might be considered bad form to try to peer through a person's glamour – particularly a girl's – but the Inquisitors wouldn't let anything like that stop them. And they would definitely recognise her if they saw her without any disguise at all. She'd solved the problem by nipping into a hairdresser's and having her hair cut short and dyed black, then walking into a clothes store and picking something more suited for a sixteen-year-old girl trying to impress her first crush than an Inquisitor. It was unlikely anyone would bother to look for anything below the surface when she was showing off so much skin.

The Arena itself was surrounded by people waiting to pass through the protective wards and find their seats. Cass smiled to herself as she found a magical family, then smiled at the oldest son, who couldn't have been more than nineteen. He promptly forgot his little sisters in favour of chatting to a desirable girl, telling her about all the advanced and complicated magic he'd learnt at the Peerless School. Cass kept her face under strict control as his bragging grew more and more elaborate, even though it was unintentionally hilarious. In her desperate quest to make something of herself, she'd mastered such spells a year or two ahead of him.

But it did help her walk through security. The guards checked wands – Cass had replaced hers with a simpler wand after leaving the Inquisitors – and then waved them through the barriers, clearly assuming that Cass was just one of the family. She didn't bother to correct them, nor did the parents, who were watching their eldest son with an indulgent eye. Her parents would have been less amused, she was sure, as they found seats and settled down, but then her parents had always been more controlling. They would never have allowed their children to speak to a member of the opposite sex without carefully briefing them on precisely what they should and should not say.

She sat down next to the young man and looked down at the Arena ... and froze. A large stone statue stood in the centre, next to a wooden podium. Vlad Deferens hadn't just defeated the Grand Sorceress, she realised; he'd turned her to stone, then placed her in the perfect place to bear witness to his triumph. Cold hatred spread through her body as she promised herself bloody revenge, then she looked at Light Spinner again. The practice of surrounding one's house with the petrified bodies of one's former enemies had gone out of fashion centuries ago, because the spells sometimes wore off or were removed. And if Light Spinner was still awake and aware in her stony prison ...

"It's going to be a great moment," the boy said. Somehow, Cass had managed to miss his name in all the bragging. Or maybe he hadn't mentioned it. If his family had been one of the Great Houses, she would have known him by sight. "We have an Emperor again!"

"I suppose we do," Cass said. She sighed, then settled back into her seat and pasted an interested expression on her face. "But what do you think that means?"

***

329

Charity had only been to the Arena once, apart from the time she'd taken Light Spinner's statue to Lady Aisling. It wasn't something that had impressed her; indeed, she knew she'd only gone because her father had been unable or unwilling to take Jamal. Watching men kill each other on the sands hadn't excited her; it had disgusted her. Magic could turn people into toads or stop them dead in their tracks, but it didn't leave people bleeding to death on the sands while people cheered or booed. Well, it *could*, yet what self-respecting wizard would bleed his opponent to death?

The Emperor, on the other hand, seemed equally bored with the Arena, but for a different reason. His chatter, which she had been trying to ignore, was all about the need for *real* challenges, about the need for real tests. What was the point, he asked, of a place where healing spells could cure anything that wasn't immediately fatal? Charity had asked if the druids actually allowed people to gain more experience, if only by learning from their mistakes, but the Emperor had sneered. People were meant to live with their mistakes, he'd snapped, if they weren't fatal. It was how they served as an example to everyone else. By the time they reached the Arena, she was feeling thoroughly depressed.

She sighed in relief as the carriage finally came to a halt – it would be too much for the Emperor to walk, even though it was only a short distance from the Imperial Palace to the Arena – and the Emperor climbed out. Instantly, the guards on the outside of the Arena prostrated themselves in front of their master, banging their heads on the stone pavement so hard she wondered if they would do themselves a mischief. Or, for that matter, if a time when the guards were looking at the ground would be perfect for assassins. But the red-robed sorcerers – and a handful of watchful Inquisitors – never took their eyes off their surroundings.

"Come," the Emperor said.

Charity sighed inwardly, then followed him through a long corridor and out onto the sands. It smelled faintly of blood and piss and worse, she realised, as the Emperor motioned for her to stand by the walls, then strode onwards, into view. The crowd starting cheering, but they seemed confused. Some of the older families had looked up the proper acclamations for an Emperor, but others were cheering as they would for a Grand Sorcerer. The Emperor didn't seem to care. He mounted the podium, then smiled winningly at the crowd. They cheered so loudly that Charity couldn't help wondering if the wards were going to hold.

"There are hustlers in that crowd, of course," a dry voice said.

Charity jumped, then turned to see Dread standing beside her, leaning on his staff. He wasn't the youngest of men, yet he'd managed to sneak up on her with ease. She scowled at him, feeling her heartbeat pounding in her chest. The Inquisitor could have stuck a knife between her ribs and she wouldn't have noticed until it had been too late.

"Oh," she said, finally. "Hustlers?"

"Men and women primed to cheer for the Emperor," Dread explained. "They know precisely what to say ... and how to carry the crowd with them."

Charity shook her head in disbelief. On the podium, the Emperor was just standing there, drinking in the cheers. The magic surrounding the wooden frame ensured that everyone saw the Emperor as looking in their direction, no matter which way he was actually facing. In fact, according to the safety briefings, the magic also placed the Emperor two metres from where he was actually standing. An assassination attempt would be difficult, to say the least.

Eventually, after what felt like hours, the Emperor raised a hand. The cheers instantly abated.

"My people," he said. His voice was quiet, but the spells surrounding the Arena made sure that everyone could hear. "It has been so long since one of my family sat in the Golden Throne, acknowledged by all as the true representative of a bloodline that derives from the blood of the very gods themselves. In that time, there have been Grand Sorcerers who have ruled, but have not built. The Empire has remained unchanged since the Necromantic Wars."

That wasn't quite true, Charity knew. It was true enough that the system hadn't changed, even if the names and faces of the people on top had changed several times. But there had been changes, she was sure, even if they were small ones. The Iron Dragons had been introduced only thirty years ago. Someone from the early years of Grand Sorcerer rule honestly wouldn't have known what to make of them.

"But now we have returned," the Emperor continued. "There will be many, many changes as the Empire seeks to grow once again. To expand and learn, to develop newer ways to work magic, to reshape the world into something remarkable. We will change!"

"Change isn't always a good thing," Dread muttered.

Charity nodded. Johan's change had been bad for the family, even if it had been good for him personally. She wondered, suddenly, if Lady Lakeside had brought her younger siblings to the Arena to hear the Emperor speak. It had been agonising, but she hadn't dared send another note to the older woman, let alone go in person to see her sisters. The former Privy Councillor would have taken one look at her and known what had happened.

"The signs of decay are all around us," the Emperor pronounced. "But we will repair the damage and progress onwards."

***

Patience was one thing Cass had learnt to master at a very early age. An impatient Inquisitor was one who would act too quickly and make it impossible for his or her fellows to close the case against the suspect. Even so, the urge to just start throwing curses at the Emperor as he babbled on was growing stronger and stronger with every passing second. He talked about change, but refused to go into specifics; he talked about honour and duty, yet failed to say what they might include. Or, for that matter, what he might want from his loyal subjects.

She glanced at the sun, mentally calculating the time. The Emperor had droned on for nearly twenty minutes and people, particularly the younger children, were getting restless. She couldn't help wondering how many parents had slapped silencing spells on their children, or charmed them into obedience. Using such spells on children was risky – and would mean heavy fines if they were caught – but none of the parents would want to risk their children making a scene in front of the Emperor. Her own parents had been chillingly obsessive about presenting the proper face at all times. If she hadn't had older brothers, Cass suspected she would have been beaten or charmed into being a good little girl in very short order.

"This is the task of my family," the Emperor continued. "We are proud to serve as the rulers of the Empire as we lead the way into a brave new world ..."

Cass glanced at the family beside her. They were lapping it up. Their teenage son wasn't even glancing at the exposed half of her breasts, because he was spellbound by the Emperor's words. Was he using a charm, too subtle for her to detect, or was he just a better speaker than Cass realised. It wasn't as if she'd been to many public meetings ...

And then a thunderous explosion echoed over the city.

Chapter Thirty-Four

Elaine had been looking at the Watchtower when it happened.

One moment, everything was normal; the next, tongues of flame were shooting out of every exposed window in the brooding fortress. She jumped to her feet, one hand grabbing at her wand, as the entire front side of the Watchtower seemed to explode outwards, throwing chunks of stone debris out over the city. The blast was so loud she found herself rubbing at her ears, trying to unblock them. Beside her, Daria shuddered in pain, covering her own ears with hands that had somehow started to become paws. If the blast was loud enough to leave Elaine's ears ringing, it would be far worse for Daria.

She hastily cast a protective ward as pieces of debris fell down over the city, striking buildings and people in the streets. The Levellers hadn't realised, she guessed, as the remainder of the Watchtower started to fall apart, that the blast would bombard the entire city with debris ... or maybe they just hadn't cared. There was no way to know, she reminded herself, as flashes of magic glittered around the peaks. The Watchtower had been part of the city's defences and now it was gone. It wouldn't be long before the remains of the protective wards collapsed completely.

"By all the gods," Johan breathed. "They did it!"

"Yes," Elaine said. She had just witnessed the birth of a whole new world. "They did."

She said a silent prayer for the people in the city as the final chunks of debris came crashing down, then led the way out of their hiding place. There wouldn't be much time before Deferens and his men managed to regain control of the city. All hell was about to break loose, she was sure, and she wanted to be gone before the riots started in earnest. Or the soldiers turned on the civilians and began killing them.

"Come on," she said. In the distance, she could hear screams. "We need to move."

***

Charity stared in disbelief as the Watchtower exploded, pieces of debris raining down on the city below. Beside her, Dread seemed stunned, the first time she'd seen the older man show any strong emotion. The Watchtower was impregnable. Everyone *knew* the Watchtower was impregnable. And yet it was now gone. A piece of debris struck the wards covering the Arena and bounced off, crashing to the pavement nearby with a terrifyingly loud crash. She heard panic rippling through the crowd as the Emperor fell silent, as if he too was stunned ...

... And then all nine hells broke loose.

***

Cass took a very quick moment to acknowledge the destruction of the Watchtower and the deaths of several of her former friends and comrades, then she rose to her feet, drew her wand and threw the strongest curse she could muster towards the Emperor. Red and green light blazed around the podium, but his protective wards repelled the curse. Cass had expected as much – there were *very* heavy protections in the Arena – and threw a second spell towards Light Spinner, then hopped down towards the sands. Behind her, a whole series of tiny explosions echoed through the giant building. The Levellers, she knew, had brought their own surprises to the Arena.

She landed on the sands, just in time to duck a stream of black light from one of the red-robed sorcerers. Cass smirked, then threw back another curse, paired up with a transfiguration prank spell. The combination caught the sorcerer by surprise; he started to block the curse, only to find himself becoming a snail before he could finish saving himself from certain death. Moments later, the remains of the curse killed him, scattering pieces of his body all over the Arena. Cass threw a second curse towards two more red-robed magicians, then looked around for the Emperor. He was nowhere to be seen.

He can't have fled in public, she thought, as she turned towards the stand. *His reputation won't survive fleeing from an assassin, even after the Watchtower fell.*

She swore under her breath as a grey-robed figure appeared in front of her, wand raised and already spitting spells. An Inquisitor ... not Dread, thankfully, but someone she knew. Gritting her teeth, she called on her memories of how Calvin moved, then threw a freeze spell at just the right moment. He shook it off a second later, but she was already close enough to punch him in the head. The Inquisitor staggered, then fell to the ground. Cass tossed a third and final spell at him, just to make sure he stayed down, then kept hunting for her target. But he was nowhere to be seen.

***

Charity stared, rooted to the spot, as the crowd panicked. There were people in the crowd waving wands ... no, those weren't wands! Whatever they were, they were doing something; she saw a guard fall, half of his head blown away by the impact. Hastily, she cast a shield ward around herself, tightening it as best she could. A second later, something struck the shield and glanced off, hitting the stone walls and landing on the ground. She stared at the metal ball, then looked up towards the fleeing crowd. Just what was going on up there?

A flash of light caught her eye and she turned, just in time to see blue-white light spinning over Light Spinner's petrified form. There was a sudden flicker, then the Grand Sorceress was suddenly standing there, her hideous face twisted with anger. Charity had a moment to see her raise her hand, then a wave of fire billowed out towards the stand, which exploded into flames. The Emperor was at risk ... Charity raised her wand, compelled by her oaths to defend him, but Light Spinner turned and casually waved a hand at her. Charity's entire body locked solid, leaving her unable to move a single voluntary muscle. It was humiliating, particularly when she couldn't lift the spell herself, and yet it was also a relief. If she could do nothing to defend the Emperor, she could do nothing to defend the Emperor ...

Light Spinner threw another wave of fire, so hot that

Charity was sure her face was going to burn, towards where the Emperor had to be. An explosion flared up, right in the middle of the Arena, then the Emperor landed nearly in front of the Grand Sorceress. He was carrying a huge staff in one hand, wielding it as easily as another magician would wield a wand. Flames danced around him as he darted forward, smashing his magic directly into Light Spinner's protective wards. And all Charity could do was stare as the two magicians collided, pressing their power directly against one another.

And then there was a flare of light as a dark-haired girl threw a curse at the Emperor's back. He sensed it coming, somehow, and jumped out of the way, then threw a wave of force at the Grand Sorceress, targeted on the sand under her feet. Light Spinner jumped backwards, allowing her magic to carry her to the other side of the Arena, just as another grey-robed figure confronted the dark-haired girl. Dread ...

The Emperor smirked, then lifted one hand. There was a sudden wave of magic that felt strange and unpleasant, as if merely to sense it was to feel dirty and used. Charity would have shivered if the spell holding her in place had allowed any motion; instead, all she could do was watch in growing horror as *something* started to press its way into reality. A flapping creature materialised above the Arena, slowly taking on shape and form. Charity could only stare as the air shook, displaced by the presence of a dragon. She'd always thought they'd died out centuries ago, hunted to extinction by humans who hadn't wanted to share their world with any monsters. And now one was back.

It was huge, easily the size of an Iron Dragon. Its wings beat the air, sending warm gusts of wind toward the remaining people in the stands. She wanted to scream as the dragon opened its mouth, revealing very sharp teeth, and the huge beast spat a blast of flame towards the Grand Sorceress. The Grand Sorceress ducked, then hurled herself forward as the flame struck the stands, blasting through them as easily as a blasting curse would go through paper. Charity stared as the entire north side of the Arena started to crumple, the crystals the Emperor had ordered placed within the Arena shattered by the attack. She caught sight of strange glimmering entities, so hard to see that she was half-sure she was imagining them, flickering and fading as the flames grew stronger ...

The Emperor shouted a filthy word to the skies, then hurled another set of curses towards the Grand Sorceress. She ducked and dodged his curses, but had to leap away as the dragon turned towards her, golden eyes packed with dark malice. Just for a second, the dragon looked right into Charity's eyes, its cruel gaze seeming to bore right into her very soul. She knew, beyond a shadow of a doubt, that it was going to bite her in half with its sharp teeth ... but then it moved on, staring at Light Spinner. Charity had never been so glad to be ignored in her life.

The rite, she thought. *It must have given the Emperor the power to summon a dragon.*

Something else pressed against reality, as if it were waiting to be born. Charity sensed it, even though she couldn't move; moments later, a second dragon shimmered into existence, as if it had slammed down from a higher plane and taken on mortal flesh and blood. It turned its scaly neck, then blasted fire over the remainder of the Arena. The handful of remaining people – mundanes with blasting sticks, magicians with wands – were vaporised before they could run for their lives. Charity watched as the dragon landed on the scorched and broken stone, then blew flames into the sky. The entire city would see the fires ...

She wanted to flee, or at least to look away. But she could no longer move.

***

"Cassandra," Dread said.

Cass gritted her teeth. If any of the Inquisitors could have recognised her, it was Dread. She had spent practically every waking moment of her apprenticeship with him, knowing that one mistake could mean the end of her career. And he'd watched her with a cold awareness of each and every thing she did, watching for signs of weakness and moral turpitude. Even her mother, engaged in one of her rants over how everything had to be absolutely perfect, hadn't been so coldly perceptive. A mere change in hair and dress wasn't going to fool him.

"Dread," she said. She didn't lower her wand. Dread might have been an Inquisitor for longer than she'd been alive, but he hadn't slowed down at all. "You're on the wrong side."

She saw – or thought she saw – the agony in his eyes. "So are you," he said. "How did you break your oaths."

"I was released from them," Cass said. "You have to stop this ..."

She threw the spell as quickly as she could, but he still sidestepped it and fired back a set of curses of his own. Cass ducked as many of them as she could, yet she still had to block three of them and they all cost her magic. The sheer power at Dread's disposal was bad enough, but when it was paired with experience and skill ... she knew the Grand Sorceress had been lucky to have Dread as an Inquisitor. If he hadn't been one of them, he might have been a challenger for the post of Grand Sorcerer.

"Give up," Dread snapped. She knew he was trying to tell her to run, pushing against his oaths as hard as he could. "You can't win this ..."

Another wave of heat washed past her as the second dragon turned, bringing its giant mouth level with her eyes. Dread jumped backwards hastily as the dragon opened its mouth and blew a long rolling breath of fire at her; she rapidly summoned water, throwing as much as she could into the firedrake's breath. There was a hissing sound, so loud she almost covered her ears, then steam exploded in all directions. Cass yelped as it stung her exposed flesh – the outfit might have drawn eyes, but it provided almost no protection at all – then threw a curse right up the dragon's mouth. It hopped backwards, like a chicken, then glared at her with two beady eyes full of malice. But the curse hadn't been enough to do more than irritate the giant beast.

She braced herself, then hurled a curse right at the creature's eye. It howled, then lashed out with one scaly claw. Wards or no wards, Cass found herself picked up and thrown across the Arena; she landed, hard enough to stun her, on a patch of scorched ground. The impact shattered her wards; somehow, she managed to pick herself up, just before the dragon threw another burst of fire towards her. It missed, barely. She lifted her wand, trying to think of something – anything – that would work. Dragons were heavily armoured – dragonskin made the best protective armour in the world – and very few magicians could hope to put a hole through it. And even if she did, it still wouldn't kill the beast.

Light Spinner landed next to her, lightning crackling around her hands as one of the dragons took to the air, its jaw hanging open as it prepared to spit more fire down at the two humans. Cass glanced at her, saw grim resolution in her one working eye, and nodded in agreement. It was time for one last stand.

"Watch my back," Light Spinner ordered. "I didn't lose everything when he took the wards."

The flying dragon hovered closer, toying with them. Light Spinner raised a hand and started to chant, in a language so old that Cass barely recognised it. For long moments nothing seemed to happen – she could swear the dragon was laughing at them – and then green light flared high overhead. She looked up, just in time to see lightning crackling from the peaks, then stabbing down at the flying dragon. The creature howled as green light tore through its body, ripping it into shreds. Pieces of steaming flesh fell to the ground and splattered everywhere.

"The weather spells," Light Spinner said, with heavy satisfaction. "They were never keyed into the Golden Throne."

The green light faded, just as the second dragon lunged forward. Light Spinner threw a fireball at its armoured chest, but the spell simply spattered off the dragon's scales. Cass summoned the strength to create a protective ward, then cursed as a well-placed spell shattered it. Seconds later, the dragon lunged at Light Spinner and slammed into her wards, knocking her flying. Cass hesitated, then threw a minor tickling hex at the dragon's rear, in the hopes it would distract the creature. But it merely breathed fire in her direction, then turned to follow Light Spinner.

A hand wrapped itself around Cass's neck, holding her tightly. She kicked out, but her captor held her too firmly to be dislodged. His magic field was overpowering hers, making it impossible to cast a spell. She knew without looking up that Dread had caught her, that it was his fingers gripping her neck. Like the other Inquisitors, he was strong physically as well as magically. And he wouldn't let her go.

She poked his skin with her fingernails, hoping to force him to let her go, but it wasn't enough to break him. His hands tightened on her neck; she looked up and saw pity in his grey eyes, as well as something else, something unreadable. Desperately, she tried to summon raw magic, but even that failed.

"I'm sorry," Dread said, so quietly she couldn't help wondering if she'd imagined it. "I'm so sorry."

And then he snapped her neck like a twig.

***

Charity saw Light Spinner land in front of the Emperor, her wards broken and twisted by the impact. The Emperor didn't give her any time to recover as his new pet crawled towards her, its eyes laden with unthinking malice. Instead, he kicked her in the chest and laughed, unpleasantly, as blood spluttered out of her mouth. The Grand Sorceress didn't seem inclined to lie there and take it; she started to pull herself upright, despite clearly having more than a few broken bones. But the Emperor didn't seem to care.

"You should have stayed down," the Emperor said. "Or a statue. You wouldn't have died so ... so unpleasantly. But women have never known what was good for them."

Light Spinner's one good eye met his, unblinkingly. "Men have never known what was good for them, either," she said. Her voice was harsh, but clear. "You should have stayed at home."

The Emperor's face changed, just for an instant. Light Spinner stared, her face suddenly horrified. Charity watched in numb disbelief as the Emperor kicked her in the ribs, knocking her back to the ground, then pressed his foot down on her chest. There was an awful crunching sound, then blood spurted up and over his boot.

"I have my Empire now," the Emperor hissed. But it no longer sounded like him. "And you will no longer live to see my works."

He looked down at the body for a long moment, then straightened up. "Well," he said, as he waved a hand at Charity. "What do you think?"

Charity's entire body jerked as the spell holding her in place snapped. She looked around, feeling panic bubbling at the corner of her mind. There were dead bodies everywhere, flames licking through half of the Arena, and a dragon standing on the sand, peering at her as a cat peers at a mouse. Whatever happened next, and she had no idea what would happen, it was clear that the Empire would never be the same again.

In the end, she could only stare at him in horror.

Chapter Thirty-Five

"Two guards," Daria said, sniffing the air ahead of them. "Several more running away towards the Arena as fast as their legs can carry them."

Elaine nodded. Magic – raw magic – was pulsing out over the city, in a manner that triggered snapshot images of the books crammed into her mind. Spells not seen since the Second Necromantic War were being unleashed into the world, summoning creatures that were best left forgotten. Anyone with any sensitivity to magic would know that the situation had become a great deal worse ... but what could they do about it? The Emperor held all the cards.

"Then we'd better go," she said. She hefted her wand, mentally gathering herself. No matter how many times she'd had to fight, she knew she wasn't a natural fighter. "Let's move."

She'd never actually seen the tunnel entrance, even when leaving the city on the Iron Dragons. Unlike the other tunnels, it was protected by a charmed fence, a handful of hex signs warning of danger and repelling children or mundanes from even going close to the tunnel entrance. The entrance itself was just a gaping gash in the sheer rock, with two pairs of rails running out of the city and into the darkness. Two guards stood beside the fence, peering towards the Arena with nervous eyes. Flickering lights, dancing high overhead, cast an eerie light over the scene.

"You," the lead guard called. "You can't come here!"

Daria growled, deep in her throat, as the second guard made to object. The first guard elbowed him, hard. Elaine couldn't help a flicker of amusement, followed by bitter guilt and even shame. The first guard was merely doing his duty, following orders. He hadn't allowed his friend to even catcall at two young women. It was almost a shame, she knew, that they would both be in deep trouble at the end of the day.

A dull roar echoed over the city. She turned and saw a giant *shape* in the air, hanging above the Arena. The sight was terrifying. No one had seen anything like it for hundreds of years, since the last dragon had been killed. There had always been stories about dragons hiding in unsettled parts of the world, but no one had ever given the stories any credence. And *Elaine* knew that dragons were summoned from another world ...

She turned back to the guards and cast a compulsion spell of her own invention. They wore protective amulets, but the spell she'd invented bypassed most protections on its way to the brain. She readied herself to launch something nastier if necessary, but the two guards fell into a trance immediately. Beside her, Daria sniffed at them suspiciously, then paced down to the fence. Elaine watched her friend go, then turned back to the guards and cleared her throat.

"Here are your orders," she said, as green lightning flashed out in the distance. "You will not prevent us from walking through the tunnel. You will remain here, on guard; when your superiors arrive, you will tell them that no one passed through the tunnel."

She waved her wand, fine-tuning the spell, then hurried down to join Daria and Johan. Johan was staring at her, his expression unreadable, but she could feel his concern through the bond they shared. He'd been hit with enough compulsion spells to be completely repulsed by the idea of using them, even on a pair of guards. Elaine agreed, particularly after what Deferens had planned to do to her, but there were no other options. Unless, of course, she wanted to kill the guards and hide the bodies.

I'm sorry, she thought, looking back at the two men. *But I don't see any other way out of here.*

She crossed the fence, ignoring the subtle prodding from the hex signs, and peered into the darkness. Up close, the tunnel was narrower than she'd realised – or, maybe, it was the awareness, no matter how flawed, that an Iron Dragon could come looming out of the darkness at any second. She listened and heard nothing, beyond a steady drip-drip-drip of water, somewhere in the shadows. But the sounds from the

Arena were so loud that it was hard to be sure it was quiet inside the tunnel.

"There's a strong stench of oil and smoke, but little else," Daria observed. "We need to move."

Elaine cast a night-vision spell over her eyes as Daria led the way into the tunnel. The interior was eerie; rough-hewn walls, glittering rails and walkways intended to allow the staff to walk along the tunnel, without running the risk of being hit by a train. A handful of spells could be sensed crawling along the ceiling, filtering the air; despite herself, Elaine was almost disappointed. There might be no magic in the Iron Dragons, but the operators still used magic in some places.

"It's to keep the poisonous gases away from the crew," Johan said, when she asked. "Some of the smoke is actually poisonous and, in this tunnel, it builds up rapidly."

"I can smell it," Daria said. "It's horrid."

"It's progress," Johan said, as Elaine hastily cast a filtering spell of her own. "And aren't there times when magic leaves behind dangerous residue as well?"

"Yeah," Elaine said, remembering the Blight. "But not for many – many – years."

But was that true? The magic she'd been taught – the magic refined over a thousand years ago – left behind little residue, but Deferens had unleashed spells from a bygone age. He was running the risk of contaminating the entire Golden City, purely for power – and the greater glory of the Witch-King. The more Elaine thought about it, the more she was sure that Deferens had been overcome by the Witch-King years ago. Even a power-mad sorcerer would have thought twice about unleashing dragons, if he'd even known how.

But the Witch-King would know, Elaine thought, coldly. *The spells were commonplace, back in his day.*

The darkness seemed to grow stronger as they walked deeper into the tunnel. It grew cold, colder than it had been in the city, even when it was snowing. Elaine cast charms to warm them, but there was something in the shadows that seemed to interfere with her magic. No matter how many charms she cast, the temperature kept dropping sharply.

Maybe it was one of the protective wards scattered around the city, she told herself, or maybe it was just her nerves making it harder to cast the spells. It was impossible to tell.

"There's a body here," Daria said, sharply. "One man, lying on his side."

Elaine followed her gaze. A man was lying on the ground, a knife protruding from his chest. Elaine was no expert, but it looked as though he'd died very recently, too early for the body to decay. Or maybe someone had cast a preservation charm on the knife. She looked closer and saw a handful of runes carved into the blade, ensuring the body would never decay as long as the blade remained there. The man could have been killed at any time after the last tunnel inspection. Hell, maybe he had been killed during the inspection. He wore the uniform of an Iron Dragon worker, after all.

"Take the blade," Daria advised. "It might be useful."

"Better not," Elaine said, slowly. She reached out a hand and sensed coiling magic under the hilt. Picking the blade up with her bare hand could be very dangerous. "I think ..."

Elaine's night vision spells failed, completely. One moment, she could see; the next, everything was pitch black. She froze, sensing Johan's shock and panic through the link; beside her, Daria growled and snapped back into wolf form. Elaine had barely a moment to sense something moving towards them at astonishing speed before Daria growled and threw herself at the newcomer. The sound of her growl was so terrifying that Elaine would have fled, if her legs hadn't turned to jelly. A terrible struggle began, all the worse for being unseen.

She hastily cast a set of spells, only to have them fail, one after the other. A flare of light, so bright that it would have blinded her if she'd been looking right at it, appeared behind her, where Johan was standing. The fight was so vicious it was hard to see the two combatants properly; she'd wondered if the newcomer was another werewolf, but he didn't seem inclined to drop into wolf form. Instead, he backhanded Daria on the snout, hard enough to draw blood, then looked up and glowered at Elaine. She couldn't miss blood dripping from his fangs.

A vampire, she thought, badly shocked. Vampires were

rare, not least because they were hated and feared more than werewolves or dark wizards. Even a *rumour* that someone was a vampire was enough to get him tied down and exposed to sunlight, just to make certain he wasn't a *real* vampire. *Where the hell did Deferens get a vampire?*

The vampire hissed, then threw himself forward. Elaine remembered, as Johan yanked her back, that vampires did funny things to magic. Their nature sucked in magic, to the point where most spells simply failed around them, unless they were designed to specifically exclude supernatural vermin. She hadn't thought to protect her wards against a vampire, if only because no one in their right mind would consider using a vampire as a guard. But Deferens was clearly not in his right mind.

Sunlight, she thought, as she cast the protective ward. Blue sparks flashed and the vampire stumbled backwards, then bared its teeth at her. *We need sunlight.*

"Close your eyes," she ordered, and cast the spell. Warm light flared in the tunnel, throwing everything into sharp relief. "I think this should work ..."

The vampire sparkled, then exploded into dust. Elaine eyed the dust for a long moment, then cancelled her spell and recast the night vision spells. Daria was just snapping back into human form and stalking over to pick up her robe. Elaine smiled at her cross face – a vampire had no scent, so Daria hadn't realised what she was sensing until it was too late – and then led the way further down the tunnel.

"That was a bloodsucking vampire," Johan said. "Where did it come from?"

Elaine shrugged. Vampires drank blood, true, but the only way someone could *become* a vampire was if they were completely drained of blood in the first feeding. The victim, if the body wasn't cremated, would rise again after three nights, lusting for blood. They tended to go for their families first, perhaps sensing what they'd lost, but after that they just drained whoever they found until they were hunted down. And that wasn't always easy. There was a whole subculture of vampire worshippers in the world, largely composed of people who had never met one. A couple of vampires had managed to take advantage of their foolishness in the past.

"Anywhere," she said. Deferens was certainly ruthless enough to capture a vampire and use it to breed more vampires, but controlling the bloodsuckers would be a challenge in and of itself. They were resistant to compulsion spells, even when the bloodlust wasn't threatening to send them over the edge and into a rampage. "But right now it doesn't matter."

The tunnel seemed to widen as they reached the halfway point. They paused, then kept walking through a network of caves that seemed to have been converted into a storage point. Elaine wondered, as she saw the boxes stored within the shadows, if the Inquisition knew it existed. *She'd* certainly thought of the tunnels as nothing more than tunnels, simple holes dug into the mountainside. But there were smaller tunnels, side-tunnels and entire chambers hidden under layer upon layer of rocky protection. Who knew just what could be hidden in the darkness?

Maybe the vampire belonged to the Levellers instead, she thought. Hawke hadn't warned them about it, but he couldn't be the only Leveller mastermind. *Or maybe Deferens just got lucky*.

They kept walking until they finally reached the end of the tunnel and saw sunlight ahead of them. Elaine covered her eyes, blinking rapidly, as they stepped out into the light, then looked down at herself. Her borrowed dress – the innkeeper's daughter was about the same size as her – was covered in soot, while neither Daria nor Johan looked much better. She couldn't resist a giggle, which faded away as a line of armed soldiers appeared in front of them, their faces cold and hard. They wore the same uniform as the other soldiers Deferens had brought to the city.

Shit, she thought, badly shocked. She'd made the greatest mistake of all, according to the books; she'd assumed her enemy was stupid. No, *she'd* been stupid. She hadn't even bothered to think about it. *Why didn't we think there might be guards at the far end?*

"Do not attempt to draw your wands," the leader said. He was a magician, she could tell, although quite a low-power one. Maybe not much more powerful than herself. "How did you get out of the city?"

"We walked," Daria said.

The magician glowered at her, then nodded to his men. "Bind them and take them to the camp," he ordered. "I want them held until the Emperor has a chance to see them."

Elaine swore, mentally, then sent a single order down the link to Johan. Johan stepped forward, clenching his fists. The soldiers saw and laughed, then exchanged comments in their own language. Elaine couldn't understand their words, but nothing they said sounded pleasant. Johan gathered himself, then unleashed his power. The world seemed to shiver on its axis for a long moment ... and then the soldiers froze solid

Daria looked up, alarmed. "What did you do?"

"Concentrated on freezing them," Johan said. He sounded as though he was trying to be nonchalant, but Elaine could sense cold hatred and fear emanating along the link. "They wanted to rape you."

Elaine gave him a sharp look. "You could understand them?"

"My father thought we should learn at least a few words from each of the major tongues," Johan admitted. "That was before he largely gave up on educating me. That one" – he nodded to one of the frozen men – "thought they should take you halfway to camp, then have some fun with you."

"Bastards," Daria said.

"Idiots," Elaine agreed. They were carrying wands, after all, and Daria was obviously a werewolf. "Come on."

She turned and started to walk along the Iron Dragon lines, casting a handful of invisibility spells over themselves as they walked. They wouldn't fool an Inquisitor, she was grimly aware, but anyone else who saw them would feel compelled to look elsewhere. She hoped it would suffice as they walked through a long stretch of fields, glancing towards the handful of buildings and homes in the distance. There was no point in seeking help from there, she suspected, not when Deferens had had ample time to billet his soldiers in the homes. For all she knew, he was massing the rest of his forces there.

Magic flickered and flared over the mountains, each spark making her want to look back. The wind blew hot and cold, sometimes throwing snow into her face, sometimes warm enough to make her think of summer, of the days when the Golden City had always been temperate. She couldn't help a pang of grief for everything they'd lost over the last six months as she paused long enough to look back at the mountains, where the Watchtower had once brooded over the landscape. Once, the Empire had seemed as solid and unchanging as the mountains themselves. Now ...

Civil war, she thought. It had been almost inevitable, once the Grand Sorceress had been replaced by an Emperor. Now, with dragons blackening the sky once again, the Empire was likely to shatter completely. *We're looking at total civil war.*

Something *twitched* in her pocket. She reached into her pocket and felt around, then pulled the life-charm out into the light. It was a simple spell; Cass had given her a snippet of golden hair, which she'd used as the core of a charm. As long as Cass was alive, the charm would show it, even though it wouldn't show anything else. It was such a simple spell that fooling it was almost impossible. But now she was dead.

Elaine shook her head, feeling tears prickling at the corner of her eyes. Cass was dead ... and that, she suspected, meant that Deferens was still alive. How many people had died when the dragons had been unleashed? Hundreds? Thousands? The memories she had from the wars told her that dragons had ripped apart entire cities ... how did one fight a dragon? A single magician could never hope to survive.

Johan looked over at her, concerned. "What is that?"

"Cass is dead," Elaine said, bitterly. The envelopes Cass had given her were burning holes in her pocket. "And if she's dead, Deferens is still alive."

"Then we will avenge her," Daria said, firmly. "But for the moment, Elaine, we need to keep walking."

Elaine gritted her teeth. It was a long way to Knawel Haldane, longer than she'd realised when she'd devised the plan. Neither Hawke nor Cass had thought anything of it, at the time, but a life spent shelving books hadn't prepared her for a ten mile walk. But there was no way they could hitch a lift, even if they happened to trust whoever they met. All they could do was keep walking.

She took one last look at the charm, then returned it to her pocket. It could be buried later, with the proper prayers said to the gods. And then ...

Bracing herself, she turned and looked back towards the city. Smoke was rising, as if a volcano had suddenly come to life, readying itself to devastate the land around it.

Somehow, she couldn't escape the feeling that the image was all too accurate.

Chapter Thirty-Six

"You didn't have to kill her," the Emperor thundered. "Why did you kill her?"

"Because she was a threat," Dread said. "She had to die."

"Of course she had to die," the Emperor said. "But I wanted to kill her personally."

Charity stared at them both in silent horror. The Emperor had refused to leave the Arena, even after the slaves had started cleaning up the mess, and he'd refused to allow Charity to leave either. Looking at him, as much as she had come to hate his smug face, was preferable to staring at the ruins of the Arena – and the scorched bodies scattered everywhere. And Dread ... she didn't know him that well, but she had the impression he wasn't quite telling the truth.

Or he isn't telling the complete truth, she thought. Her mother, back when she'd been a *real* mother, had had a remarkable gift for separating truth from lies. *There's something he isn't saying.*

"She needed to die," Dread said. The *former* Inquisitor, Charity guessed. "And so I killed her."

Charity shook her head, bitterly. Too much had happened for her to take it all in. The Watchtower had been destroyed, the Emperor had almost been assassinated ... and the Emperor had summoned *dragons* to his defence. She turned and looked at the remaining dragon, which was casually sitting in the centre of the Arena, licking its claws with a long jagged tongue. It struck her, perhaps because she was too tired to think clearly, that a tongue-lashing from a dragon might be far worse than a lecture from her mother. Somehow, the thought almost made her giggle.

"You killed her to keep her out of my clutches," the Emperor hissed. "Admit it."

"I did," Dread said. He seemed completely unruffled, even though he'd just confessed to something akin to treason.

"She deserved better than to die at your hands. It would not have been an easy death."

The Emperor glowered at him. "And if I told you that you should die in her place?"

"I would die with pleasure," Dread answered. His voice was faintly mocking. "You are the Emperor, after all. Death in your service would be a honour."

"We shall see," the Emperor said. He turned and strode towards the dragon, which peered at him through beady eyes. "My new pet will see to it that my reign lasts a thousand years."

"You won't be very sane at the end of it," Dread said, following him. "No one can cling to life that long without going mad."

"I can," the Emperor said. He reached up and stroked the dragon's skin. "I can do anything."

Charity looked from one man to the other, puzzled. It sounded as though they were talking about something, without ever quite coming out and saying *what* they were talking about. She looked at the Emperor, who was showing remarkable courage as he stroked the dragon, and then at the grim-faced Dread. It struck her, suddenly, that the Emperor's plans had gone completely off the rails. He couldn't have expected the Watchtower to be destroyed.

As if he'd read her mind, the Emperor turned on her.

"Charity," he said. "What happened to the Watchtower?"

"I don't know," Charity said. She had always believed the Watchtower to be impregnable, utterly indestructible. "Magic?"

The Emperor's face darkened, but Dread spoke first. "Nothing magical could get into the Watchtower without being noted and logged," he said. "And something powerful enough to destroy the fortress would have been detectable halfway across the city."

"Then I don't know," Charity said. Tiredness made her voice more whiny than she might have preferred. "How do you expect me to guess?"

"You never know what someone knows these days," the Emperor observed, archly. He turned to survey the damage, his hands clasped behind his back. "Whoever planned this really did a great job."

Charity and Dread exchanged glances. "Really," Dread said. "Because, from where I'm sitting, over two thousand people are dead."

"Perhaps more than that," the Emperor said, without looking back. "How many bodies were burned to ash by my magnificent pets?"

"I do not know," Dread said.

Charity shivered. It was illegal to preserve a person's body, for fear of necromancy, but each of the Great Houses had their own funeral rites, spoken over bodies before they were burned to ash and scattered in crypts. None of them would be happy at having the bodies destroyed by the Emperor, even if there *had* been an attempt to kill him. And then ... what if Lady Lakeside *had* brought her sisters to the Arena? They might all be dead and she wouldn't have a clue.

"I cannot even guess," the Emperor agreed. He walked over to where one of the would-be assassins had fallen, then picked up a long hollow stick from the ground. "And what is this?"

Dread took it and frowned. "I do not know," he said, again. "It looks like a blowpipe."

"But it killed people," the Emperor said. He sounded, for the first time, disturbed rather than amused. "And there's no magic in it at all."

He turned as a red-robed sorcerer ran into the Arena, carrying a heavy parchment scroll. Charity watched as the Emperor turned to meet him, then looked at Dread. The Inquisitor looked ... tired, and oddly furious. She wondered, suddenly, how *he* was coping with the situation. Losing the Watchtower had to sting badly. The gods alone knew how many Inquisitors had died in the blast.

"Lady Lakeside, it would seem, has decided to stick a knife in my back," the Emperor said, rolling up the scroll. "She has called an emergency meeting of the Great Houses and the remaining members of the former Privy Council, with the declared intention of unseating me."

Charity swallowed. No one had ever successfully unseated a Grand Sorcerer, not since the first Grand Sorcerer had established the rules. They would not only have to fight the most powerful magician in the world, but the Inquisitors as well. But now, with the Watchtower gone, just how many Inquisitors were *left*? She knew Dread was alive, and there had been a handful of others in the Arena, but what had happened to the remainder? Had they been on the streets or in the Watchtower?

"This is treason, of course," the Emperor said. He turned his head, locking eyes with the dragon. There was a brief moment of mental communication, then the dragon hurled itself into the sky, wings beating frantically as it struggled for attitude. "We will have to do something about her, now."

"Your Majesty," Charity said, before she could finish thinking of a plan. "Is that wise?"

The Emperor turned to face her. "To allow traitors to go unpunished?"

Charity thought, as fast as she could. "Your Majesty, the Great Houses may have more magical power than yourself," she said. "I think ..."

The Emperor backhanded her, slapping her right across the face. Charity tasted blood in her mouth as she stumbled, almost falling to the ground. Her parents had walloped her from time to time, when they'd grown tired of endless lectures, but she'd never been slapped so brutally. It felt almost as if he'd knocked out a couple of teeth.

"You will not question my judgement again," the Emperor hissed. "Or would you like a demonstration of what happens to uppity bitches in my homeland?"

Charity stared at him, then shook her head. Part of her wanted to provoke him into killing her, but the oaths wouldn't let her try to wriggle out of his service that way, any more than they would allow her to kill herself. And besides, she had a feeling that his demonstration would be painful and humiliating, but not fatal. There was no point in allowing him to torture her ...

But the kids, she thought, as the Emperor turned away. *What can I do for them?*

Dread passed her a handkerchief, then cast a light healing spell on her jaw. The pain faded rapidly to a dull throbbing, no worse than the toothache she'd once had as a child. Her father had forbidden her to use any painkilling potions, pointing out that she'd ignored his advice, time and time again, to actually brush her teeth. He'd said, she recalled, that the pain might teach her a lesson. It had, in many ways, but she'd still hated him at the time.

She closed her eyes for a long moment, then followed the Emperor through the arch and out onto the streets. They were deserted, save for a handful of soldiers and red-robed sorcerers, but the Emperor didn't seem to mind. This time, instead of climbing into a carriage, he walked towards the Great Houses, the dragon flying high overhead. Charity looked up as its shadow fell over her and shivered.

"It's hard to kill a dragon," Dread muttered. "A single sorcerer would never be able to do it."

"I know," Charity muttered back. All of the legends surrounding dragons claimed they were nearly invincible. Light Spinner had killed one, but only by drawing on the immense power stored in the city's protective wards. "Can the Great Houses kill one?"

"I don't know," Dread said. "Did they have time to make any preparations?"

Charity knew it was a rhetorical question. A dragon attack had been rated about as likely as the Grand Sorceress snapping her wand, then insisting that everyone else snapped theirs too and give up magic for life. Whatever protections there were surrounding House Lakeside, they wouldn't be enough to stop a dragon. What sort of paranoid fool would waste time and effort constructing wards against purely imaginary threats?

But they're not imaginary, she thought, as she looked at the dragon. *That threat is all too real.*

She sighed and rubbed her jaw as House Lakeside came into view. It was one of the oldest buildings in the city, built during the time of the first Grand Sorcerer, something the Lakeside Family never allowed anyone to forget. They had an unbroken line of powerful sorcerers, skilled druids and resourceful alchemists who were responsible for some of the most fascinating magical breakthroughs since the first laws of magic had been codified. If they hadn't produced a Grand Sorcerer, they'd certainly produced hundreds of people who had managed to steer events to their satisfaction.

And maybe that was what they wanted, she thought, as the small army came to a halt and surveyed the mansion. The Lakeside Family was so wealthy that they actually had a small garden surrounding their home. *Not to have the appearance of power, but the cold hard reality.*

"Well," the Emperor announced, as his sorcerers poked at the wards surrounding the mansion. "It seems the rats have sealed themselves into their lair."

He snickered, then looked up at the dragon. Soldiers and sorcerers scattered back in alarm as the dragon's mouth lolled open, then a long stream of flame cascaded down and struck the wards. Fire rolled over the wards, licking against the magic and searching for any weaknesses. Charity realised, to her shock, that the flames were actually threatening to set the wards on fire, burning away the magic that held them in place. No wonder dragons had been considered so fearsome, so many years ago. The flames they produced were the most effective weapon against magic known to exist.

The temperature rose, sharply, as the dragon kept pouring fire down onto the wards. Charity hoped – prayed – that the other houses were fireproof as the garden caught fire, the flames spreading rapidly and reducing the trees and hedges to ash. Inch by inch, the wards began to splutter and die, then snap out of existence. Charity moaned inwardly as the dragon roared, then edged closer to the mansion. The final wards were starting to break under its flames ...

A wash of magic pushed her back as the family launched a counterattack. She watched, lifting her wand, as a stream of magicians emerged from the wards and attacked, throwing curses into the midst of the army. The Emperor laughed, then sent a new set of commands to the dragon. It stopped pouring fire onto the wards and turned its attention to the newcomers, incinerating them all in a blaze of light. And then it returned its attention to the mansion.

"They died for nothing," Dread said.

Charity shuddered. She'd known a couple of the Lakeside Family's children from her time at school. One daughter had been both smart and pretty; the boys had flocked round her like bees to honey, while the girls had hated her silently. The other had merely been pretty; Charity had known her long enough to be sure she didn't have an original bone in her body or thought in her head. She'd heard the latter girl had been sent out of the city after her graduation, perhaps to somewhere where intelligence was considered less vital than good looks. It had certainly taken her out of the running to become Prime Heir.

But Dread was right. The dead had died for nothing.

The wards sputtered violently, one last time, then died completely. Flames licked along the side of the mansion, burning off the ivy and other climbing plants that the family had used as a form of protection, but the entire building didn't catch fire. The dragon lunged forwards, claws extended, and tore right through the stone, ripping the building open as easily as a human might cut into a piece of meat. Charity realised, as the dragon plucked up a couple of defenders and swallowed them whole, that the family had planned to fight through the house, room by room. But the dragon had ruined all their plans.

But they could have run, she thought, as the soldiers and sorcerers ran forward and plunged into the house. *Why didn't they run?*

The Emperor watched and smirked as House Lakeside was ruthlessly torn apart by his men, while the dragon perched on a nearby house and peered down at the scurrying humans as if it was considering which one to have for lunch. Charity wanted to look away, but she forced herself to watch as the handful of survivors – mainly children too young to fight – were pulled out of the house and dragged in front of the Emperor, while the serving maids were taken into half-intact rooms and brutalised. The handful of adult survivors were killed out of hand.

"Well," the Emperor said. "I believe you will want to see these three."

Charity knew what she would see before she looked. Jolie, Chanel and Chime stood there, staring at her in absolute horror. They would see the mark on her face, she knew, and ... and who knew what they would think? Offhand, she couldn't recall her father ever slapping her mother, not when her mother was a powerful magician in her own right. Even their loud arguments over Johan's ... *condition* hadn't ended with physical violence. But sometimes the maids had been slapped ...

"Your sisters, I presume," the Emperor said. "What should I do with them?"

"Let them go back to school," Charity pleaded. "They're too young to be dangerous."

"Ah, but children grow into big strong threats," the Emperor observed. "One day, one of these young ladies may even try to kill me."

"You have a dragon," Charity reminded him.

"There are ways to kill dragons," the Emperor countered. He was enjoying watching her agony. "And it isn't as if I need to keep you happy."

"Please," Charity said, falling to her knees. The children stared at her, as if they didn't quite understand what was happening. "Please. Spare their lives. I'll do anything."

"You would do anything for me now," the Emperor pointed out. He reached for her hair and stroked it, as one would stroke a cat. "But their lives will be spared, for the moment."

He looked at one of his sorcerers. "Take them to the Peerless School," he ordered. "They can stay there until I send for them."

"Thank you," Charity said, as the children were marched off. "I ..."

"Oh, you'll pay for it," the Emperor assured her. "In fact ..."

He broke off as a messenger ran up to him and threw himself into full prostration. Charity blinked, then realised that the news had to be bad. The Emperor hadn't started killing messengers yet, but it might just be a matter of time.

"Get up," the Emperor snarled. "What's happened?"

"Two women and a man made their way through the tunnels, evading the ... special guard," the messenger reported. "They froze an entire troop on the other side, then vanished."

The Emperor's face purpled. "Your brother would seem to be alive," he said, to Charity. "Who else could do that to an entire troop?"

He turned to look at Dread. "Get after them," he ordered. "I want the Head Librarian alive; once you've taken her prisoner, kill the other two and get her back here. Do you understand me?"

"Yes, Your Majesty," Dread said, stiffly. "I understand."

Charity shuddered. She knew that Dread and the Head Librarian had worked together in the past ... was it possible they were friends or lovers? But it didn't matter, she knew; Dread, bound by his oaths, would carry out his orders. And if they were friends, he would have to bring her back to a fate worse than death. Unless he could find a loophole ...

... But was there one to be found?

"Go," the Emperor ordered. He beckoned one of the sorcerers over and muttered orders in his ear, then turned back to Charity. "Go back to the Palace and wait for me there."

"Yes, Your Majesty," Charity said. Her sisters were alive. Her sisters would *stay* alive. And she would do whatever it took to *keep* it that way. "I'll be there."

"Of course you will," the Emperor said. He watched Dread leave, then smirked at her. "You will do whatever I say."

Chapter Thirty-Seven

Johan wasn't quite sure *what* to make of Knawel Haldane.

On one hand, it was a city far – far – larger than the Golden City. There were no mountains hemming it in, nor were there any society rules about what counted as a decent place to build a home. Instead of towering apartment blocks, pressed in together by the sheer weight of the population, there were smaller homes and apartments that he'd been told were surprisingly affordable, while the population seemed much less stressed than the folk he recalled from the Golden City. But, on the other hand, there was an ever-present stench of human waste that refused to fade from his nose.

"I think I hate the smell here," he said to Daria, as they waited outside the Town Hall. "We need to move on."

"It could be worse," Daria said. She wrinkled her nose. "Believe me, it could be worse."

Johan shuddered at the thought, then looked across at a handful of guardsmen on the other side of the square. They seemed nervous, unsurprisingly. There might be no stream of refugees from the Golden City – yet – but they had to have heard rumours about everything from riots in the street to live dragons. Hell, the moment they'd entered the city, a guardsman had asked them to report to the Town Hall. Elaine, reluctantly, had agreed.

"I'll take your word for it," he said, finally. Elaine's emotions were always tightly controlled, but he could feel her irritation and impatience jumping down the bond. "Why did we come here again?"

"Because we need horses and supplies," Daria said, patiently. "Are you always so impatient?"

Johan smiled at her. "Are you always so calm?"

"Always, except when the full moon rises," Daria said. "Don't pick a fight with me then if you value your life."

"I won't," Johan said. He looked up at the darkening sky,

nervously. "How long do we have until the full moon?"

"One week," Daria said. "Maybe I'll go howling through the woods for the night – each night."

Johan opened his mouth to reply, then closed it as Elaine came out of the Town Hall, looking irked. "They're unwilling to do anything," she said. "They're scared halfway to death."

Daria nodded as she rose to her feet. "I could smell it from out here," she said. "Didn't they believe you?"

"I told them most of what had happened," Elaine confirmed. "Some of their people saw the dragons, briefly. But I couldn't tell them everything."

Johan sighed, inwardly, as they found their way through a maze of streets to the address Hawke had given him. Not entirely to his surprise, it was another pub, crammed with nervous-looking customers. The chatter grew louder as they pushed open the door, then made their way over to the bar, but it was impossible to pick out a single word. They were using so many privacy wards that even unprotected conversation was garbled.

"Hey," he said, waving to the bartender. "I have a note for you."

The bartender glanced at the note, then waved to a waitress wearing a long shapeless dress that was buttoned all the way up to her neck. She nodded to Johan – her sour pinched face barely twitching – and then led the way into a smaller room. It was so completely empty that there wasn't even a table, let alone chairs or a sofa.

"Wait here," she said, in a voice so tart it could sour lemons. "Do you want drinks?"

"No, thank you," Elaine said. "We'll wait."

Johan frowned as Elaine leant against the wall. He'd walked for hours, the few times he'd managed to get out of the house, and Daria was a werewolf, but it was clear that Elaine wasn't used to walking very far. Her entire body was aching and she wanted nothing more than to sleep, but he doubted that sleep was an option. The crisis in the Golden City was only ten miles away, after all. A team of men riding an Iron Dragon could be there within an hour, perhaps much less.

Should have sabotaged the rails before we left, he thought, grimly. *Why didn't we think of that?*

"The waitress is strongly religious," Daria commented. "Her sect aren't supposed to have any form of sexual relationships, outside procreation."

Johan blinked. "How can you tell?"

"The way she dresses, the way she moves," Daria said. "And her smell, which is completely unblemished by any man. I dare say she would rather be working somewhere else, but has to work here for some reason."

She broke off as the door opened, revealing a tall man wearing an apron and carrying a small bag in one hand. Johan eyed him, feeling uncomfortably reminded of his father; the face was different, but there was the same attitude of absolute superiority he'd hated seeing on his father's face. The man wasn't a magician, he thought, and yet he was still convinced he was in charge.

But these are the Levellers, he reminded himself. *They will not honour a magician just because he is a magician.*

"No names, not here," the man said, as he closed the door behind him. "I have been asked to give you all the help I can. What do you need?"

"Horses, food and a map," Elaine said. "And, if you have it, permission to use the Emperor's Roads."

"That will require a heavy bribe," the man said. "But I can get it for you. When do you want to leave?"

"As soon as possible," Elaine said.

"I can get the horses and permits to you within two hours," the man said. "Any quicker and you might be better off requesting them from the council."

"Two hours would be fine," Elaine assured him.

"I'll see to it," the man said. "I'll have food and drink sent here for you now, too. Travel food is rarely nice."

He nodded, then stepped back out of the door and closed it behind him. "Nice guy," Daria said, "but also very nervous. I guess he's heard the rumours too."

"Probably," Elaine said. She sat down, resting her back against the wall. "Is it normal to ache so badly?"

"It's your muscles being stretched for the first time in ... years," Daria said, as Johan sat down next to Elaine. "You could do with stretching a few more muscles too."

"I hate you," Elaine said, without heat.

"Here's another question," Daria said. "How long has it been since you rode a horse?"

"I learnt at the Peerless School," Elaine said. "The beasts never liked me."

"I'd better make sure yours stays in line," Daria said. "But I'd be much happier running beside you, in wolf form."

She nodded, then paced out of the room. Johan watched her go, then looked at Elaine. She seemed tired, but he could feel the stress, guilt and shame running through her mind. Johan understood, in a way; he'd liked Cass and to have her die, perhaps for nothing, was horrific. It was hard to blame Elaine for feeling guilty. Cass would have survived if Elaine had insisted she come with them.

But Cass was also a strong magician, Johan thought. *How could we have stopped her from going?*

"We'll avenge her," he said, putting his arm around her. It was never easy to know what to say, but he meant it. "One day, we will kill Deferens and his master."

"I hope so," Elaine said. She relaxed into his arm for a long moment, then straightened up. "I have a letter she wanted me to give you, if she ... if she didn't make it. I don't know what it actually says."

Johan blinked. "For me?"

"One of them," Elaine said. She pulled it out of her pocket, then passed it to him. "It will be charmed so only you can read it. Make sure you don't let anyone else open the letter, or handle the paper."

"My father taught me that much," Johan said. "But why would she write a letter to me?"

Elaine shrugged.

Johan examined the paper closely, then pressed his fingertip against the rune Cass had drawn on the back. Magic sparkled around his finger for a second and the envelope grew warm, then the heat suddenly died. Shaking his head, he opened the envelope and pulled out a scrap of paper, followed by a heart-shaped pendant. He put it down sharply – who knew what spells were attached to it? – and scanned the letter quickly. Cass had clearly been in a hurry when she'd been writing and it showed.

Johan.

If you're reading this, I am dead. Anything less will not alter the charm I have given your mentor, or the hex I placed on this letter. Should someone – even you – have tried to open it prior to my death, the paper would have been destroyed. Your magic is strange and unpredictable, but even you should be unable to read this letter early.

I have a confession to make. We are related.

I don't know if you knew, although you certainly did not know my pedigree. Like most of the Great Houses, House Lakeside had a habit of trying to mate its cadet branches with children from lesser bloodlines or new blood magicians. My great-great-grandfather, a third son of the House, was married to a daughter of House Conidian. At the time, your family was considered very lowly indeed; important outside the Golden City, minimally important within the mountains. I do not know if your father knew of the connection – I never had a chance to check the records and see if he'd worked with House Lakeside – but I was certainly not aware of it until after you manifested powers and we looked into your bloodline.

Inquisitors are expected – required – to sunder all ties to their families when they place the ring on their finger for the first time. I do not believe that many of my former comrades knew of my family history, and if they did they would not have considered it important. Daughter of House Lakeside or not, I was no longer in line for either power or inheritance. In the unlikely event of me having children, they too would not be part of the family. We may share a faint biological link, but the family magics long since separated us.

And yet I feel guilty.

I knew nothing about you until the incident outside the Imperial Palace. Your father was quite successful in covering up your existence. I suspect that much of your early development was simply attributed to your brother – helped, of course, by the fact you lived well away from the Golden City. Few people in the Golden City really cared about your family, although – as you know – rumours did get out. I thought nothing of it when your family arrived in the Golden City, although we were trying desperately to clean up the mess after Kane by then.

I could have said something when we were thrust together. Maybe I should have done.

But I saw your treatment of your sisters and thought better of it.

I understand your anger at your family. In many ways, I was equally angry at mine. They did not expect me to be anything more than a decorative piece of window dressing, then an ornament hanging from the arm of some elderly wizard, willing to trade his blood for the family name. But I had power and drive, while you lacked power. I had options that were simply not, at the time, open to you.

But what you have to decide, sooner rather than later, is what you want to do with your newfound power.

Your sisters treated you badly. I don't blame you for being traumatised – and I don't blame you for wanting revenge. But they were – are – children. A child lacks the ability to tell right from wrong, to understand when a joke is no longer funny, to see the fine line between pranks and outright bullying. I will concede they were set a bad example by your parents and your older siblings. But tell me – what do you want to become?

You have shattered their lives already, for better or worse. Your parents are gone, your older brother has fled and your sister is Deferens's slave. I do not care to imagine what will happen to your younger siblings if they too fall into his hands. They may be unhurt, physically, but their minds will be torn asunder. I have met Deferens in my working capacity and I can say, after hours of observation, that he holds women in total contempt. In many ways, he is far worse than your older brother. A rapist – even a serial rapist – would be a far better person to encounter than Vlad Deferens, particularly if he believes he holds the whip hand. Charity's submission to him will not have impressed him. Indeed, he will only hold her in greater contempt because she gave up her freedom to save her life.

So tell me ... what do you want to become? The bully who terrorises his siblings as they terrorised him, or the child who rises up above his early life to be a truly great man?

I had Dread to tell me when I was being a fool – and he

did, believe me. There was never a day when he didn't find something to criticise, never a day when I didn't do something wrong in his eyes. I hated him at the time, let me tell you. There were times when I seriously considered throwing a hex at him or simply telling him where to go and leaving for good. But I stuck with it ... and, at the end, I realised what he'd been trying to tell me all along. I made mistakes – everyone made mistakes – but that doesn't matter so much as how you handle yourself when you make one. Do you realise you made a mistake and do what you can to fix it, or do you try to deny the possibility that you could ever be wrong?

And it gets much harder when you're dealing with other people's mistakes.

Your father made a thousand mistakes when dealing with you and your siblings. He spoilt Jamal, because Jamal was the first-born and always special in his eyes. He treated you like dirt, because you seemed to have no power and were thus useless to his dreams of dynasty. He treated Charity like I was treated, to some extent; she was prepared for marriage to a suitable partner, not to be Prime Heir. And I suspect the same happened to your younger siblings. Their role was to carry out your father's plans, not to be young men and women in their own right.

I've seen the results of far too many mistakes in the years I spent on duty, Johan. It isn't pleasant.

You have to deal with your father's mistakes – but you have to do it without making mistakes of your own.

If you will accept advice from your great-great-cousin (or whatever the precise term for our relationship actually is) *either mend fences with your siblings or leave them behind for good. Right now, you're as much of a bogeyman – perhaps more – to them as Jamal ever was. Worse? You took magic from both their father and their older brother. A terror to any magician – and maybe that was why I didn't speak to you when I was alive – but far, far worse to them. They knew you, after all.*

You think they deserve it. Maybe you're right. But does that mean that you should be a bastard to them – or worse? All I can tell you is that the choice is yours.

I like to think I would have done something to help you, if I'd known. I could not have claimed Right of Blood, as I severed myself from the family magics, but there were other options. There were ways to separate you too from the family, so your existence posed no threat. But I didn't know. How many people have I heard say the same thing? It feels no better to say it myself, than to hear it from someone who should have known and didn't.

The pendant I've included in this letter is the sole heirloom I kept from my mother, when I left House Lakeside. The magic was removed when I took the skull-ring and, right now, it isn't really worth more than twenty pieces of silver. However, I would like you to have it and gift it to your future wife, when – if – you marry.

There's nothing else to write, save this. If I died – and I must have done, if you're reading this letter – I hope I died well.

Yours

Cassandra Lakeside, Inquisitor 1st Class

Johan looked down at the letter. "She was related to me," he said. "Was that true?"

"She said so," Elaine said. "What did she tell you?"

"That ... I don't know what to make of it," Johan said. "Can you read the letter?"

Elaine shook her head. "You can read it to me later, if you like," she said. "But she charmed it against prying eyes."

The door opened, revealing Daria, carrying a small tray of food. Johan suddenly felt ravenous; he folded the letter, placed it in his pocket and then reached for the closest sandwich. Ham and cheese wasn't his favourite, but it tasted wonderful after walking so far. But he couldn't help feeling melancholy. He hadn't known he'd had a decent relative. No one had known.

"We should honour her," he said, finally. "Can we say something?"

Elaine reached out and rested her hand on his for a long moment. "We can and we will," she said. "Once we're out of the city, we'll stop long enough to bury the charm."

Chapter Thirty-Eight

Elaine couldn't help keeping a wary eye on Johan as they finished their meal, then waited for the innkeeper to escort them around the back of the inn, where the horses were kept ready for clients. On the surface, Johan looked normal, but she could tell he was lost in his own thoughts. Apart from the request to hold a proper ceremony – or as close as they could – for Cass, he hadn't said anything.

"I'm no good at horses," she said, in the hope it would cheer him up. "I used to keep falling off."

"She's a well-trained beast," the innkeeper assured her. "Just trade her in at the next inn, or keep her for yourself, if you wish."

"I can handle her, if necessary," Johan said. He sounded tired and worn. "Just climb onto the back, then hold the reins."

Elaine did as she was told, although she was nervous. She might have learnt how to ride at the Peerless School, but she wasn't used to riding; indeed, she hadn't ridden a horse since she'd left the school, years ago. The horse gave her a look that promised mischief, then settled down when Johan scrambled onto the other horse. Perhaps, Elaine decided, the horse could sense someone who knew what he was doing.

Or perhaps she is just biding her time, she thought, sourly.

"Thank you," she said, to the innkeeper. "You might want to go elsewhere for a while."

"I have work here," the innkeeper said. "But good luck."

Daria scrambled up behind Elaine, then hung on for dear life as Johan led the way out onto the streets. Elaine gritted her teeth, then held the reins as tightly as she could; Johan didn't seem to have any problem steering through the streets, then out into the countryside. The population shot them dark looks as they passed, but did nothing. Elaine was almost pitifully relieved.

"Here will do," Daria said, once the city was out of sight

and the fields were closing in around them. "Don't worry about the horse. I'll catch her if she runs away."

Elaine snorted as Daria dropped to the ground, then pulled off her dress and passed it back to Elaine. The horse neighed uncomfortably as Daria snapped into wolf form, then started to slowly canter after Johan, Daria loping along behind it with casual ease. Elaine suspected the horse wasn't even remotely comfortable with a werewolf following in her footsteps, but there was nothing to be done about it. Besides, Daria was right. If the horse *did* decide to run, a werewolf could catch her before she managed to throw Elaine off.

It was nearly an hour of hard riding before the fields were replaced by forest, flickers of wild magic sparkling through the trees. The wind blew colder, threatening them with gusts of snow or sleet, although it still seemed warmer than the Golden City. Elaine shivered, cast warming charms around herself, then allowed the horse to keep following Johan. Her apprentice was brooding, she sensed, but she didn't know what to say. What had Cass said to him, in her letter? Elaine's imagination provided too many answers.

"This would be a good place to stop," Johan called back, as they reached a small clearing. There was a large pond in the centre of the clearing, slowly icing over as the weather cooled. "I think she'd like it."

Elaine wanted to ask what made him say that, but instead she just pulled the horse to a halt and slid down to the ground. Her legs felt weak, after riding for so long, yet it was a relief to stand on solid ground again. Johan gave her a concerned look as she started to rub aches and pains out of her body, then turned to look towards the pond. There were animal tracks all around it, suggesting that nothing dangerous lurked within the murky water. Or so she thought. It had been years since she'd taken any classes on surviving outside human settlements.

"There's a nice patch of ground over there," Daria said, pointing to a gap in the trees. "That would be suitable, I think."

Johan nodded, tied the horses to the trees, then walked over to the grass. There was something about it, Elaine decided as she followed him, that was definitely charming, a sense of agelessness in a world undergoing rapid change. She lifted her wand and performed a simple charm, looking for hints of wild magic that might interfere with the rites, but found nothing. Once she was sure the place was clean, she reached into her pocket and produced the life-charm. Cass's once-golden hair was now rapidly decaying into dust.

"Deferens will not have kept her body," she said, as Johan turned to face her. "I think he would have simply ordered it cremated."

"No doubt," Johan agreed. He knelt down, then dug a small hole in the ground with his fingers. "Do you know what to say?"

"Only in general terms," Elaine said. "I have no idea what gods she worshipped – if she worshipped any."

"She was from House Lakeside," Johan said. "Wouldn't they have household gods?"

"I wouldn't know their names," Elaine said. The Great Houses rarely shared such details with outsiders, even outsiders who had married into their families. "Besides, Lady Lakeside isn't here to bury her."

"Call on them, if you can," Johan urged. "I don't know if my family's gods would accept her."

Elaine swallowed, then knelt down beside the tiny grave. "Gods of Lakeside, we speak to you, even though we are not of your family," she said. There was no way to address the prayer more precisely, not without knowing specific names. "We ask you to take unto yourselves the soul of Cassandra Lakeside, who was born into your family and died upholding your family's finest values. We bear witness, before you and our own gods, that she is worthy of the name she bore. We could not honour her more had she lived and died as one of us."

She took a breath, feeling tears prickling at the corner of her eyes. "Cassandra saved my life," she said, simply. "She sacrificed much to save me from a fate worse than death. For that and so much more, I do her honour."

Johan cleared his throat. "Cassandra saved my soul," he said. His voice was even, but Elaine could sense the bitter guilt that flowed through his mind. "For that, and so much more, I do her honour."

"Cassandra accepted me for what I was," Daria said, after a

long moment. "For that, and so much more, I do her honour."

Elaine held the life-charm over the tiny grave, then dropped it into the earth. There was a flare of light as it touched the soil, which faded rapidly into nothingness. Elaine wiped the tears from her eyes, then carefully picked up a piece of soil and dropped it into the grave, covering the life-charm. Johan and Daria did the same, burying the life-charm until there was no sign that anything had been buried there at all. Elaine lifted her wand, sketched a hex sign in the earth covering the grave, then rose to her feet.

"I'm sorry," she said, quietly. "You deserved so much better."

She had gone to five funerals in her life; three of them for children who had died at the orphanage, one for a co-worker who had been killed by a book sent to the Great Library and one for the Inquisitors who had been killed during Kane's attack on the Golden City. She had felt guilty as a child – they had *all* felt guilty – at being torn between grief for their lost friends and relief that they were gone, that they would no longer be consuming food that was sparse enough as it was. The other funerals had been better, but still poignant And they had all been attended by more than three mourners.

"She would have understood," Daria said, quietly. "She knew she could die in the line of duty."

Elaine shook her head. Cass had had no obligation to risk her life, not after the Grand Sorceress had released her from her oaths. She could have escaped the city in the chaos caused by the Watchtower's destruction, escorting them all the way to the border if necessary. Instead, she had stayed, fought and died. Deferens had had to summon a *dragon* – two dragons – to deal with her. There were times when Elaine wished she had had that sort of courage, when she'd been in school. But maybe it came with the power. No one could ever have accused Cass of lacking in magic.

"Maybe she would have understood," she said, as she looked towards the grave. "But it still feels sad."

She looked over at Johan, then walked towards where he was sitting, staring down at the freezing pond. He smiled weakly at her as she approached, then rose. Elaine hesitated, then gave him a tight hug. He started in surprise, then returned it.

"I was never good with emotions," Elaine admitted, "but do you want to talk about what you're feeling?"

Johan frowned as he let go of her. "Am I turning into Jamal?"

Elaine blinked. "Is that what she told you?"

"Not really, but close," Johan said. He passed her the letter, but it was blank to her eyes. "I ... she told me that I was terrorising my family."

"You weren't very nice to your sisters," Elaine said. She wondered, suddenly, what had happened to the young girls. Lady Lakeside might just have taken them to the Arena ... or she might have handed them over to someone else, if she didn't feel like taking care of them any longer. "But I've never had sisters, so I don't know if they deserved it or not."

"You grew up with sisters at the orphanage," Johan said. "Didn't you?"

"They weren't *real* sisters," Elaine said. "I always knew they would snatch the bread from my mouth if they had a chance – and I would do the same. We were always competing, hoping to be chosen by a family and taken home ... one day, a girl would be with us; the next, she would be gone. Your family will always be part of you."

Johan rubbed his eyes. "She could have told me she was related to me," he said, finally. "I could have taken it."

"You scare people," Elaine said.

"I don't scare *you*," Johan objected.

"I know you," Elaine reminded him. "I know you're a decent person, under the anger issues and the determination to prove yourself, but most people don't know you. Your very existence threatens everything they hold dear."

"I didn't want to be anything but a person who lived his own life," Johan said. "Is that wrong?"

Elaine sighed. "I don't think so," she said. "But fate handed you a different set of cards."

She sat down on the hard ground, shivering before she managed to cast yet another warming charm. "A couple of hundred years ago, I wouldn't have been invited to the Peerless School," she said. "My magic wouldn't have been reckoned strong enough for generalist training. I would have either apprenticed myself to a potions brewer, if I'd been lucky, or been offered a chance to serve as breeding stock for one of the Great Houses. They would have taken me for a very weak bloodline, but with some careful breeding my grandchildren might have amounted to something.

"If I'd been born in Deferens's homeland, I would have been raised to worship men and do whatever they told me," she added. "I would have been sold to a man in need of a wife, or sent out of the country if they realised I had magic. They would never have taught me to read and write, let alone do anything beyond cooking, cleaning and churning out babies. I would have lived and died without ever realising there was a bigger world beyond the walls of my home – my prison.

"If I'd been born to one of the Great Houses, they might have considered me an embarrassment too ..."

"No," Johan said. "You have magic."

"Not very much of it," Elaine said. "Would I still have been allowed to go to school? Or would they have given me a little private tutoring, then passed me to someone who needed a wife who might share her gift with their children?"

Johan started to pace, angrily. "I wish I'd known," he said. "If I'd known she was related to me, I would have listened to her ..."

"Or would you have snapped at her?" Elaine asked gently. "You cannot say what *would* have happened when you have the benefit of hindsight."

"I don't know what to feel," Johan admitted. "What *should* I feel?"

He stopped in front of her, his eyes pleading for understanding. "I don't regret what I did to Jamal, or my father," he said. "Is that wrong of me?"

Elaine considered it. "I think I don't blame you for lashing out at them," she said. "And I know you did it, at least in part, to avenge what you thought was my death."

"But I don't regret it," Johan snapped. "I don't feel guilt!"

"Tell me," Elaine said. "Do you think you should?"

"*I don't know,*" Johan insisted.

Elaine understood, better than she wanted to admit. She'd been bullied, yet her bullies hadn't been members of her family. Johan, on the other hand, had been bullied endlessly, merely for having been born without magic. He'd been so badly abused that he lacked any real empathy for his tormentors – and only a moron or a monster would expect him to have any. It was hard, so very hard, to blame him for ripping that precious gift out of their bodies, even though it had terrified the entire city. The magicians she knew would sooner castrate themselves than lose their magic.

She reached up and caught his hand, holding it gently. "I once cast a tripping jinx on Millicent," she said. "She was walking down the stairs at the time and she almost broke her neck."

"Good," Johan said, after a moment.

"I thought so too," Elaine said. "Until it dawned on me, afterwards, that I could have killed her."

She didn't know who had reported her, but *someone* had. Serving a month of detentions had been bad enough, she recalled, yet the lecture had been worse. The Administrator had pointed out, in exacting detail, just how close Elaine had come to being a murderess. A few inches further and Millicent would have been past all help, even with the strongest druids on call. She would sooner be beaten to within an inch of her life than endure a second such lecture.

"*They* could have killed me," Johan said.

"But they didn't," Elaine countered. "I think you need to decide, now, what you're going to do, the next time you see them. Are you going to let it pass or are you going to lash out at them again."

"I don't know," Johan said. "I want revenge ..."

"You can take it," Elaine said. "But will it be worth the effect it will have on you?"

She looked back towards where they'd buried the life-charm, then sighed. "I went to Ida, once," she said. "That was about six months before we met, a week after I became a Bookworm. Dread followed me there."

"He must have been interested in you," Johan said, mischievously. "You are quite pretty."

Elaine felt her face heat. She glared at him, then went on.

"We talked about what power could do to people," she recalled. "I didn't understand what he was trying to say at first. It was an odd conversation, you see. I didn't realise that he thought *I* might have had a power boost, rather than ... well, rather than having the Great Library dumped into my head. He pointed out that people who suddenly gained power tended to go a little insane."

"I'm not insane," Johan said. "Am I?"

"And then there was one of my co-workers," Elaine continued, not answering the question. "Her husband won favour – I don't know how – and got promoted up a rank or two. It came with quite a decent pay rise, enough to put him in the upper middle class. But it turned him from a nice man into a complete asshole."

Johan frowned. "Are you sure *she* wasn't the one who changed?"

"I didn't notice any change in her," Elaine said. She had to admit he had a point. Sudden wealth could ruin a woman as easily as it could ruin a man. "Point is: he'd been jumped forward too quickly, so he didn't adapt slowly to the change in circumstances. You have the same problem. You started out as a young man without magic, then you gained magic ... and not just *any* magic, but something radically different from anyone else. Right now, you could become a champion of righteousness ... or you could become a monster."

"I won't become a monster," Johan said. He gave her a look that spoke of endless trust and respect. "You won't let me."

"I will certainly *try* to keep you sane," Elaine said, "but ..."

She broke off as she sensed a flicker of magic. Someone was standing by the grave, hidden behind a complex concealment charm.

Johan looked down at her. "What ...?"

And then a rock flew out of nowhere and struck Johan neatly between the eyes. Elaine almost blacked out herself as her apprentice crumpled, hitting the ground with a terrifying thud. The shock stunned her, but she shook it off, somehow. She didn't dare collapse now, not when she knew, beyond a shadow of a doubt, who was standing behind the charm.

"Dread," she said, pulling herself to her feet. Her legs felt wobbly, but somehow she managed to remain standing upright. "Fancy meeting you here."

Chapter Thirty-Nine

Daria growled, low in her throat, as the Inquisitor made his appearance.

"Elaine," he said. He looked older, somehow; older and angrier. "I would like you to accompany me back to the Golden City."

Elaine eyed him warily, holding her wand in one hand. His wand was dangling from his belt, but she didn't relax. She knew, all too well, that he didn't need it to work magic. He wouldn't have become an Inquisitor without becoming proficient at working magic without a wand.

"I must respectfully decline," she said, although she knew it was futile. "The Emperor is a pawn of the Witch-King."

The flash of frustration she saw in his eyes confirmed her worst suspicions. He *knew* what was happening, yet he couldn't break his oaths and intervene. If Vlad Deferens was the Emperor, then Vlad Deferens was the Emperor ... and, no matter what he did, Dread had to do as he was commanded.

"The Emperor has ordered me to bring you back to the Golden City," Dread said. He hadn't moved, but that too meant nothing. Dread was old enough to be her father, yet he was both stronger and faster than her. "I can leave your friends here if you come with me now."

Elaine thought rapidly. She didn't dare allow him to take her back to the city – and yet she didn't dare try to fight him. Dread wasn't a mad Dark Wizard; he was a trained Inquisitor, with more power and experience than she could imagine. And he'd been smart enough to knock out Johan first, before his presence was completely blown. The greatest threat to him had been neutralised before they knew they were under attack.

"I can't do that," Elaine said. She hesitated, then gambled. "If the Witch-King is using Deferens as a puppet, do you have to obey him?"

"The oaths admit of no such loophole," Dread said. "He is the person sitting in the Golden Throne. He must be obeyed."

"But it's madness," Elaine protested. She stared at him, willing him to understand. "The Witch-King wants me to set the seal on his victory."

"I know," Dread said. His entire body quivered. "But I can delay no longer."

Daria snapped into wolf form and attacked, lunging forward at terrifying speed. Dread raised a ward, then ducked, snapping out a spell as he moved. Silver dust appeared from nowhere, surrounding Daria like a deadly cloud. It would be deadly too, Elaine knew, as she hastily cast a counterspell. Silver dust wouldn't be immediately fatal to a werewolf, not like a silver knife to the heart, but it would condemn Daria to a slow and unpleasant death. Daria choked, even as the dust started to fade, then roared angrily. Dread threw a spell at her and blasted her wolf body right across the clearing, right into a tree. Elaine took advantage of his distraction to fire a spell at him, but he blocked it without apparent effort.

"This is pointless," he said. He sounded as though he was trying to talk down to her ... and yet there was a hard edge to his voice she didn't quite understand. "You don't stand a chance against me. Let me take you back to the Golden City and your friends can be left here."

Elaine shuddered as he threw a freeze spell at her. It was the simplest of charms, used by students at the Peerless School, yet there was so much power behind it that blocking the spell required all of her concentration. Dread looked bored, rather than surprised, as she batted it aside, then simply threw another one. This time, Elaine ducked and dodged the spell, allowing it to zap over her shoulder and strike a tree. The fireball she hurled back at him struck his shields and vanished.

"Pointless," Dread repeated.

He was toying with her, Elaine knew. It was odd, yet somehow heartening. No normal Inquisitor would stoop to toying with an opponent, not even when the opponent was so much weaker than him. Dread was fighting his oaths, doing just enough to satisfy them without actually *winning* ... and trying to buy her time to produce a victory. But she honestly didn't know how to win.

She launched another fireball at him, then cast a second charm on the ground below his leather boots. It turned to mud; he started to sink, slipping and sliding as he tried to take a step forward. Elaine braced herself, then cast another freeze spell, turning the ground to ice and trapping his feet in the ground. Dread looked up at her, then flicked his finger. Elaine found herself picked up by an invisible force and slammed against the nearest tree.

"Pointless," Dread said, again.

Elaine muttered a charm under her breath. The force holding her in place twisted and threw itself back at Dread. He held up his hand, deflecting the wave of magic, then yanked his feet free of the ground and took a step forward. Elaine cast another spell, this time sucking up dirt and earth from the soil and throwing it right into his face. A wash of muddy water came back at her, soaking her dress. Dread stepped through the haze, smiling coldly. Elaine hastily created a dozen images of herself, each one accurate in every detail, but the Inquisitor was not fooled. He just kept walking towards her.

And this is him trying to lose? she thought, dazed. *How the hell do I stop him?*

She hefted her wand and launched a lightning bolt, striking him directly on his wards. Light flared around him, but he seemed unharmed. She gritted her teeth, formulated a second spell, then hurled another lightning bolt. As magic sparkled around his wards, she launched the second spell into his protections. Piece by piece, they started to untangle his protections, converting them into raw magic. Few magicians could hope to cast such a complex spell, she knew; fewer still could hope to cancel it in the midst of a fight. But Dread had an unfair advantage. He knew her, all too well.

"Not bad," Dread said. "But dangerous."

He ignored the spell in favour of throwing another one at her. This time, it struck her protections and punched right through, slamming into her bare skin. Elaine screamed as she felt her body warp and twist, then start to shrink. It was no prank spell, she knew, as it did its dirty work; it was designed to allow Inquisitors to capture and transport prisoners without resorting to either compulsion spells or handcuffs. Somehow, despite the pain, she managed to counter the spell, then reverse its effects. But she collapsed to the ground as soon as the spell was cancelled.

Dread looked down at her for a long moment, then started concentrating on the spell attacking his wards. It had done a great deal of damage in a few seconds, Elaine noted, despite the throbbing pain running through her body. Even Dread, for all of his skill, was having problems removing it. He'd need to drop his wards altogether if he wanted to do it quickly, she told herself, but he knew better than to do it with potential threats all around him.

She forced her mind to focus, drawing on what power she could to repair the damage to her body. It ached in so many places, after the spell and forced landing; it was all she could do to push the pain into a small corner of her mind. The link she shared with Johan didn't help; she cursed the irony mentally, even as she stared up at Dread. The Inquisitor's mental struggle was all-too-visible behind his eyes.

"I'm sorry," he said. "But there are no loopholes left."

Elaine winced as he grabbed her arm and hauled her to her feet, then pushed her into the nearest tree. His movements were calm and unhurried, despite the spell that was still attacking his remaining wards. Elaine would have been impressed if she hadn't been ruefully aware that he was going to take her back to Deferens, to face him one final time. She knew she wouldn't survive the final meeting.

"I'm sorry too," she said.

She summoned enough magic to cast an itching hex, then aimed it through a chink in his wards. Dread swore – she couldn't recall him ever swearing before – and let go of her dress, just enough to let her cast a second spell. The world grew around her rapidly, her dress falling down around her, casting everything into darkness. Dread yanked the dress back and stared down at her tiny shape, then reached for her with a hand the size of an Iron Dragon. Elaine ran, her tiny legs taking her into the tree, then out of reach. He would have to shrink himself to come in after her ...

The tree shook, then was violently yanked out of the ground. Elaine swore as pieces of wood crashed down all around her, then ran, trusting in the dirt and dust to conceal her movements. She found herself falling forwards as the ground shook – Dread had dropped the tree – and landed in the mud. A hand grabbed for her, but she managed to dodge, then cast a complex summoning charm of her own. Dread looked down at her from a very great height, then looked away. A large fox was running towards him at speed, followed by dozens of other animals. The summoning charm was used by hunters to attract game, everything from foxes to deer. It looked as though it had done its work too well.

She took advantage of the distraction to snap back to normal size, then looked around for her friends. Johan was still lying stunned, while Daria was choking and coughing. The silver would have burned her throat, even if she had managed to banish it before it was fatal. Elaine hesitated, cursing her own uncertainty. She wanted to help her friend, but she knew the only person who could stop Dread was Johan. Bidding her friend a silent apology, she ran over to Johan and looked down at him. There was a nasty gash on his forehead where he'd been hit, leaking blood. She hesitated – a blow to the head could have caused brain damage, which needed a specialist druid to heal – and then cast a healing spell. Magic soaked through the gash, slowly knitting together the damaged skin. But she didn't know if it would be enough.

"Wake up," she breathed, drawing on the link. Her legs wobbled as she sent him all the energy she could. "Please."

A flash of magic flared up as Dread banished the animals, then turned to face her. Elaine felt a moment of pity – his face was scratched and bleeding, while one of the larger creatures had taken a bite out of his leg – then ducked sharply as he threw a fireball at her. It shot over her head and blew a tree into flaming debris, which clattered down behind her. She ignored it as she lifted her hand and summoned her wand. It smacked into her palm a second later.

"Come back with me," he said. The struggle in his eyes was growing stronger. "Please."

Elaine shook her head, then launched a series of complex

hexes and charms she'd devised herself, using the knowledge from the Great Library. She'd stripped out all of the unnecessary sections, ensuring the spells could be cast with the bare minimum of power. Dread battered them away, as easily as a batsman would knock away balls thrown at him by his teammates, but every one of his counterspells drained magic from his reserves. And yet, she knew it wouldn't be enough.

She retreated, drawing his attention away from Johan. The cold wind felt chilly against her underclothes – it struck her, suddenly, that the fight was completely undignified – but Dread didn't seem distracted. He'd probably had experts trying to seduce him, she thought, as she cast the next set of spells. He was definitely stalling, trying to give her as much time as he could to win the fight, yet if Johan didn't wake up ...

"I'm sorry about the Watchtower," she said, hoping to keep him distracted. "They didn't deserve to die."

"None of them deserved to die, but they would not have wanted to live," Dread said, as he walked towards her. She knew what he meant; like it or not, the Inquisitors had wound up serving a monster. Their oaths prevented them from leaving Deferens, betraying him or even killing themselves to escape their shame. "The Levellers came up with something, I take it."

Elaine's eyes narrowed. "How did you know?"

"It was not hard to deduce," Dread said. He gave her a humourless smile. "Whatever destroyed the Watchtower had to be taken through the wards. Everything even slightly tinged with magic would have been noted by the wards, and checked if it was powerful enough to do serious harm. But the attackers got something through the wards, without bringing them down. Simple logic leads to the conclusion that the attack was not carried out with magic, but something else."

"Elementary," Elaine said.

"Quite," Dread agreed. "But also futile. The Emperor remains in control."

Elaine met his eyes. "How long will his Empire survive?"

Dread lifted his wand. "As long as he can hold it together."

"That may not be long," Elaine said. She was expecting the hex and dodged it as soon as she sensed the flare of magic. "He brought back the *dragons* in front of the Court Wizards! I dare say the entire world knows by now."

"Those who survived are being held," Dread said. "I dare say they will make the proper reports when they contact their tame monarchs."

He cast another hex, slamming it into Elaine's weakened wards. They held, but pins and needles ran down her fingers and she almost dropped her wand. Dread eyed her, sheer desperation clearly visible in his eyes. He couldn't toy with her much longer before his oaths pressed him forward ...

... And then she sensed Johan slowly staggering back to wakefulness.

Wake up, she thought at him. *Hurry*!

"I dare say they will," she said, trying to keep Dread focused on her. "But what about everyone else? Is he going to sacrifice the whole city?"

"I ..."

Dread stopped, then hurled a nasty spell at her. Elaine tried to dodge, but this time she moved far too slowly. The spell slammed through her wards and knocked her to the ground, while her wand flew off in the opposite direction. She grunted in pain, then gasped as Dread caught her and rolled her over, pressing her face into the muddy ground. Her hands were yanked behind her back and cuffed. Moments later, she was rolled over again, helplessly staring up at him. The charms on the iron cuffs prevented her from using magic.

"You mustn't take me back," she said, knowing it was still futile. Dread's oaths would no longer allow him any leeway. "He cannot be allowed to destroy everything we've built."

Dread reached for her, then stopped. His hand shook, then his entire body started to tremble violently. Blood trickled from his nose and eyes, dripping down and splashing on her bare chest. He was fighting, she realised, and the fight had reached a point where the magic he wielded was turning against him. He'd played games with the oaths until they'd finally caught up with it.

She stared. *No one* could resist such oaths. And yet Dread

was trying ...

Behind him, she saw Johan rising to his feet. *Take his magic, quickly*, she thought at him, hoping and praying it would be enough. It should be – mundanes had no magic to swear on – but would it save Dread? And would he want to live after losing his magic. *Hurry.*

Dread shuddered violently, but kept his mouth firmly closed. He was trying not to scream, Elaine saw; she wanted to look away, yet her head refused to turn. Magic was crackling around him now, ripping into his mind and body. And yet, it could all end if he just carried out his orders. Oaths existed to enforce themselves, after all. They didn't kill people who abided by their word.

But he isn't my father, Johan thought at her. She sensed waves of panic and guilt – and pain – accompanying the thought. *I shouldn't take his magic.*

He'd done it before, Elaine knew. He'd taken magic to save his father's life. But his father's mind had snapped, and then he'd left the city. Or so she had been told. Charity Conidian might have been ruthless enough to have her father killed as soon as control of the house had passed to her.

You must, she thought back. *Save him!*

Johan concentrated. This time, because of the bond, she sensed the rush of his magic. She'd been right, she realised; Johan's magic was driven by emotion, rather than the precise control she'd been taught at the Peerless School. He might never learn control ... not the way he was, but he didn't need it. And yet, his magic was odd. His reluctance to hurt Dread was actually making it harder for him to save him.

"Do it," she pleaded. She could draw on the bond to compel him, but she knew he would never forgive her if she did. He'd been humiliated too often by his family. *"Please."*

There was a flare of magic. Dread opened his mouth, spewing up blood, then collapsed on top of her. His entire body shook one final time, then he blacked out.

Johan stumbled over to them and fell onto his knees. "Is he dead?"

"I don't think so," Elaine said. Her hands felt constricted in the cuffs, as if they were blocking her circulation. "Help me get these things off, then we'll tend to him. And Daria."

Chapter Forty

"Well," the Emperor said. "You look good."

Charity scowled at him, then prostrated herself. The Emperor's maids had greeted her when she had returned to the Imperial Palace, then informed her that the Emperor expected her to wear a certain outfit until he said otherwise. It consisted of two translucent strips of red silk, so pale they were almost transparent, covering her breasts and groin. The rest of her body was bare. She'd never worn anything so daring at the Peerless School, let alone at a High Society gathering. She would almost sooner have been naked.

"Thank you," she said, through gritted teeth. No one would ever take her seriously again, after they saw her prancing around like a cheap whore. "I bring news from your sorcerers."

"You may rise," the Emperor said. "What news do they have?"

"Inquisitor Dread has not returned," Charity informed him. For once, she would have preferred to keep her face firmly fixed to the floor. "He was never an easy person to track with magic, but now he has vanished completely."

"So he is dead," the Emperor said. He sounded ... placid. "He has failed in his mission?"

"It would seem so," Charity said. Dread ... had been kind, even though they'd both been slaves. She would miss him. "And the Head Librarian seems to have made her escape."

"Maybe she has," the Emperor said. He didn't seem angry. Charity had half-expected a temper tantrum, perhaps followed by a brutal beating. "But where is she going?"

"I don't know, Your Majesty," Charity said. She had never thought she would be *worried* about someone *not* beating her, but his calm acceptance that something had gone wrong was surprisingly unnerving. "She merely ran from the city."

"Ah, but what can she do," the Emperor asked, "if she

doesn't know where to go?"

"Nothing," Charity said.

The Emperor smiled. "I trust that your siblings have returned to the Peerless School?"

"Yes, Your Majesty," Charity said. She wanted to scream in frustration. It was worth any price to keep her sisters safe, but she knew – all too well – just how easily the Emperor could end their lives. "They look forward to resuming their classes."

"What little swots," the Emperor observed. "Were you like that at school?"

"I worked hard," Charity said. It hadn't helped that far too many people remembered Jamal – and not in a good way. "But I'm sure they will become skilled magicians who can serve you well."

"I am sure of it too," the Emperor said. "I trust that you have seen the plans for the invasion?"

"I am no military officer," Charity protested. It struck her, a moment too late, that it might have been better if she *had* commanded the operation. "But I know where Dread kept the plans."

"Then we will commence the operation as soon as this city is secure," the Emperor said. "*That* will teach the petty kings not to pick fights with me."

Charity frowned. She *was* no military officer, but *Dread* had warned of the dangers of heavy casualties from storming Ida and she trusted his judgement. Losing half the army in an attack on a minor kingdom would be pointless – worse than pointless. It would be actively fatal, once the kingdoms started building up their own forces. Whatever else had happened, the dragons and the destruction of the Watchtower would fatally undermine the Empire's illusion of invincibility.

And what did Ida have that was worth the risk?

She kept that thought to herself, even as she rose to her feet and backed out of the Throne Room. If the Emperor wanted to waste his men by battering them against a mountain kingdom, who was she to stop him? It might even shatter his power, once and for all.

And that, she knew, was greatly to be desired.

***

Johan had never had to handle a medical emergency before, not when his entire family knew healing spells that could cope with almost everything short of major brain damage. Elaine detailed him to feed as much water as he could to Daria while she worked on Dread, attempting to save the Inquisitor's life. Johan wasn't sure he liked the Inquisitor as much as Elaine did, but he did as he was told. Besides, it kept him busy, with no time to brood.

"You smell of guilt," Daria said, once she managed to return to human form. "What have you done?"

"It must be impossible to get away with anything in your family," Johan muttered. He rose, then started picking up pieces of wood for a fire. The darkness was falling rapidly now and he knew better than to sleep in a forest without some source of light. "Your parents must always have known who to blame."

"Only if that person blamed themselves," Daria said. She didn't bother to don her robe, merely joined him in picking up sticks. "You have to know the difference between right and wrong to feel guilt."

"I took his magic," Johan said, very quietly. "It's my fault."

"He would have taken Elaine otherwise," Daria told him. "And perhaps killed the pair of us."

Johan sighed, rubbing his forehead. He'd been compelled before; Jamal had been very fond of forcing him to abase himself, or perform humiliating acts in public. He knew what Dread had been feeling, forced to lay hands on a friend and arrest her, even as every fibre of his being struggled against the commands. Taking Dread's magic had been the only way to save his life, yet ... yet it hadn't been anything like lashing out at his father. Dread hadn't deserved to be crippled.

He looked at Daria's naked body, admiring it in an abstract way that puzzled him. She was covered in scars, reflections of the internal damage her wolf form had suffered, yet she was moving as easily as ever. He knew he should be attracted to her – still attracted to her – and yet he felt nothing beyond casual admiration. He'd felt attracted even after knowing she was a werewolf, so why was he no longer interested in her now?

Shaking his head, he glared at the pile of wood and tried to set it alight. There was a flash of light, followed by a wave of heat that sent him stumbling backwards. When he looked, the first pile of wood was rapidly being devoured by the flames. He shrugged, then started to gather more wood and add it to the blaze.

Johan, Elaine sent. *I think you should talk to him.*

Johan turned and saw Dread, standing beside the grave. He was turned away from them, but Johan could see iron determination in the way he held himself. Johan hesitated, unsure of what he wanted to say or do, then walked over to the former Inquisitor. Dread didn't look round until Johan was standing next to him, peering down at the unmarked grave. The hex sign had been disintegrated in the fighting.

"Thank you," Dread said.

Johan felt his mouth drop open. He'd never considered that *anyone* would thank him for removing their magic. He knew, all too well, that to be Powerless was to be powerless, to live with the knowledge that, one day, a magician could upend your life and there was nothing you could do about it. And Dread had been *powerful*, perhaps one of the most powerful magicians in the world.

"I would have died if you hadn't saved my life," Dread said. "Or spent the rest of it in service to a monster. You saved me from that fate."

"I wish I felt that way," Johan admitted. "It feels like I killed you."

"But you didn't," Dread said. "I never anticipated an Emperor claiming the Golden Throne. None of us did. It simply never occurred to us that our oaths could be turned into weapons and used to turn us into monsters. Or that we would have no choice but to serve a monster."

"It might have been short-sighted of you," Johan said. His father had been fond of horror stories about people who had sworn oaths, then discovered that they'd sworn oaths that could be twisted or used to make them do horrific things. Jamal had always found them amusing. "Or Charity, for that matter."

"Your sister is a slave," Dread said, flatly. "And, when you see her again, don't forget it."

Johan looked at him, then revised his opinion. Powers or no powers, Dread was *formidable*.

"I won't," he promised. "But what are we going to do now?"

He turned as Elaine walked up behind him. "Cass left a letter for you," she said, holding it out to Dread. "Johan – do you want to help me cook dinner?"

Johan gave her a puzzled look, then understood. Dread would need some privacy to read the letter. Nodding to the older man, he walked beside Elaine to the fire, where Daria was carefully placing pieces of rabbit on a stick. Elaine looked unhappy at having to cut up the meat, but did it without complaint. Johan sat down next to her and held the pieces of meat over the fire.

"He thanked me," Johan said, quietly. "Will he be all right?"

"I hope so," Elaine said. "But give him some time to himself, I think."

***

There was very little information, even in Elaine's head, on what happened to magicians who lost their powers. Some magicians lost their magic as they grew old and died, but they were already senile; others, very rarely, lost their powers and went mad shortly afterwards. It was a confidence issue, Elaine suspected. No matter the crimes, very few magicians would willingly agree to strip another magician of his powers.

She kept a wary eye on Dread as he walked back to the fire, expecting everything from helpless anger to a potentially-lethal bout of depression. Instead, Dread seemed calm and composed, eating his share of the rabbit without complaint. In some ways, she realised, he was almost *relieved*. Whatever happened in the future, he wouldn't have to serve Deferens any longer.

"The Emperor was planning to invade Ida," Dread said, after they'd finished the meal. "He was practically obsessed with the tiny kingdom."

"One of his opponents in the contest came from Ida," Daria muttered. "Do you think he's just taking a pitiful kind of revenge."

"I thought so," Dread said. "It's just the sort of thing he would do. And besides, Ida simply isn't very important. He may feel that making an example of the state would keep everyone else in line."

Elaine started to laugh, hysterically, as the pieces fell into place. "Not very important," she repeated, between giggles. "Not very important?"

Dread frowned. "It isn't," he said. "They don't have any territory or influence outside the mountains ..."

"It doesn't matter," Elaine said. "Ida was one of the places that held out, wasn't it? One of the places that were completely surrounded by the Witch-King's forces during the war. And they held out, despite being attacked by dragons and basilisks and every other creature the Witch-King could summon into being. How did they survive?"

Dread's eyes narrowed. "You think they made a deal?"

Elaine nodded. "I think their ruling family made a deal," she said. "And I think that, if we go to Ida, where it all began, we will find the hiding place of the Witch-King."

End of Book III

The Story Will Conclude In:
Full Circle

Elsewhen Press

delivering outstanding new talents in speculative fiction

Visit the Elsewhen Press website at elsewhen.press for the latest
information on all of our titles, authors and events; to read our blog; find
out where to buy our books and ebooks; or to place an order.

Sign up for the Elsewhen Press InFlight Newsletter at
elsewhen.press/newsletter

The Royal Sorceress
Book I of the Royal Sorceress series

In an alternate history, the principles of magic, discovered in the 1770s, saw Britain win the American War of Independence. Master Thomas, the King's aged Royal Sorcerer, needs a successor with mastery of all magical powers. The only candidate, untrained & unacknowledged, is perfect in every way but one: the Royal College of Sorcerers has never admitted a girl before.

But even before Lady Gwendolyn Crichton can begin her training, London is plunged into chaos by a campaign of terrorist attacks co-ordinated by Jack, a powerful and rebellious magician.

ISBN: 9781908168184 (epub, kindle)
ISBN: 9781908168085 (400pp, paperback)

Visit bit.ly/TheRoyalSorceress

The Great Game
Book II of the Royal Sorceress series

After the uprising in London, Lady Gwendolyn Crichton is settling into her new position as Royal Sorceress and fighting the prejudice against her gender and age that seeks to prevent her from fulfilling her responsibilities. But when a senior magician is murdered in a locked room and Gwen is charged with finding the culprit, her inquiries lead her into a web of intrigue that combines international politics, widespread aristocratic blackmail, gambling dens and personal vendettas... and some of her discoveries hit dangerously close to home.

ISBN: 9781908168375 (epub, kindle)
ISBN: 9781908168276 (400pp, paperback)

Visit bit.ly/TheGreatGame

Necropolis
Book III of the Royal Sorceress series

The British Empire is teetering on the brink of a war with France that may, for the first time, see magicians in the ranks on both sides. As Royal Sorceress, Gwen will be responsible for the Empire's magical resources when the time comes. But her adopted daughter Olivia, the only known living necromancer, has been kidnapped. Intelligence soon establishes that it was Russian agents who took Olivia, so an incognito Gwen joins a British diplomatic mission to St Petersburg.

ISBN: 9781908168726 (epub, kindle)
ISBN: 9781908168627 (416pp, paperback)

Visit bit.ly/RSNecropolis

About the Author

Christopher G. Nuttall has been planning sci-fi books since he learnt to read. Born and raised in Edinburgh, Chris created an alternate history website and eventually graduated to writing full-sized novels. Studying history independently allowed him to develop worlds that hung together and provided a base for storytelling. After graduating from university, Chris started writing full-time. As an indie author he has self-published a number of novels, but this is his seventh fantasy to be published by Elsewhen Press. The third instalment in the bestselling *Bookworm* series, *Bookworm III: The Best Laid Plans* continues Elaine's story. Chris is currently living in Edinburgh with his wife, muse, and critic Aisha and their son.